"Defiance" is an action packed thriller with a fascinating twist of suspense, conspiracy and science fiction that's so believable you'll watch for it on the evening news.

In an atmosphere of civil unrest not seen since the days of Abraham Lincoln, a brilliant scientist makes what could be the most significant scientific breakthrough of the 21st century. Her discovery has the potential to bankrupt global businesses and decimate the economies of several nations. Threatened by governments, mega-corporations, and organized crime, Dr. Ann Ford finds unexpected and powerful allies in her quest to introduce her technology into the free market.

Defiance

Fall of an Empire Series
Book One

By Tom Ryker

ISBN-10: 0615594638
ISBN-13: 978-0-615-59463-7

I would like to dedicate this book to my adorable wife Leslee, for believing in me and for all the wonderful advice she gave that went into its pages.

Acknowledgements

I would like to thank all those who assisted me in the research and writing, all who took the time to edit and proofread, and all the wonderful people who gave of their creative ideas and inspiration so that this book could come to fruition. These include but are not limited to: Aaron & Teisha Preece, Amberlee Cope, Annie Morgan, Brooke Tolman, Camden Hansen, Annie Morgan, Alex Richard Tolman, Elise Brown, Jason Cowley, Francine Sorensen, Glenn Beck, Gina and Steve Griffiths, Heidi Bardsley, Jeff and Michelle Ahnder, Kathy Ellis, Jon Tolman, Jaynalee Peterson, Kassy Bonham, Kathy Jacobs, Kayloni Hansen, Maren Dunn, Marcus Daley, Mike Sorensen, Omar Filippelli, Talei Lawson, and Wayne Sorensen.

Special thanks to my friend and agent, Randy Jones, and his creative wife, Kathe; to my editors, Genevieve Perenelle and Lindsay Woolf Jones; to Kellie Preece for a great cover; to Paul Cheney for a great website; and to all my family—Ben, Carson, Collin, Kellie and Sheii—for their love and support.

Defiance

Fall of an Empire Series
Book One

By Tom Ryker

...and to institute new Government, laying its foundation on such principles and organizing its powers in such form, as to them shall seem most likely to effect their Safety and Happiness. Prudence, indeed, will dictate that Governments long established should not be changed for light and transient causes; and accordingly all experience hath shewn, that mankind are more disposed to suffer, while evils are sufferable, than to right themselves by abolishing the forms to which they are accustomed. But when a long train of abuses and usurpations, pursuing invariably the same Object evinces a design to reduce them under absolute Despotism, it is their right, it is their duty, to throw off such Government, and to provide new Guards for their future security...

Declaration of Independence – 1776

Table of Contents

Table of Contents

Chapter One

"Breakthrough of the Twenty-First Century"

"I did it!" she burst out as she rinsed the soap suds off the last coffee mug. Ann had never felt such a huge sense of personal satisfaction and accomplishment in her life. She smiled broadly as she twisted the water out of the dish rag and draped it over the towel rack to dry. "Seven years of research, three grants, a thousand late nights, and a hundred dead ends... but it actually works!"

Whenever she had a lot on her mind and needed a quiet moment to think things through, she did the dishes by hand. There was something about a soft dish rag, warm soapy water, and an unobstructed view of the Colorado Rockies that brought her clarity. Today, the dishes were not having their desired effect. Ann was so excited she could hardly contain herself. To her students she was Dr. Ford, but her family and friends all called her Ann. Raw intelligence exuded from her hazel-brown eyes—which intimidated many who didn't know her—but she was adorable to those who did.

For the past few years, Ann had been doing research in the field of hydro-electrolysis, and like all the scientists before her, had made very little progress—up until last night. Even she'd been blown away by the incredible simplicity of her late night epiphany, which was about to explode into a media frenzy.

Imagine filling up a car with hydrogen for twenty or thirty cents a gallon, and the exhaust being water vapor, she thought, shaking her head in amazement. *If I hadn't seen it with my own eyes, I wouldn't believe it!*

Most firms who'd invested in hydro-electrolysis research had concluded it couldn't be done economically, and had limited their investments in the research. Ann had proven them all wrong with a solution that was so simple it could be reproduced in any decent high school lab.

She plopped into her grandmother's rocking chair and stared at the mountains rising in the distance. *I love the mountains this time of the year,* she thought as she admired the scarlet and gold colored trees that cascaded down the foothills behind her home. Her eyes followed a ridge line that meandered its way up into the snowcapped peaks in the distance, and she wished she had the day off to hike it. There was nothing like a good hike to bring clarity to a situation, but she knew it would be impossible to find substitutes for her classes at such late notice.

A virtually free energy source is about to make its entrance onto the world stage. What will it mean for the oil industry and all the countries that depend on oil for their revenue? What will it mean for Americans who work in the industry? Ann shrugged her shoulders and continued rocking back and forth in the old chair. In her mind's eye she visualized commercials where people were filling up their cars, trucks, SUVs, boats, four wheelers, furnaces, motorcycles, and barbeque grills with water from a garden hose, using a simple hydrolyser that they'd purchased online. She smiled at the idea.

Despite her exhilaration, Ann was anxious about the commotion her discovery would unleash, and the negative effect its publicity would have on her and her family. She worried about how to package and release her research so it couldn't be suppressed by government or big business. She didn't have any concrete evidence that they'd been keeping tabs on her, but the word on the street in the scientific community was that big brother was listening.

A shiver of excitement ran up her spine and pushed away her trepidation. Her mind reeled with scenario after scenario of what might unfold after she made her discovery public. She wondered what effect it would have on the world's volatile markets. How many businesses would fold overnight and what kind of opportunities would emerge to take their place? *Could federal and state governments get along without the billions of dollars they routinely collected from gas leases and taxes?*

Ann had no answers, but she was confident the economy would find balance just like it did when Henry

Ford put the wagon, harness, and horse currying industries out of business.

She'd moved to Fort Collins, Colorado after accepting a teaching position at Colorado State University. Her move from the west coast was precipitated by California's sick economy and catastrophic weather, among other things, but mostly by an insatiable desire to find a more peaceful and simple place to live.

The entire country was in a funk. The federal debt had soared past twenty trillion with no end in sight, and many states were facing bankruptcy. Fort Collins, Colorado, on the other hand, had survived the economic downturns and unpredictable weather without too much trauma. Snow removal costs were at an all-time high, but the Eldora ski resort and its patrons were not complaining. Fort Collins had turned out to be a perfect fit for Ann—small, quaint, and clean, with little need for more than a sheriff to keep the peace. It was home to CSU, a quiet little university of thirty-five thousand students that offered undergraduate and advanced degrees in many fields.

Since the beginning of her tenure at the university, Ann had taught undergraduate and graduate classes in both chemistry and physics. Nirvana for Ann would be to retire from CSU, do research, and spend the rest of her time hiking, biking, skiing, snowshoeing, and watching great movies with her husband, Jack.

The old rocking chair creaked a little faster as her mind drifted back to the moment the night before when she'd made her breakthrough... *Trial #1579, Monday, September 8, 11:41 p.m., increased vibration intensity by .012 percent, and lowered water temperature by one degree,* she recorded. She hadn't anticipated anything spectacular happening because her adjustments were minor and it was her fifteen-hundred-and-seventy-ninth attempt. Ann gave the apparatus a once-over, then flipped the switch to see if her modifications would have any effect. As usual, her heart quickened in anticipation as she watched the process begin. A perfectly shaped stream of very cold water poured into a vibrating, cone-shaped laser funnel. Her heart had almost stopped when five gallons of ordinary distilled water separated into hydrogen and oxygen in less than a second. She'd stood there staring at the rudimentary hydrolyser, not believing what she'd just witnessed.

"Have I done it...?...I... I think it actually worked!" She remembered having a hard time breathing. She'd forced herself to carefully and cautiously inspect every component of the hydrolyser, not daring to touch anything, for fear of changing something. Not trusting herself, she'd run upstairs to get her camera so she could take a hundred pictures just in case she'd missed something. After she was completely satisfied that she'd thoroughly documented the hydrolyser's current state, she tested the purity of the oxygen and hydrogen that had been siphoned off from the five gallons of water. The hydrogen tank registered 99.916 percent pure hydrogen, and the oxygen tank was perfect as well. She documented the figures into her digital voice recorder.

Ann gazed at the apparatus, shaking her head. She was a little miffed at herself for changing the water temperature and the intensity of the vibrating lasers at the same time, because she wasn't one hundred percent certain which one had done the trick, but she didn't care. It worked! She'd been scared to death that she wouldn't be able to repeat what she had seen, and that it would turn out to be a one-time fluke caused by factors she would never be able to identify. She remembered her heart throbbing as she reloaded the water tank and waited for it to chill to 31.85 degrees. The hair on her arms stood on end as she waited. Never in her life had she felt so much anticipatory anxiety, and it seemed like it had taken forever for the water to chill.

As the water cooled to the perfect temperature, she recorded the trial number and date into the digital recorder. *Trial #1580, Tuesday, September 9, 12:13 a.m., repeating trial #1579 configurations and set up... pictures taken of #1579...* She put the recorder down and walked around the hydrolyser, memorizing every setting and configuration, and checking for anything that looked out of the ordinary. She'd been working on the apparatus for years and knew it like the back of her hand, but she wanted to make sure every detail was seared into her mind.

She jumped when the temperature gauge beeped, indicating that the water in the tank had reached its magical temperature. She remembered standing with her finger resting on the switch that would release the water into the vibrating laser funnel. Her heart felt like it was going to pound right out of her chest, and she remembered looking up at the ceiling and saying, *please God, let this work again.* She hesitated for a few more moments before she had the courage to flip the switch.

Time stood still as a crystal-clear stream of water hit the laser funnel and disappeared into hydrogen and oxygen. Her knees buckled under her and she collapsed into the reclining chair Jack had bought her for Christmas. She remembered feeling dizzy as her mind tried to process the fact that she'd just accomplished the impossible.

Who would've thought that the laser mesh had to be vibrating at a frequency fine-tuned to the thousandths? I could have been here for another ten years. She looked up at the ceiling and mouthed, *thank you.*

Ann had forced herself to run several more trials to ensure that her experiment really did work before she collapsed back into the chair, exhausted from sheer exhilaration. She'd called Jack, who was on a business trip in Kuwait, and left him a benign message, letting him know she needed to talk to him. She didn't dare say anything about her breakthrough for fear that someone from the federal government might be monitoring the call with their stress and anxiety analysis software—which wasn't uncommon given the amount of terrorist activity that was plaguing the United States.

Ann's grandfather clock struck 8:00 a.m. with its slow, majestic tone, bringing her reminiscing mind racing back to the present. She glanced up at the atomic clock to confirm that the time announced by the century-old time piece was correct. "Tuesday, September 9, 8:00 a.m." was the reading on the clock.

"Damn!" she muttered under her breath as she bounded out of the antique rocking chair. *I'm going to be late for my nine o'clock freshman chemistry class.*

Dashing into the bathroom, she stripped off her warm-ups and jumped into the shower. Water streamed down her furrowed brow as she scrubbed shampoo into her hair. Despite her euphoria at having discovered a solution for the twenty-first century's energy crisis, she couldn't stop worrying. For better or for worse, God hadn't blessed her with a great deal of naivety, and she knew precisely the danger her discovery would put her and her family in. She was painfully aware how far oil producing corporations, cartels, and countries would go to control her discovery, or just destroy it all together.

Maybe I should just be content knowing that I figured it out, she thought for a moment. *Then I won't have to deal with the greedy, power hungry people it will attract.* Although the idea was sorely tempting, her principles wouldn't allow it. She was determined to give her research to the entire world—for free.

In conversations she'd had with Jack, they'd decided not to tell anyone about a breakthrough in her research, should she ever have one, until they'd determined the perfect medium for releasing the results to the world.

It was critical to Ann that her research be widely available, so the smallest, most economically deprived communities would be able to reproduce and develop it.

The only hitch was that they'd never decided what their plan of action would be. Perhaps it was a lack of faith on Ann's part, or the fact that she'd been working on the project for several years without any success, that they weren't better prepared for this day. Regardless, it was here, and she had to deal with it. About the only thing that they had decided on was a secret phrase Ann could use if something happened while Jack was out of town, and she hoped Jack would remember it.

Her eyebrows bunched together as she tried to remember the exact words they'd agreed on – *I burned a batch of cookies and almost burned down the whole house.* She smiled at how simple it was in light of the breakthrough it represented.

Ann debated her options as she picked out an outfit for the day. Her naturally happy face was puckered with a frown, and she was exhausted from lack of sleep. Several times during the night she'd been jolted awake by nightmares where she and Jack were being chased by people in dark suits who were trying to kill her and steal her research.

I wish Jack were here. He would know exactly what to do. His self-confidence and MacGyver personality made her feel safe. She ran through several possible courses of action in her mind, but didn't like any of them. She decided to do nothing until she could talk to her husband. Despite her best efforts to reassure herself that her research was safe, she couldn't shake the feeling that it wasn't, and she wasn't prone to ignoring her gut instincts. Looking in the mirror, she made a few adjustments to her hair and outfit until she was satisfied. Her face had that determined look on it, the way it did when she had made a decision she wouldn't back down from.

She turned away from the mirror and walked resolutely to her lab, quickly disconnected her laser equipment, and put it on the floor. After jumping up and down on it several times to make sure nobody could reconstruct it or reverse engineer the calibrations, she put the pieces in a box. She removed the hard drive from her computer and put it in the same box, then gathered up her research notes and put them on top of the hard drive. She looked around the room to see if there was anything else that contained sensitive information she may have missed. Her eyes settled on her camera and voice recorder, and she threw them both in the box on top of her research notes. She lugged the box up the stairs and placed it in front of the family room fireplace.

This should make some black smoke, she thought to herself as she piled logs onto the grate, and placed the box on top of them. Carefully, she positioned as many logs around and on top of the box as she could, then she took down the carton of fire starters and wedged several of them in-between the logs. Lighting a match, she held it to the closest of the sap saturated starters and watched as it ignited and dripped onto the surrounding logs.

Yellow flames curled their way up the side of the box as the hardwood logs caught fire. She closed the glass doors on the fireplace and lingered just long enough to make sure that the box filled with her most treasured secrets was engulfed in flames. Satisfied that her research was well on its way to becoming a pile of ash, she walked down the hall to the closet and picked out a jacket that went with her outfit. *If God wants my research to be free to the public,* she thought, *He's going to have to preserve it in my head.* Ann had a great memory and she was confident she could reproduce her notes and equipment configurations anytime she wanted.

Chapter Two

"A Suspicious Invitation"

Painfully aware of the time, Ann grabbed her Subaru keys off the copper hook in the pantry and walked briskly to the garage. "Dammit," she mumbled and turned back to the pantry. The Subaru was in the shop having snow tires put on it and Jack had left his Porsche 911 Turbo for her to take to work.

She hurried and swapped her keys for the Porsche keys. Holding them in one hand and her coat in the other, she locked the kitchen door and armed the security system. It started to beep, letting her know that she had one hundred and twenty seconds to exit the house and shut the garage door. The Porsche idled in the driveway while she waited for the garage door to close and the LED light on the security panel to flash red.

Ann pumped the gas and the twin exhaust pipes of the Porsche rumbled with raw potential energy that brought a mischievous smile to Ann's lips. She felt grateful to have a husband who would take a cab and leave her this beautiful machine. The 911 smelled like leather and Jack's cologne, and for a second her mind flashed back to when they had first met. She'd been sitting in the food court with her blond bombshell friend, Charli, when Jack walked by. Unless she'd been mistaken, he'd nearly spilled his lunch tray taking a second look at Charli. Without an invitation, he'd sat down across from them.

He later claimed he'd never even noticed Charli, but Ann knew better. Generally speaking, it was hard for any man to get past her endlessly long legs, which she happened to be showing that day. Before the meal was over, he'd asked Ann to accompany him to a dinner party where he was the keynote speaker. According to Charli, it had been love at first sight for both of them.

Most men were intimidated by Ann's PhD, forthrightness, and quick wit, but not Jack; he was somehow attracted to it like a moth to a flame. Charli had predicted they'd be married within the year, and she'd been right. Ann didn't discover that she'd married a multi-millionaire until after the wedding. Other than his car, nothing Jack owned screamed of money. With his laidback attitude and sometimes-wrinkled professor's wardrobe, no one would guess he was loaded, and she loved him for it.

Several years before marrying Ann, Jack had developed some technology that could assess the depth, breadth, quality, and quantity of subterranean oil reserves with amazing accuracy. North Star Energy had taken an interest in the technology and had offered him ninety million dollars, plus a half a percent of future sales for exclusive rights to use the device. The only hitch in the contract was that Jack had to stay on the payroll for five years as a senior consultant.

Dwindling oil reserves had made Jack's device worth every penny North Star paid for it. Ann smiled at the thought. *North Star Energy would not be happy with Jack if they knew that his wife had just put them out of business!*

Ann was one of two women in the testosterone-rich CSU Chemistry Department, and the only female Ph.D. Most of the professors in the department were friendly, but they sometimes forgot to include her in their primitive theoretical debates. She'd decided they couldn't handle her intellect and sarcastic wit, which in and of itself gave her some satisfaction. She thought about the staff meeting later in the afternoon and was tempted to take the first few minutes whiteboarding her late night discovery. Had she been more egotistical, she'd have derived immense satisfaction watching their faces as they skeptically peeled back the layers of her research and uncovered the incredible simplicity and elegance of the solution. She grinned at the thought and a dimple appeared, then disappeared, on her face. Tempting as it was, it wasn't her style, and she dismissed the idea.

The thirty-five minute drive to the university went by in a flash. Needless to say, her mind was not on her driving, and before she knew it, she was cornering into the faculty parking lot a little too fast. The tires on the 911 squealed enough to raise the eyebrows of a campus security guard and get the attention of every car-loving kid within earshot.

Ann parked the Porsche, turned off the engine, and reached into the passenger seat for her attaché case. "Ah crap," she mumbled, "I left it on the kitchen table." *I'm such an airhead,* she mused as she opened the car door.

Luckily she'd been teaching the 101 freshman chemistry class so long she could handle it without lecture notes. Glancing at the time on her cell phone, she walked briskly to the chemistry building auditorium. It was filled with students who were glancing at the wall clock, wondering if they'd waited long enough to be justified in leaving.

She paused a moment at the door, looked at the clock on the wall, then walked down the aisle to the podium and began her lecture. "You were hoping I wouldn't make it, weren't you?"

"No, Dr. Ford," chimed the students in a unanimous lie. Ann smiled, remembering perfectly well what it was like to be a freshman. Without missing a beat, she asked who had finished their homework.

A buff-looking kid on the back row raised his hand in a cocky manner, so she promptly asked him to recite his answers to the class while she took a minute to collect her collegiate senses.

"Thank you," she said, "but does anyone have a better answer for questions five and fifteen?" A smart-looking brunette on the third row raised her hand.

"Yes, what do you have?"

"Five is 'eight protons, eight neutrons, and eight electrons,' and fifteen is '11,456,432.'"

"That is correct," said Ann, guessing that Angie was right based on the number of heads bobbing in confirmation of her answer.

How would it be to have the worries of a freshman again? Ann had been teaching the majority of her adult life, so an hour of ad-libbing to a 101 class wouldn't normally have been difficult for her, but that wasn't the case today. She was having a hard time keeping focused on the class. *Using hydrogen as our primary fuel source will require massive infrastructure and distribution changes, or maybe not,* she thought. *If the hydrolyser can be produced and sold on-line... Just think of all the adjustments that we'll have to make. This means I'm going to have to talk to the press....ugh. I wonder if I could release my research notes under an alias...*

Ann had little respect for press. *I guess we're better off with them than without them,"* she conceded to herself.

"Are you ok, Dr. Ford?" asked a student on the front row.

"Uh, yes, I'm fine," Ann muttered. *Focus, you idiot,* she told herself.

Ann stayed on topic the remainder of the class and concluded by giving the next homework assignment from the chemistry textbook. Some PhD's on campus avoided teaching freshmen classes, leaving them to suffer at the hands of an inexperienced teaching assistant, but not Ann. She loved their untainted views on life, and made a point to alternate teaching assignments with her assistants.

"Please do the even questions at the end of chapter..." she was saying as a tall, nice-looking man entered the auditorium. He took a seat on the back row.

Where have I seen him before? He's probably a course auditor, she thought, as she searched her memory for his familiar face. *Thank goodness he wasn't here at the beginning of class to see me come in thirteen minutes late... or did he just come back?*

She finished giving the students their assignment and answered a few lingering questions, all the while keeping a watch on the visitor on the back row. Out of the corner of her eye she saw her uninvited guest stand and begin to walk down the auditorium steps towards her.

He was a handsome man by any measure—not as handsome as Jack, of course—and had one of the most contagious smiles she'd ever seen. *He can't be a course auditor with a smile like that,* she concluded as she said good-bye to the last student.

Turning, she faced the mystery man and stuck out her hand. "Hi, I'm Dr. Ford," she said with a smile. "How can I help you?"

"It's nice to finally meet you, Dr. Ford," said the tall stranger, taking her hand.

Finally meet me? She wondered as she released her hand from a firm handshake.

"I am Dr. Sellers from the University Of Southern Texas School of Chemistry," he said, letting the words sink in.

Ann looked at him quizzically. "Well, Dr. Sellers... you wouldn't happen to be the Dr. Ben Sellers who won a 2008 Nobel Prize, would you?"

"Guilty as charged," he said, looking down at his black crocodile-skin cowboy boots.

He raised his eyes and refocused the conversation on Ann. "The University has been keeping tabs on you and your work for over a year, and we figured it was high time we made an offer of employment."

Ann was aware of the high standards the University of Southern Texas had for their professors and looked at Ben in disbelief. When Ben didn't say anything, Ann smiled broadly. "So what *really* brings you to our lovely Colorado campus?"

"I'm not kidding; I'm only here to see you. My boss, Dr. Conner, who is the dean of the College of Chemistry, and Dr. Kane, the president of the University of Southern Texas, asked that I fly out and extend an employment offer to you. I know it's a little sudden and all, but we like to deliver these things in person with as little fanfare as possible."

The sincerity and frankness of Dr. Sellers's explanation surprised her, and she wasn't easily surprised. The university was notorious for its unorthodox hiring practices—and unless Dr. Sellers was pulling her leg—the rumors were true! Not only had Dr. Sellers's approach surprised her, but the timing of the university's interest in her was alarming. The events of the last twenty-four hours already had her on pins and needles, and Dr. Sellers's visit pushed her beyond that.

Ann's mind raced as she tried to make sense out of his visit. *Why would the University Of Southern Texas want to make me an offer unless they thought I'd had a breakthrough in my research*?

Intellectually, Ann knew there was no way for anyone to have knowledge about her progress, but the chances of the University of Southern Texas turning up today and making her an offer was a huge coincidence. She fought down the feeling of panic that was starting to churn in her gut. *How could they know?*

Dr. Sellers squinted his eyes at Ann. "Are you all right?"

"Ah...yes...I'm fine. You just caught me off guard." She hated losing her composure and fought to maintain it by focusing her attention on every word he was saying. Ann forced herself to smile. "Tell me more about your offer."

"I'd prefer it if you'd call me Ben."

"Same here... I mean... Just call me Ann."

"Ok, Ann. We would like to offer you a teaching position at our Corpus Christi facility and a seat on one of our research subcommittees."

Ann's eyes widened slightly. Most professors would do anything for a teaching position at UST. "What department would I be teaching under?"

"You would be reporting directly to Dr. Conner."

Ann's eyes widened even further. Dr. Conner's research was well-known in the scientific community. She fingered the collar of her blouse while she processed Ben's proposal.

"We'd start you at a salary that is one-and-a-half times whatever CSU is paying you now, and we'll buy your home at its market value or swap it for one of similar size in the heart of our fifty-thousand acre Corpus Christi collegiate community. Most of our professors live there considering how safe and tranquil the area is."

Ann's body language betrayed everything she was thinking, which made Sellers chuckle.

"What?"

"Your response to my offer is not too dissimilar from the one I had when Dr. Conner approached me."

"Is it that obvious?"

Ben smiled. "There are numerous other benefits enjoyed by our teaching staff that I won't elaborate on right now, but they're all spelled out in your official offer letter."

Ben handed Ann a manila envelope containing the information.

Ann took the envelope and held it against her chest. "Well, I, ah… I'm surprised and pleased all at the same time," she said with a smile. "I'm definitely interested, but I'll need some time to think it over."

Ben chuckled. "I certainly didn't expect an answer now. You have all the time in the world to think it over. When you've made a decision, please call me at the number printed in your offer letter and I'll fly up to discuss it. The internet, snail-mail, and phone systems aren't as secure as they once were, so we always discuss our offers in person."

Ann frowned. "It is unfortunate that it's come to that."

"It is indeed." Ben apologized again for his unsolicited visit, then turned and started walking towards the exit.

"Won't you stay for lunch?" Ann blurted out.

Ben paused and turned with a smile, "I would, Ann, but I don't want to interrupt your day any more than I already have. If your answer to our offer is favorable, we'll have plenty of time for lunch, Texan style."

He started to turn away, but then turned back. "I forgot to ask how your research is coming. I believe I read a paper you published a few years back."

He raised a finger in the air like he was trying to remember what her research was about. "Hydro-electrolysis, right?"

Ann's gaze sharpened and she looked into Ben's eyes, searching for any clue that he knew more than he was letting on, but his innocent look convinced her that he didn't.

Ann responded carefully. "You know how research is. I'm always hoping that tomorrow will be the day I get the results I want."

"I hear that!" said Ben. He smiled, then turned and took the auditorium steps two at a time until he disappeared into the hallway filled with bustling students. Ann watched him leave with a puzzled expression on her face.

Everyone knew that UST recruited the best talent in the world, but she'd never considered herself overly talented. She remembered reading an article in NewsWeek about how the university recruited its unique blend of professors. They prided themselves on being able to identify brilliant, tenacious, happy, secure, balanced, objective, humble people. She shook her head; in her estimation, it was an impossible set of characteristics for any human being to have.

For a minute, she wondered if UST thought she had the coveted array of personal attributes. She shrugged and shuffled a stack of homework into a more manageable pile. *They obviously don't know me very well or they've lowered their standard.*

Ann hardly noticed the student-packed hallway as she walked to her office. The space had never looked so inviting. She slipped in, hoping that nobody would notice she was there, and sunk into the sofa. She'd never felt so exhausted and exhilarated at the same time.

Chapter Three

"Stress and Anxiety Levels"

Exiting the Chemistry Building, Ben made his way to the lot where he'd parked his rental car. He revved up the Chevy Malibu engine and followed the directions his GPS provided back towards the Denver International Airport.

After he'd made a couple of turns in the right direction, he docked his cell phone on the dash and said, "Call Dr. Conner."

"Dr. Conner's office," answered a familiar voice through the car speakers.

"Dr. Conner, is that you?"

"It is," said Dr. Conner on the other end of the line. "How did it go with Dr. Ford?

"As usual we caught our candidate by surprise… but she seemed excited about the offer."

"Good," said Dr. Conner. "Thanks for sending her DNA to me so quickly."

Ben winced. "I didn't have a chance to read your text other than the part that said 'Go ahead with the offer.' How did she score?"

"Her preliminary G-Score was in the high nineties."

Ben wasn't too surprised, knowing what he did from the research his team had done on her.

"You realize you sent over two DNA samples, don't you?"

"Yeah, there were two hair types in her brush, so I scanned them both to be safe. I wasn't sure if she'd colored her hair or was sharing her hairbrush with a girlfriend."

"Worked for us," said Dr. Conner, "We were able to figure which one was hers by deducing her age from the sample and comparing it to the age on her birth certificate. Do you have any idea who the other hair sample might belong to?"

Ben shook his head. "No clue."

"Well, whoever it is has one of the highest G-Scores we've ever seen."

"Interesting," responded Ben. "Maybe I should have brought two offers."

Ben glanced at his GPS readout to make sure he was headed in the right direction. He'd arrived late the night before so he didn't have a clue where the I-25 exit to the airport was.

Dr. Conner interrupted his concentration. "Did she say anything specific about our offer?"

Ben chuckled, "She said she was surprised, but pleased."

"That's a hopeful sign," replied Dr. Conner. "If I remember right, you had a similar reaction when I approached you."

"Your memory serves you well," Ben replied, recalling how he'd reacted.

Ben and Dr. Conner had grown very close over the past few years. Ben trusted him more than any man he knew aside from his own father. Dr. Conner was one of the most brilliant, well-balanced, hardworking people he had ever had the opportunity of associating with, and his wisdom had proven infallible over the years.

"Well, what did you think of her?" pressed Dr. Conner.

"She'll be a great fit for the department if she accepts."

"Good… good. Did you ask her how her research was progressing?"

"I did, but she stone-walled me with a benign response."

"I wonder if she's further along than we think," said Dr. Conner, half to himself.

"Who knows," responded Ben. "I am sure of one thing. She had a lot on her mind or was in the middle of a hectic day."

"Why do you say that?"

"She was very distracted during the tail end of the class I attended."

"I would be too if a six-foot-four-inch man wearing cowboy boots barged into one of my classes!"

"There was more to it than that," said Ben. "She seemed seriously distracted about something; and from what we've gathered, that is not like her."

There was silence on the other end of the phone, and Ben took advantage of it to check his navigation.

"Do we know if she and Jack are getting along ok?" asked Dr. Conner.

Ben smiled, "Like a couple of love birds, according to our sources."

"Hmm," responded Dr. Conner. "If she's had a breakthrough in her research, it might be enough to put her on edge, considering how disruptive it will be."

"What do you mean?" asked Ben, who had not really considered how Ann's research would affect the economy.

"Ask me tomorrow," said Dr. Conner solemnly. "I'm talking about the possibility of trillions of dollars' worth of oil revenues going down the toilet."

Ben whistled, "A lot of people wouldn't like that, would they? On a positive note—regardless of whether she's made any progress with her research, she'll make an awesome addition to our team."

"I agree," said Dr. Conner, trying to sound less anxious. "Did we find out anything new about her husband?"

"We know he graduated from Yale at the top of his class, then taught at CSU for twelve years. He was the dean of the College of Natural Resources for six years."

"Interesting," responded Dr. Conner.

"A few years ago he finished research on a radio-sonar based petroleum detection device that he sold to North Star Energy for around ninety million dollars."

"Is he working for CSU at all anymore?" asked Dr. Conner.

"No, I don't think so. His contract with North Star Energy requires him to work for them exclusively as a consultant."

"Sounds like a pretty intelligent guy."

"More laid back than intellectual, though."

"Did she say when she'd get back to us?"

"No, and I didn't push her for a time frame."

"Ben," said Dr. Conner slowly, "my gut's telling me she's closer to a resolution with her research than we think. For some reason I can't get past the reports our Department of Criminology put together on Dr. Ford. It looks like everyone and their dog is tapping her phone or has tried to hack her computer ever since she released that white paper on her research a few years ago."

He was speaking of the regular analysis the university's Department of Criminology did on a candidate professor's phones, internet access, and internet community involvement. It was a standard part of the hiring process the university did on every person they were interested in. Ann had been on the 'candidate professor' list for over a year so the university had sizeable history on her. During the comprehensive background check, the university discovered that her home and cell phones had been tapped from time to time by the FBI and someone else they couldn't identify. They also discovered that several unknown entities had tried to hack the Ford's personal computers, but failed.

"How high was her stress level?" asked Dr. Conner.

"Oh, I almost forgot about that," said Ben, pulling a Stress Analyzer out of his coat pocket. "Wow!" he exclaimed, "She is definitely agitated about something. Is it possible that my visit might have caused this much anxiety?" Ben looked at the readings on the device again to make certain he hadn't misread it.

"What is the ANXT reading?" asked Dr. Conner.

"Sixty-Seven," said Ben.

"How about the TENSE and the QUIV readings?" fired Dr. Conner, who was sounding more alarmed.

"Eighty-two and eighty-eight," responded Ben.

Dr. Conner didn't say anything while he compared the readings with the ones they had on file for Ann.

"She's off the scale compared to normal," said Dr. Conner. "Something's going on. That's way out of the ordinary for her. Has she had anybody close to her die?"

"I don't know about that, but her parents both passed away several years ago."

"Does she have any siblings?"

"She has a sister who is in good health who she has regular contact with."

UST's Security Department had developed some software that allowed them to ascertain a person's stress and anxiety levels from live, phone, or text message conversations. An older legacy version was widely used by federal and state law enforcement agencies across the country.

"We assigned a couple of GA's to her sometime after she published her last paper, didn't we?" asked Dr. Conner.

"Yes, they've been in place for about thirty months," responded Ben.

"How close are they to Ann?"

"I'm not certain of all the details," said Ben, "but I've been told they're very close."

"Can't be too close for me!" said Dr. Conner, sounding a little more worried. "We absolutely cannot allow Dr. Ford's technology to fall into the wrong hands or be suppressed by the federal government."

"I couldn't agree more."

"If there is the slightest chance she's pulled off what I think she has, her life and the well-being of her family are at risk. How good are the GA's we have looking after her?" asked Dr. Conner.

"Our very best," reported Ben confidently.

Dr. Conner's angst didn't dissipate in the least. *If she's blown the lid off this thing by creating a hyper-economic solution, nobody can protect her,* he thought. *Ten of our best GA's couldn't protect her.*

The university staff jokingly referred to their undercover security team members as GA's—guardian angels. For several years, the university had found it necessary to keep a plain clothes security detail near or around their key people and some of their candidate professors. For some reason, every time they showed interest in recruiting someone, it was as if they'd painted a big sign that said, 'this person is a genius and is about to invent something that is worth billions,' and pasted it on their back.

"I hope I'm not over analyzing this, but my gut tells me we'd better increase Dr. Ford's security coverage to Tier One. It's better to be safe than sorry. Make sure our satellite jockeys keep an eye on her twenty-four-seven."

"We'll do our best."

"Do you think I'm overreacting?"

"Maybe a little, but I wouldn't bet a dime against your intuition."

"You're very kind," said Dr. Conner smiling. "Regardless of whether I'm right or wrong, it doesn't hurt to be overly protective when we can afford it."

"I agree."

"Well, drive safely and have a good weekend, Ben."

"Thanks," responded Ben as he hung up the phone, not knowing that his weekend was about to become nonexistent.

Chapter Four

"G-Scores and a Pulitzer Prize"

Ben arrived at the Denver International Airport and pulled into the rental car return lane, the tire rippers clicking behind him. He unloaded his luggage and pulled it over to where the shuttle bus was waiting. Five minutes later he was at the terminal, doing his best to dodge the workers who were replacing the airport's landmark canopy roof.

A freak hail storm had obliterated it a month earlier, causing forty-nine million dollars worth of damage.

He reached the security gate and waited for his turn to be processed, praying that he wouldn't be delayed by a more invasive search. Increased terrorist activity made getting through security a major ordeal. If you packed well and did everything by the book, it only took an hour and a half. If you screwed something up or looked remotely suspicious, it could take three hours to get through.

Terrorist tactics had changed in the years since 9/11. Rather than attack targets as large as the Twin Towers, they were targeting buses, restaurants, rental cars, subways, and less secure public buildings. Some areas in the US were as bad as living in the Middle East.

Ben didn't mind the wait because it gave him time to unwind so he could sleep on the plane—as long as he didn't have to take his pants off for some guy working for TSA. His prayers were answered, and he cruised through security without a mishap and boarded his flight. After stowing his briefcase in the overhead compartment, he pushed his first-class seat back as far as it would go and relaxed.

At least Dr. Conner flies me in style on these kinds of trips, he thought as he positioned his head on a pillow.

As the plane taxied away from the gate, Ben mulled over the possible causes for Dr. Ann Ford's elevated anxiety. It annoyed him that such a small handful of cowardly and corrupt people could cause so much stress and anxiety for everyone else on the planet.

What would this world be like, he wondered, *if all criminals were banished to a colony on Mars?* Ben pondered the social and economic ramifications of such a possibility. For all intents and purposes, Dr. Conner and President Kane had almost pulled this off in the micro-economy of the University of Southern Texas.

His mind lingered on Dr. Conner's G-Score research that had made it possible. His 'Goodness Score' research—G-Score as it was commonly called—had won a Nobel Prize and had been the catalyst for a worldwide paradigm shift for measuring a person's character among sociologists, psychologists, and human resource departments.

Ben smiled as he remembered Dr. Conner's humble, yet provocative acceptance speech. He'd applied his research to a sample of twenty-five million people and had proven that a person's true character at any given point in time could be determined by analyzing the emotional chemical imprints left on the cells of the body.

He'd demonstrated that if a person were regularly sarcastic for example, the chemicals triggered by sarcastic emotions would leave a detectable imprint on that person's cellular structure. If the chemical triggered by sarcasm made repeated imprints on one's cellular structure over a two- to three-year period, the imprints would become as permanent as the impressions left on the hoodoos in Bryce Canyon National Park, and were just as difficult to change. Positive attributes also left imprints that were easily identified and leveraged by the G-Score tests.

Dr. Conner discovered that every emotional- and character-related imprint could be accurately read and interpreted from a simple human DNA sample. As his research became more commonly used, all of the major emotions and states-of-minds for billions of people had been repeatedly trended, cross-referenced, and validated since his initial thesis. Happiness, sadness, stress, ego, self-assuredness, intellectual arrogance, pride, fear, kindness, humility, tenacity, love, compassion, anger, selfishness, denial, peace, charity, envy, hope, hopelessness, faith, jealousy, creativity, spite, prejudice, laziness, tolerance, honesty, optimism, etc., had all been meticulously catalogued, tested, and retested for accuracy.

Dr. Conner had figured out how to compile the results of his character tests into a meaningful array of outputs that culminated in what he referred to as a G-Score. The G-Score wasn't perfect, but it had turned out to be a surprisingly accurate way of determining a person's general character.

Considering the nature of his research, Dr. Conner was remarkably non-judgmental. He regularly gave people the benefit of the doubt and plenty of opportunity to change their G-Scores. He often quoted Viktor Frankl who said, "Everything can be taken from a man but ...the last of the human freedoms—to choose one's attitude in any given set of circumstances, and to choose one's own way."

Prior to Dr. Conner winning the Nobel Prize, Dr. Carson B. Kane—the President of the University Of Southern Texas—adopted the G-Score test as a source of information used to evaluate potential hires. Since the introduction of the G-Score tests, the staff at UST had undergone a remarkable transformation. Professors who ranked high on the G-Score test out-performed those that ranked low by as much as forty to fifty percent. They seemed to work smarter and have significantly higher student approval ratings than their lower-scoring counterparts.

An unpredicted characteristic of this group of professors was their insatiable desire to assist, collaborate, and share ideas with their students, associates and colleagues. The results of using G-Scores to qualify professors was so remarkable that the university implemented the technology as part of the student application process.

A byproduct of having such an amazing staff and student body was UST's uncanny ability to win a high percentage of the available private, corporate, and government-funded research projects. Hardly a year went by without a professor, student or alumni of the university winning a major award or making a significant contribution to the scientific community— and it showed in their robust financial statements.

UST had become a melting pot of people from different cultures, nationalities, and religions who had amazing synergy. Ben continued to think about the positives and negatives of G-Score technology until he drifted off to sleep.

Chapter Five

"Burned Cookies"

Ann closed her eyes, wiggled her shoulders, and sank further into her office sofa. The events of the last twenty-four hours seemed less important as she drifted into the space between semi-consciousness and sleep.

Unfortunately, her phone rang, and brought her abruptly back to reality. Sitting up, she yawned, stretched, and searched for her phone, which had fallen somewhere between the cushions in the couch.

With as much enthusiasm as she could muster she answered, "Hello, this is Dr. Ford."

"Hey baby, it's Jack," the voice said on the other end of the line, "I noticed that you tried to call a couple of times, and you sounded a little anxious. How are things in Fort Collins?"

Ann didn't know what to say. All of the emotions she had been dealing with surfaced simultaneously. She remained silent, trying to gather her thoughts and marshal her emotions.

"Hello, anybody home?"

"Jack, I'm so glad it's you! When is that North Star Energy contract going to be up?" she burst out.

"I love you too, baby, but wasn't it North Star Energy that put ninety million in our pocket?"

"Yeah..." She paused for a minute to gain some composure. "I'm sorry, Jack. I've just had the most unbelievable twenty-four hours of my life, and I need you here."

"Not possible, sweetheart, the last twenty-four hours couldn't possibly have topped our two week honeymoon in New Zealand!" said Jack, grinning on the other end of the line.

Ann sighed... typical man, alluding to sex during a serious conversation.

Given campus and Home Land Security phone taps, she had to be very careful how she was going to word what she so desperately wanted to share with him. Had she been more familiar with complexities behind voice stress and anxiety analytical science, she wouldn't have taken Jack's call at all. Unknown to her was, three separate computer programs were monitoring her call, and that would be notifying a number of people that her 11:27am MST call had generated anxiety and stress metrix that were off the charts.

Knowing that someone might be monitoring her call, she tried to bring some humor into the conversation with her husband. "I've got some good news and I've got some bad news. Which do you want to hear first?" There was a momentary pause on the other end of line.

"Hit me with the bad news."

"Promise you won't hate me?" Ann asked.

"How could I hate the most intelligent, beautiful, and adorable woman on the planet? Hit me with the bad news, baby."

"Well... ah... I... ah... totaled the 911," she teased with a believable stutter. She let the news sink in for a few seconds before she continued, and Jack bought it hook-line-and-sinker. "Just kidding... Gotcha didn't I? You love that car more than me, don't you?" She hoped her tactics would hide any anxiety she might have expressed earlier and fool anyone that was invading her privacy.

There was silence on Jack's end, followed by a weak but audible laugh.

"Ann, that one's going to cost you. You won't know when, and you won't know where, but I promise the pay back is going to be well thought out. So what's going on?" Jack could tell by the tone of Ann's voice that something out of the ordinary was up, and it made him a little nervous.

"Well," sighed Ann, trying to sound casual, "I would much rather tell you in person, but since you are not going to be home for another five days, I will tell you now." *I only wish that we had a more secure line to talk on,* she thought to herself. "I had an interesting visit today from Dr. Sellers from the University of Southern Texas," she said matter-of-factly. "He offered me a job with a salary one-and-a-half times what I'm making now, and said that I would be reporting directly to Dr. Conner. He also offered me a seat on a research subcommittee."

Again there was silence on the other end of the line. Jack sensed that Ann was doing her best to remain calm, and he understood why. The last thing they needed was an agent from Home Land Security asking questions about the overseas call they were making.

"Is that the good news or the bad news?" asked Jack.

"That is the bad news."

"What is so bad about that? You just got an offer to work for one of the most prestigious universities in the world, among the most admired people in your field, delivered by a Nobel Prize winner. Good hell, girl, I hope you said yes."

Jack was so proud he thought the buttons where going to pop off his shirt. From the first day he met Ann, he was certain she was the most incredible person he had ever known, and now UST seemed to be sharing the same sentiment. He wasn't sure his wife was aware of the rigorous background checks, character screening, and IQ analysis that preceded such an offer. He'd even heard they did some kind of genetic test to measure a person's character.

"I've never been so proud of anyone in my entire life," said Jack, barely restraining the urge to shout. "Are you still there, Annie?"

"I'm still here," she said, and a tear dropped off her eyelash onto the phone. She paused for a moment, wiping the phone on her blouse. *Listen very carefully Jack because I'm only going to say this once. I hope you remember this is code for 'I had a major breakthrough,"* she thought, as she tried to calm her voice. "Oh, and another thing, I burned a batch of cookies this morning and almost burned down the whole house."

Jack didn't say anything and Ann thought she may have lost the connection. "Jack?"

Jack slowly and carefully repeated back the words. "You burned a batch of cookies and almost burned down the whole house?"

"Yes," articulated Ann slowly, "I burned them so bad that we're going to have to have our home fumigated." She could sense the excitement in Jack's voice and hoped he had the wisdom to choose his words and tone wisely.

"You're telling me that, *you burned a batch of cookies, and almost burned down the whole house*? Wow..." responded Jack with constrained emotion, "You have had a busy day. I'll see if I can arrange to come home a little early and help you clean up the smoke damage."

"I would really like that," said Ann, her eyes brimming with tears. "Just come home as soon as you can. I'll wait until you get here to make a decision about the UST offer. I love you," she said, and hung up the phone.

Ann felt like she had just confessed a lifetime of sins to a priest. She sank back into the couch, wishing she could disappear into its comfortable cushions until Jack got home. The thought of sleeping another night without him made her feel sad. She closed her eyes and breathed in and out slowly. It felt good to share her secret with another person, and somehow her burden felt lighter now that Jack knew what was going on.

Chapter Six

"Half the Truth"

A recognizable and obnoxious knock on her office door jarred her to a sitting position. *Charli and lunch,* she thought. She brushed a lingering tear off her face, straightened her hair, then slowly opened the door.

"You've been crying, girl!" Charli said, plopping onto the couch and pulling her best friend down beside her. "Did Jack dump you?" she asked, "Because if he did, I can have him killed."

Ann half-believed her, considering the size of her twin brothers. "Let's get some lunch and you can tell me all about it," Charli teased, pulling Ann to her feet.

"All right," said Ann with a heavy sigh, "but can we go somewhere off campus for a change?"

"As you wish," Charli answered, flourishing her hand as she steered Ann out the door.

"I hope you didn't mind me using your brush and makeup while you were in class," said Charli. "I misplaced my gym bag somewhere this morning and needed a little touch up."

"Not at all," said Ann, knowing full well Charli could go a month without makeup and still look good.

Ann and Charli had begun their teaching career at CSU the same semester and become acquainted in one of the new professor orientation seminars. By the end of the fourth day they were best friends.

By all definitions of the word, Charli was a bombshell. Ann loved to be out in public with her just to watch men fall over themselves to say hello. It was the most pathetic commentary on the physically stronger of the sexes that Ann had ever witnessed, and she got a kick out of watching it. What Ann didn't realize was that she also was easy on the eyes, and that the pair of them were more than most men could handle.

"Why don't I drive?" suggested Ann, knowing how much Charli lusted after Jack's 911.

"Ok with me, heiress, have it your way. I don't mind being chauffeured around after a rough morning. On the other hand, my morning wasn't so rough that it made me cry, so perhaps I should drive."

"Nah, I got it covered," said Ann.

Arm-in-arm they headed into the parking lot. Ann pulled out Jack's key fob and pushed the start-engine button. Eight cars away, the Porsche 911 roared to life.

"No way!" yipped Charli, "Jack left you the 911?"

"Yes way," Ann said, grinning at her friend. "I'll let you drive if you won't tell." Ann's eyes twinkled.

"On the grave of my dead grandmother and before God and all his holy angels I swear, double swear, and triple swear—I won't breathe a word," said Charli, and she snatched the dangling car keys out of Ann's hand.

Charli opened the driver's side door and slid behind the wheel. "Ouch!" she yelled as her knees jammed against the steering wheel. In her excitement, she forgot that she was a full eight inches taller than her best friend and most of it in legs, as any of the males on campus would attest to. Not too many years ago she'd been a volleyball super star, which explained her current position as the head coach of the women's volleyball team at CSU. What most people didn't know was that she had brains as well as looks, which her master's degree in genetics confirmed.

Fumbling with the power seat controls, she finally wiggled into a comfortable position. For a moment, she stared with delight at the control panel of the 911.

"Whee," she giggled as she played with the lumbar support and heated seat controls.

"Are we done yet?' snarked Ann, who had been comfortably buckled in for over a minute.

"Not quite," sighed Charli as she adjusted the mirrors and brushed a long strand of naturally blonde hair away from her eyes.

Taking a deep breath, she backed the 911 out of the parking stall and then gingerly put it into first gear. Accustomed to rodding around her little red Mazda MX-5, she was totally unprepared for the power unleashed by the turbo-charged 911. With a bit of a spunky look and a toss of her head, she revved the engine and let the clutch go. Having made a similar mistake earlier in the day, Ann grabbed her seat with both hands, praying Charli wouldn't put a ding in Jack's car. The 911 responded precisely as Professor Ferdinand Porsche intended, and both rear tires smoked the pavement for twenty yards. In absolute panic, Charli slammed on the brakes, throwing both of them forward in their seat belts. The 911 promptly left another eight feet of skid marks before coming to a steaming halt. Ann was laughing so hard, tears were streaming down her face.

"Oh, shut up," Charli said as she struggled to regain a smidgen of composure before bursting into laughter. "Why can't I find a man like this?"

"Give me the keys and step out of the car," said Ann through a fit of laughter. Ann motioned for the keys with an outstretched hand.

"Please, please, please, give me one more chance," begged her friend.

"This isn't your mama's mini-van or your toy Miata, so give up the keys!" snapped Ann, pretending to be mad.

Charli gave Ann her patented baby-face look, and shook her head sideways.

"All right," sighed Ann, "but so help me, if you put a single dent in this car or another flat spot on the tires, I'm driving!"

With a lot less gas and a lot more finesse Charli drove out of the parking garage.

Minutes later, she pulled into the parking lot of their favorite restaurant. As soon as they were settled, Charli started in. "Let's talk about the tears I saw in your office."

Her comment brought Ann careening back to the events of the last few hours. She wished she could share her recent research breakthrough with Charli, but she didn't want to put her in danger. They ordered two mouthwatering French dip sandwiches and ate them slowly, telling each other about their day. Ann told Charli about Dr. Sellers's visit and offer. The perfect fall day turned cloudy, and it started to rain. Ann couldn't think of anything she would rather be doing than chatting over lunch with her best friend. Rain fell against the restaurant window, distorting their view of the distant mountains.

Chapter Seven

"Looking Back"

Jack hung up the phone and lay back on the hotel bed, positioning his head between two goose down pillows. "Unbelievable," he breathed. "She actually did it."

He wondered if she'd had time to think through the immensity of her discovery. His heart pounded so fast he had to stand up and walk around the hotel room. He was certain that Ann hadn't told a soul about her progress, and was confident she'd be safe for the time being.

Our lives are about to change forever, he thought with a scowl, *unless we can figure out a way to take this thing public without associating Ann's name with it.*

Jack loved his comfortable, low profile lifestyle and had no intention of changing any of it.

We have a ton of money, he theorized, *and we got it without any publicity, so we ought to be able to figure out how to keep this out of the press as well... What an awesome girl,* he thought, smiling to himself. He still couldn't believe she'd said yes to his proposal of marriage. He remembered seeing her around campus from time to time, but had never had the opportunity to speak to her. For some reason, he had always assumed that she was married.

He grinned when he remembered how he'd stumbled upon the fact that Ann was single. Every kid on campus had been talking about the hot new volleyball coach, and during a lunch break he'd noticed that she and Ann were sitting together in the cafeteria. For the sole purpose of creating a stir among his male students, he stopped to ask Charli to accompany him to a charity event where he was scheduled to be the keynote speaker. He remembered the conversation well. "Hello, ladies," he'd said. "I'm Dr. Jack Ford, the dean of the College of Environmental Science. Half my students have informed me that the man who can get a date with the new volleyball coach would be considered the luckiest man on campus."

"Why would they say such a thing?" asked Charli, acting aloof.

"Well, I imagine it's because they believe she has a dizzying intellect," he'd said smoothly.

Ann had looked at Charli and raised her eyebrows. The grin that had tugged at the corners of her mouth suggested that Jack might be interesting enough to talk to.

"Nothing to do with legs or looks then?" asked Charli innocently.

"Not at all," he'd quipped, deflecting the sarcasm. "What good are legs or looks if the woman they belong to can't have an intelligent conversation about genetics or molecular biology?"

He'd looked right into Charli's eyes, waiting for a response. Although he'd not dated seriously since his wife's death, he'd always been attracted to intelligent women, and it appeared that Charli fit the profile.

He remembered glancing at Ann before he sat down and thinking it was too bad she was married. The thought made him glance down at her ring finger. *No ring!* His heart skipped a beat. *Damn college rumors*, he thought, trying to remember who had told him she was married, but was interrupted by Charli who continued to roast him.

"Well said," chirped Charli, warming to the man in front of her.

Jack barely heard a word she was saying. Yes, she was attractive, but not even close to Ann. He gathered his thoughts and tried to respond intelligently to Charli's last remark while looking at Ann.

"It is my duty as the dean of Environmental Science to be aware of the university's biomoleculer environment, especially as it relates to protecting any rare, beautiful, and intelligent species with masters and doctorate degrees."

"Why doctor, it's nice to know someone with such a deep intellect is concerned about the safety of the Ph.D.s on campus," said Charli, who raised her left eyebrow when she realized that Jack's interest had shifted to Ann.

Jack blushed, knowing he had to bail out of this conversation quickly before it turned into a train wreck. "I, ah… that's not exactly what I was implying," he responded, trying not to let the conversation rattle him.

"What *did* you mean, Dr. Ford?" asked Charli, who nudged Ann under the table with her foot.

Jack remembered trying to decide how to respond. He knew his next sentence would make or break his chances of taking the most eligible doctor on campus to the benefit dinner, and he wasn't thinking of Charli.

"To be clear, I feel it is my sacred duty as one of the deans at this fine university to send a strong message to the rest of the campus yahoos that it's quintessential for a woman to be courted because of her intellect rather than her mere beauty."

"Did you just say that I'm beautiful and intelligent?" asked Charli kicking Ann again.

It didn't seem possible for Jack's face to turn any redder, but it did. In a desperate effort not to be outmaneuvered by the smooth-talking female, he responded, "You are indeed a rare beauty, and from what I gather, extremely intelligent, but I was referring to the beauty and intelligence of Dr. Archer, and I was wondering if she would do me the great honor of accompanying me to a benefit dinner this very evening?"

Jack's response caught both Charli and Ann completely off guard, which he'd enjoyed immensely. They'd looked at each other in surprise and then gave each other the '*yeah, he is interesting enough to go out with*' nod.

"It would be my pleasure to accompany you, Dr. Ford. However, I must warn you that I fall asleep and snore loudly during boring speeches."

"Then I will do my best to prepare something that will titillate your intellect," said Jack, putting a slight emphasis on the word "titillate" as a last ditch effort to even the score with Charli.

It worked, and both women blushed slightly.

"I will pick you up at 7:15 pm sharp, then?" he confirmed, trying to suppress a grin.

"That would be fine," said Ann, who noticed for the first time how ruggedly appealing Jack was.

"Do you know where I live?"

"It shouldn't be hard to find," said Jack, "I will just follow my heart."

He remembered saying thank you, then walking away being grateful he'd broken even on the conversation. He'd cursed himself for not asking for an address and for his ridiculous closing remark. *I must have come across as extremely forward,* he reflected as he took off his tie. Ann had quickly become his best friend, the center of his life, and one year later, his wife.

Jack didn't mind traveling for North Star, other than it took him away from Ann. On numerous occasions he'd tried to get her to quit her job and travel with him, but she refused. Ann hated to travel unless it was to explore locations of ancient origin or to see extraordinary geological formations. Unfortunately, Jack's travels did not take him to such places very often, so he traveled alone. *It's worth the ninety million,* he told himself, but he couldn't wait until his contract was over.

North Star had approached him about staying on another five years, but he turned them down without a second thought. He valued his time with Ann more than anything else in his life, and all he wanted to do was to spend less time working and more time with her. Ann filled a deep and profound void left by his first wife when she had been killed with her parents in a terrorist attack. Marrying Ann had been the beginning of the healing process for Jack. She'd become the light and joy of his life, and a new reason to live.

Chapter Eight

"Solicitation from the CIA"

A few months before asking Ann out on their first date, Jack was eating lunch at a local diner when he was approached by a handsome young man wearing a well-kept suit. The man stuck out his hand and introduced himself as Matt Dalton, an agent for the CIA. Curious, Jack had offered him a seat. Matt asked how he was doing since his wife's death, then offered his condolences.

Jack wasn't too surprised by the visit because the FBI and the CIA had called on him several times following the attack. He was one of only a handful of people who had been standing across the street from the bus terminal where the terrorist bombing had occurred.

Matt made an attempt to impress Jack by telling him he'd flown to Colorado to see him face-to-face.

"You could have called," said Jack sarcastically.

"You would have said no on the phone."

Jack half-smiled. "No to what?"

"No to what I'm about to ask you."

"If I would've said no on the phone, I'll say no to you now," said Jack.

Agent Dalton then tried to sell Jack on the idea that being an undercover civilian operative for the CIA was a good thing and a great opportunity. "We know you don't need the money, but we could really use your expertise on several cases involving the petroleum industry."

"How much money are we talking about?" asked Jack, only because he was curious.

"Two hundred and eight thousand dollars a year."

Jack looked at him as if he were bone stupid. "You're right, I don't need the money. And since you seem to know I have over a hundred million in the bank then you know what your 'opportunity' sounds like, right?"

Matt expected this response and played another card. "With oil prices over twelve dollars a gallon, the country is in dire straits. If we don't find more oil resources within this country in the next forty-eight months, we are screwed."

"Not only am I not interested in your opportunity, but my oil research is under exclusive contract to North Star, and I'm not interested in breaking it."

"We're not asking you to share or talk about your technology," countered Matt. "All we need you to do is to keep your eyes and ears open during the normal course of your business and report any information that might affect the United States' domestic and foreign oil reserves."

"The answer is still no," said Jack.

Matt had expected this response as well. He had only one card left to play, but decided not to play it until their next visit.

Standing up, Matt straightened his coat, making no effort to conceal his Berretta, the CIA's weapon of choice.

"Looks like a new issue," Jack commented sarcastically. "I've never had a job offer from a guy carrying a gun before."

"Then you'd better say yes the next time we meet, or I'll be forced to use it," retorted Matt, putting his hand on his gun.

Jack didn't know what to think, so he just stared at his hamburger.

"I'm totally kidding, professor," said Matt dryly as he retracted his hand and headed towards the door.

Matt visited Jack a half a dozen times during the following year, and each time had been told no. Every time he visited, he asked enough questions that Jack felt like he was already working for the CIA, and Matt wasn't the kind of guy who was shy about pushing for more.

During one of Matt's visits, Jack decided he had had enough. "Look, you pump me for information almost every month. For all intents and purposes, I'm working for you now. You owe me approximately three million dollars in consultation fees, and I'm not meeting with you again unless you start paying your bill."

"How did you come up with three million?"

Jack shrugged. "It's easy math. I charge a dollar a question."

"Sounds fair," responded Matt, smiling slyly. "I knew I would eventually wear you down."

"You know this is harassment, don't you?"

"Pretty much," said Matt, not looking the least bit concerned. "Where would you like me to send the check?"

"Deposit it in this bank account," Jack said, handing Matt a piece of paper, "and make damn sure it looks like it's coming from an oil company I'm consulting for."

Jack had never told Ann about his arrangement with the Central Intelligence Agency. He knew he needed to come clean about the extra $208,000 he received from them every year, but he didn't want to cause her undue stress. It was the only thing in their marriage he had hidden from her, except for the Berretta they gave him that he had stashed in the trunk of his car.

Chapter Nine

"Ransacked"

Ann and Charli finished their relaxing lunch, which culminated in a resolution. Ann would accept the teaching position at the University of Southern Texas and keep an eye out for an opportunity Charli might be interested in.

They waited in the doorway of the restaurant for a lull in the rain, and when it slowed momentarily, they made a dash for the 911. Ann drove back to the university feeling a little calmer about the events of the day, thankful for good friends.

"See you tomorrow, then, for lunch?"

"Yep!" said Charli, and she waved as she walked down the sidewalk to volleyball practice.

Ann walked in the opposite direction to teach her final two classes of the day, holding a paper over her head so her hair wouldn't get wet. Despite all that was on her mind, the graduate chemistry and compound disposition classes flew by without incident. At the end of the last class, she fielded a few questions, then headed towards her office, and finally, the car.

After a few minutes, the air blowing out of the Porsche's vents warmed up and blew the fog off the front windshield. The rain picked up tempo and started pounding ruthlessly on the Porsche roof and windshield—so much so that the windshield wipers could barely keep up with the onslaught.

"A perfect day for a crackling fire, a warm blanket, and cup of hot cocoa," she said out loud. "The only thing missing is my man, Jack." Shifting into first gear, she pulled out of the parking lot and onto the road for home. The rain intensified and Ann had to turn up the volume on the radio several notches to hear over the flip-flop of the windshield wipers and the pounding rain.

Why can't they make the windshield wipers purr like the engine? she thought as she plowed through the horrific weather.

Twenty minutes into the drive home, the Porsche 911 lurched hard to the left, interrupting Ann's favorite singer, Sheii Lindley, on the radio singing, "Goodnight Mr. Moon." Ann turned off the radio and slowed down so she could hear if there was a problem. The unnerving sound of rubber making a loud thumping sound could only mean one thing—a flat tire. She slowed to a stop and turned on the emergency flashers, then pressed her forehead against the steering wheel. *Unbelievable! Thank goodness Jack insisted on teaching me how to change a flat on this little monster,* she thought before she got up enough courage to face the pouring rain. She popped the trunk from the inside of the car and tentatively opened the door. *No way to avoid getting wet,* she thought, *so I might as well get on with it.*

Ann maneuvered through the rain to the front of the car to open the deck lid. She ran her fingers under the edge until she found the release latch and pressed it. Inside the dimly lit interior, she could see the spare tire and the jack assembly cover. Luckily, Jack didn't have anything in the trunk except golf clubs and an emergency kit, which she put on the ground in the rain. Opening the spare tire cover, she squinted to see how to free the tire from the compartment.

"You've got to be kidding me!" she burst out. To her absolute dismay, the compartment contained a very flat spare tire.

Truly unbelievable, she thought. *God must be testing my patience and I'm getting a C-.* She stood with her hands on her hips, staring into the trunk. *Now I'm going to have to thumb a ride home with a stranger.* Up to this point, she hadn't had time to be scared, but a thread of fear began to wind its way through her belly.

Despite Fort Collins's lower-than-average crime rate, it was not without its problems. Taking her cell phone out of her pocket, she held it close to her mouth and said, "Charli," and then waited for the phone to dial. The phone rang eight times then flipped over to Charli's answering machine.

"Hi, this is Charli... I'm sorry I missed your call, but please leave a message after the beep, and I will return your call as soon as I can."

"Not soon enough, girl," Ann shouted into the phone, "not soon enough. I'm stranded on I-287 with a flat tire and a flat spare, so if you don't hear from me soon, call the cops."

Ann hung up the phone and slipped it back into her pocket. She lifted the spare tire out of the trunk and put it on the ground so she could take it into town and have it repaired. She was about to throw the emergency kit and the golf clubs back into the trunk when she noticed a six-by-ten metallic box lying near where the spare tire had been. Curious about what it might contain she picked up the box and turned it over. It was heavier than she expected and slipped out of her wet hands, spilling its contents into the trunk.

"What the...!" she gasped in surprise. A two-inch roll of Ben Franklins, a hand gun, and a sheaf of passports bound together with a rubber band lay exposed on the floor of the trunk.

Good hell, Jack, what are you thinking? Handguns had been outlawed across the country without a special federal permit, and she couldn't think of a single reason why Jack would have one. The only people she knew who were qualified to carry a handgun were law enforcement authorities, which Jack was not. The penalty for carrying or possessing an illegal hand gun was a $20,000 dollar fine and up to five years in prison, no questions asked.

Ann was processing the reasons Jack might have a handgun, passports, and a roll of hundred dollar bills in his trunk when she noticed that a car had pulled up behind her. She turned to see a highway patrolman motioning her over to his cruiser through his rain drenched windshield.

Her heart pounded in alarm. "Damn, damn, damn, damn, damn," she said under her breath. She pretended not to see the officer as she pushed the handgun and shells into the spare tire compartment and closed the cover. Then she casually put the roll of money and the passports into her pocket and returned the clubs and emergency kit to the trunk and slammed the lid.

When she turned towards the lights of the patrol car, she could see that the police officer had left his car and was only ten feet away from her and closing fast. At this point, she didn't even have to pretend to cry.

"Looks like it hasn't been your lucky day," shouted the officer over the traffic and rain. Examining the flat tire and the flat spare, he asked, "Where are you headed?"

"Home," replied Ann, "I live west of here, off of I-14." The pouring rain mixed with her tears and ran down her cheeks.

"Why don't you sit in my cruiser and I'll jack your car up so you can have both tires repaired at the same time."

"Sounds really good," said Ann in a panic, "but I'm late for an appointment."

The last thing she wanted was to try and explain why she was driving around in a car that had a handgun in its trunk which neither she or Jack was authorized to carry.

"Would you mind giving me a lift home with just the spare?"

"It will only take me a minute to get your car jacked up so you can take both tires in for repair," said the officer.

"No, no, really, it's ok!" said Ann, with increased anxiety.

"There are a few hundred people who will be wondering where I am in the next forty minutes if I don't show up. I'm the guest speaker at a benefit dinner," she lied, hoping desperately that he wouldn't insist on jacking up the car and find the revolver and five hundred rounds of ammunition sitting next to the tire jack.

"Well, if you're in that big of a hurry..." He grabbed the spare tire and headed towards his car. "I'm not a bit sad about not having to change a tire in this downpour," he yelled over the rain.

"Thank you very much," Ann replied with an audible sigh.

As they pulled onto the highway, Ann took one last look at the Porsche and shook her head in disbelief. *Oh do you have some explaining to do, Mr. Ford!*

"Nice car," said the patrolman, trying to make conversation with an obviously cold, wet, and irritated lady.

"Yes," said Ann, "it's my husband's. He left it for me to drive while the snow tires are being put on mine."

"Not many guys would do that," said the officer, trying to be friendly. "Your husband must be a pretty nice guy."

I'm not entirely sure what he is at the moment, she thought to herself. The tension of the last twenty hours was starting to crescendo into a storm of anxiety in her mind, and she fought down the urge to scream.

"Isn't it a little early for a speaking engagement?" asked the officer, looking at his watch.

"Not really," responded Ann, shivering from cold and wondering why the officer would think that. Her mind felt like it was going a thousand miles an hour to keep up with the officer's questions. She desperately needed her lie to be believable. The fifteen minute drive home seemed like an hour, but she was able to answer the overly inquisitive officer's questions to his satisfaction. Finally the cruiser pulled in front of Ann's home.

"Do you want me to wait and give you a ride to your speaking engagement," queried the officer.

"Thank you, but no," said Ann. "I'll get a ride with my neighbor. Thank you so much for the ride home."

"Not a problem," responded the officer. "Let me get your spare tire for you." The officer put the cruiser in park, then pulled Ann's spare tire out of his trunk.

"Where do you want me to put this tire?"

"I'll take it from here," said Ann and took the tire.

"Ok, then," said the officer, "it looks like you have everything under control." The officer could sense that his services where no longer appreciated, and he retreated to his car.

"Are you sure you are going to be all right?" he asked through an open window.

"I'll be fine, and thanks again," responded Ann, forcing a smile.

Ann stood in the rain in front of her house, shivering from the cold. Being cold and wet wasn't nearly as annoying to her as the fact that she had left her keys sitting in the seat of the Porsche. She collapsed on the porch and leaned against the door, trying to remember where they had put the spare key, and felt the front door slowly push open under her weight. *What the...? I know I armed the alarm this morning!* She stumbled to her feet. Every nerve in her body was tingling as she pushed the door the rest of the way open and groped for the light switch. The sight that greeted her was so shocking it dropped her to her knees. The house had been ransacked! From where she knelt she could see her sofa had been gutted and the stuffing was all over the floor. Every picture was torn from the walls and her Victorian bookshelf was smashed to pieces.

Fearing that the culprits might still be in the house, Ann ran back into the street and started walking towards the first house that had lights on. Her heart was racing and every muscle in her body was tense.

"Why would someone want to break into our home?" she gasped. *Maybe someone did find out about my research.* Ann was on the brink of mental exhaustion. All she could think about was finding someone she trusted so she would be safe. *Is it possible that someone figured out the meaning behind the conversation I had with Jack on the phone? No way,* she thought, but her nerves were at DEFCON one. *Maybe Dr. Sellers's visit tipped someone off...?* She tried to convince herself that this was a random act of violence and that nobody had targeted her directly. Ann took her phone out of her pocket and dialed Jack's number. "Sorry, all lines are busy. Please try your call later," said the fake lady on the other end of the line.

"I hate you," she said to the fake lady and put the phone back in her wet pocket. Her anxiety level was so high she barely noticed when her phone started to ring. Searching through her soaked coat, her cold fingers found the phone, and she squinted at the LCD hoping it was Jack. It was Charli.

"Thank you, thank you," she said under her breath. "Charli, can you hear me?" she gasped. "My car had a flat tire, my spare tire was flat, there was a gun in Jack's trunk with a bunch of hundred dollar bills and a stack of passports, and my house has been broken into and, and... it's totally trashed..."

"I'm on my way," said Charli. "I'll be there in fifteen minutes. I want you to clear your head, and do exactly what I tell you to do. Who are the neighbors you like so much?"

"The Joneses," said Ann between sobs.

"I want you to walk across the street to the Jones's house, knock on their door, and ask if you can stay with them for a few minutes until I get there. Do not call anyone until I get there and do NOT, I repeat do NOT tell anyone what you just told me about the gun in the Porsche! Do you understand?"

"I understand," whispered Ann, who had already started running towards the home of Mark and Linda Jones.

"I will stay on the phone until you get there and they answer the door."

"Thank you…"

Chapter Ten

"Anonymous Call"

The earliest that Jack could get out of Kuwait was 3:25 PM, so he decided to attend his morning meetings. He looked out his hotel window at the blue waters of the Arabian Gulf as he finished packing. *So pretty, but so dry*, he thought. His phone started to ring, and he fished it out of his pocket to take a look at the caller ID. When he saw it wasn't from anyone he knew, he put it back in his pocket. He needed to catch a taxi, and he didn't have time for a conversation with a stranger.

Jack put the papers he needed for his meeting into his briefcase and left his room for the lobby. Just as he stepped into the elevator, his phone started ringing again.

I don't have time for this, he thought. *I've got to get through my meetings today and figure out how I'm going to convince North Star Energy that they don't need me here during the next few days.*

He pulled his phone out of his pocket and looked at the number. It was the same as before. Half way down the elevator the phone rang again. *703,* he thought. *What state has the area code of 703? Washington, D.C.? Virginia? Who's trying to reach me from Virginia?* "If I don't know you, you can wait or leave a message," he mumbled under his breath.

Jack exited the elevator and pushed his way out the front door of the Ritz Le Meridian Hotel. He hailed a cab and then stood on the curb thinking about the phone conversation he'd had with Ann.

She'll be all right until I get there, he kept telling himself. *After all, she's one of the calmest people I've known. Besides, no one knows anything about her progress or what she has been doing. For that matter, I don't have a clue about her progress either! Why didn't she tell me she was getting close?*

A taxi pulled up to the curb and the driver popped the trunk lid. He motioned for Jack to give him his briefcase. Jack declined and pointed towards his suitcase instead. *Why do they always assume I want to put my briefcase in the trunk?* he wondered, a little annoyed.

Jack opened the door of the cab and sat down in the rear seat. "Ouch!" he shouted. "Lucky I'm wearing cotton pants or I'd be fused to your damn Naugahyde seat." He glared at the cab driver, who didn't look a bit concerned. Jack wasn't certain, but he thought he'd seen the cab driver smile with pleasure at his discomfort.

"Where to, American man?" asked the cab driver in broken English. "The KOC Building," responded Jack.

"Ok, I know it," said the cab driver as he whipped the cab into traffic.

"What you do in Kuwait?" asked the cab driver.

"I'm here to consult with the Ministry of Oil," said Jack.

"Ah then, you a big man?"

"Not really," chuckled Jack, "but I consult the big man."

"I see," said the cab driver, flashing a smile. "You know big man?"

"I suppose so," said Jack, his butt still burning from the taxi's hot, sticky seats.

His phone started ringing again, and he looked at the caller ID. *703-356-8477*, it read, but there was no name. He clicked through the phone numbers he'd received in the last half hour. *703-356-9377, 703-356-1700...*

That's strange. All the numbers were coming out of the same location. It was almost like someone was calling from different pay phones in a shopping complex or a train station. *Do they even have payphones anymore?* Intrigued, he answered the call.

"Hello?"

"Jack, is that you?" said the voice on the other end of the phone.

"Who is this?"

"A friend," said the voice.

"Is this a joke?" asked Jack intensely.

"Shut up and listen," said the caller. "Your wife is in danger and you need to return home immediately! I will protect her for as long as I can, but the danger she's in originates at levels in the federal government that are well over my pay grade. I have intel suggesting that she's attracted the interest of several major oil cartels...

Trust only UST," said the voice, and the phone went dead.

Before Jack had time to process the information, the cab had arrived at the KOC Building. "UST?" he said out loud. The acronym meant nothing to him. "UST," he repeated. "University of South….. Southern…..Tennessee…..Texas! The University of Southern Texas!"

"That will be forty dollars, if you please," said the cab driver with a grin. Jack fumbled for his wallet, handed over an undeserved Ulysses S. Grant, and stepped onto the sidewalk with his luggage. His mind raced as he searched in vain to match a face or a name to the voice on the phone, but nothing came to mind.

"Trust only UST?" *But everybody trusts the University of Southern Texas,* he thought. *How would anyone know that Ann had received an offer from the University of Southern Texas in the first place, unless they'd tapped Ann's cell phone? Could someone have found out that Ann had made a major breakthrough in her research?* Jack searched his memory for anyone in Washington who knew his cell phone number. Agent Dalton at the CIA had his cell phone number, but the caller didn't sound like him.

He reviewed the phone call he'd had with Ann the night before, but couldn't think of anything that would have clued anyone else in on her success.

He dialed Ann's number, but the line was busy. He hit redial but got a message telling him that "all circuits were busy and to try again later." Jack tried redialing one of the phone numbers that had been left on his missed-call phone log, but there was no answer. Jack could feel his stress level starting to peg. *If anything has happened to Ann...* he couldn't even finish the thought.

He ran inside the KOC Building and interrupted the conversation the lobby attendant was having on the phone.

"I need to see Mr. Ahmadi now!" The look on Jack's face and the tone of his voice must have said a thousand words, because the man behind the desk hung up the phone and dialed Mr. Ahmadi. Less than a minute later, Mr. Ahmadi came bustling from the direction of the elevator. When he saw Jack, he changed direction and jogged towards him.

"Jack, how are you! Is there a problem?" he asked, trying to interpret the look on Jack's face. Ahmadi had obviously been prepped by the man at the desk.

He quickly explained the phone call he had received in the taxi and told Mr. Ahmadi that he would need to cancel the North Star Energy meetings. To Jack's relief, Mr. Ahmadi nodded his head vigorously.

"Jack, if I were in your shoes, I would already be running to the airport. We do not take such things lightly in my country." Mr. Ahmadi took Jack by the arm and hustled him to the door. He waved to the driver of a long black limo parked in the shade of the KOC Building, and was barking orders in Arabic before the vehicle came to a halt.

He turned to Jack, "I have known you and your beautiful wife for many years. There are few men that I respect more than you, and fewer still that I would help as I will help you now. "This man," he said pointing at the driver of the limousine, "works for me and will take you to the airport. When you get to the airport, there will be a man waiting at the curb to escort you to my personal jet, which will then fly you directly to the United States to an airport of your choosing. We'll conclude our business another day, when your wife is safe. Our oil is not going anywhere soon," he said. "I just need you to tell me where to dig my next thousand holes! I will remember you at Salat—now go, and may Allah protect your wife and family and curse any that would do them harm!"

"Thank you so much," choked Jack, trying to smile, but his emotions were running too high. With a grim face, Mr. Ahmadi spoke rapidly to the limo driver until he was certain he understood. Jack sank back in the seat—his heart and mind racing.

"Hurry! This is a serious situation," said Mr. Ahmadi in English for Jack's benefit.

"Yes, Prince Ahmadi," responded the driver.

Mr. Ahmadi wasn't kidding when he said he would arrange everything. Jack's limo hadn't even come to a complete stop before a man in a turban was opening his door and pressing his itinerary into his hand. "You follow me," the man said, touching his chest. "You must hurry, sir, you only have ten minutes to board your plane."

Jack dug in his wallet for a tip.

"No tip, no tip!" said the limo driver in an offended tone. "Follow him now!" he said pointing at the man wearing the turban.

Jack didn't question further, and ran to catch up with the man. The man walked briskly up to the security line, shouting something in Arabic. The security officers parted like Moses parting the Red Sea, and Jack followed him through the scanner on the run.

"This way," said the man as he jogged down the corridor.

Eight minutes later, Jack was boarding a private jet bound for the Denver International Airport.

Chapter Eleven

"Meltdown"

"What do you mean, her notes and hard drive are gone?" yelled Reggie Southerland, Deputy Director of the CIA, "She's just a professor of chemistry. Why in the hell would she burn her notes and hard drive? And how do you know they didn't get there before us?" he shouted, the veins bulging out on his neck. "Get me some concrete information on this now!" he spat, and hung up the phone.

Matt Dalton, who was lingering outside, waiting for the conversation to end, decided not to eavesdrop anymore and pushed his way into the office.

"Bad day?"

"It's nothing," said Southerland, who failed miserably to hide the fact that he was totally pissed off.

"Need to know only?" queried Matt.

"Something like that," retorted Southerland irritably. "How long has it been since you touched base with that guy from Colorado?"

"Who are you talking about?" pried Matt, trying to gauge the importance of the conversation.

"That guy who works for North Star...I think his last name was Ford. What's he up to these days?" probed Southerland intently.

"I haven't spoken to him for over a month. He rarely has anything of value to tell us. Why the sudden interest?"

"Oh, nothing." Southerland stood up behind his desk, indicating that Matt's visit was over. "Why don't you touch base with him and let me know how he is doing? I want to know everything—how his invention is working for North Star, how much oil he has located with the thing, how his relationship with his wife is, what she is doing, you know—everything!" Southerland didn't try to hide his irritation, and physically pushed Matt towards the door.

Matt had never really seen eye-to-eye with the Deputy Director, but their working relationship was as good as any. In Matt's humble opinion, Southerland had a hard time distinguishing between what was best for him and what was best for the country.

Matt was curious about Southerland's sudden interest in a rich retired professor who provided boring updates on worldwide oil reserve locations. He started to walk away from Southerland's door, but stopped when he heard Southerland's voice increasing in pitch again.

I wonder if he knows how thin the walls are around here? Matt loitered near the water cooler, pretending to get a drink. It was his third and fourth drink that began to make the secretary suspicious.

"I don't care what you do," Southerland was yelling, "but if they get her research, the President will have both our heads! Neither the government nor American businesses are prepared to handle trillions of dollars of lost revenue!"

Matt walked slowly over to the water cooler, put down his notepad, and filled a fifth cup of water. The secretary wagged her pen at him as if she were going to tattle on him.

"These guys are worse than the mafia!" yelled Southerland. "They're protected by a network of legitimate global corporations who are drunk with power. They've already got us by the balls, and I don't like it! If they get their hands on Ford's research, they'll have sole control of the energy supply of this planet!"

"We don't even know if she's got an economic solution," said a voice on the speaker phone.

Southerland was nearly screaming now, and Matt had run out of reasons to linger. "If she hasn't done anything noteworthy, then why in hell was her house ransacked? And why did she torch her own lab?" Southerland's voice faded as Matt walked farther down the hall.

Ford? he thought. *Do I know anybody by the name of Ford that is doing energy research?* Jack Ford's invention was pretty good at locating dwindling pockets of oil. Maybe he'd come up with another ninety-million-dollar invention.

His legs moved faster as he resurrected his conversations with Jack. He remembered Jack telling him that his wife worked at Colorado State University as a professor. "I wonder what her area of expertise is?"

he muttered as he approached the hallway leading to his office.

Has Southerland duped me into thinking that he's interested in Jack when in reality he's been interested in his wife all along? He pressed his thumb against the biometric reader outside his office door, and then again on his computer.

Why is the CIA involved in this anyway? He typed in Jack's name and scanned through the file. Wife, mother, and father-in-law killed in terrorist attack, married to Ann Archer, no children, sold oil detection device to North Star Energy for ninety million. Doctorate in... Matt exited out to the main screen and typed in the name Ann Archer Ford.

The screen went blank except for some black text in a red box that read, "Access denied. Security clearance insufficient to view this file." *Why on earth would an average professor's file be restricted? Why does the CIA care about Ann Archer Ford—isn't that FBI territory?*

Matt turned off his computer, and took the stairs to the first floor. He knew someone who had higher security clearance than he did, and it was time he called in a favor. He and Sam had played high school basketball together back in the day when the world was a simpler place. Sam had worked for the bureau for twenty years, serving the last ten as the Director of Information Technology.

Matt and Sam ate lunch together at least twice a week, where they reminisced about old times. Both were guilty of living off their athletic glories of the past. Matt had coordinated several projects that required heavy IT involvement, so their close association had gone unnoticed. Matt pressed his thumb against the bio-reader and the door to the IT department slid open.

"Hi Matt," said Dixie, the office manager, "looking for Sam?"

"Yeah," said Matt. "Is he around?" Very few people in the Agency had access rights to the CIA's bank of computers, but the Director of Information Technology was an exception.

"I'll page him for you," said Dixie, as she dialed Sam's number.

"Sam, there is a young man here to see you. "Would you like me to send him in?"

"Only if he's not any younger looking than me," retorted Sam. They had never told Dixie which of them was younger. She had no idea why they were so close, but those were questions one didn't bring up around the CIA these days. There were a lot of people checking and rechecking employee backgrounds in the center, and it didn't pay to ask too many questions.

There were rumors that the FBI and the CIA had been infiltrated by an unsavory cartel referred to as Mcorp. There was very little concrete evidence that Mcorp even existed, but there were open cases at the CIA and FBI, and resources were being applied to find out for sure. Some had surmised that Mcorp was originally organized by American businesses to protect American oil interests from unfair import/export pressures from OPEC.

Both the FBI and CIA had information suggesting that Mcorp had grown to a point where it had sufficient power to unlawfully influence government trade policy at many levels and across global industries. Nothing had been proven in court, but evidence was building that Mcorp had infiltrated even the top levels of the CIA,

FBI, Homeland Security, Federal Reserve, Congress, Wall Street and even the White House.

"Tell Sam that I want to get an early lunch," said Matt, rubbing his stomach.

Dixie did as he asked, and Sam soon appeared around the corner wearing the child-like grin Matt had known for years.

"What's up?" asked Sam, raising an eyebrow.

"Is there anything wrong with being hungry?"

"At 11:20 in the morning?"

"Yeah, well, I didn't get breakfast," Matt lied.

"I'm game," responded Sam, his interest peaking. "Where to?"

"How about a deli sandwich in the park?" suggested Matt.

Sam shrugged. "Works for me." Then he rolled his eyes and gave his friend a sideways glance. It'd been raining off and on, and he could not imagine why Matt would want to sit on a damp bench, unless he had something interesting on his mind.

They'd made it a point to have lunch and stretch their legs in the park every once in a while so that nobody at the agency would find it unusual. They ordered their usual footlong sandwiches, bags of chips, and root beers, and talked while they walked across the street to the park. Matt told Sam about his official and unofficial conversations with Director Southerland. He also told him about his work with Jack Ford, and asked if he'd heard anything about him or his wife, Ann.

"Ann Ford?" Sam looked startled the second Matt said her name.

"Yeah, Ann Ford."

Sam groaned. "Tell me you're yanking my chain."

"Not yanking your chain," breathed Matt quietly, trying to walk a little closer to his friend.

Sam looked around nonchalantly to make sure nobody was within earshot. "Her name has been coming up all over the place."

"Since when?"

"Since yesterday when Dr. Sellers visited her on campus and her house was broken into by Mcorp."

"In what order did these events happen?" urged Matt, his interest skyrocketing.

"Dr. Sellers visited her on campus around 10:00 AM, and her home was broken into a short time later."

"How long have you been keeping tabs on her?"

"Officially, she became a person of interest ever since she wrote that paper on hydro-electrolysis a couple of years ago and Mcorp started showing interest in her work, but we didn't take her seriously until yesterday," said Sam. "There are a half a dozen oil companies who are members of Mcorp that would rather see her dead than have her reveal a plausible replacement for oil."

"Why are we involved at all?" asked Matt. "Aren't Mcorp and UST domestic players?"

"Several big dogs in the CIA believe that if Dr. Ford's technology falls into the wrong hands, the balance of power on this planet will shift in a very unhealthy way. If she really has figured out how to crack H_2O super-efficiently, then there are trillions of oil and tax dollars at risk, and we believe the government has the right to weigh in on how the technology is released—if at all."

"Last I heard," said Matt, "this country allowed its citizens to do whatever they wanted with their ideas and technology. Isn't it the United States' protection of intellectual property and the rule of law that makes it great?"

Sam shrugged, "Yeah, but we don't just let anyone have a nuclear reactor in their backyard, or a submachine gun in their closet, do we?"

Matt shook his head. "Do you really believe the US Government won't try and suppress this technology?" He didn't wait for an answer. "I, for one, am tired of riding the bus because I can't afford to fill my car up with gas."

"Oh, I think the government will release the technology, but on their terms and according to their time frame."

Matt changed the subject. "I think Southerland believes the FBI has been compromised by Mcorp and is incapable of protecting Dr. Ford or making an objective decision around her technology."

Sam looked Matt in the eyes. "What do *you* think?"

Matt shrugged half-heartedly. "They've had quite a few security breaches lately. Do you think she's safe?"

Sam shook his head in disgust. "Not by a long shot. We don't even know where she is for sure. With Mcorp on her trail, she's far from safe. Mcorp totally destroyed her house looking for the reason she would get a visit from Dr. Ben Sellers."

"Did they find anything?"

Sam laughed. "Not a single thing."

"What's so damn funny?"

"Before she left for school, she burned her documentation, including the hard drive on her computer. It was almost as if she knew someone would ransack her house."

"Do you think Sellers and the University of Southern Texas tipped her off?"

"Doubtful," said Sam, "that's not their style; besides, what would they know about Mcorp?"

"I've heard they have technology that rivals what we have."

"That's a myth," responded Sam, with a hint of annoyance.

"Then who tipped her off? You don't just wake up in the morning and decide to burn several years of research on a whim."

Sam raised his eyebrows. "We don't know, and I agree it's not possible she just happened to burn her notes and hard-drive a few hours prior to Mcorp ripping her house apart. Apparently she put enough wood on the fire to melt metal."

"Where is she now?' asked Matt.

Sam shook his head. "Seriously, we don't know, but we have a fleet of agents headed to Fort Collins as we speak."

"Why is the IT department involved on this one?"

"We were asked to do some special work with our satellite imagery so Southerland can track her."

"He wants to track her visually?"

"Yes, her every waking move. He's also trying to pick up her heat signature so he can track her by that as well. The minute we get a lock on her, we'll bring her into protective custody."

"I'm sure that's exactly what she wants," responded Matt sarcastically.

They walked back to the CIA building without speaking, both in deep thought. Sam said his good-byes and went in the building, and Matt waved down a taxi. He had an urgent desire to get to a safe phone and warn Jack about what was going on.

Chapter Twelve

"The Principals"

As always, they'd rented a room anonymously from a high-end hotel and had it equipped to meet their needs. A huge boardroom table filled the center of the room, surrounded by high-backed leather chairs. The exterior of the room was filled with matching leather sofas and chairs, and a large bank of monitors dominated the wall at one end of the room, each framing the face of a professional-looking person.

The eight men and women seated around the table were all engaged in conversations with someone else present or someone on a monitor. The subdued talking came to a halt when a broad-shouldered man named Hauzer entered the room and strode to the head of the table facing the monitors.

"I appreciate all of you coming together for our monthly meeting. Generally, because of the risk, we try not to meet as an entire body unless we have urgent business to attend to that requires the principals' buy-in. I've determined that this is one of those times."

He looked around the table to make sure he had everyone's attention. "As you know, we keep an eye on numerous enterprises, developments, and research projects around the world. What you probably don't know is that we've been particularly interested in several independent scientists who are doing research in the area of alternative fuels. One of these scientists is Dr. Ann Ford from Colorado State University."

Several of the people in the room and on the monitors were double tasking and not paying attention. He smiled, knowing that what he was about to say next would get their full consideration. "The reason Dr. Ford's research interests us is because it may threaten over a trillion dollars of next year's revenue."

Every head in the room snapped in his direction. "Yesterday, before leaving her home, Dr. Ford burned all of her research notes, including the hard-drive to her computer. Shortly thereafter, at the end of her first period class, Nobel Prize winner Dr. Ben Sellers from the University of Southern Texas paid her a visit. An hour after Dr. Sellers' visit, Dr. Ford received a phone call from her husband, Jack, that pegged our monitoring software. Normally, this type of thing would hardly be noteworthy; however, since trillions of dollars are at stake we decided to look into it."

"That's it? You risked having a meeting with all the principals because of this intel?"

"You're damn right I did! What are the chances of all these things happening on the same day? Our sources within the CIA and FBI have told us that the Feds are keeping a very close watch on her as well. We have evidence that suggests Black Gold is also watching her, so yes, I called a meeting of all the principals!"

"I'm still not impressed. Hasn't she been working on this for several years without any progress? I thought our scientists determined that her research was crap."

An elegant-looking woman on one of the monitors interrupted. "Let's be realistic. If Black Gold is interested in her, we'd better be too, or the Middle East will control the energy supply for another thousand years. Dr. Ford's actions today are very suspicious."

"I agree with Silvia. You don't just wake up one morning and burn the research you've been working on for the past seven years."

Hauzer brought the meeting back to order. "There are a couple of things we know for sure. She tried to call her husband on Monday night, but could not get through to him."

"That was prior to burning her notes, right?"

"Yes, and when we broke into her home we found this," said Hauzer and tossed a twisted piece of metal onto the table.

"What is it?" asked someone on one of the monitors.

"It's her hard drive."

Everyone looked at the scorched piece of twisted metal lying on the table. A man on one of the monitors squinted as he tried to get a better look at it. "Would you hold that thing up so we can see it better?" After he'd taken a good look at it he swore, "If Ford has successfully created a hyper-efficient solution, it will literally obliterate our oil revenues overnight. We could easily lose over a trillion dollars a year from petroleum and petroleum bi-products if this thing is for real."

A woman on one of the monitors spoke up. "My people estimate that an economic hydro-electrolysis solution is worth over one hundred trillion dollars during the next few years, not to mention the leverage it would give to whoever controls it. We cannot afford to let this technology get into the wrong hands."

"Does our competition in Russia, the Middle East, or Asia know about this?"

"Black Gold in the Middle East knows something is going on, but we haven't seen any sign of activity from anyone else."

"What are you proposing we do?"

"Secure the technology or destroy it immediately, regardless of the cost."

"Where is Dr. Ford now?"

"She hasn't returned home from school yet."

"Do we have any idea if she has a copy of her research stashed somewhere?"

"More than likely it's on a thumb-drive with her."

"Is there a chance she didn't make a copy and just memorized it?"

Hauzer shook his head. "Given the complexity of the algorithms involved, we are quite certain she has to have a copy of her notes somewhere. Nobody could retain that much information."

"Dr. Ford has a couple of safe deposit boxes in banks we own, so we'll search them first. If nothing turns up there, we will have to bring her in. Like I said earlier, she's got to have it on an external drive, and I'd bet anything she has it on her."

"What will we do if she won't cooperate?"

"She'll either cooperate to the tune of one billion dollars, or we will have to kill her," said a deep voice as if he were talking about an everyday business transaction.

"No one turns down a billion dollars, but if she doesn't cooperate, I agree, we'll have to kill her."

"Didn't her husband invent the oil repository locater that North Star is using?"

"I believe so," responded another voice at the table. "I was told they paid him nearly a hundred million for the device."

"Ninety million, to be more accurate," said a deep voice at the table.

"She doesn't need the money then, does she?"

"She'll take the billion, or she'll be pushing up daisies."

"Have our scientists made any progress improving the efficiency of our hydro-electrolysers?"

"No, our scientists have hit a brick wall with their research—just like everyone else who has been working on it."

"Maybe we need better people."

"We have the best," someone retorted defensively.

"If Dr. Ford cracked the H_2O molecule in her basement with limited funding and equipment, then we obviously don't have the best," chuckled an objective voice.

Hauzer shrugged. "Whether Dr. Ford is a genius or just got lucky is irrelevant at this point. Let's get her research or bring in the good doctor. I want someone tailing her every second of the day until we either control or have destroyed this technology."

"Yes, sir," responded two men seated near the door.

Chapter Thirteen

"Surprising Technology"

The Boeing 737 touched down and shuddered to a halt on the tarmac at Houston's George Bush International Airport. The braking of the big jet woke Dr. Ben Sellers from a very pleasant dream. He checked his cell phone messages as the jet taxied up to concourse 'A.' To his surprise, there were two urgent messages from Dr. Conner. The first message briefly explained Ann Ford's situation, and the second message gave him explicit instructions on where to board a Citation X Jet—owned by the university—that would be leaving for Fort Collins, Colorado the minute he arrived at the terminal.

After the airliner had rolled to a stop, Ben grabbed his sports coat and trotted up the gangway. He nearly ran over a man holding a sign that read 'Dr. Sellers.' He followed the man to an electric cart where Justin, the university's Director of Security, was waiting. Ben sat down, and a second later the electric car was dodging in and out of pedestrian traffic.

"I didn't know they let just anyone drive these things."

Justin smiled. "They don't."

"Where do I sign up?" asked Ben. Justin's cheshire grin and flushed face told Ben that he didn't have permission to be driving the cart either. "You're going to get us both arrested."

"Just don't look directly into the cameras," retorted Justin. "I'll bet you a hundred bucks they won't even notice."

Justin masterfully steered the cart through the throngs of people until they reached their destination. He pointed to a Citation X sitting on the tarmac. "That's our flight."

Ben looked through the glass and could see the turbines on the jet starting to turn. "Is Dr. Ford all right?

"She's on her way home from school and may not even know that her home's been trashed."

Ben looked alarmed. "Who's responsible?"

"All we know for sure is that our satellite surveillance picked up three thugs entering her house around 11:00 this morning."

"Didn't we have someone in the area who could've stopped them?"

"Our people were trailing you and Dr. Ford on campus when it happened," said Justin.

"Were we able to figure out who they work for?"

Justin shrugged. "Their MO matches some guys who have done work for Mcorp in the Denver area in the past, but we aren't a hundred percent positive yet."

"Do we have any idea what their motive was?"

"We aren't sure," responded Justin, "but we think they may have read way too much into your visit with Dr. Ford."

"Who will be going back?" asked Ben.

"Six, including you, me, and the pilot," said Justin. "We also have a modified, souped-up Bell 429 helicopter that is an hour or so away from Fort Collins to guarantee we have maximum flexibility."

Ben whistled softly. "Cool... So why do you need me to go back with you?"

"Because you're going to talk Dr. Ford into coming back with us," said Justin with a smile. "You're going to persuade her that returning with us to Corpus Christi is her safest and best option."

"You're expecting me to persuade her to leave her home and fly to Texas today? Is the situation really that critical?"

"This is by far the most tenuous situation we've ever had. Dr. Ford has somehow attracted the attention of two extremely corrupt organizations. We believe that both Mcorp and Black Gold are convinced that she has come up with an energy solution that will put a trillion dollar dent in their oil revenue."

Ben looked puzzled. "I talked with her this morning, and I don't know if she has come up with a viable solution or not. Her anxiety levels *were* abnormally high, though."

"There are a couple of things you may not know. Before she left for school this morning, she burned her research notes, hard drive and all, and incinerated her equipment in the family room fireplace. She also left a message with her husband last night and had a conversation with him this afternoon where her anxiety and stress levels were off the charts."

Ben raised his eyebrows. "Maybe she *has* done it."

"Regardless of whether she has or not, Black Gold, Mcorp, and the United States Government think that she has, and they will feed off of each other until one of them has control of the technology or they've destroyed it."

Ben was beginning to feel a little stressed. "I hope I didn't cause this whole mess."

Justin shook his head. "Dr. Ford's early morning barbeque started this mess—you only threw gas on the fire."

"That makes me feel a lot better," said Ben, glaring at Justin as they walked towards the jet. Ben couldn't help admiring it. "I suppose we own this as well?"

"Yes, we have few of them positioned around the globe for use with our clients, customers, and for research. We've modified them to fly as high as fifty thousand feet and as fast as 800 knots, which means we should be on the ground in Denver in less than an hour."

"Wow," said Ben, "That's a little faster than the 737 I just arrived on. I didn't know we had a fleet of helicopters and supersonic jets."

Justin couldn't help grinning at Ben's naiveté. "We don't exceed Mach 1, but it's nice knowing it's under the hood if we need it."

Ben shrugged. "I can see where I am in the pecking order. Who else did you say is coming along for the ride?"

"I will introduce you once we're in the air," said Justin, motioning for Ben to board. Ben had to duck to get through the jet's door, but once inside it accommodated his height without any problem. Justin bounded up the stairs behind him taking them three at a time. After everyone was seated, he made the obligatory introductions so the team would know who was going to Denver and why. The jet bumped along the tarmac as the pilot taxied the souped-up Citation-X onto the runway and waited for his turn to take off.

"Can we protect her if she chooses to stay?" asked Ben hopefully.

Justin shook his head. "No way. We'll be lucky if we can protect her in Corpus Christi."

"Why not let the Feds protect her?"

"We think there is more to their agenda than just protecting her. There's a high probability that they'll try and suppress her technology to protect the billions of dollars they receive in gas taxes and leases every year. Even if they didn't suppress her research, with all the infiltration problems they've had, we don't think they can protect her any better than we can."

"Well, I hope I can talk her into coming back with us."

"I do, too," said Justin. "But if she chooses not to come, there is nothing we can do about it."

Chapter Fourteen

"Friends or Foes?"

Ann's wild dash to Mark and Linda Jones' house had left her out of breath. Under the light of their front porch, she put her hands on her knees while she caught her breath. Her teeth were chattering as much from being emotionally shaken as from being wet and cold, and she could barely hold on to her cell phone. To her surprise and relief, the door opened before she could get the strength to ring the bell. She raised the cell phone to Mark Jones, indicating she needed to say something before she came inside. "I'm here," she said to Charli.

"Good, and don't say anything about what you found in the Porsche until we've had a chance to talk about it!"

Ann's teeth were chattering. "I got it." she said and hung up the phone. She looked up at the large muscle-bound figure of Mark Jones that framed the doorway. "I...I... need help," she gasped between breaths.

Pushing Mark aside, Linda Jones put her arm around Ann's shoulders and pulled her inside.

"Get a towel and a blanket," she barked, and Mark disappeared into the house.

"Sit on the couch while I get you some coffee," ordered Linda and she went into the kitchen.

Ann slowly regained her composure as her body warmed up and her mind slowed down. The hot cup of coffee felt good in her hands, and she sipped it slowly. With both hands wrapped around the coffee mug, she shared a conservative version of the evening's events, starting with the flat tires on the Porsche and ending with how she had discovered her home had been ravaged.

She trusted the Joneses, but not enough to include the details about her recent innovation, the offer she'd received from UST, or the handgun in her husband's trunk. Nor did she mention the roll of one hundred-dollar bills and packet of passports that bulged in one of her pockets.

"Was anything of value taken from your home?" asked Mark.

"I didn't stay inside long enough to find out," said Ann. "I didn't want to risk running into the intruders."

"Smart move," said Linda.

"Mark, is our perimeter secure?" asked Linda, who had turned off the living room light and opened the drapes.

"As far as I can tell," he said, acting as if the question where routine. They could see the front of Ann's home, but there was nobody in sight.

"Did you turn the front entry lights on?" asked Mark, looking at Ann.

"Yes," she responded, "that is as far as I got before I saw the damage."

"How bad is it?" asked Linda.

"From what I could see from the doorway, the chairs, couches, and pictures were all ripped up, and every drawer in view had been thrown on the floor."

"Would you like us to call the police?" asked Mark.

"No," responded Ann, "I would like to wait for Charli to get here first."

"Charli, the volleyball coach?" asked Linda tensing slightly.

"Yes," said Ann. "She is a good friend of mine from CSU."

"You have mentioned her before, but is she someone you trust?" asked Mark. "How long have you known her?"

"I've known her for nearly five years," said Ann, wondering why he was so concerned.

"From everything you have described to us, I recommend that you restrict your communication to your most trusted and loyal confidants," suggested Linda earnestly.

That's good advice. Ann was beginning to wonder how well she knew Mark and Linda Jones. They'd moved into the neighborhood sometime after she'd begun teaching at CSU, and had always been helpful, trustworthy neighbors. Ann and Jack had double-dated, had backyard barbeques, and skied with them dozens of times since they first met, and had always found them to be enjoyable company. On occasion, they'd asked Mark and Linda to keep an eye on their home and water their plants when they'd gone on vacation. *No reason not to trust them,* thought Ann.

Just as Ann's anxiety began to fade, there was a rapid knock on the front door.

"Is that Charli?" asked Mark, flipping on the TV monitor in the living room.

"Yes, and her twin brothers," said Ann, looking relieved.

Mark switched the monitor through eight additional views that showed the entire periphery of his home.

"It looks like we are clear," he stated in a matter-of-fact tone.

Linda opened the door, and Charli rushed in and gave Ann a hug, nearly spilling her coffee.

"How are you holding up?" she asked in a worried tone.

"Ok, considering my car broke down and I've been robbed," she said, looking up at Charli.

"Everything is going to be all right," Charli promised, trying to buoy Ann's confidence. She gave her a squeeze, then turned her attention to Mark and Linda Jones.

"These are my brothers, 280 and 290," she said pointing to the twins.

"I was thinking more along the lines of 300 and 310," laughed Mark. "It's not too often I meet someone bigger than myself."

"Hi, I'm John, and this is my brother, Jake," said John, extending a huge hand.

"I'm Mark, and this is my wife, Linda."

"Nice to finally meet you folks," said Charli smiling, "Ann has told us so much about you."

Ann rehearsed everything that had happened to her since she'd left the university earlier in the day so everyone was up-to-speed. The only details she left out were those related to the things she'd found in Jack's trunk. By the time she had finished, her hair had dried and she'd stopped shivering. She stood up and stretched her legs and answered a barrage of questions from her concerned friends about the day's events. After several minutes their questions petered out, and they were satisfied that they hadn't missed any important details.

"You guys are great! Thanks for being here for me."

"It is our pleasure," said Linda Jones, "what are friends for anyway?"

"We wouldn't have missed it for the world," echoed John and Jake.

"I've got a hunch this thing isn't over yet," said Charli, giving Ann a supportive nudge.

Ann smiled weakly. "I've got the same feeling. I guess we'd better get this show on the road and call nine-one-one."

Mark handed Ann a cordless phone. She steeled her nerves and dialed the number.

Chapter Fifteen

"Narrow Escape"

Rist Canyon Road had never seen so much activity. Within forty minutes of Ann's nine-one-one call, the street in front of her home was buzzing with CIA, FBI and local police officers with their flashing lights and badges. Rarely had the CIA and FBI both made such a formidable showing in Fort Collins, Colorado.

Flanked by John, Jake, Linda and Mark Jones, Ann walked arm-in-arm with Charli to face the onslaught of flashing lights.

"Hello, Dr. Ford," A traditionally dressed FBI agent greeted Ann. "I'm Agent Porter and I will be handling this case," he said, flashing his badge.

"How did you know she was Dr. Ford?" asked Linda suspiciously.

"I was wondering the same thing," echoed Mark.

"Well, uh… you see… We thought you might have been injured, so we took a picture of you off the university's website and gave a copy of it to all our people so we'd recognize you."

"I didn't indicate I was injured when I called nine-one-one," responded Ann.

"In situations like this, we don't take any chances," said Agent Porter.

"Why are the FBI and the CIA interested in a residential robbery in Fort Collins, Colorado," asked Linda, looking straight into the man's eyes.

Before the man could answer, her husband fired a question. "I'd like to know how the FBI and CIA found this many people to respond so quickly to a nine-one-one burglary call in Fort Collins, Colorado with only forty minutes notice?"

The rapid series of questions caught Agent Porter off guard, and it was obvious he wasn't prepared to answer them. He was a good man just trying to do his job.

"Isn't this a local police matter, or do you know something that we don't?" asked Linda.

Porter paused to process all the questions before he responded. "We believe this robbery may involve an element of organized crime, so we got involved."

"And you got all that from my nine-one-one call?" asked Ann.

"Not exactly," stammered the FBI agent, "but we have several other cases that involve organized crime in the intermountain area, and your call triggered an alert to us, so we brought the men we had in the area to the scene."

"And do you have a similar explanation for the CIA's presence here as well?"

"You'll have to speak to one of them about that," said the agent looking over his shoulder for his CIA counterpart.

"I would like to see my home." Ann smiled to take the edge off her demand.

"Follow me, Dr. Ford." The agent turned and walked briskly towards the front door of the house, grateful for the excuse to avoid any more questions.

The amount of damage that had been done to Ann's home was more than she initially imagined. The place had literally been torn apart. Every cupboard and drawer had its contents thrown on the floor. The couches and chairs were all gutted and ripped to shreds. It was obvious that whoever had perpetrated the attack was looking for something other than artifacts to be sold on the black market.

Ann gasped when she discovered her heirloom grandfather clock in pieces. She was not prone to anger, but she could feel the emotion starting to stir within her. She tenderly picked up the pieces of the clock and set them on a table. "I loved this clock… it was my grandmothers…"

"We'll find someone who can put it back together," said Charli confidently.

Ann hoped she was right. After twenty minutes, she concluded that absolutely nothing had been taken from her house. "They didn't take anything, so why did they do this?" she asked, looking around at the agents who were within ear shot.

No one had a plausible answer except Ann, and she didn't verbalize it. A chill rippled through her body as she realized how vulnerable she was. She had no idea who she could trust outside the group of friends that were with her now, and half of them she hadn't known for very long. She knew Charli trusted her brothers, but could she? Ann's grip on Charli's arm tightened unintentionally. "Ow!" squealed Charli. "What's wrong?"

"Nothing," said Ann, "I'm just a little shaken.

It was then that Ann remembered the fireplace, and guided Charli into the family room where she had torched her research notes. She hardly dared look to see if the box full of her research had burned. A surge of relief poured through her when she saw the pile of ash and twisted metal.

Silently she thanked God for prompting her to burn everything. Had she not done so, her life would have been of no value to whoever had been looking for her research. If they'd found it, they would've killed her to monopolize her breakthrough. *Thank goodness the high efficiency fireplace did its job! God willing, I'll be able to find someplace to land so I can get it out of my head and onto the internet.* Ann tensed again at the thought.

"What?" asked Charli, looking quizzically at Ann.

Ann shook her head at her friend and mouthed the words, "Ask me later." Charli nodded that she understood. *At least they didn't find what they were looking for,* she thought with immense satisfaction. *Whoever they are, they'll never profit from my research! I just hope and pray it puts whoever is responsible for this out of business for good.*

Agent Porter appeared in the doorway leading to the basement with a puzzled look on his face. "Any idea what these guys were looking for? Did I hear you say that you don't think anything is missing?"

"So far nothing appears to be missing. It's almost as if they tried to destroy as many of my personal belongings as possible without taking anything."

"Apparently they got scared off before they could break into your safe," said another agent.

"They didn't get into it?" asked Ann.

The agent shook his head. "Do you have the combination? We'd like you to check to see if the contents are intact.

I bet you would! You think my research is in there don't you? Ann ignored the agent's question about the safe. "How about you, Agent Porter, what do you think they were looking for?"

"We're not sure either," he lied.

"Charli, would you and your entourage mind escorting me downstairs?" asked Ann quietly.

"Sure thing, girl."

"What about the safe?"

"I'll look at it in a minute, but first, I would like to see what they did in the basement.

The agent looked at Agent Porter and shrugged.

Ann squeezed Charli's arm. "Have I told you how much our friendship means to me?"

"You don't need to, heiress! I felt the depth of your appreciation when I was behind the wheel of your hubby's 911 this afternoon!"

"Seriously, Charli, thanks for being such a great friend. Next to Jack, you are the closest friend I have."

Changing to a more comfortable subject, Charli asked, "Where is Jack, anyway?"

"He's in Kuwait," said Ann, the corners of her mouth turning down. "He's trying to catch an earlier flight home."

"So have you been able to get a hold of him since the last time he called?"

"No."

"Knowing Jack, he's probably already on a flight home," said Charli smiling. "You know you need to tell him about this before he gets here, right?"

"Believe me, I've tried," said Ann.

"Why don't you try again? He may have phone service on the plane."

Letting go of Charli, Ann found her cell phone and flipped it open. "Jack," she said into the receiver. The phone rang six times, then went to his voice mail. "Hi, this is Jack, I'm sorry I missed your call..."

Ann let the recording finish, then left a message. "Jack, this is Ann. I hope you were able to get an earlier flight home. I'm assuming you did since I cannot get a hold of you. I don't want you to be alarmed when you get here, but someone broke into our home today and totally trashed the place. Please call me the minute you've landed so I can fill you in. I'm ok, and will be staying at Charli's home tonight. Charli and I will pick you up at the airport, so call me the minute you land. Remember you don't have a car because you left the 911 with me. I love you..."

Ann hung up the phone. "I hope he gets my message before he shows up here."

"Me too," agreed Charli, "or he'll have a stroke."

"To the basement then?" asked Ann. "Let's see what the vandals did down there. Ann's emotions were numb as she tiptoed through her personal belongings. The basement was worse than the upstairs. It looked like every nut and bolt in Ann's lab had been dismantled and thrown into a pile on the floor. Even the recliner that Jack had given her for Christmas was completely dismantled.

"What were these guys looking for?" asked Charli.

Ann squeezed Charli's arm and gave her a warning look, then mouthed the words, *later.* "I don't know," replied Ann in a bewildered tone that was just loud enough for the FBI agent who was lingering in the basement to hear.

"Did you and Jack keep any of your millions stashed in the house?" asked Charli.

"Are you kidding," laughed Ann. "Jack's so tight, he doesn't keep more than fifty dollars at a time in his wallet!" *Except for the wad I found in the Porsche*, she thought.

Charli and Ann climbed the stairs back to the kitchen where John, Jake, and the Jones' were talking to an agent.

"Is this Ann?" he asked.

"Who are you?" responded Ann cautiously.

"I'm Agent Bishop from the FBI," he said, flipping open his wallet and exposing a badge.

"Can I see your badge again?" asked Linda Jones. "Sure," said the agent confidently. Linda looked closely at the badge. "This isn't a legit FBI badge!" she blurted out, looking at her husband, Mark. "Who are…"

The agent didn't bother to respond. He grabbed Ann around the neck and put his Beretta to her head. "Red team, red team, the party has been crashed," he said into his wireless. "Plan Alpha-B is in progress. I could use some help in here!" The man pretending to be an FBI agent backed slowly towards the basement door but didn't take his eyes off Ann's friends. "Listen very carefully, and no one will get hurt." The Berretta was steady as a rock in his hand and he looked like the kind of man that wouldn't hesitate to use it. He was so focused on the three big brutes in front of him that he didn't see Agent Porter walk back in the front door.

Agent Porter raised his hand and was starting to speak when he noticed the man holding a gun to Ann's head. "Hey, what is going on?"

The man with the gun shifted the barrel of the Berretta from Ann's head to the FBI agent in the doorway and pulled the trigger. The shot knocked Agent Porter against the door jamb and he stumbled out the front door.

Before the gun could recoil—and faster than Ann had ever seen a man move before—Mark Jones grabbed the gun hand of her assailant and shattered his wrist against the granite countertop. The man screamed in pain, but his scream died in his throat when Mark hit him in the windpipe, smashed the man's face against his knee, and then again on the granite countertop. The man collapsed to the floor, unconscious.

A flurry of gunfire erupted from the front lawn. "Take her alive," commanded a voice through the unconscious agent's wireless, "it's imperative that she be taken alive!"

The voice was drowned out by the deafening roar of automatic gun fire.

"On the floor and follow me!" commanded Mark. Mark crawled rapidly toward the basement doorway, dragging Ann with him. He pushed her down the stairs in front of him, and everyone else followed.

"John and Jake, grab something big to block this door!" yelled Mark, as he swung the door leading to the basement shut. "Bring me that lamp, Ann," he bellowed like an army general.

Ann tossed the lamp to him, and he promptly ripped off the cord and tied it from the door knob to the hand rail. John and Jake had Ann's workbench in hand and wedged it against the door.

"Perfect," said Mark, inspecting their work. He leaped down the stairs and grabbed Ann by the arm. "I know you don't know who to trust right now, but if you want to live to see tomorrow, you'd better trust me."

Ann's ears were still ringing from the gunshot that had gone off three inches from her head. Her mind raced through alternative options, but in the end she found herself nodding her head in the affirmative. For reasons she could not explain, she trusted the big man.

"Follow my instructions and we might get out of here alive!" Mark looked at John, Jake and Charli. "I don't mean this to sound shallow, but if Ann dies, we all die, so keep her alive at all costs. These guys don't give a damn about anybody but Ann. I want everybody to gather near that sliding door," he said pointing to the other side of the basement, "but don't go out until I tell you to. Find something you can use as a weapon. We may have to fight our way out of here."

John grabbed Jack's old hockey stick off the wall, and Jake helped himself to an aluminum softball bat that was in a sports bag in the closet. They huddled next to the sliding door behind Mark, waiting for his command. "We are going over the back fence into your neighbor's yard. Do they have a dog?"

"None of our neighbors have a dog," said Ann.

"Good, because this neighborhood is surrounded, and we'll be lucky if we can get out undetected. Linda, get on the phone and tell Justin we need a pick-up somewhere on that mountain," he yelled, pointing up to the moonlit ridgeline. The automatic gunfire coming from the front of the house had not subsided, and it was hard to hear.

Mark looked at the group huddled behind him. "I don't know what's going on out there, and I don't know who to trust. We'd better leave our cell phones here or anyone that's tech savvy will be able to track us."

Everyone placed their phones on the carpet. Mark quietly slid the door open and stepped onto the back patio, letting his eyes adjust to the darkness. He pointed to his eyes then at John and Jake, and raised two fingers in front of his face indicating that there were two people in the back yard. Carrying the baseball bat and hockey stick they'd found in the basement, John and Jake stepped up next to Mark. Mark looked at their weapons and whispered, "Nice choice."

Mark motioned for Ann to get closer to him. "I don't know how we are going to get out of here and I might have to improvise, so trust me and follow my lead."

"I'm putting all my eggs in your basket," said Ann, smiling weakly. She was horrified that her worst nightmare was about to come true and regretted not having made a copy of her research.

"Ok, let's do this. Follow me close..." he said, looking at John and Jake. He made eye contact with Charli and Linda. "Give us ten seconds then run towards that toolshed against the fence."

Charli and Linda's eyes were wide, but they nodded their heads that they understood. Mark looked like he was going to say something else, but shook his head and stepped off the back patio and onto the lawn towards the two men. He held Ann's wrist in an iron grip as if she were his prisoner. "I've got her," he said, trying to be heard over the gunfire, but not too loud that everyone else could hear. The two agents jogged over to apprehend Ann. Just as they were about to take her from the big man, a huge explosion startled them all. The Ford house had burst into flames, shattering glass, and throwing bricks and wood in all directions. The explosion couldn't have been timed any better, and John and Jake dispatched the two agents with a single swing each. "That's going to leave a bruise," said Mark. "Nice work, boys!"

Ann's eyes stung and she coughed from the black smoke that swirled around them. She clung to Mark's hand, trusting that he would lead her to safety. "What happened?"

"I don't know," yelled Mark. "A bullet must have hit a gas line."

Mark pointed to the back fence. "We've got to get out of here… Let's go over the fence there," he said pointing. He hoisted Ann over the fence with ease, then vaulted over himself. John and Jake gave Linda and Charli a leg over, and then climbed over themselves. Mark put his finger to his lips, and they crouched in the darkness while he listened intently and scanned the area for more agents. "I'm sorry about your house, Ann, but that explosion may have just saved your life."

Ann grimaced. The thought of everything she had just lost left a void in her heart, but she didn't have time to think about it. More gunfire erupted from the front and side of the house, then there was just the crackle of fire and voices yelling in confusion.

Mark moved quietly around the neighbor's house, and paused near a lilac bush. After checking the street in both directions, he motioned for them to make a run for the aspen grove across the street. Black smoke billowed from the Ford's house, masking their retreat into the foothills. Once in the aspens, Mark didn't stop. He pushed them up the mountain until they were easily a mile away from the house. "Let's stop for a breather," he said.

Ann looked back the way they'd come and could see her home burning in the distance. They'd gained enough elevation that they could see the entire valley. A myriad of flashing lights surrounded her home, and in the distance she could see dozens more approaching from the interstate.

"Will they think we're dead?" she asked, her voice shaking from the adrenaline rush.

"They might be fooled until morning, but they'll eventually find the two agents we knocked cold in the back yard, and they're going to talk. Unless it rains really hard, they'll find our tracks leading up this mountain as well. The good thing is they won't know who walked up this hill until they've finished with all the autopsies.

"So you think someone may have been killed in the fire?" asked Ann.

"I hope not, but the guy that was holding a gun to your head wasn't going anywhere on his own. If the help he requested made it into the house, they may not have made it out."

"What do we do now?" asked Ann, trying to sound calm. The day's events had her system on overload, and she didn't know how much more she could handle.

Mark had been dreading this question, but he figured it was better to come clean now rather than later.

"First, Linda and I need to tell you who we work for so you can decide whether you want to take our advice going forward."

Charli raised an eyebrow, "This should be rich. I was wondering who Linda was going to arrange a 'pick-up' with earlier.

Ann dropped her head in her hands. John and Jake moved a couple of steps closer so they were standing directly behind her.

"Great," said Charli in distaste. "We are surrounded by people that we don't really know. Let's get out of here, Ann."

"Let's hear them out first. I want to know who all the players are so I can weigh my options. Besides, what are they going to do with John and Jake standing here?"

"Good point. Let's hear it," said Charli curtly, glaring at Mark and Linda.

"We work for the University of Southern Texas, under the direction of Justin Woodward," said Linda, with a weak smile. "For the past several years, the university has been forced to provide a security detail for most of our senior staff. Every year, we have a professor or two who are either seriously threatened or are targeted for blackmail. Our people have a propensity to give technology away, which isn't very popular in today's world. Similarly, the people we make offers to are often exposed to all kinds of unfavorable attention.

"That's nice," said Charli.

Linda shrugged. Take you, for example," she said, tossing her head towards Ann. "We've reason to believe that Dr. Sellers's visit may have triggered a number of organizations, including the US Government, to increase their interest in you. We've been down this road so many times. We were forced to develop a highly advanced and well-trained security department to deal with it."

Mark could see that Ann was listening, which was a positive sign, so he added his two cents to what his wife was saying. "A few years ago, you published a paper that suggested lasers and high frequency vibration would be the key component in developing a hyper-efficient electro-hydrolysis solution. At the time your paper was published, UST had no research under way related to hydro-electrolysis, but our scientists found your paper extremely helpful in solving a problem related to another initiative. Our interest in your work sparked some unsolicited curiosity from a number of unsavory scientific circles, even though they didn't have a clue as to why we were intrigued with your approach."

"How did they figure out that UST was interested in my work?"

"Either from a leak on campus, or by hacking one of our internal blogs or tweets," said Mark.

"Regardless, the university has been considering making you an offer for over a year now," added Linda.

"So what's the holdup?" asked Ann curiously.

"The delay was caused by Dr. Haslam's indecision around his retirement plans. His retirement would've created the perfect opening for someone with your interests and expertise, but he decided to keep working until his latest project was completed."

"So has he formalized his retirement plans any further?" asked Ann.

"No," said Linda. "But, the board decided not to wait any longer, and made you an offer anyway. If you accept it, we will be able to shield you from a lot of the riff-raff we've been discussing."

"How would working for UST shield me or protect me in any way?" asked Ann.

"Well, that's a long story," Linda responded. "The short of it is that our campus community is the safest place to live in the world, and we figured if you accepted our offer, we could protect you better than anyone else."

"I find it hard to believe that a private university can afford that kind of security," said Ann.

"Have you ever heard UST make a claim that it couldn't back up?" asked Mark.

Before Ann had a chance to respond, Charli chimed in. "Actually no, I haven't." Charli blushed slightly as the focus switched to her. "I hate to admit this, but a hobby of mine has been keeping up with UST news and politics, and you guys don't say anything lightly. A few years ago, somebody wrote an article in NewsWeek where they tried to estimate how much revenue the university was bringing in from private contracts, technology sales, federal and private funding, and revenue sharing."

"How much was it?" asked Ann.

"Keep in mind this was a few years ago, but the article estimated the university's yearly revenue at over forty billion dollars."

"Ok... so maybe you can afford a little security," conceded Ann.

"Speaking of amazing UST security," said Linda, "perhaps a little demonstration of our technology might help make our case."

Linda snapped her fingers and motioned to something lurking in the trees. A small, virtually silent, remote-controlled vehicle emerged from the shadows of the aspens, and positioned itself in front of her. It was round on the top like a jellyfish. On two sides of the rounded top were inscribed the letters UST #1002.

"This is a security drone. It's being piloted by one of our trusted associates in Corpus Christi. It's well-armed with everything from lasers to lethal darts, and is capable of taking down anything from a human being to a full-sized aircraft. We've had two of these in the vicinity of your home for the last few months. I apologize if this seems excessive, but our faith in our local and federal security forces has dwindled to almost nothing, and we've had to make up the difference with technologies like these to keep people safe."

Ann, Charli, John, and Jake didn't hear a word she was saying. They were all staring at the security drone as if it was the most amazing thing they'd ever seen.

"How does it float like that without making a sound?" asked Jake.

"Don't ask me," said Mark, "I'm a field agent, not a scientist."

"I'd hate to go up against that thing in a fight."

"Why didn't you use one of these things down at the house?" asked John.

"We are trying to keep the strength of our security force a secret, and we didn't want to broadcast where you were headed. If things had escalated any further, we would have been forced to engage anyone who tried to take you, and would risk making the front page of tomorrow's news."

"Does the government know about these things?" asked Charli.

"Yes," said Linda. "They know, but they regard them as 'toys' rather than viable security assets." Linda waved the drone back into the trees and continued talking.

"During the last few hours, you've been protected with our highest level of security, which means we're tracking you by satellite visually, with infrared, imaging technology, and with feet on the street. We decided it was necessary after discovering that the CIA and FBI had you under VSS."

"What is VSS?" asked Jake.

"Visual Satellite Surveillance," responded Linda.

"Can they legally do that?" asked Ann.

"Ever since 9/11, a lot of disturbing things have become legal," said Linda.

"How did you find out they had her under VSS or whatever?" asked Jake.

"Like I said, our security and intelligence people are the best in the world. We regularly monitor what other organizations are doing so we can protect ourselves. Our satellites have been tracking you ever since you got in your car to come home this evening."

"That's how you knew to open your door before I knocked."

"Yes, and Mark followed you all the way home from work too."

"Why didn't you help me out with my tire?" asked Ann.

"Our orders are to protect you, but not intervene unless absolutely necessary."

"That's just great," said Ann, "so you would have watched me put on my spare tire all alone!"

"Um, yes," said Linda. She changed the subject quickly. "Perhaps one more demonstration of our technology would be helpful?" Linda spoke into her phone. "Buckley, how many people can you see within a mile of me?" Then she held her phone out for everyone to see. Within a few seconds, text appeared on her screen. "We can see you, Mark, Dr. Ford, a Swedish model, and two huge gorillas."

"I find that very offensive," said John, feigning shock.

"Shut up," growled Charli, who was trying to get her mind around what she was seeing. "Either that's the smoothest illusion I've ever seen, or UST is really well-connected."

More text started to show on the phone Linda was holding. It read, "You guys need to get moving. The feds and local authorities have figured out that someone jumped the North fence and headed West into the mountains. They have a couple of dogs that are yanking pretty hard on their chains, so you need to get moving."

Linda snapped the phone shut. "Well, it appears that we are out of time. If you want to know the difference between us and them," she said, waving her hand in the direction of Ann's burning house, "We will stop watching you if you ask us to. Give us the word, and you'll never see or hear from us again."

Ann looked at Mark. "What are my options from your point of view?"

"You have all the options you had yesterday," said Mark. "All UST has really done is added one more. You can return to your home and trust your federal, state, and local authorities, or you can come with us. All we can promise is to overlay their security with our own."

"So I could stand up right now and walk back to my home, and you wouldn't try and stop me."

"That's right," said Mark. "And your life as you know it will resume, except you'll be under the protection of the FBI, CIA, and local police force."

Ann stood up and brushed the grass, dirt, and leaves off her pants. She looked down at Charli and offered her a hand up.

Mark and Linda didn't say a word, but Mark dug in his pants pocket for something. "You might want these," he said, and tossed Ann's Porsche 911 keys to her.

Ann snatched them out of the air and led her friends far enough away from the Joneses that they couldn't be overheard.

"I hate it when people aren't completely honest with me," blurted Charli.

"They may have saved our lives back there," John countered.

Charli gave him the evil eye and he stopped talking.

"How long have you known them, anyway?" asked Jake.

"Over two years."

"Are you telling me that they've been tailing you for two years and you never noticed?"

"That's what it sounds like," sighed Ann, shrugging her shoulders.

"That's some serious dedication," observed Jake.

"Or some really whacked out craziness," countered Charli. "Have you ever heard of a university with enough money to fund the kind of security force they're describing?"

"None that I know of," said Jake. They stood in a group and looked at each other.

Jake broke the silence. "We've got company," he said, pointing down the mountain.

A group of people with flash lights had started up the hillside in their direction. Two dogs were barking their heads off.

"They really do have dogs," observed Jake, raising his eyebrows.

"How far away are they?" asked Ann.

"At least a mile or more," estimated John.

"Well, do we go down and meet them, or shack up with Mark and Linda?" asked Charli, looking at Ann.

"Last time we were in the company of the CIA and FBI, we had a hard time figuring out who was friend or foe. At least with Mark and Linda, we know who is who... I think..."

"I'm not entirely certain about that either," said Charli, looking a little skeptical, "but if they really do work for UST, they are definitely our best option."

John looked at Ann. "You probably have about fifteen to twenty minutes before they reach us on foot, but I bet they put a helicopter in the air before that."

"Well, what would you guys do?" asked Ann.

"That depends," said Charli. "Have you really cracked the H_2O nut?" she asked, putting her hands on her hips and grinning at Ann.

Ann's first impulse was to lie, but she didn't think it mattered anymore.

"I got lucky," she said, with a hint of excitement in her voice.

Charli leaped forward grabbing Ann's hands in hers and swung her around and around. "You did it! You actually did it! Why didn't you tell me?"

"I wanted to, but I was afraid it would put you in danger." Ann let out a huge sigh. "I can't tell you how good it feels to tell someone besides Jack." Ann marched over to where John and Jake were sitting, looking a little bewildered. "If you guys tell anyone about this I'll have to kill you," she said, looking as stern as should could at the two brutes.

"Yes, ma'am," they said in unison, trying to hold back smiles.

John raised his hand. "Yes, John," responded Ann, as if she were giving a lecture to a class. "Do you have a question?"

"Yes, ma'am," said John, trying not to look stupid. "What does it mean to 'crack the H_2O nut?'"

Ann and Charli burst out laughing and did a little jig with their elbows locked together. "It means, dummy, that Ann is the smartest person in the world," said Charli giggling.

"I've been burned, beat up, shot at, and lied to, and all I want to know is why," said John.

"Well, it means that I figured out an economical way to get the hydrogen molecule out of water so it can be used as a fuel source. How would you feel about paying twenty cents a gallon for fuel?"

"No way," the twins shouted in unison.

"It also means that all war being waged over oil will become meaningless. Nobody will give a damn about the price of oil anymore!"

"Wow," said Jake, "there is a smart girl on the planet."

Without hesitation, Charli punched him in the arm, then turned to Ann.

"Make up your mind, girl!"

Ann closed her eyes and tried to sort through her feelings. She took one last deep breath and said, "My gut tells me to throw in with Mark and Linda."

"I agree!" said Charli.

Ann, Charli, John, and Jake found Linda and Mark sitting on a log, looking glum.

"Who is the last person I talked to from UST, and what did he say to me?" queried Ann, looking at Mark.

"Well," he stammered, "if my information is correct, Dr. Ben Sellers met with you this morning after your 9:00 AM class that you were thirteen minutes late for, and offered you a job at UST. I believe he offered you a seat on one of the research sub-committee boards, and proposed a salary that was one-and-a-half times what CSU is paying you."

"You are correct. Now let me talk to Ben," she said.

Mark fumbled with his phone, punched in Ben's number, and handed it to Ann. The phone rang three times and a familiar voice answered.

"Hello, Mark. Things aren't looking so good down there. What's the hold up?"

"This is not Mark," retorted Ann, "this is Dr. Ann Ford."

"Holy cow, Ann, are you all right?"

"Does it look like I'm all right?" asked Ann sarcastically. "It appears that your visit this morning stirred up a hornet's nest. Do you always cause this much misery in a person's life when you make them a job offer?"

Ben was speechless. "Usually things go a little smoother than this," he said sheepishly. "What do you want me to do?"

"What I want you to do is get me off this mountain before some stupid knot head kills me!" she said passionately.

Mark's head jerked up when he heard the tone of Ann's voice, but his angst quickly dissipated when he saw the tired grin on her face.

"Give the phone to Mark," said Ben, "and we'll have you out of there in no time."

Ann handed the phone back to Mark. "Nice work, Mark," said Ben.

"I had little to do with it. We are lucky to be alive, and even luckier that Black Gold or Mcorp didn't kill her."

The voice on the phone changed to that of Justin Woodward, Mark's commanding officer. "Mark, I need you to climb another six hundred yards up the mountain to your right. Follow the security drone and it will lead you to a helicopter that is prepped to fly you out of there. Stay in the trees as much as possible because the FBI has a bird equipped with infrared that will be flying over your location in five or ten minutes.

"Will do," said Mark, flipping the phone shut. "Follow me. We've got about six hundred yards to go before we are home free."

They climbed the next six hundred yards faster than Ann had ever climbed a mountain in her life. *Thank goodness I've been jogging,* she thought through gasps of air, *or they would have to carry me.*

"There," said Mark, pointing through the trees.

Squinting, Ann could see a black helicopter against the back drop of aspens, and they started running towards it. Mark waved his hand in the air in a rotating motion, and the pilot fired up the helicopter's twin turbo engines. By the time they reached the chopper, it was ready to lift off. The minute they were buckled in, the helicopter left the ground with ease, and the pilot banked to the north. Ann watched as the hillside fell away beneath them. Mark Jones was talking on the phone, but the roar of the helicopter was too loud for her to hear what he was saying. She assumed he was getting some kind of directions.

"Look for three flares on I-2, northeast of your current position. We've got the traffic stopped in both directions so you can land."

The chopper tilted forward, flying at its maximum speed just twenty feet above the tree line. It was tilted at just an angle that Ann could see through the front windshield. She strained her eyes hoping to recognize the terrain below, but it was too dark. Suddenly, a few miles away, three flares lit up the night sky, and the pilot banked slightly and headed towards them.

"We can see you," said Mark, speaking into his phone.

"What are you going to do about the FBI's chopper?" asked John.

"I was hoping nobody would notice," said Mark, "but since you have... we are going to blast it with an EMP burst and force it to land. If that doesn't work, we'll have to be more aggressive."

"You can do that?" asked John.

"Yes," said Mike grinning, "but I'm not sure they'll appreciate it or classify it as a legal activity."

John looked behind them and watched the FBI helicopter trying to keep pace with them. Suddenly, it dropped like a rock to the ground, landed with a thud, and slowly rolled over on its side, its rotors beating the ground until they stopped.

"Looks like 'Plan A' worked!"

"Good thing," responded Mark. "We don't like putting people in harm's way unless it is absolutely unavoidable."

A few minutes later, they were on the ground next to a small jet aircraft. "Aren't you coming with me?" asked Ann when Mark, Linda, Charli, John, and Jake didn't get out of the helicopter.

"No," said Linda, we have lives here that we need to wrap up so nobody gets suspicious."

Ann was disappointed, but hadn't really expected Charli or the Joneses to go gallivanting off across the country with her. She grabbed Charli's hand. "Thanks for everything you did tonight! I'll call you when I get there. Please do me a favor and pick up Jack tomorrow. If he got my message, he'll be a mess," she said forcing a smile. "Fill him in on all the details, then have him call me."

"I'll take care of Jack for you," said Charli.

Ann looked at Mark and Linda Jones. "I might be dead right now if it wasn't for you two. Thank you so much for risking your lives to protect me."

"That's what we do," said Mark.

"Are we chopped liver?" asked John and Jake, doing their best to look offended.

"Thanks, you guys. Thanks for clubbing those two blokes down in the yard who tried to take me."

"That's what we do," said John and Jake, grinning.

"Oh shut up you two," said Charli, throwing an elbow at her two brothers. "Call me the minute you get there."

"I will," said Ann.

"Call her on this," said Dr. Sellers, emerging from the darkness.

Dr. Sellers handed Charli a cell phone and a slip of paper with a phone number scribbled on it. "This is the only secure way you'll be able to contact Ann."

Charli looked at him a little puzzled.

"It's a satellite phone that transmits through our private network," he said, answering the question she hadn't verbalized. "I'm sorry to be bossy, but unless you guys want the CIA and FBI to get a bead on your location right away, I wouldn't make any phone calls from your homes or use a credit card. Here," he said, handing Charli an envelope. "There's a couple of thousand dollars in there you can use until we figure out how to secure your safety. In the meantime, do you have somewhere safe you can stay?"

Charli looked at John and Jake, then nodded at Dr. Sellers. "We've got a cabin we can stay in where nobody will bother us for weeks."

"Perfect," said Ben, "pick up enough food for a few weeks and wait for me to call you. Don't go out unless you absolutely have to."

"Don't forget Jack," said Ann.

"I'll color my hair and pick him up," said Charli.

"That should work," said Ben, "but you two gorillas stay out of sight, you hear? There's nothing you could do with your hair that would disguise you."

John and Jake smiled and nodded.

Ben looked at the group of people before him. They were all exhibiting various levels of anxiety, which was totally understandable. "During the next few days, the CIA and the FBI are going to uncover who Ann's friends and neighbors are, and they will try to get in touch with each of you. It would be a great service to Ann if the FBI and CIA didn't know where she was until she gets to Corpus Christi, where we can protect her. So I apologize in advance for asking you to do this, but lie about her whereabouts if they do happen to get to you. Tell them she went to visit her great aunt in Minnesota."

"Not a problem here," said Charli, and John and Jake agreed.

"Ok... We've got to leave or our fake highway workers are going to get stoned," said Dr. Sellers, pointing at the men in orange vests who were being abused with hand gestures and foul language.

"Thanks for all you've done," said Ann to her friends. "If I don't call you by tomorrow, you'll at least know who abducted me." She was only half-kidding.

"I'll be waiting for your call," said Charli, holding up her new phone. Ann boarded the Citation-X with Dr. Sellers, and Justin secured the door behind them. They lifted off of Interstate-287 like it was the tarmac at the Denver International Airport and banked to the south.

Dr. Sellers looked across the aisle at Ann. A tear made its way down her cheek as she looked out the window. She wiped it away, hoping that he didn't see it.

"I'm so sorry about your house."

Ann glanced at him, forcing a smile. "Everything we owned was in that house... everything," she said softly. "It's hard to believe someone could be so cavalier about another person's personal belongings and their life."

Dr. Sellers couldn't think of anything to say that would comfort her, so he looked out the window too.

Ann could see Charli and her twin brothers getting into an old pickup truck and the Joneses climbing into Jack's Porsche.

"Hey, how did you get Jack's Porsche out here?" she asked, digging the keys out of her pocket.

"You just took a ride in a twenty million dollar helicopter, you're headed to Texas faster than the speed of sound, you saw one of our drones, and you're asking me if we have the technology to hotwire a Porsche?" teased Dr. Sellers.

"We even had the two flat tires fixed," said Justin, who'd been listening in on the conversation.

"Ann, this is Justin, our head of security. Justin, this is Dr. Ann Ford."

"Nice to finally meet you, Dr. Ford," said Justin. "We've been keeping an eye on you for so long, I feel like I already know you."

Chapter Sixteen

"Jammed Communications"

"What do you mean the satellite transmission has been disrupted?" yelled Director Southerland of the CIA.

"A few minutes before the house exploded into a fireball, we lost our satellite feed," responded the agent into the phone. "It was almost like someone was jamming our signal, or a huge bird flew in front of the lens."

"Did Dr. Ford get out alive?"

"We don't know," said the agent.

"Does the FBI know if she's alive?" shouted Southerland.

"We don't know that either, sir. We do know that they had a helicopter trying to track her, but it went down due to some unexplainable electronic problems. It almost sounded like they were hit with an electromagnetic pulse of some kind."

"That can't be a coincidence…"

"What was that, sir?" asked the agent.

"Nothing," said Southerland. He had a sick feeling in the pit of his stomach that was telling him someone was toying with the FBI and playing cat-and-mouse with the CIA. The idea annoyed and alarmed him, but his pride would not allow him to accept the possibility. His irritation bubbled to a crescendo and he snapped at the agent on the phone, telling him not to call again unless he had intel worth more than the cost of the call. He slammed the phone into its cradle. *Something about this whole Ford thing is not right*, he told himself, *something about it is rotten to the core*. He couldn't put his finger on it, but he was determined to burn tax dollars until he figured it out.

Chapter Seventeen

"Speculation"

A smaller group of people sat around the large table in the rented conference room. This time the monitors on the wall were blank.

Hauzer, the general manager of Mcorp, was clearly in charge. "Did we get her?"

"No, the place was crawling with FBI and CIA agents. We couldn't get close to her." Another man in the room spoke up. "Someone besides the FBI and the CIA was on site because there was a hell of a lot of unexplained gunfire right before and after the explosion."

"What do you mean?"

"Just as we tried to distract the FBI and CIA by shooting a couple of their agents, a shot was fired inside the house, then all hell broke loose, and not all the shots were fired by us."

"Who lit up the house?" asked Hauzer.

"It wasn't us."

"We think Dr. Ford was killed in the fire because she was in the house when it blew."

"Talk about opportunity loss," said one of the men.

"Are we positive she's dead?"

"We won't know until the FBI is done with their autopsies. Nobody knows anything right now."

"Let us know the minute the results are back," said Hauzer.

Those around the table sat in silence, each weighing their options.

"We are better off losing Ford's hydro-electrolysis solution than trying to restructure our organization to control it."

"That's a bunch of bullshit!" snapped Hauzer. "It's the next logical step in the evolution of global energy, and we'd be crazy if we didn't take control of it now! If Ford's solution is lost, it's only a matter of time before someone else comes up with something similar!"

"Are we certain Dr. Ford didn't stash her research results somewhere?"

"We have no way of knowing for certain, but we do know it's not in her safe deposit boxes or in her house."

"Did we get her safe open?"

"Yes, sir. We had it opened before we ransacked her house. There was nothing in it that was worthwhile."

"Let's take every precaution to ensure that Dr. Ford didn't leave a copy of her research with her husband, the university, or another family member," said Hauzer in a serious tone.

The men at the table nodded their heads silently. They were accustomed to being in complete control, and in this situation they were far from it.

"I'll call another meeting when the results of the autopsies are in or we have better information on Dr. Ford's whereabouts," said Hauzer, standing up from the table. "In the meantime, keep me in the loop."

Chapter Eighteen

"Hidden Assets"

"So where exactly are we headed?" asked Ann, as the jet leveled off at forty thousand feet.

"The UST headquarters in Corpus Christi, Texas," said Ben. "We have a fully furnished home in our fifty thousand-acre collegiate community that is being set up for your temporary use as we speak."

"Temporary?" asked Ann curiously.

"Until you decide whether you're going to work for us or not, the house is yours temporarily."

Just like that? thought Ann. She was skeptical of anything that appeared too good to be true. Experience had taught her that anything that was worth having or achieving generally required a great deal of effort. "You know what my father told me about things that are too good to be true?" said Ann.

"Yes," said Ben, "probably the exact same thing my father told me."

"So what does UST plan to do with my research if I sign on?"

Ben smiled broadly at the way Ann had phrased the question. "First of all, we don't know for sure if you have anything that is even worth talking about, and second of all, the university never decides what to do with someone else's work."

"What will you do if I decide to give my research away and decline your employment offer?"

"Well," Ben paused as he tried to come up with the perfect answer. He desperately wanted Ann to accept the position they had offered her, and didn't want to say something that would dissuade her. He made the mistake of looking over at Justin, who was grinning from ear to ear. "What?"

"Nothing," said Justin, with a chuckle. "I just thought it was a great question."

Dr. Sellers cleared his throat, "We would be very disappointed because we think you would be a great addition to our team."

"What would happen if I decided not to share what I have learned about hydro-electrolysis with the university?" repeated Ann.

"Again, we'd be disappointed, but that's your decision, not ours."

"Would you still want me to work at the university if I declined to share the information?"

"Of course, Ann, we didn't make our offer of employment to you based on the potential of your research. We made you an offer of employment because we think you're a brilliant, well-balanced scientist who would be a great addition to our staff. We take great pride in hiring the best and the brightest," he reiterated, "and we think you're one of those people."

Ann looked Ben in the eye and watched to see if his body language jelled with what he had just said. It did, which was good, because there were several things about the university and the whole situation that bothered her. She couldn't comprehend how they could possibly have access to so many resources when most universities were struggling to fund their athletic and agricultural departments.

As was Ann's style, she purposely didn't sugar coat what she was about to say. "It seems like UST has an unusual amount of money and resources for a private university."

Dr. Sellers didn't respond right away, so she pressed him with another question. "How could UST possibly afford to keep multi-million dollar satellites in orbit above my house, fund the most advanced security team I've ever seen, and buy high-tech airplanes and helicopters? Don't think I didn't notice how easily you brought down that FBI helicopter that was tailing us. What did you use, some kind of EMP burst?"

Again, she watched Dr. Sellers's body language intently for a sign he might be lying or exaggerating the truth, but he was as calm as a summer's day as he answered her questions. "On the surface, the University of Southern Texas appears to function like any other university, but once you dig into our finances and get your mind around the volume of specialized research we do, it all makes sense."

Dr. Sellers could see that Ann was still skeptical. "Over the last twenty-five years, our research and development teams have generated unprecedented donations, revenue and royalties from private and government entities around the world. We hold thousands of patents and copyrights, and have hundreds of thousands of shares of stock in companies we've partnered with over the years. Last year, the university had revenues in excess of ninety-six billion dollars, which is almost three times what General Electric posted, and similar to what Exxon Mobile disclosed."

"So Charli was right," said Ann. "Maybe you *can* afford your own fleet of planes and a satellite or two."

Dr. Sellers raised his eyebrows and shrugged. Ann turned and looked out the window, trying to decide if what Dr. Sellers was telling her was feasible. She shook her head in amazement as she processed what he had told her.

From the look on her face and the defensive posture of her body, it wasn't hard for Dr. Sellers to guess what she was thinking. "I know all this is hard to believe, but I promise that if anyone has the resources to protect you and your intellectual property, it is the University of Southern Texas. I never felt like my family was safe and secure until I started working for the university," he said sincerely.

Ann looked at him, but didn't say anything, so he continued, "Speaking of family, remind me where your sister lives.

"Kiera lives in Portland, Oregon with someone she thinks she's in love with. You probably already knew that."

Justin nodded.

"I hope you have a security detail looking out for her, now that the lid has blown off this thing."

"We didn't until a few minutes ago," said Justin. "Mark and Linda Jones will fly up tonight to take that assignment, and we've assigned a satellite team to look after her as well."

"Thanks," said Ann gratefully. "I should probably call and warn her that she's about to have neighbors who are spies for the University of Southern Texas."

"Spy... is a strong word," said Justin, "but we were hoping that you would at least call her and let her know that someone has threatened you, trashed your home, blown it up and is trying to steal your research."

"So you don't want me to tell her about Mark and Linda Jones?"

"No, not yet. Let's wait for a few days and see if things simmer down. More than likely she'll be fine once you make your research public, but it wouldn't hurt to give her a heads up." Justin raised an eyebrow. *She didn't deny that she was ready to make a public announcement... hmm.* He looked over at Dr. Sellers to see if he had picked up on the comment, but he was looking out the window.

"Ok," said Ann.

Using the phone that Dr. Sellers had given her, she called her sister. Kiera was shocked at all that had happened, but didn't buy into the theory that someone was trying to steal her research. She blew off the rogue FBI agent incident as a major communication debacle, but she wholeheartedly congratulated Ann on the employment offer from the University of Southern Texas. Ann wrapped up the phone call with her sister, feeling totally exasperated. She couldn't understand how someone so smart could be so naïve about what was going on in the world around her.

"What an airhead! You'd better triple the security detail you have keeping an eye on her."

"I've got a little brother who sees the world the same way your sister does," said Dr. Sellers, smiling. "Do you have any other family we should be worried about?"

"No. Jack and I have no immediate family who are living except for my little sister and a couple of great aunts that I haven't seen for years."

"I'm sorry to hear that," said Dr. Sellers sympathetically.

Ann's brow furrowed with worry. "Do you think Charli and her brothers are in any danger?"

"Considering what's gone on in the last few hours, I'd say that anyone who is close to you is in danger. Don't worry about Charli and her brothers though; we have them covered with our highest level of security, and the cabin they are staying in is perfect."

Ben changed the subject. "Did anyone help you with your research?"

"No, I did all the research myself," said Ann. "Jack and I decided to keep the details of my research between the two of us, for obvious reasons."

"You mentioned that you'd left Jack a voice message."

"Yes?"

"Did you say anything about Charli, the Joneses, or your research?"

"Mmm... I may have mentioned I was planning on staying at Charli's house tonight and I may have said I was going over to the Joneses..." Ann did her best to remember what she'd said in her conversations with Jack, as well as details about the message she'd left on Charli's phone shortly after she discovered she had a flat tire on the Porsche. They listened intently.

Justin looked at Dr. Sellers, then turned back to Ann. "Would you mind if we deleted all the messages from you and your husband's phones?"

"You can do that?" she asked incredulously.

"Only with your permission," said Justin.

"Please do, if you think it will protect Charli and Jack."

"It's probably too late, but there's no reason to leave them around for someone to stumble upon."

"Fine by me," said Ann, yawning. The adrenaline that had pumped through her body earlier was gone, and the lack of sleep from the night before, as well as the horrors of the day, had finally caught up with her.

"You'd better sleep," said Dr. Sellers. "I have a feeling that tomorrow is going to be a busy day."

"I should probably let someone at CSU know I won't be in tomorrow," she said sleepily. "I ought to call the Fort Collins Sheriff's Department as well so none of my neighbors are worried about me."

Justin frowned. "I wouldn't talk to anyone about this situation except for the people who are already involved. The last thing we need is for a bunch of feds to be crawling all over campus while we're trying to figure out what to do next. I recommend you wait at least a day. I'll have someone call in a sick day for you at the university so they don't worry about you, but I'd let the local and federal authorities stew until we get things figured out on our end."

"That works for me," said Ann. She looked out the window and watched the city lights pass below. Her nerves had finally begun to settle down, and she stretched her neck and shoulders until she found a comfortable position in the luxurious leather chair.

"That chair reclines into a bed if you want it to— the controls are on the lower right side."

Ann turned the chair so she could see Dr. Sellers without turning her head.

"Who was the guy with the fake FBI Badge?"

"We are not certain," said Ben, "but we think he might have been employed by Mcorp or Black Gold."

"You really think Mcorp is involved? I thought their existence was mostly myth?"

Dr. Sellers hesitated to respond, not wanting to alarm Ann. "Oh, they're not a myth... that much we do know. In fact, we linked some of the taps on your phone to a source controlled by them, and the people who trashed your house have been employed by Mcorp in the past.

From the description Mark and Linda gave us and from a satellite image we took before he entered the house, the guy who put a gun to your head was working for Black Gold, or at least he has in the past."

"Is it possible that he was acting on his own?" asked Ann.

"Not a chance," said Justin, "he had too much backup. After your home blew up, there was a firefight in your yard between the FBI, the CIA, and his crew. Eight people were killed," said Justin, looking out the window again, "so he was definitely not working alone."

Dr. Sellers frowned. "The FBI and CIA will insist on questioning you," he said flatly, "because four of the eight people who were killed tonight were federal agents, and they are going to pull this thing apart until they figure out who is responsible for their deaths."

Justin sighed, thinking of all the red tape the university was going to have to wade through when the FBI and CIA discovered that they'd assisted Ann with her getaway. "By now, the FBI knows that they were infiltrated—again—and in front of a dozen local police officers and the county sheriff's department. It'll be interesting to see how they spin this evening's events in tomorrow's news."

"Who is Black Gold? I've never heard of them before."

"They are similar to Mcorp. Everything you have heard about Mcorp could be applied to Black Gold, except Black Gold runs out of the Middle East, rather than New York City. They are rivals on the global crime stage. Rumor has it that Black Gold financed 9/11 and handpicked the Twin Towers because Mcorp had a presence there."

Ann shook her head in concern, and Ben rolled his eyes at Justin and mouthed the words, *thanks for that.*

All the talk about Mcorp, Black Gold, and the agents who had been killed had Ann frightened, and she shivered involuntarily. "How confident are you that you can protect me and Jack?" she asked again.

"Our security isn't completely foolproof," said Justin. "Nobody's is, but I believe we have the best technology and the most trustworthy personnel in the world."

I wish I knew the university better, Ann thought to herself, and she shuddered again. Dr. Sellers stood and walked over to a bank of cabinets located behind the cockpit, pulled out a couple of blankets, and handed one to Ann.

"Thanks," she said, and threw it over her legs and body.

Ann gazed out the window at the wing of the Citation-X. Her eyes grew heavy as she watched the lights from some unknown city below appear and disappear between the clouds.

Chapter Nineteen

"Agency Clash"

Brushing the CIA Director's assistant aside with a wave of his hand, Rick Jefferson stormed into Reggie Southerland's office. "Why in the hell is the CIA involved in the Ford case?" Jefferson, the Director of the FBI, was obviously furious.

"I could ask you the same thing," retorted Southerland casually. "Clearly, the case has expanded into a Central Intelligence issue considering how many of our foreign allies will be affected by Dr. Ford's research. Besides, we have reason to believe that Black Gold might be involved, and they're on top of our foreign corporate espionage list."

Director Southerland's intel on Black Gold was sketchy at best, but made perfect sense because Ford's research had the potential to totally destroy their empire. In an effort to get more information about the case out of the FBI, he purposely provoked Jefferson, hoping something of value would shake loose. "So why didn't you tell me the minute you suspected Black Gold was involved?"

Jefferson was stunned. *How could the CIA already know about Black Gold's involvement in the Ford case?* He tried to hide his surprise, but the look on his face had already betrayed him.

Now it was Southerland's turn to be surprised. He'd not expected Jefferson to fold so easily, nor did he have any concrete evidence that Black Gold was involved at all. He glared at Jefferson. "Are you telling me that you knew a well-known foreign crime organization was operating on American soil and you didn't contact me?"

"Well, ah… we don't know for sure," stammered Jefferson.

"What do you mean you don't know for sure?"

"Well, we did arrest a man nosing around in Fort Collins, Colorado who we suspect might be one of their operatives," confessed Jefferson, who wasn't about to tell Southerland that the man had put a gun to Dr. Ford's head.

"And just when were you going to inform me about this?" fumed Southerland, all pretense of calm gone.

"That's what I came over here to talk to you about," lied Jefferson, trying to back-pedal into a more comfortable position.

"I look forward to meeting this guy," said Southerland. "Have you run his DNA?"

"It's being processed as we speak," responded Jefferson.

He's lying, thought Southerland to himself, *he's already got proof the guy is a Black Gold operative*. Southerland sat back in his chair and stared at Jefferson.

"We will turn him over to your people when we are done with him," said Jefferson with resentment, but not breaking eye contact.

Southerland was peeved; the trust between the CIA and the FBI had disintegrated over the last couple of years and something had to be done about it, but he had no idea what.

"Where is Dr. Ford now?" asked Southerland, fishing for more information.

"We think there is a good chance she was killed in the fire," said Jefferson. "We won't know for sure until we get the results of the autopsies from our forensic team. So far we've recovered nine bodies, but some of them are burned beyond recognition. We are missing a couple of agents, so we're assuming some of the bodies are ours. The others either worked for you, someone else, or they are Dr. Ford and her friends."

Director Southerland blew out an exaggerated breath. "Let me know when you have something concrete. Do you need some help with the forensics?" he asked sarcastically.

"No!" snapped Jefferson, trying to think of a comeback but failing to do so.

"So I heard the guy was sporting a fake FBI badge," Southerland taunted, probing for more information.

Jefferson had hoped Southerland didn't know about the rogue FBI agent. The agency was aware it had a problem and was doing what it could to fix it, but severe budget cuts had hampered their progress and made it impossible to hire and train the people they needed. "We don't know if he had an FBI or a CIA badge, he lied, "but he definitely was dressed like an agency man."

Southerland grinned. He'd already received intel that proved the guy was either FBI or pretending to be FBI.

Jefferson's head throbbed from a headache that seemed to be rooted right behind his bloodshot eyes. *At least Southerland doesn't know where she is either,* he thought, rising to leave. Jefferson didn't tell the CIA Director about the footprints in the backyard, or the landing site they'd found up the hill. He'd let him figure it out on his own.

"I'll have the man we believe is associated with Black Gold turned over to your people after we process him." He smiled weakly at the CIA Director, then turned and left the office. *At least he doesn't have a clue about the other Black Gold agents we killed on the Ford's front lawn.* Jefferson smiled to himself as he walked out of the CIA headquarters in Langley.

Chapter Twenty

"Confrontation"

At exactly 10:45 AM on Tuesday—thanks to a supersonic flight over the Pacific—Ahmadi's private jet touched down on the tarmac at the Denver International Airport. It was ahead of schedule, but not a minute too soon for Jack. A malfunction in the jet's onboard phone-communications system had made it impossible for him to make a call during the flight, so he tried to call Ann the second he had signal bars on his phone.

"Why isn't she picking up?" Jack couldn't remember being so anxious. He was unconsciously clenching the phone so tight his knuckles were white. He navigated through the phone's applications to see if Ann had left him a message. He thought he'd seen one come across, but he couldn't find it. He hoped she'd received his message about his arrival time or he'd have to take a taxi home.

The second the door to the plane was open Jack was running down the loading ramp towards the passenger pick-up area. He sprinted through the doors, knocking unsuspecting travelers all over the place, looking frantically in every direction for someone he recognized.

His peripheral vision picked up on a tall, cute brunette waving at him vigorously and yelling his name. *Who is that?* he wondered as he moved through the crowded sidewalk in her direction.

"Jack, over here!" she was yelling.

"Charli...is that you?"

"It's me," she yelled back.

Jack shouldered his way to her car and jumped in. He didn't have time to shut the door before she punched the gas and the little Mazda MX-5 shot away from the curb.

"What did you do to your hair?" asked Jack, still out of breath. "If you hadn't been waving and yelling my name, I never would have recognized you." Jack's heart was still beating a hundred-and-ten beats a minute. "Where is Ann and how did you know I'd get here early?"

"I've been waiting for hours because we didn't know exactly when you would get in."

"Oh...you didn't get my message?"

"Nope."

"How much do you know?" yelled Jack over the road noise and radio – his agitation showing on his face.

Charli jabbed the button on the radio turning it off. "I don't know much more than you do about what is going on, but I'll tell you what I do know. Someone wants to control production of hydrogen in this country enough to kill for it."

"She told you?"

"Yes, we discussed it while she was deciding whether or not to trust the University of Southern Texas."

Jack fell silent and Charli took the opportunity to fill him in on what had happened from her perspective. She recapped the events of the previous day, starting with details of Dr. Sellers's visit to the university. The only thing Charli didn't tell him about was Ann's discovery of his handgun, ammunition, cash, and passports in the trunk of his Porsche. She decided to let Ann nail him on that one. She knew Jack well enough to believe there was a valid explanation.

"Wow!" exclaimed Jack in disbelief. His lips kept moving but no words came out. He swallowed several times, trying to digest everything that Charli was saying. "A man can't even leave his wife alone for a week without her blowing up the house," he said dryly, trying to cover up his anxiety.

"You might want to wait a couple of years before you use that line on Ann," suggested Charli, with a sarcastic smile.

From the look on Jack's face, it was obvious he was having a hard time deciding what to do next. "Ann really flew down to Corpus Christi with those guys?" he asked with noticeable irritation. "Are you sure it was UST that took her?"

"Unless someone is a Dr. Ben Sellers look-alike, it was them. Ann was convinced it was them," said Charli, trying to measure her own certainty.

"The rogue FBI agent incident must have really shaken her up."

"That, and the house blowing up," responded Charli.

"Why didn't she call and leave me a message?" asked Jack.

"She did, but the University of Southern Texas erased all her messages in case someone was eavesdropping."

"She called me the minute she landed in Corpus Christi. Why don't you give her a call now?" asked Charli.

"I tried when I landed, but the call wouldn't go through." Jack started to dial Ann's number on his cell phone, but Charli stopped him.

"Call her on this," she said, pulling a cell phone out of her pocket with a piece of paper taped to it.

"What's this, a bat phone?"

Charli rolled her eyes as Jack took the phone.

"Why do I have to use this?"

"It's the only secure way to reach Ann, according to the UST," said Charli. "They told Ann that her phone had been tapped and gave her a phone just like this one so we could talk to each other."

"You've got to be kidding me." Jack punched in the number on the paper. The phone only rang once before Ann picked it up.

"Charli, is that you?"

"No babe, it's me, Jack. Are you ok?" he asked, pressing his ear against the receiver.

"I'm okay," said Ann, "But it's been a scary couple of days."

"Where are you?" asked Jack.

"I'm in a hotel in Corpus Christi, Texas."

"Are you safe?"

"I think so. The university has a couple of guards outside my door and a security drone of some kind outside my window."

"Do you trust them?' asked Jack earnestly.

"Yes, more than I trust anyone else at this point. Did Charli tell you about the guy posing as an FBI agent who pointed a gun at my head and tried to take me hostage?"

"Yes, she told me everything. I'm so sorry I wasn't here for you. It sounds like you've been through hell and back in the last forty-eight hours. I… I can't believe you actually did it!" said Jack, unleashing the excitement he'd suppressed on their earlier call.

Ann ignored Jack's enthusiastic comment because she'd just started to rant. "Did she tell you about the handgun I found in the back of your Porsche?"

"That part she left out," he said, glaring at Charli.

"What's gotten into you, Jack? Do you know that a police officer wanted to help change the flat on the

Porsche last night? If he'd have looked in the trunk I would be in prison right now. Is there something you would like to tell me?" All the fear, anxiety, and frustration she'd been feeling the last two days bubbled to the surface, and it was starting to show in her voice.

"Baby….ah….it's like this—the CIA talked me into being their eyes and ears in the oil industry during the course of my normal work. They thought it best that I have some extra cash on hand and a couple of passports in case I got into trouble. This arrangement all happened before I met you."

"So I'm married to a spy?"

"No… it's nothing like that."

"What about the gun?"

"That was their idea too. I hate the thing, so I hid it in the trunk. I actually do have a legal permit to carry the gun, if that helps. Open up the passports and you will find it sandwiched in between one of the pages." Jack could hear Ann rustling through the passports on the other end of the phone.

"Humph," she said when she found it. "Why do some of your passports have 'Mr. Talbot' printed under your picture?"

"That's only for emergencies."

"What, in case you need to be a spy?" Ann's voice was shaking. "Is your real name even Jack? What else have you been hiding from me?"

"Ann, Annie… that is the only thing I have been hiding from you, other than that the CIA has been paying me a little to keep my eyes and ears open."

"How much have they been paying you?" snapped Ann.

"Only… two hundred-and-eight thousand a year and change."

Jack's face was flushed and he didn't know what to say next. A muffled laugh was coming from the driver's side of the Mazda MX-5. Charli was enjoying the conversation and was finding way too much pleasure in his discomfort. Jack held the phone against his chest and gave Charli a bone-melting glare.

"Thanks a lot." He mouthed to her.

Charli burst out laughing.

"Baby?" he started to say into the phone.

"Don't call me baby. You know how much I hate it when I'm mad!"

"Annie?"

"Don't call me Annie either! You can refer to me as Dr. Ford until I decide if I like you."

"Dr. Ford," said Jack, humbly, turning away from Charli so she couldn't see him grovel, "what would like me to do?"

Jack could hear sobbing coming from the other end of the phone. "I'm so sorry that all this has happened and I'm sorry about the gun, ok?"

"Is there anything else you haven't been straight with me about?" she asked.

"*Ah, you know that ninety million I got from North Star* Energy?"

"Yeah," said Ann hesitantly.

"Well, it wasn't ninety million exactly; it was ninety million, one hundred-and-one thousand, five hundred dollars and six cents."

"Oh, shut up, Jack," she said a little less vehemently.

Neither one of them spoke for a moment, though both of them were relieved that the other was safe. Jack broke the silence, "Oh, and I'm also driving around with a tall brunette who has long legs and drives a poor man's sports car."

"Tell her thanks for helping me out last night while I was husbandless. And tell her thanks for picking up my fathead husband."

"I'll be sure and tell her, and I'll call you back once I've seen the house."

"Ok," Ann said softly. "Then I want you to fly out to Corpus Christi so we can figure out what to do next."

"Ok, I'll call you a little later. Love you..." said Jack and he hung up the phone. Jack was grateful he'd at least got an invitation to see his wife again. He handed the phone back to Charli with a glare. "Thanks a lot!"

"What...?"

"You could've given me a heads up that she knew about the gun!"

"And miss hearing you grovel? No way."

"What's with the brown hair?" asked Jack.

"Didn't you listen to a word I said? I was the last person seen with your wife, and I don't want to stick out like a sore thumb."

"And you don't think your long legs will be a dead giveaway? Try putting some pants on if you don't want to stick out like a sore thumb.

Charli blushed and tried to pull her skirt down below her knees as she sped down the freeway towards Fort Collins, Colorado. It didn't work.

Jack's thoughts were racing faster than the Miata. He couldn't get his mind around the idea that the University of Southern Texas had so much capital invested in security. *How can they possibly protect her from the CIA, the FBI, or Mcorp? Hell, what am I saying? Why should she need protection from the FBI and the CIA?*

Charli interrupted his thoughts. "You've been quiet for a while. What's going on in that *fat* head of yours?"

Jack chuckled. "I can't believe you heard that. He was quiet again for a moment, and his look became serious. "Charli, do you think the CIA, the FBI, and this Mcorp or whatever they're called know that Ann's in Corpus Christi?"

"No, according to UST they don't have a clue. Apparently they're still waiting for the autopsy results from the people killed in the fire."

"Damn, those university folks are on the ball. They must be sitting on a boatload of money to be able to do what they did yesterday. Do you trust them?" asked Jack again, looking at Charli intently.

"I've heard nothing but good things about them," she said, "but the jury is still out on how well they can protect Ann."

"If the jury's is still out, why did you let her fly down to Corpus Christi?"

"Ann's a big girl and it was her decision. Besides, what else were we supposed to do, trust our fake FBI and CIA friends? Who has a better reputation than the University of Southern Texas?"

"Good point," said Jack, remembering the advice he'd received from the anonymous phone call.

"So, what's our story going to be?" asked Charli, her fists clenching the steering wheel at ten and two.

"What do you mean?" asked Jack, looking puzzled.

"Well, in about twenty-five minutes you are going to be surrounded by FBI, CIA, and local police authorities who are going to be asking you a ton of questions. They'll want to know where you have been, if you've seen or heard from your wife, do you have any known enemies, who started the fire in the lab… yada, yada, yada."

Up to this point, Jack hadn't worried about what he was going to tell the authorities or the press. The thought hadn't crossed his mind.

"I don't know for sure," said Jack. "The FBI and the CIA will figure out that Ann's alive sooner or later, but I would prefer not to offer any information on her whereabouts yet. Let's see how long it takes them to figure it out." Jack changed the subject. "How bad is the house?"

"It was a total loss from what I could see," said Charli. "It burned the whole time we were up on the mountain last night."

Jack tried to think of anything that might have been destroyed that he couldn't live without. *At least we have all our pictures backed up on the web.* His mind shifted gears to the Jones.

"I still can't believe the Joneses moved into our neighborhood for the sole purpose of keeping an eye on Ann. Who would do that?"

"That is hard to believe," said Charli, grinning slyly, "but I've known my best friend's husband for nearly five years and just barely found out that he is a spy." Charli put her hand on Jack's arm. "You'd let me know if you were double agent for the Palestinians or Chinese, wouldn't you?"

"Would you shut up about the 'spy' stuff already?" snapped Jack. He wasn't in a laughing mood and was trying to figure out what he was going to say to the FBI in a few minutes. He'd always held his cards close to his chest, and loathed sharing details about his personal life or finances with anyone but Ann. He wondered if the FBI agents on the ground in Fort Collins knew he was employed by the CIA. He decided it was not information he would volunteer. He looked over at Charli. "I'd prefer not to tell the authorities at my home anything at all. I'm not going to let on anything they don't already know until Ann and I have had a chance to talk first."

Charli looked pleased. "I was hoping you'd say that."

They drove in silence for a few minutes, each lost in their own thoughts.

"If push comes to shove, we'll tell them that Ann decided to stay at the home of a friend until things get sorted out. We certainly don't need to tell anyone where she is until we are damn good and ready. We especially don't need to tell anyone how she got there," said Jack, rolling his eyes.

"Agreed," said Charli.

"Who else knows where she is and how she got there?"

"My brothers, Jake and John, and the folks on the University of Southern Texas payroll."

"Will they keep their mouths shut?"

"I can only speak for John and Jake," she said, "and I assume that it is in the interest of the University of Southern Texas not to disclose their involvement either."

Charli told Jack about the precaution she and her brothers had taken with their cell phones and credit cards. She told him about the cabin they had rented with cash, and what their plans were for the next few days.

Before long they were rounding the corner onto the street where Jack's house had once stood. Neither one of them was prepared for what they saw. The street had been blocked off, and there were dozens of local and federal vehicles parked all over the place. Both the FBI and the CIA had a trailer on site, and the smoldering ruin of Jack's home was crawling with agents. It appeared that they were looking for something of tremendous value.

"Wow!" said Jack, "Annie really did a number this time."

A year ago, Ann had blown a hole in the basement ceiling when one of her tests had gone awry. Jack smiled as he remembered trying to explain what had happened to the fire department. Charli pulled the MX-5 up to the blockade and waited patiently for an officer to come to the car.

A burly policeman approached the car, squinting through the driver's side window in an effort to identify the occupants. "What can I do for you, ma'am?" he asked, looking at Charli and hardly noticing Jack.

"Well," she said with an innocent look, "I just picked up Dr. Ford from the airport and thought I'd bring him home."

"Dr. Jack Ford?" asked the officer, unable to conceal his excitement.

"Yes sir, the one and only," said Charli.

In his agitation, the officer knocked his radio off its clip and it fell to the ground. Charli, unable to suppress a giggle, snickered out loud.

"What's so funny?" asked Jack, his eyebrows knit together.

"Nothing," said Charli, "other than these guys seem pretty excited to see you."

Jack soured. "At least he loves his job." Jack put his hand on the door latch and paused for a moment, gazing sadly at the pile of smoking rubble that used to be his home. Trying to lighten his own mood, he winked at Charli. "Let the games begin," he said, and opened the door and stepped onto the asphalt.

The police officer motioned Jack and Charli to follow him to a twelve-by-forty-foot aluminum trailer that had FBI plastered all over the side. The officer knocked loudly on the door, which was opened by a man wearing a traditional FBI jacket. One of his arms was in a sling, but he extended his good arm to shake their hands.

"I'm Agent Porter," he said, "the agent in charge." He was a narrow-shouldered man, but he looked Clint Eastwood-tough. "You are Dr. Ford, I presume?" Agent Porter knew full well who he was from the pictures he'd passed around to his associates.

"I am."

"Let me start by telling you how sorry I am for your loss."

Jack shrugged. Agent Porter motioned for them to follow him into the trailer, which opened up at one end into a small sitting area. "Who is she?" asked agent Porter, jerking his head towards Charli.

"A close friend of the family," said Jack.

"Does she have a name?"

"No," said Jack, with a straight face.

"Hmm," grunted Agent Porter, looking at Jack. "Would you mind if we had a word in private?"

"Not at all," said Jack, waving for Charli to take a seat.

"Alone, doctor, if you don't mind."

"I mind," said Jack, motioning more passionately for Charli to sit down. Jack and Charli sat down in the cramped trailer and waited for Agent Porter to get the ball rolling.

"Coffee?" asked Porter.

Jack and Charli both accepted a cup, more to keep their hands warm than anything else. Jack grew impatient waiting for Agent Porter to brew up another pot. "Why are the FBI and CIA here at all?" he asked. "It's not every day that the president sends out his best and brightest when a house burns down."

"Missing and dead people will always bring out the FBI, especially if one's the wife of a federal employee."

Jack was a little surprised that the FBI knew he was working for the CIA, but didn't show it. *They must be cooperating today for a change,* he thought. "Don't give me that line of crap. People die in fires all the time and the FBI doesn't show up. Why are you really here?"

"No other reason than that," lied Porter.

"If the only reason you are here is because you think my wife is missing or dead, then you had better pack up your bags and go home," said Jack, smiling slyly.

Charli looked at Jack in surprise. She thought they'd decided to keep that a secret. Obviously Jack had changed his mind.

"What are you talking about?" stammered Porter.

"She may be missing or dead to you, but I just spoke with her twenty minutes ago."

"You made no such phone call," said Agent Porter before he could stop himself.

"So you are monitoring my personal phone calls?" snapped Jack, escalating his voice.

"Yes, well."

"Yes, well, what?" pushed Jack.

"It's not uncommon for the FBI to tap a suspect's phone when a person close to them is perceived to be missing or dead."

"How can I be a suspect if my wife isn't missing?" asked Jack. "Are you forgetting that I was in Kuwait when this all went down?"

Jack was livid, and too uncomfortable sitting down, so he stood up. Charli stood beside him.

"Where is she then?" asked Agent Porter.

"That is none of your damn business," snapped Jack.

"Actually it is," said Porter, "because until we can confirm that she's alive or dead, she will be classified as 'missing,'" he said, emphasizing the word *missing*.

"Did you consider me 'missing' before I showed up here?" asked Jack loudly.

The walls of the trailer were thin, and their voices carried into the yard. A man opened the door and asked Agent Porter if everything was all right. Agent Porter assured him that everything was under control, and the man shut the trailer door. Agent Porter changed his tactics in an effort to settle Jack down. He continued calmly, "The last time I... we... saw your wife, she was being hustled down the basement stairs of your house by three very large men."

"Hustled?"

"Well, they appeared to be pushing her."

"What happened after that?" asked Jack, trying to ascertain how much the FBI and the CIA had figured out.

"I'm not entirely sure," said Agent Porter, "because your house exploded a few minutes later."

"Why weren't you killed in the blast if you were in the house long enough to see my wife being hustled down the stairs?" asked Jack.

"I was knocked out the front door just before the house blew up," said Agent Porter, trying not to divulge anything he didn't have to.

"So, you're the agent my wife told me took a bullet in the chest?"

Agent Porter's mind raced as he tried to figure out how Jack could have possibly known that he was the agent who had been shot, unless he really had spoken with his wife. Up to this point, the FBI had assumed that Ann Ford had been killed in the fire.

"Don't look so surprised, Agent Porter, I told you I spoke with my wife not more than twenty minutes ago and she told me the whole story. Besides, that explains the bandages sticking out over your shirt collar, and your arm sling. Tell me, who was the rogue FBI agent who tried to kidnap my wife?" asked Jack, trying to back Porter into a corner. Porter squirmed like a stuck pig, and Jack knew he had him against the ropes.

"Well... I... ah... we aren't exactly sure yet," he stammered, looking embarrassed.

"Was the man that tried to kidnap my wife one of yours turned bad or an imposter?"

"That is confidential information," said Porter. He quickly tried to pull himself together and regain control of the conversation. "Who were the three big fellows I saw going down the stairs with your wife?"

"That is confidential information," parroted Jack through clenched teeth. "Who was the fake FBI agent who had a gun pointed at my wife's head working for?"

"That is confidential information," repeated Agent Porter.

"Well, then, you may never know the names of the gentlemen who protected my wife when the FBI couldn't," said Jack frostily.

"There were a couple of ladies with your wife last night—one of them a tall blonde. Do you have any idea who they were?"

"No idea," lied Jack, starting for the door. "Let's go, Charli, these guys don't have a clue what is going on around here or they are lying through their teeth."

"Not so fast," warned Agent Porter, his hand resting on his gun.

"Oh, give me a break! Are you going to shoot a guy who works for the CIA in an FBI trailer?"

"I need confirmation that your wife is alive; otherwise, I can't let you go."

"You can't let me go?" questioned Jack, looking Porter in the eye.

"Unless I have empirical proof that your wife is alive and not being held against her will, I cannot let you leave," he restated firmly.

"On what grounds are you going to hold me?" asked Jack.

"Kidnapping and attempted murder," said Agent Porter.

Jack looked like he was going to grab Agent Porter by the throat, but Charli put her hand on his arm. He shook his finger in Agent Porter's face. "Here is what we are going to do," he said, holding up his cell phone. "I'm going to let you speak to my wife for one minute, and then I'm going to walk out of here before I do something I'll regret."

Agent Porter eyed Jack, considering the offer. "You are a hard man, Dr. Ford, but I can live with that."

"You'd do the same thing if you were in my shoes," said Jack, trying to control his voice, "especially if you suspected that the FBI and the CIA had a hidden agenda and were being less than honest."

Porters face was rigid, confirming that what Jack had said was true. Jack flipped the lid of the cell phone open and pushed the redial button. The phone rang a few times and Ann picked it up.

"Is that you, Jack," she asked, sounding relieved.

"It's me," responded Jack trying to sound calm. "Why are you breathing hard?"

"I just got back from a run," said Ann.

"Is that safe?"

"I think so, since nobody knows where I am, and I was followed by a couple of security guards."

"Be careful, Annie," said Jack anxiously.

Jack wanted to say more, but he was afraid he might slip and give away her location, so he got right to the point. "I'm at the house and there's an FBI agent calling himself Porter who wants to talk to you."

"What does he look like?" asked Ann.

"He's about 5'11", a little-scrawny looking, with wavy blond hair, and green eyes." Jack wasn't about to say he looked like Clint Eastwood.

"That sounds like the agent who greeted us, but I saw him get shot in the chest," said Ann.

"He must have been wearing a bulletproof vest or just got grazed," said Jack.

"You're probably right."

Jack held the phone to his chest. "Agent Porter, would you mind if we had a minute alone?"

"Not at all. I'll be right outside the door." Porter opened the trailer door and stepped outside. Jack grabbed a piece of paper off the desk and wrote a quick message to Charli. *Is Agent Porter the FBI agent who greeted you in the street last night and was shot in the chest?*

Charli nodded.

Are you 100% positive? scribbled Jack.

"Yes," Charli whispered. "One hundred percent positive."

Jack wadded up the paper and put it in his pocket.

"You can come back in now," yelled Jack. "Ann, are you still there?"

"I'm here," she responded.

"Agent Porter is going to ask you a few questions and take an audio sample of your voice so he can confirm that you are who you say you are. Don't answer any questions that make you feel uncomfortable, or hint at where you are located."

"We're on the same page," said Ann.

Jack handed the phone to Agent Porter. Porter turned on the cell's speakerphone and laid it in a cradle on the table.

"Hello, is this Dr. Ann Ford?" he asked.

"It is," said Ann.

"Would you tell me about the last time you saw me?"

"Well," said Ann. "The last time I saw you, you had just come through my front door and you looked in my direction and yelled, 'what's going on over there.'"

"Why did I yell that?"

"I hope it was because you were surprised to see a government agent pointing a gun at my head."

"What happened after that?"

"The FBI agent who had his gun pointed at me turned and fired a shot into your chest."

"Then what happened?"

"One of the gentlemen I was with grabbed the FBI agent's gun arm, snapped his wrist, then smashed his face into the kitchen counter."

"How did you know he snapped his wrist?"

"Because I heard the bones break," said Ann, grimacing at the memory.

"Who were the three men that hustled you into the basement?" asked Agent Porter.

"That is one of those questions I will not answer," said Ann.

"Who were the two women with you in the street when we first met and what happened to them?"

"That's another one of those questions I won't answer."

"Who were they?" repeated Porter forcefully.

"I'm sorry, but I already told you I can't answer that question," responded Ann. "All I can tell you is that they are concerned citizens of Fort Collins who do not have names at this time."

"Why the secrecy?" asked Agent Porter, slightly agitated.

"Why the fake FBI agent?" retorted Ann, matching his agitation. "How can I possibly trust you guys?"

"Sorry about that," said Agent Porter. "That man is in custody and we are questioning him at this time. Now back to my questions, Ann. Do you have any idea who blew up your house?"

"That is a question I'm hoping you can answer, Agent Porter, because I lost everything in that explosion. Maybe a bullet from the little war you were having in my front yard hit a gas line? What was going on out there?"

Agent Porter didn't respond to Ann's theory but apologized about the house. "Sorry ma'am, you have my deepest sympathies. Thanks for taking my phone call, Dr. Ford. I don't have any other questions. I hope you are safe, because the FBI cannot protect you unless we know where you are."

"My confidence in your organization is very weak at the moment," said Ann, "I think I'll take my chances on my own."

"I don't think that is wise, Dr. Ford, especially given the caliber of people we think are trying to find you."

"And who would they be?" asked Ann.

"I cannot discuss that right now," responded Porter.

"Then I cannot tell you where I am."

Porter was noticeably agitated. He was certain he was talking to Ann Ford despite the poor connection, and couldn't wait to get off the phone to see if his associates in the other trailer had successfully traced the call. "Again, thanks for taking my call, and please don't hesitate to contact me if you need to," said Agent Porter hurriedly. He folded up the cell phone and set it on the table.

An FBI agent opened the door and gave Agent Porter a thumbs-up. "You are free to go, Dr. Ford, but I wish you would let us provide your wife with the protection she needs until we figure this all out."

"How do you know it isn't me who needs protection?" asked Jack, looking deep into Porter's eyes.

"I just assumed…"

"You didn't assume anything," said Jack. "The FBI and the CIA have an agenda of their own related to my wife's research and you know it."

Agent Porter didn't answer. Jack grabbed the cell phone off the table and headed towards the door.

"I'll need to keep that cell phone," said Agent Porter.

"Like hell, you will," said Jack. "This is my only link to my wife, and it's going with me, unless you want to pry it out of my dead hands."

Agent Porter was a little taken aback but didn't stop Jack and Charli from leaving the trailer with the phone.

"That went well," said Charli sarcastically. "What's next?"

"Let's take a look at the house," said Jack. They walked around the perimeter of the house, amazed at the amount of damage the explosion had caused.

Agents were still swarming over the debris searching for clues that would tell them how it started.

As soon as Jack and Charli left, Agent Porter went to the other trailer where he was soon engulfed by FBI technicians who'd been assigned to trace Jack's call. They huddled around a large array of computers at the back of the trailer, chatting excitedly.

"Where is she?" asked Porter, his patience running thin.

"We are tracing the call now," said one of the technicians. He traced the screen with this finger, then his brow began to furrow.

"That's not possible," he muttered under his breath.

"What's not possible?" asked Agent Porter.

"This piece of crap software says the call originated in Hobart, Tasmania!"

"Isn't that just off the southern tip of Australia?" asked another technician.

"Why isn't that possible?" asked Agent Porter, his time and distance math a little rusty.

"Well, on a perfect day, when all the planets are in alignment and you had your airfare purchased in advance, it would take you at least twenty hours to get from Fort Collins, Colorado to Hobart, Tasmania. You said the last time you saw Dr. Ford alive was last night around 8:45 PM."

"That's about right," said Agent Porter, slamming his fist down on the desk, "not quite enough time to arrange an unplanned trip to Tasmania."

"This software isn't making any sense. Unless..." The technician muttered to himself as he tapped a pencil on the screen.

"Unless what?" demanded Porter.

"Unless the call was routed there on purpose then dead-ended, but not many people have the technology to pull that off."

"Please explain what you mean in terms I can understand."

"Was there any delay in Dr. Ford's response to your questions? What I mean is, did it seem like you were talking to someone who wasn't hearing your question for a second or two after you asked it?"

"Now that you mention it, yes," answered Porter.

"Damn," said the technician, "somebody is good—very, very good."

"I still don't understand," said Porter.

The technician explained further. "Somebody routed the call through the traditional cell phone network all the way to Tasmania. When the signal got there, it was taken off the network and uploaded to a private network, then sent to wherever Dr. Ford is currently located."

"Who has the technology and money to do that?" asked Porter. "More importantly, who would Dr. Ann Ford know that could possibly assist her like this?"

"I don't know," answered the technician, "but whoever they are, they are good."

"Keep working on it," said Agent Porter, his frustration showing.

"There's nothing to work on, sir, the trace went dead in Tasmania."

That was not what Agent Porter wanted to hear. His superior at the Bureau had no patience for incompetence or failure, and for reasons that Porter did not entirely understand, he was more interested in this case than any he'd worked on during the last decade. He was so interested that he'd asked Porter to call him twice a day with an update.

Porter watched Jack and Charli poke through the smoking rubble for a minute, then forced himself to go back inside the trailer to make the dreaded phone call. His anxiety showed as he waited for Director Jefferson to answer.

"Hello, Deputy, Director Jefferson's office, how may I be of service?"

"Amy, this is Agent Porter calling from Colorado."

"Hi, Porter. Director Jefferson has been waiting for your call. Whatever you're working on down there has him all riled up," she whispered. "Oh... he's glaring at me... so let me patch you through, sweetie."

She's way too nice to be working for the Director, thought Porter as he waited.

"What have you found out, Porter?" asked Jefferson in a gruff, but eager voice.

"I made contact with Dr. Ford."

"How did you do that?" asked Jefferson.

"Her husband, Jack, showed up on site and let me talk to her using his phone."

"Are you sure it was her?" asked Jefferson.

"One hundred percent sure. We got a perfect voice match."

"Where is she now?"

"We don't know, sir."

"You don't know?"

"The call was routed through a series of satellites and we were unable to determine the point of origin," said Porter, simplifying the story.

"How is that possible?" asked Jefferson.

"We are not sure, but it has been a long time since we have seen this kind of technology."

"Is it just me, or does it seem like the Fords are getting outside help?" asked Jefferson.

"That's exactly what I was thinking, sir."

"Have the phone transmission analyzed by our best people, and get back to me with the results." Porter had already done that, but he would call Jefferson back with the data he had already found out later on in the afternoon. "It's quintessential that nobody knows she's alive until we pinpoint her location. Let the CIA keep thinking she's dead until we get the autopsy results back on the bodies we found in the fire."

"Those results should be back in a few hours, sir, and then the cat will be out of the bag."

"I expect you'll be able to find out where she is before then!"

"Yes, sir, we will do our best."

"Doing your best is not good enough!" said Jefferson, raising his voice. "There is too much at stake here not to figure this out. Put the best people you can find on it and I'll foot the bill," said Jefferson, "even if you have to work with someone from the private sector."

"Yes, sir," said Agent Porter.

"Oh, and Porter, if you haven't put two and two together yet, every detail of this case is to be kept highly confidential."

"Yes, sir," said Porter, with as much conviction as he could muster. The Director was asking the impossible, but he'd gladly waste another ten million dollars of taxpayers' money to keep his boss happy.

Chapter Twenty-One

"The University of Southern Texas"

Ann sat on the balcony of the hotel eating a cobb salad and thinking about the call she'd just had with Jack and Agent Porter. The satisfied look on her face confirmed that the chef had gotten the ingredients just right and that she was happy with how the call had gone.

The temperature was a perfect sixty-eight degrees according to the fancy thermometer on the balcony, but the humidity was a little too high for her liking. The sun warmed her body, which had a calming effect on her rattled nerves.

I hope Jack is ok, she thought as she put her salad bowl and fork down on the table. She wiped a smudge of ranch dressing off her lower lip and adjusted the folding deck chair until it lay all the way back. Still not satisfied, she kicked off her shoes, peeled off her socks, closed her eyes, and stretched out in the sunshine.

I must be absolutely crazy, she thought. *I'm sitting on a balcony in a city where I have no friends, feeling safer than I have for a couple of days.* She let her mind relax and wander. The sun felt so good on her skin she rolled up her sweat bottoms to expose her legs and get more of the warming sensation. Ann enjoyed the feeling for a few more minutes, but the comfortable recliner and the warm sunshine were no match for the anxiety she was feeling. Her gut was telling her she needed to make her research public as soon as possible, but she didn't want to do it without Jack at her side.

She ratcheted herself up in the chair and fretted about what she should do next. Initially she'd planned on staying put until Jack arrived, but she was feeling so uneasy she decided to visit the university. She put the chair into a sitting position and went into the suite to call Dr. Sellers.

The phone rang a couple of times and a pleasant sounding person the phone.

"Hello, this is Dr. Sellers's office."

"Hi, may I speak with Dr. Sellers?" responded Ann boldly.

"He is in a meeting at the moment; may I ask who is calling?"

"This is Dr. Ford from….."

"Oh, hi Dr. Ford, Dr. Sellers said you might call today. I will let him know you are trying to get a hold of him."

"When can I expect a call from him?" asked Ann.

"In about five minutes," responded the receptionist.

"Thanks."

Ann went back down to the chair on the balcony, and before she knew it, had dozed off into a fitful slumber. She was so tired that she hardly noticed the security drones hovering just off her balcony in a defensive array. Their near-silent rotors beat the air like the wings of a dozen humming birds. Eight minutes later, she awoke to the sound of ringing. It took her a few seconds to get her bearings, and when she did, she hurried into the bedroom to locate the phone. "Hello?" she answered a little sleepily.

"Did I wake you up?" asked a familiar voice. "You deserve a nap after all you've been through in the last couple of days."

It took a second for her mind to shift into a conscious gear, then she recognized the voice. "Is this Dr. Sellers?"

"It is, but you need to go easy on the doctor stuff," he chuckled. "Call me Ben."

Ann skipped over the small talk and cut right to the chase. "I think I'm ready to take you up on your offer to tour the university."

"Excellent! Why don't we meet in the lobby in a few minutes and I'll give you the grand tour?"

"Perfect," said Ann. "Are you guys keeping a close eye on Jack?"

"Absolutely," said Ben, "although he doesn't seem like a guy who needs much help."

"He is very capable," said Ann, "but I don't think he fully understands what he's up against yet. For that matter, I'm not sure any of us do."

Ann had not been able to shake the gnawing fear in her gut that there were people in high places doing everything in their power to get their hands on her research.

Ben had been having a similar feeling, and prayed that the university would be able to protect her. He was relieved that she wanted to visit the university sooner than later. "Don't worry. We have our best people looking after both of you. See you in a few minutes?"

Ann hurried into the bathroom to brush her hair and freshen up. She was the kind of girl who looked good in about anything and with very little make-up, which was fortunate because she was on her second day in the same clothes. She tossed her hair to one side and took the stairs to the hotel lobby, trailed by two capable-looking security guards. Her emotions surged from anxious, vulnerable, and skeptical to thankful. She felt sincere gratitude for the interest and security the University of Southern Texas was trying to provide, but she was skeptical that they would be able to keep her safe when the FBI and the CIA could not. She'd watched one too many movies where snipers hit targets from over a mile away, and she couldn't comprehend how they could possibly have sufficient security expertise to protect her. But they had a great reputation and they were all she had.

Clinging to that hope, she forced herself to move towards the familiar face in the lobby.

Ben stood there smiling. "You're right on time."

"Yes," said Ann, her elevated anxiety showing. "You're sure we're safe?" she asked as she glanced around the lobby at all the people she didn't know.

"Our security team has checked out every single person within a mile of this hotel. So far there have been no suspicious characters out and about that we are aware of."

"That's comforting," said Ann with a weak smile.

"Shall we go?"

"I would like that very much."

"I was just thinking how nervous you must be feeling. I mean, you don't really have any contacts at the university, we've only known each other for a few hours, and you are playing cat-and-mouse with the FBI. If I were you, I'd be stressed out of my mind."

"You pretty much nailed it," said Ann. "I'm still having a difficult time not feeling naive by placing too much faith in a university's security department. No offense, but when I think of campus security, James Bond 007 isn't the first thing that comes to mind."

Ben laughed. "That's understandable. Until I met Justin Woodward, I felt the same way about campus security. The quicker you feel comfortable, the happier you'll be, so don't hesitate to ask questions. If I don't have an answer, then we'll find someone who does. Nothing is off limits."

"You may regret your offer, because I have a lot of questions," said Ann.

"And it's my job to answer them. Speaking of security, I need you to hold this umbrella above your head every minute you are outside from here on out."

"But it isn't raining."

"You're right, but that's not its purpose. It's designed to block heat signature and image recognition satellites from being able to get a read on you."

"Are you serious?"

"Dead serious. We have several satellites equipped with this technology, as do the FBI, the CIA, and several other organizations. Unless you want them to know where you are, you need to keep this over your head while you're out doors.

Ann frowned but followed Ben out the lobby and across the street holding the umbrella over her head. A decorative but sturdy-looking wrought iron fence blocked access to one of the most beautiful gardens that Ann had ever seen. "Who owns that?"

"This is the northwest gate into the university," said Ben as they walked up a cobblestone drive to the ornate gate. The wrought iron gate was flanked on both sides by two English-style guardhouses. The guardhouse exteriors were a combination of rock and brick, accented by a rustic, green-tinted copper roof. As they approached the gatehouse, a nice-looking gentleman emerged and greeted Dr. Sellers.

"Hello Ben, it looks like you have company."

"Indeed," responded Ben. "Steve, I would like you to meet Dr. Ann Ford."

"Good afternoon, Dr. Ford, how has your stay been so far?"

"Very nice, thank you," said Ann, pleased with the genuine and sincere greeting.

"If I could get you both to put your hands on the bio-reader, it would be much appreciated," said Steve.

"Bio-reader?"

"It's required for entrance into the university for all students, visitors, and faculty," said Ben. "It helps us keep track of everyone who is on campus and assists us in promoting public health and safety."

"What kind of information does it gather?" asked Ann, before putting her hand on the glass.

"It matches your fingerprints and DNA to your public record, and retrieves the allergies, medications, and lifestyle preferences that you have recorded there."

Ann placed her hand on the glass surface of the bio-reader. It was warm to the touch.

"Now you have enough data to calculate my G-Score, don't you," stated Ann matter-of-factly.

"Yes, ma'am," said Steve.

Ann's DNA, G-Score, and other assorted information had already been added to the university database from the hair sample Ben had taken from her brush when he had visited her in Fort Collins a few days earlier, but Steve refrained from mentioning that fact, and ducked inside the guardhouse for something.

"Aren't you guys being pretty presumptuous, offering me a job and a seat on the Research Board before knowing what my G-Score is?" asked Ann curiously.

Ben looked uncomfortable, "I... we, ah... I already got a sample of your DNA from a brush in your office before I met you in class the other day."

The thought of Ben poking around in her office looking for a DNA sample annoyed Ann. "You could have asked," she said, glaring at Ben. Ben looked embarrassed so Ann didn't say what she was thinking. *At least he's honest. I'll give him that,* she thought.

"To be completely honest," said Ben, "taking people's DNA without their permission is one practice this University has that I don't entirely approve of. I don't mind requiring a DNA scan as a part of a resume," Ben continued, "but obtaining one without a person's permission is a little outside of my comfort zone."

"Then why do you do it?

"I am truly sorry, Ann—I should have asked you."

Steve returned and interrupting the uncomfortable exchange. "If you'll step through the entrance, I'll give you a day pass," he said, motioning them towards the gate with his hand. Ann stepped through the entrance and a small swoosh of air let her know that she'd just gone through another security check.

"What are you checking for now?" asked Ann, her curiosity growing by the minute.

"Everything that Home Land Security checkpoints look for and a thousand things more, and we do it in a fraction of the time they do," he said, betraying a little pride.

"Interesting. How much more?" she asked, pressing for more information.

"Well," responded Steve, "between the bio-scan and security check we can detect diseases, drugs, weapons and explosives, stress and anxiety, G-Score Factors, viruses and the flu. All of this information is now online for your review if you are interested."

It took Ann a second to digest the implications of what Steve had just said. "Impressive! Was this technology developed here at the university?"

"Yes, and I was part of the subcommittee that sponsored the project a few years ago. We've developed our prototypes to a point where we think they might have application in the medical industry to diagnose disease," he said, the excitement showing on his face. "We are almost through piloting a scanner that can do a complete MRI and a blood workup without pricking the skin."

"Nice," said Ann, "I hate needles and get claustrophobic in an MRI tube. Is this one of the prototypes?"

Steve blushed as if he had divulged a trade secret. "Yea, but we'd like to keep that to ourselves for a while until we go public."

Steve's enthusiasm made her smile. "Not a peep from me," said Anne trying to suppress a laugh.

"You can see your scan info on line if you want to."

Ann nodded and Steve handed her a business card. "Go to this website and type in the password on this card." Ann's day pass printed and Steve handed it to her. "Have a great day Dr. Ford... and make sure you change your password."

"Thanks," said Ann, "I'll be sure to go online and check it out." Ann's curiosity about her own test results nagged at her as she walked up the cobblestone path to campus. She made a mental note to stop and talk with him on her way back to the hotel, then turned to Ben. "I noticed a couple of security drones by the gate. Are you expecting trouble?"

"Considering what happened in Fort Collins, we're certain that the FBI and the CIA will have a response the minute they find out where you are and how you got here. We're also a little worried about a couple of unsavory characters we found lurking around downtown Corpus Christi, so we've raised our security level to compensate."

"How would anyone be able to find me?

"They could identify your heat signature, or simply twist the arm of someone who knows where you are."

"That's not comforting."

Ben glanced at Ann and could tell he wasn't projecting the level of confidence she needed to hear. "I promise we'll protect you better than the Feds."

"I'm counting on it." said Ann.

"Each of our security drones is controlled by a highly skilled and qualified security officer who reports up a command chain. In situations where critical decisions need to be made, there are several sets of eyes and ears to assist each drone controller.

"Are they all remote-controlled?" asked Ann.

"Yes. Each one has its own operation team."

"Why do you use drones for security rather than people?"

"We use both, but the drones keep our people out of harm's way. They help our security team scale. Each drone can fly up to one hundred miles an hour and successfully navigate altitudes as high as fifty thousand feet. It's almost like stuffing three human beings into the body of a peregrine falcon. At a thousand feet, a single drone can secure a very large area. Each drone is equipped with a camera system that projects a three-hundred-and-sixty-degree image into our control center. They're armed with tear gas, pepper spray, and a fifty-round Rohypnol/Ketamine synthetic tranquilizer that has enough oomph to knock down an elephant and a laser that can punch a hole through about anything. They're powered by a hydrogen fuel cell that..."

"Where did you get your hydrogen fuel cell technology?" asked Ann, interrupting Ben's effort to make her feel better.

"We developed it here, but it's not cheap."

Despite the drone's lethal appearance which didn't quite fit in with the exquisite landscape of the university, Ann was glad that they were there.

"Are you ok?" asked Ben, who noticed Ann eyeing a cluster of drones.

"I feel a little better knowing there are humans driving those things," she said, smiling. Ann's attention shifted to the amazing array of flowers along the cobblestone walk way. "Who takes care of the university grounds?"

"The agriculture and botany departments do. This is their lab," he said gesturing to the surround area.

"They do an amazing job!"

They walked towards the center of campus for a minute without talking. Ann didn't mind because it gave her a few minutes to admire the flowers. Ann shook her head in amazement. "I can't believe the agriculture and botany departments do all of this."

"There are hundreds of students that help out. We have a number of alumni and emeritus professors— some of whom have a lifetime of experience in landscape and gardening—who dabble as well."

"I don't think I've even seen Butchart Gardens look this good," said Ann.

Ben had an aunt who lived on Vancouver Island, so he understood the significance of the compliment.

"What in the world...?" exclaimed Ann in surprise, and she veered off the cobblestone sidewalk to look up into the sky. She kept walking, dodging shrubbery and flowers, with her eyes glued to the tallest flagpole she had ever seen. "How big is that thing?"

Ben had to run to catch up with her. "What did you say?"

"How big is that thing?"

"Oh... the flag. Years ago we had a couple of history students that got it in their minds to build the largest American flag and tallest freestanding flagpole in the world. If I remember correctly, the flagpole is several hundred feet tall."

"That is absolutely breathtaking," said Ann as she walked up to the base of the flagpole and looked up at the billowing flag. She'd seen the flag lit up by lights the night before, but hadn't appreciated its size. The base of the flagpole was huge and shadowed by the surrounding trees, and morning sun lit up the flag high above like a beacon of hope.

"That flag is the first thing in the morning, and last thing in the evening to see the sun," said Ben.

"Wow!" said an still gazing updward.

The pole was centered in the middle of a huge brick courtyard, ringed with dozens of ornate brass and hardwood benches. In front of each bench, there was a large bronze plaque. Every plaque was a different size, each embossed with raised lettering which was easy to read.

Curious, Ann walked over to the closest plaque and began to read the inscription out loud. "When in the Course of human events, it becomes necessary for one people to dissolve the political bands which have connected them with another..." Her fingers traced the raised bronze lettering, which seemed to bring the historic text to life. "...We hold these truths to be self-evident, that all men are created equal, that they are endowed by their Creator with certain unalienable rights, that among these are life, liberty and the pursuit of happiness. That to secure these rights, governments are instituted among men, deriving their just powers from the consent of the governed. That whenever any form of government becomes destructive to these ends, it is the right of the people to alter or to abolish it, and to institute new government... The Declaration of Independence," she said, pleasantly surprised. The Declaration of

Independence was one of her favorite works. Every sentence inspired a collage of historical images in her mind.

Ben stood over one of the larger brass plaques. "This one is the Constitution."

Ann walked to where he was standing and read the words, "Congress shall make no law respecting an establishment of religion, or prohibiting the free exercise thereof; or abridging the freedom of speech, or of the press; or the right of the people peaceably to assemble, and to petition the Government for a redress of grievances... They even included the Amendments!" she said nodding her head in approval.

"That one over there is the Gettysburg Address," said Ben.

"Is Martin Luther King's 1963 speech from the Lincoln Memorial here?"

"I believe it is," said Ben as he walked around the perimeter of the courtyard scanning the plaques.

Ann found Dr. King's famous speech before he could locate it. She gently ran her fingers over the raised lettering until she got to the last paragraph. "Let freedom ring. And when this happens, and when we allow freedom to ring - when we let it ring from every village and every hamlet, from every state and every city, we will be able to speed up that day when all of God's children - black men and white men, Jews and Gentiles, Protestants and Catholics - will be able to join hands and sing in the words of the old Negro spiritual: "Free at last! Free at last! Thank God Almighty, we are free at last!""

Ann paused for a moment with her finger resting on the word *last*. Somehow, being able to feel the raised lettering of each word as she read them was more powerful than just merely reading the words.

"I love this speech," she said, "I wonder if the human race will ever live up to his dream?"

"We do our best around here," said Ben, trying to mask the stress he was feeling for not having Ann indoors yet. It had been twenty minutes since he had left the hotel and he was going to get heat for it. He was sure that Dr. Conner was beginning to wonder where they were.

"What do you call this place?" asked Ann.

"Most of us refer to it as the Freedom Memorial," answered Ben quickly. Ben didn't want Ann to sense his anxiety but he had to get her inside. "Dr. Ford... at the risk of sounding pushy, we need to get going. The security team was expecting us over thirty minutes ago, and considering all that is going on in your life, I'm certain they would prefer I get you inside."

"You should never create an expectation you can't deliver on," said Ann, a twinkle in her eye.

"Seriously," said Ben, "we cannot protect you to the extent we would like to unless you're inside." The stern tone in Ben's voice caught her a little by surprise. She was not accustomed to being in any kind of danger, and Ben's seriousness was a cold reminder of her situation.

"We'd best not keep President Kane and Dr. Conner waiting a minute longer then," said Ann, trying to ease the tension.

Ben guided Ann away from the Freedom Memorial towards the university's administration building. They walked up the steps so quickly they both were out of breath by the time they reached the top.

"Here we are," said Ben, motioning towards the entrance to the building. Before they could reach the double doors, a handsome man sporting a well-groomed white beard came bursting through the entrance.

"You must be Dr. Ford," he said, extending his hand. "I'm Dr. Conner."

Ann put down her umbrella and extended her hand. "It is nice to finally meet you."

"I feel the same," said Dr. Conner. "I apologize for the increased security, but we are deeply concerned about your safety. We feel partially responsible for the attention you and your family have been getting the last day or so, and we want to do everything we can to compensate for it."

The trio entered the administration building and the door was promptly locked behind them by a security guard. A sign on the door stated that the building was undergoing some modifications and would be closed until further notice.

"Is your husband flying down to join us?" asked Dr. Conner.

"Yes," said Ann, "he should be here around 8:00 or 9:00 this evening, if all goes well."

"Good. Forgive me for being so forthright, Ann, but I need to know why someone ransacked and blew up your home. Have you published more information in regards to your research that I'm not aware of, or is everyone just jumping to conclusions?"

Ann could not help smiling. "That's the question, isn't it? Will my answer affect the offer of employment the university has made to me?"

The question caught Dr. Conner off guard. "Of course not!" he responded, laughing out loud. "The premise of this university's existence is not to hire people with great ideas, but to hire great people who will inspire great ideas! I can see that Ben hasn't had time to fill you in on our philosophy yet. We discovered that if we hire enough great people, great ideas will follow as naturally as summer follows spring. So... did you figure out a hyper-economic energy solution or not?"

Ann put her hands on her hips and just grinned at Dr. Conner.

"Well?" he persisted, with great anticipation.

Dr. Conner was a little too pushy for her taste, but there was something about him that she liked. *What can it hurt to tell him?* she thought. *Besides, everyone who has meddled in my life in the last forty-eight hours assumes I've done something amazing...* "I would prefer to keep this information absolutely confidential until Jack and I have decided what to do with it. I also need your word that you will abide and uphold any course of action that Jack and I determine is best for us and my research," said Ann, "even if it means not sharing it with the University of Southern Texas.

"Your research is yours, and yours alone to do with as you will," said Dr. Conner. "If you decide you want to work for us, we will help you develop a commercial application for the solution if that's what you want to do. Ben may have already told you that our teaching contracts give the university unlimited 'internal use' rights to any inventions that are developed by a professor during their tenure at the university."

"What exactly does that mean?" asked Ann.

"It simply means that all professors working for the university sign an agreement to allow the university to use any intellectual or technical advancements internally at the university."

"If I sign on at the university and then decide that I want to give my energy solution to the world for free, can that be arranged?"

"A number of our people have opted to do that in the past," responded Dr. Conner. "In your case, the university would want to leverage your technology to build a hydrogen-based energy plant to power the campus, which means we'd build a commercial grade hydrolyser in the very near future."

Ann thought she understood what Dr. Conner was saying, but decided to restate the university's position to be sure. "So the university would reserve the right to use my research internally, but I'd be the sole decision maker on how it is distributed outside the university?"

"That is correct," said Dr. Conner. "And we do allow professors to change their minds," he concluded with a smile.

"I can live with that."

"So... did you do it or not?"

Ann smiled again. "Oh, I did it all right, and the efficiencies I achieved are going to blow you away."

"Excellent!" thundered Dr. Conner, and he pulled her into a bear hug. His response surprised both Ann and Ben. "I've been dreaming of this day for many years! I just didn't know who would pull it off or if I would be alive to see it. What do you intend to do with it?"

"I'm going to give it away to the world," said Ann, watching Dr. Conner for his reaction.

"Interesting," said Conner. "I believe I would have done the same." He tucked Ann's arm through his like an old-fashioned gentleman and escorted her up the steps of the rotunda to the second level where his office was located. "What kind of efficiency did you achieve?"

"You may want to sit down," said Ann.

"I think I'll be fine," responded Dr. Conner, "Not much surprises me anymore."

"My hydrolyser burns about one BTU of hydrogen for every 1251 BTUs it produces."

"You're kidding!" gasped Dr. Conner, stopping so fast that Ben plowed into him from behind. "You're telling me that you figured out how to create 1251 BTUs of hydrogen for every BTU required to power your hydrolyser?"

"Yes," said Ann, enjoying his reaction.

"I think I'm going to have a heart attack," said Dr. Conner, who'd put his hands on his knees trying to regain his composure. "Twelve hundred and fifty-one to one," he muttered in amazement.

His demeanour changed from exuberance to dead serious. He hadn't considered a breakthrough of this magnitude and his mind was having a hard time processing it.

Kellie, Dr. Conner's office manager, heard the commotion in the hall and poked her head out the doorway. "Is everything all right, sir?" Seeing him bent over had her worried.

"I'm fine," he assured her, waving a hand in her direction and straightening slowly.

"Would you clear all appointments from my calendar for the next few days? Dr. Ford and I have a great deal to talk about. Oh, and please keep a look out for her husband. He should be arriving on campus in the next hour or so."

"Yes, sir," she said, craning her head to get a better look at who was in the hallway and to make sure everyone was really ok.

Dr. Conner was speechless as he led Ben and Ann into his office. When they were all inside, he shut the door and locked it. Both Ben and Ann looked at him curiously. He paced back and forth as if he was the only one in the office, eyebrows scrunched together with a worried expression on his face.

"How can we possibly protect you?" he was muttering under his breath.

"Protect who?" asked Ann.

"You!" he said, wringing his hands. "I thought you may have come up with a solution that was marginally better than what's already out there," he moaned, "but you had to blow it out of the water! You do realize that at the efficiency levels you just described means you've uncovered a viable replacement for oil don't you?"

"That was my goal," said Ann. She understood the thought process Dr. Conner was going through, because she had been there herself not too many hours earlier.

"I can't believe you actually discovered a replacement for oil!"

"Isn't that a good thing?" asked Ben, looking a little confused.

"It's good all right," said Dr. Conner, "but there are a hundred organizations out there and twenty countries that would wage a war just to stop this information from going public! What would you do if your country's revenue was about to plummet by ninety-five percent because of some new technology? How many people know about this?"

"Like I told Ben earlier, John, Jake, Charli, my husband, and your people."

"That's a lot of people," said Dr. Conner, looking concerned.

"My people won't say a word," replied Ann. "Are you worried about any of your people?"

"Not really," said Dr. Conner, "but money has corrupted a lot of good people." Dr. Conner leaned over the phone on his desk and punched in Kellie's extension.

"Kellie, is Justin back in town yet?"

"I believe he is, sir. Would you like me to ask him to drop by?"

"Yes, please," responded the professor, "and tell him it is urgent. Would you let President Kane know that Dr. Ford is here on campus and that I need to see him immediately?"

"I'll let you know when I've contacted them."

"Thank you." Dr. Conner sat down, leaned back in his chair, and swiveled towards his window, which had a panoramic view of the campus. Ben looked at Ann and shrugged. After a minute or so, Dr. Conner turned to face them.

"May I give you some unsolicited advice, Dr. Ford?"

"I've been looking for someone with good advice for about two days now," said Ann.

"It is imperative that you publish your solution as soon as humanly possible; and I'm not talking about in the next few months, I'm talking about the next twenty-four hours."

"I couldn't agree more," said Ann, looking pleased that she and Dr. Conner were on the same page. "If I can make my research public in the next few hours, it should relieve a lot of pressure." She nodded her head as she was speaking as if it would make what she was saying come true. "Instead of everyone wanting to steal or destroy it, they'll be trying to figure out how to capitalize on it."

"Exactly," said Dr. Conner.

"So what do we need to do to make this happen?" asked Ann.

"In order for it to be believable, you are going to have to publish a schematic of a working model, or nobody is going to believe you, not even if you announce it from the steps of this university.

"That's going to be a little bit of a problem."

"Why is that?"

"The only schematic of how it works is in my head."

Dr. Conner's face turned pale. "Please tell me you're kidding."

"Not kidding," said Ann. "I decided that it was too risky having a copy of my research anywhere but in my head. Had I done anything else, I would already be dead, and somebody would be monopolizing hydrogen production rather than sharing it."

"So if you die, it dies with you?"

"That's right."

Dr. Conner leaned over his phone. "Kellie, I need to see Jason Woodward in here sooner than later. It is an emergency!" He looked at Ann. "You're not going to die on my watch. We will engage every resource we have to keep you safe and get your research published." He thought for a moment about what he was going to say next.

"Here is what I propose. Let's do our best to keep your location a secret until you have documented and published your research on the internet and sent a copy to every university, scientific syndication, and network we can think of. In order to pull this off, we will have to reproduce your research notes along with a working model as soon as possible. How long would it take you to reproduce notes, schematics, and a working model from scratch?

"If we start this afternoon, I should be able to release something by tomorrow or the next day, depending on what kind of materials and resources you have available."

Dr. Conner's eyebrows arched, "Seriously? It can't be that easy."

"It's that easy," responded Ann, looking pleased.

"You're going to turn this world on its ear aren't you? As far as equipment and resources go, we we'll put anything and anybody at your disposal to get this done.

Ann did a few calculations in her head. "Well, in that case I could probably build a rudimentary hydrolyser in eight to ten hours."

Dr. Conner smiled broadly and shook his head in disbelief. "Perfect! Why don't you make a list of what you will need, so we can start rounding things up."

"Sounds great," said Ann. She grabbed a sheet of paper from Dr. Conner's desk and started writing down the equipment and the kind of expertise she would need. She filled up one page and had just started on another when she thought of Jack. "My husband was planning to fly into Corpus Christi in a roundabout way sometime this evening. Please let him know where I am the minute he arrives."

"Do you still have the phone Ben gave you?" asked Dr. Conner.

"Yes."

"Give him a call and tell him to wait until the last minute and then not board his flight. Instead, have him drive south on I-287 and we'll pick him up before he runs out of gas. Make sure he doesn't use his credit card for any reason."

"How will he know where you'll pick him up?"

"There will be a fancy black helicopter at a rest stop when his gas gauge is nearing empty." Dr. Conner grinned. "Give him those instructions for now and we'll call him again with more details later."

Ann walked over to the window to make the call. She started to press the numbers, then stopped. "Would you mind if Charli and her brothers tag along with Jack? I'm worried about their safety."

"We better bring them in separately, or they'll attract too much attention."

"What about your sister?" asked Ben. "I'm not certain how long we can protect her."

"She won't come," responded Ann.

The door to Dr. Conner's office opened and Kellie stuck her head in just long enough to announce that Justin and President Kane would be arriving in a few minutes.

Ben hadn't said much during the exchange between Dr. Conner and Ann, and he was antsy to be doing something. "Dr. Conner, I don't seem to be of much use here. Would you mind if I left and made arrangements for Dr. Ford to move from the hotel to the campus community? I'll also get the ball rolling on having a lab set up for her."

"I'd rather have Justin set up the housing accommodations and you set up the lab with the equipment that Ann has specified. If you'd get Dan Johnson from NBC News in here to do a newscast sometime in the morning between six and ten, it would be awesome?"

"Will do," said Ben. "What do you want me to tell him?"

"Tell him it's the most amazing breakthrough that will come out of this university this century."

Ben waved at Ann to get her attention.

Ann put her hand over the phone. "Where are you going?"

"I have a couple of things to take care of, plus I need to set up your lab."

Ann mouthed 'ok' and handed him the list of materials.

President Kane and Justin arrived in Dr. Conner's office just as Ben was leaving and Ann was finishing her call. "We meet again," she said, looking up at Justin.

President Kane extended his hand towards her. "Hello, Dr. Ford. I'm Carson B. Kane. Some folks here call me president, some refer to me as Carson, and I'm sure there are a few who use less complimentary terms."

Ann laughed. She didn't care what people called him, she liked his easy-going style right off the bat. "So what does the 'B' stand for?"

"Beck... My dad named me after President Beck."

"He was one of my favorites," said Ann. It's a pleasure to meet you."

"How have my people been treating you?"

"Well, since I've been introduced to your people I've had two flat tires, my home broken into, a handgun pointed at my head, my house blown up, and had a fake FBI agent attempt to kidnap me. Then I was whisked away from my burning home in a fancy helicopter by a man I didn't know, to a place I've never been, where I might not live through the night."

President Kane's eyes twinkled, his cheeks turned a little pink, then he burst out laughing. It took him a few seconds to regain his composure. "Nothing like brutal honesty without a spoon full of sugar! If you're as optimistic as you are honest, we are going to get along famously!"

"She is," said Dr. Conner. "She claims to have solved the world energy crisis, which may inadvertently solve world hunger."

"That's what I've been hearing," responded President Kane, then his voice took on a more serious tone. "I sincerely apologize if the university played any role in putting you and your family in harm's way. We'll do our best to protect you in the future. It is not our policy to cause so much drama when we make a candidate professor an offer; although, it might be something to consider in the future if it works in your case," he said with a straight face.

Ann could not help laughing.

President Kane turned to Justin, "Please raise the security level at the university to a level 'one' until things simmer down."

"A one, sir?" asked Justin, lifting an eyebrow. "We've never actually done that before. It means cancelling all classes for tomorrow and pretty much locking down the whole campus."

"And we've never had to protect the most brilliant technology breakthrough of the century and its creator before either. It's about time we had a 'level one' security drill, don't you think?"

"I was just about to suggest the same thing," said Dr. Conner.

"Then we are all on the same page," said President Kane. He looked out the window for a few seconds. "If the FBI is as hot and bothered about this as we think they are, and they figure out where you are, they'll have personnel on campus by tomorrow morning. Let's assume the worst and lock the campus down for the next couple of days. The students and faculty are going to wonder what is going on, but we can't risk being completely transparent with them until Ann has released her research."

"What's our story for locking down the campus going to be until then?"

President Kane shrugged. "Half of the truth. We're preparing for the press release of a highly sensitive breakthrough and we could not risk an information leak until press time."

"That should get the campus buzzing," said Dr. Conner.

"It's better than lying or leaving them completely in the dark," responded Kane. Turning to Ann, he quizzed her on her intentions related to her research. Ann reiterated what she'd told Dr. Conner and President Kane nodded his head in approval. "I agree that giving the solution away is the only option, so if you're comfortable with that decision, let's get this show on the road."

"I've been planning to give it away since I started my research," said Ann.

President Kane looked down at his watch, then back at Ann. "If you really think you can have a working prototype up and running in eight hours, we'd better get cracking if we're going to make the morning news."

"If you have the equipment and personnel I need, we'll be ready for the six o'clock news," said Ann confidently.

Ann was feeling surprisingly comfortable around the University of Southern Texas's Nobel Prize winners, and was starting to feel like she might actually fit in. Her confidence in her research was solid as a rock, but she was anxious to get it out of her head and into the hands of a few more people.

"I have a few things to finish up in my office," said President Kane, "but I'll come down to the lab and help you out the minute I'm finished. Please feel free to request anything you need to get a prototype up and running. Trust me, once the word is out that you're here and that you've made a significant breakthrough, there will be no shortage of highly qualified volunteers who are willing to help through the night."

Ann's excitement showed on her face. "Just show me how to get to the lab, and I'll get started."

President Kane smiled a big Texan smile. "I've never seen anyone so excited to throw a wrench in the world's economy. If you've done what you claim you've done, it will be more profound than all the world wars combined. Hell, I'm not sure anyone will be able to find a legitimate reason to fight anymore.

I'm honored just to be a part of it… good luck and Godspeed."

The excitement and anticipation around Ann's project was palpable. The meeting in Dr. Conner's office broke up and people hurried out to fulfil their assignments leaving Ann and Dr. Conner standing alone. Kellie came in and offered to show Ann a semi-private ladies room where she could freshen up.

"It's no longer safe for you at the hotel, so I'll have your luggage packed up and brought over. There's a conference room with an attached bathroom where you can lock the door and crash if you need a few minutes alone until we find you a more permanent residence."

"That sounds great to me," said Ann.

Chapter Twenty-Two

"Missing"

Mcorp didn't have a location they called their headquarters. They were a virtual organization made up of top executives from some of the most influential corporations in America. They'd started out as a handful of companies in the oil business who joined forces to counteract the influence of OPEC. Since the their inception in the 1950s, they'd remained hidden from the world and functioned in absolute secrecy. During the last decade, membership in Mcorp had swelled to include non-oil-related companies, members of the Senate, the House of Representatives, and other high-ranking officials from within the United States Government.

Initially, Mcorp's intentions were good, but as more and more people of influence joined the organization, they became very powerful. Eventually, power bred corruption, and Mcorp turned into one of the most sophisticated factions of organized crime in the world.

Even though Mcorp was a virtual entity, they were well-organized. Every ten years, a general manager was selected by popular vote from among the men and women who were principals in the organization. The general manager was in charge of high level operations and coordinating all meetings, agendas, and recruiting across the organization.

Marlon Hauzer was the GM of Mcorp and had been for the last six years. Up until this point in his tenure, everything had run smoothly, and Mcorp had successfully protected the interests of the people and companies he represented.

The atmosphere in this particular meeting was charged, as one question after another was asked by the principals who had been invited to attend.

"She's not dead?" asked a voice wrought with annoyance.

"Where is she?" asked another voice.

The associate assigned to find Dr. Ford shook his head. "We don't know. Even the FBI can't figure out where she is. One of our sources within the FBI says that an Agent Porter spoke with her on the phone and confirmed that she's alive."

"Didn't they trace the call?"

"They tried, but they lost the trace somewhere in Australia... Her husband apparently called her using his personal phone, and for some reason they couldn't trace the call to its origin."

"They let him contact her using his own phone?" asked a voice incredulously.

"It gets better," said the associate. "Not only did they let him use his own phone, but he took the phone with him when he left."

"They let him leave with the phone?"

"Yes."

"No wonder they're so easy to infiltrate!"

Hauzer looked at the man delivering the information. "What else do we know?"

"The FBI has quarantined a five-mile corridor from the burn site to where a high-tech helicopter landed in the trees up on the mountain. They've determined that six people walked up the mountain the night Dr. Ford's house burned down and they were flown somewhere."

"They don't know where?"

The man shook his head again. "The helicopter had some kind of jamming device on board, and they couldn't track it.

"Dammit!" said another voice, "We have totally lost control of this situation!"

"To be frank, sir, we were never in control. The tracks leading up the mountain indicated that all parties involved walked up without a struggle."

"You're telling me that this whole thing was planned?" asked a principal in the room.

"No doubt about it. It looks like Dr. Ford met her benefactors in her backyard and they flew her out by helicopter."

"Unbelievable!" said a principal on the call. "If it wasn't the FBI or CIA that helped her escape, then who was it?"

"We're not sure; but whoever they were, they were well-financed."

"What makes you say that?" asked a female voice from one of the monitors on the wall.

"The fact that their helicopter out-flew an FBI chopper, jammed its circuitry with an EMP burst, and was never seen on radar. It would take a well-healed, souped-up twenty-million-dollar helicopter to do what this bird did. It feels like a Black Gold stunt to me."

Nobody in the room, least of all Hauzer, liked being outmaneuvered, but he shook his head skeptically. "From what we know of the doctor, she would have had nothing to do with Black Gold, and they're too rough around the edges to have been able to fool her. Besides, the timing doesn't add up. She made a 911 call and twenty minutes later was surrounded by local and federal authorities. Then less than ten minutes after the Feds meet and greet her, she gets whisked away in a high-tech helicopter that disappears completely? Something stinks, and it isn't Black Gold. They may have been in the area, but they didn't do this. It's too far outside of their method of operation."

"They were on site!"

"I don't care if they were standing next to her. This is too sophisticated and too smooth, even for them."

"We are trying to get to the bottom of it, sir, but we don't have much to go on at this point. We do have a report that a small supersonic jet aircraft used a highway five miles north of the pick-up site as a landing strip. Several eye witnesses said they saw a medical helicopter in the same vicinity, so we're pretty sure that whoever was picked up by the helicopter got a ride on the jet a few minutes after they left the mountain."

"And this all happened right under our nose and it wasn't picked up by radar?"

"Yes sir, and right under the noses of the FBI and the CIA. From what we can gather, neither organization has a clue as to who assisted Dr. Ford."

There was silence on the conference bridge for twenty seconds. "Does the FBI still have the Black Gold agent in custody?" asked Hauzer.

"No, they've turned him over to the CIA."

"Get rid of him."

"We don't have anyone in the CIA that can get within ten miles of him."

Hauzer glared at the man tasked with gathering information. "Use one of our regulars and kill him! We can't risk having any intelligence about Dr. Ford's research getting back to Black Gold."

"They're already going to be pissed when they find out the FBI shot five of their operatives at the Ford house. If they find out we assassinated one of their guys, it could mean war."

"What are you talking about? We've been at war with them for thirty years."

"It's been a while since we openly killed one of their operatives."

Hauzer looked at the man in disbelief. "Then kill him in a way that won't raise suspicion! I can't believe we are having this discussion! Do I need to tell you how to do your job?" Hauzer shook his head. *We have no clue what's going on... Hell, we figured out how to bring the stock market to its knees and make billions doing it, but we can't kill a guy being held by an organization we've infiltrated or find a damn college professor... I'm going to have to do it myself!*

The principals argued about what action should be taken next. They were a cold, calloused, and practical bunch who placed very little value on human life.

Hauzer listened for for a minute, then brought the conversations back on track. "We agree that there's no way Ford pulled this off on her own. She might have money, but there's no way she or her husband could have coordinated a getaway this elaborate on such short notice. I want to know who they are working with. If Dr. Ford won't cooperate, then we'll have to eliminate her from the equation."

"Find her, and spend whatever it takes!" said a principal heavily invested in the banking and oil industry. "My organization will fund the whole project if need be."

Hauzer took a note and nodded to the man in appreciation, then turned to an associate sitting at the conference room table. "Get every infrared and imaging satellite we own or can influence trained on the areas a supersonic jet can travel using a single tank of fuel. We have Dr. Ford's heat signature and image profiles in our database, so we know what we're looking for. She can't stay undercover forever, so find her."

"We are on it"

Hauzer looked around the room. "I'll keep all of you informed of our progress, but won't call another meeting until we've uncovered something substantial."

Chapter Twenty-Three

"Person of Interest"

Director Southerland at the CIA hadn't slept for twenty-four hours. Every time he got close to REM sleep, he was interrupted by a phone call. Everyone from the President on down was getting wound up about the Ford case. After midnight the phone stopped ringing, but he'd lain awake until 2:00 AM trying to figure out who had flown Dr. Ford off the mountain in Colorado.

At 4:00 AM he gave up on sleep, showered, dressed, and went back to the office. He sat in front of his computer for a couple of hours, searching for clues on who had orchestrated Dr. Ford's flawless getaway.

He was in the middle of cross referencing the list of people who had contacted her during the last sixty days when Director Jefferson from the FBI barged into his office again. His secretary pushed past Jefferson and announced sarcastically, "Director Jefferson from the FBI is here to see you again…"

We need to move farther away from Washington, D.C., he thought. *Being within ten miles of each other is too close for me.* "Thanks," said Southerland, looking up at Jefferson, who had bellied up to his desk. "You look like hell. Have a seat."

"Where is she?" asked Jefferson in an accusing tone. "There's no way Dr. Ford knew her house was going to be blown up and just happened to have a twenty-million-dollar helicopter parked up the canyon!"

"Slow down," said Southerland, pushing his chair back from his desk. Jefferson was crowding his personal space.

"Do you have her?" demanded Jefferson, his voice elevating.

Southerland stood up and leaned over his desk defensively. "Your incompetence is disgusting." The veins in his face were bulging, and he looked right into Jefferson's eyes. "I wouldn't tell you if I did because it would get her killed!"

"Do you have her?" yelled Jefferson, looking like he was about to come over the desk. Southerland leaned forward a few more inches. "I'm sorry, Director Jefferson, but that is none of your damn business."

"It will be after I escalate the incident to the Director of National Intelligence."

"Good luck with that," said Southerland. "Unlike you, he is in the loop." Southerland knew full well that nobody knew where Ford was, but he had no intention of telling that to Jefferson. The FBI Director gave his CIA counterpart a venomous glare, stomped out of the office, and slammed the door behind him.

After a minute, Southerland opened his door to make certain that Jefferson had gone, then motioned his secretary into his office. "Nancy, I know the walls are pretty damn thin around here, so please keep everything you've heard about Dr. Ford to yourself."

"Yes, sir," she responded.

"I need Matt Dalton up here the minute he shows up for work."

"Will do, but remember he had a late night apprehending that dirty congressmen and was planning on coming in late."

"He's young and can handle it. Call him and tell him to get his butt into work ASAP—I need him sooner than later."

"Ok," she said, but didn't raise her eyebrows until she had her back to her boss.

Matt had just finished exercising and was about to step in the shower when his phone rang.

"Matt, the Director wants to see you right away," Nancy said, her voice a bit strained.

"I'll shower and come up the minute I'm in the office and have had my cup of coffee."

"I would skip the coffee and shower if I were you," said Nancy, not trying to hide the stress she was feeling.

"Ok then, he must be pretty worked up about something. If his undies are in that big of a bunch, I'll come right over. Tell him I'll be there in twenty minutes unless he wants to send a chopper for me. If I get a ticket, he's paying for it and ..."

Nancy tried to control a nervous snicker, but was unsuccessful. Director Southerland scowled through the door in her direction.

"Just hurry up, please!" she whispered urgently, and ended the call.

"Was that Matt?" asked the director.

"Yes, sir."

"Is he in the building yet?"

"No, but he will be here in twenty minutes."

"What else did he say?"

"Just small talk, sir,"

"Out with it, Nancy, I want to know what is so damn funny this morning."

"He said the only way he can get here sooner is if you send a helicopter for him," she said, doing her best not to smile.

"If he wasn't so damn good, I'd fire him!"

Southerland turned back to his computer and scowled at the screen. Nobody on his list of people and organizations that had contacted Dr. Ford in the last sixty days had the connections to orchestrate her getaway. *Who could it be? Would Mcorp or Black Gold have sacrificed several of their own operatives and risked killing FBI and CIA agents for Ford's technology? Maybe...* Southerland threw up his hands in frustration. *Who would risk so much exposure for research that might not be worth the paper it's written on, unless... they knew for certain that it worked?* Southerland turned his attention to the pile of field notes on his desk and started digging for clues.

Agent Matt Dalton made it to the office in record time. He bounded up the stairs, but slowed down as he entered the director's office, doing his best to appear attentive and calm.

"What have you heard about the Dr. Ford situation?" inquired Southerland.

"Not much," said Matt, who wasn't about to discuss what he'd learned from his high school buddy, Sam. "I know he's been consulting with the government of Kuwait as well as a couple of major oil companies there."

Southerland looked irritated. "I meant Dr. Ann Ford, Jack's wife."

"Oh," said Matt, doing his best to act surprised. "The only thing I know for certain is that she's been employed by Colorado State University for the last few years."

"Listen, Matt, she's become a person of interest in a very high profile case. Rumor has it that she's come up with a way to extract hydrogen from water that's so efficient it will put the oil companies out of business and destroy the economies of several countries. The scary thing is that she disappeared from her home in Colorado a day ago and we haven't been able to find her. I had some agents on site in

Fort Collins just to keep an eye on the FBI and the situation, but two of them got themselves killed when Dr. Ford's house blew up. I've also had the IT guy, what's his name?"

"Sam?"

"Yeah Sam. He's doing some high-tech surveillance trying to locate her with our heat and image recognition satellites softwares. He's got every satellite in the system programmed to find her."

Matt whistled, "It's been a while since we went to this much effort to find someone."

Southerland ignored the comment. "I'll work this case from my level, but I need you on the ground figuring out what in the hell is going on. Put a small, competent team together. Spend what you need to, and find Dr. Ford. Do whatever it takes to keep her alive. Find out the last time she was at work, the last time she used her credit card, the last time she used her gas card, the last time she went to the spa, and the last time she brushed her teeth! I want you to find out everything you can about her whereabouts. I want to know the last time she took a pee, and I want a sample! Work with Sam and make sure our technical crews are on top of their game. She was at her house two nights ago and then she disappeared, so start there and work your way out. Oh, and report your findings directly to me."

"You got it," replied Matt, opening Southerland's office door.

"Not a word to anyone! Not the FBI, not the president, not your mother!" he said harshly, pointing his finger at Matt.

"Yes, sir!" said Matt over his shoulder.

"Hey," said Southerland, "Aren't you going to take Dr. Ford's files?" Southerland nudged the pile of folders on his desk. "Do I need to do this myself?"

Matt didn't say anything as he shouldered the stack of files.

"And try taking a shower once in a while," said Southerland. "It will do wonders for your career."

Matt rolled his eyes but didn't respond.

"This could be the most important assignment you have ever had, so don't screw it up!" Matt turned to leave. "And another thing," said Southerland, "when she left her house the other night, she was traveling faster than the speed of sound."

"What?" asked Matt, raising his eyebrow.

"Somebody flew her to a highway north of her home, then flew her away in a supersonic jet."

"Sounds like she's got some law-bending friends," responded Matt.

"That's the understatement of the year," said Southerland irritably. "We think they may have used an EMP blast to bring down an FBI chopper."

"I'll find her," said Matt confidently. "There can't be too many jets like that flying out of Fort Collins."

"What are you still standing here for?" asked Southerland.

Matt hesitated like he had something else to say, "Ah... never mind..." He decided to keep it to himself until he did more research.

Southerland watched him walk down the hall. "Young, cocky agents," he muttered.

Chapter Twenty-Four

"Ruins"

All that was left of his two-story home were the foundation walls and a bunch of smoldering timber. Jack and Charli stared in disbelief at the devastation. Jack searched the rubble, moving debris around with his boot, looking for anything recognizable, but could find nothing. "It's hard to believe that this pile of ash used to be my home."

"No kidding," said Charli.

The presence of the CIA and FBI poking and prodding through the timbers annoyed Jack. He felt like they were poking and prodding his privacy.

Charli tugged at his sleeve. "Over here," she said, pointing.

Jack stumbled through the rubble, following Charli. She leaned over and brushed the ash off the metal face of Ann's grandfather clock. "I'll keep that," said Jack. "It might be the only recognizable thing we find. Besides, Ann inherited it from her grandmother."

Jack looked over at the agents again. He wished they'd all go away so he could look through the rubble alone.

"Doctor Ford," an agent yelled, interrupting his thoughts. "Doctor Ford, I believe we found your safe!"

This should be interesting, thought Jack. *Won't they be disappointed when they discover there is only a thousand dollars in tens, a couple of car titles, and Ann's passport.*

"Do you mind if we open it, sir?" asked the agent.

"I doubt you'd have asked if I hadn't been here," muttered Jack under his breath. "Go ahead and pry it open," he yelled. The agents working on the safe looked a little too eager for a couple of guys who weren't looking for something specific. *It must be killing them not knowing where Ann's research is,* he thought smugly.

When they finally got the door open, their disappointment was palpable. "Is this what you expected?" asked an agent.

"Pretty much," replied Jack with a grin. "That's all we ever keep in there."

"This is a mighty big safe for a couple of car titles, a passport and a grand."

"What did you expect?" asked Jack sarcastically.

"Well... I don't know. Most people keep a gun, documentation, or valuables of one sort or another in their safe."

"Sorry to disappoint," said Jack. "I'll take the grand though so it doesn't get lost in your paperwork. The officer handed the money, car titles, and passport over to Jack, who tucked them away in his coat pocket. Jack took Charli by the arm and guided her in the general direction of her car. "Let's get out of here before Agent Porter makes another grab for my phone. When he finds out he can't trace the call, he's going to take it from me at gun point."

"Good idea."

"Hey... Thanks for waiting for me to fly in this morning. I really appreciate the company and a second pair of eyes and ears. Was it just me, or did those guys look noticeably disappointed when they saw the contents of my safe?"

"I was wondering if you had noticed," said Charli.

"They opened that safe with the excitement of a five-year-old on Christmas morning," said Jack with a chuckle.

"I bet they were hoping to find a stack of papers that included Ann's research."

"Oh well."

Jack opened the driver's side door for Charli and shut it after she slid into the seat. He waved in the direction of Agent Porter, signaling he was about to leave, but he had his back turned to him.

"Should we leave without saying good-bye?"

"I think so," said Jack.

"To the airport then?" asked Charli.

"To the airport," said Jack.

A commotion near the FBI trailer caught their attention. They could see several FBI and CIA agents having a heated discussion. Jack and Charli strained to hear what they were saying, but could only picked out a couple of words, "...how long have you known she was alive? ...Did you get the phone...?"

"Too many cooks in the kitchen," said Jack with a grin. "We'd better get out of here."

Charli sped out of the subdivision and headed towards the freeway on-ramp.

Chapter Twenty-Five

"Found"

Agent Porter was a little frustrated with the
Larimer County Sheriff and the Fort Collins Police
Chief. They couldn't understand why he wouldn't
share every detail of the investigation with them.
Porter admitted that the detail about Dr. Ford's body
not being among the deceased was an important
distinction for the sheriff to have, but didn't think the
information was as time sensitive as the sheriff.

I should have got the phone, he thought as he
retreated back to the command trailer to bark orders
to his satellite and forensic technicians. There was a
noticeable buzz coming from a group of technicians
at the rear of the trailer. He pulled up a chair next to
the technicians and sat down. "What's up, guys?"

"We found her!" they said enthusiastically.

"Hold that thought." Agent Porter cleared the trailer of all nonessential personnel, and sat back down. "Are you sure it's her?

"Ninety-nine-point-nine percent sure! We got a positive heat and facial image match."

"Where is she?"

"Corpus Christi, Texas," said the technician.

Agent Porter sighed with satisfaction. "It's about time."

"Keep every bird we have focused on that area until we pick her up. We cannot afford to lose track of her again. Remember this is highly classified information so it better not leave this trailer. Not a word to anyone!

The technicians nodded in unison.

"I'll relay this information to headquarters myself," said Porter.

"Sir, there is something else you need to know."

"What?"

"She's on the campus of the University of Southern Texas."

Porter sat back in his chair and let out a slow breath of air.

"Dammit…"

"What, sir?"

"Nothing, just keep every satellite we have pointed at the university until you hear otherwise. I'll take it from here."

All the pieces of the convoluted case started to fit together. The University of Southern Texas had the resources to fly Dr. Ford out of harm's way, but how did they get the timing right? Unless… they had been up to their counterespionage games again and had security people on the ground in Fort Collins before the incident.

"Damn them for meddling in our affairs!" During the last couple of years, Porter had suspected the university of extending their security detail to protect employees who were traveling off campus. He didn't care if the university had a security detail, because most universities did, but he didn't like the idea that their intel was better than his. *It's sad when the private sector is better funded than the FBI…*

Porter loathed having to make the call to Director Jefferson. *Hey, at least we found her,* he thought, *so the call shouldn't be too painful. He* stepped out of the trailer into the crisp mountain air to make the call. The phone only rang once before Jefferson picked it up.

"Did you find her?"

"Yes, sir."

"Where is she?"

"Corpus Christi, Texas."

"Where in Corpus Christi?"

"We picked up her signature as she walked into the University of Southern Texas administration building."

"Those bastards. I've had about enough of their meddling!" said Jefferson in a threatening voice.

"Who, sir?"

"The University of Southern Texas," snapped Jefferson irritably.

"Have they done anything like this before?"

"Nothing this bold, but I always feel like they know as much as we do."

"How many people were with her?" asked Jefferson.

"Three," said Porter.

"Did it look like she was being moved by force?"

"Can't tell for sure, but she was using an umbrella that was blocking our satellites from getting a read on her."

"Dammit!" said, Jefferson. "Put together a group of our best agents and get them organized somewhere near the campus before nightfall."

"Are you sure you want to do that, sir? This is the University of Southern Texas we're talking about."

"I'm damn sure," said Jefferson. "We think she might have the biggest discovery of the last two hundred years sandwiched between her ears, and we need to make sure she's safe."

Agent Porter wondered about Jefferson's sincerity because it was starting to sound like he was more interested in her research than her safety.

Jefferson interrupted his thought. "I want a play-by-play on this one! I want to know who she's with, where she is, what she is eating, and when she bends down to tie her shoe laces."

"Yes, sir."

"If you detect any other agencies or local police on campus, notify me immediately... and keep your eyes open for operatives from Black Gold or Mcorp."

"Black Gold and Mcorp, sir?"

"If you've found her, there's a chance they've found her as well," said Jefferson, pacing back and forth in front of his desk. "Black Gold tried to take her once and sacrificed five men and maybe a sixth doing it. You can bet they'll try again if have the opportunity. And watch your back; you did kill a couple of them yourself."

"Understood."

"Book the Presidential Suite at the Corpus Christi Hilton, along with enough rooms on the same floor for our agents. I think the Hilton is right across the street from the university, which will make it a perfect command center. Get a secure wireless satellite link set up in a room before tomorrow morning so we can handle input from our imaging and infrared satellites. Our satellite technicians need to be on high alert and ready for operations over Corpus Christi by tomorrow morning."

Porter scribbled a few notes on a piece of paper he had taken out of his pocket. "Will you be joining me in Corpus Christi?" he asked tentatively.

"I've been thinking about it," said Jefferson. "I will let you know what my plans are sometime this evening. Anything else?"

"No," said Porter and hung up the phone.

Jefferson sounded way too intense, and the thought of having him on site put a knot in Porter's gut. Even though Jefferson preached the value of delegation, trust, and accountability, he was a micromanager to a 'T.' He even insisted that all his direct reports CC him on all their email. Truth be known, he had major trust issues and wasn't comfortable enough with himself to allow others to lead. *I don't need him here making us all crazy...*

Jefferson was so agitated he couldn't sit down. His shoulders were tensed and rigid, and he was thoroughly pissed off. *"How in the hell..."* He muttered under his breath. UST had too much money and too much technology for his liking. He was fairly certain that the university had coordinated Dr. Ford's helicopter pick-up in the foothills behind her house, and was suspicious that they had engineered the explosion as a diversion.

It doesn't sound like they are holding her against her will though, so she must have contacted them when she discovered her house had been broken into. But how had they been able to respond so quickly...?

The more Jefferson thought about the situation, the more irritated he became. *I better do this myself. I can't trust anyone with something this big.* He pushed the button on his intercom impatiently. "Nancy, get me on the next flight to Corpus Christi! I'm going to handle this case personally."

Chapter Twenty-Six

"Kidnap or Kill"

"Is the line secure?" asked Hauzer.

"Yes," said the voice of the monitoring technician.

"Go ahead with your report then."

"The FBI found Dr. Ford!" It was obvious the speaker had been walking fast or running, because she was out of breath.

"Are you sure?"

"Absolutely sure."

"Where is she?" asked another voice.

"She's on the campus of the University of Southern Texas," said the informant. "The FBI has positioned their geostationary imaging, infrared, and

surveillance satellites over the area, and is mobilizing a ground force across the street in the Hilton hotel.

"Unbelievable!" said a deep voice on the call. "How did she end up down there?"

"We don't know for certain, but we think the university may have flown her down on a private jet. One thing we do know is she didn't fly commercial or with an aircraft that logged a flight plan."

"How long has she been there?"

"We aren't certain," said the messenger, "but it can't have been for more than a few hours. Last night, at the earliest, if the jet was supersonic and they left in good time from Fort Collins."

"UST is more formidable than I imagined," said the deep voice. "I'm impressed."

"We need to get control of this situation," said a female voice. "We have no option other than to kill her."

"It may not matter, if she's already shared the details of her research with the university."

"Doubtful," said another voice. "As much as the university will want to believe her research is real, they won't risk backing her until they see a working prototype. It might take days or weeks to reproduce it.

"There's also the possibility that the university will try and commercialize a solution themselves."

"Either way, we have to stop her research from getting out," said Hauzer.

"What are the chances that we can take her alive while she's on campus?"

"We could pull it off, but the risk is extremely high."

"Why are we so wound up," said an objective voice, "we have absolutely no evidence that Dr. Ford has come up with an economical solution."

"We've been over this before," said Hauzer. "If the FBI, CIA, Home Land Security, Black Gold, and a prestigious university like UST are interested in her, then the chances are pretty damn good she's on to something."

"Listen," said an authoritative voice. "She was late for work, she took the time to burn her lab… and she's never late. All her actions suggest that burning her lab was a last minute decision, and it was more important than standing up fifty freshman students. There is no doubt in my mind that she had a breakthrough."

"I agree," said the woman's voice. "Let's eliminate her and be done with it before she builds a prototype. We could've taken her out while we were sitting here talking about it."

"Remind me never to get on your bad side," said Hauzer.

"Have our satellites been able to confirm her location yet?"

"No, but if she makes a move out of the building, we'll have her."

"Why not kidnap her and find out how successful her efforts have been before we do anything rash?

"That would be my vote as well," said another voice.

"Mine, too," said someone who hadn't participated in the conversation previously.

"Ok," said Hauzer. "If we're going to do this, it has to be done now. There's an excellent chance she hasn't had time to share her secrets with the university, and I can have our best operative on campus within an hour. My instructions to him will be to offer her one billion dollars, with the caveat that she has to leave the campus immediately. If she doesn't go for the billion, he has instructions to abduct her. If he can't get her off campus and runs out of options, he has the green for termination. His pay will reflect our desire to have her taken alive."

"I want that thumb-drive," said the principal in charge of Mcorp research.

A principal on the phone cleared his throat as if he had something to say. "There is one other possible resource that might come into play."

"What's that?" asked Hauzer.

"The university always uses the same news crew for making major announcements. We've blackmailed one of the crew before, and we might want to get him on the hook again if he's called on to break the news on Ford's research. It's a long shot, but it may be a last ditch effort to kill her if we have to."

"Let's ramp him up just in case," said Hauzer, "but our assassin friend doesn't need to know anything about it. Understood?"

"Understood."

Hauzer looked around the room. "I need a vote from all the principals on this course of action." One by one they all gave their support and Hauzer recorded the vote on his phone.

When the call was over, Hauzer left the boardroom and headed for his car. Once he was on the road, he called a number that he hadn't used in a while. "You have a go."

"It took you long enough to make up your minds."

"There have been a few developments that you are not aware of," said Hauzer. "She was aided in her escape by the University of Southern Texas and is on campus."

The line was silent for a minute.

"Them again?" he said, his voice dripping with disdain. "Last time they tried to protect a professor, I killed him on their doorstep. What are my orders?"

"Make a billion dollar offer, kidnap her, or kill her before tomorrow morning at 8:00. We'll fly you to Corpus Christi immediately."

"How much?

"Five million for a kill, twenty million for a kidnap, and fifty million if you can talk her into taking the billion-dollar offer and leaving campus with you."

"Your oil and banker buddies are really stepping up this time... what did she do?"

"She hasn't done anything. It's about what she might do, and that's all you need to know."

Lunt took the hint but was curious nevertheless. "Is your plane in Fort Collins or Denver?"

"It is sitting on the tarmac in Fort Collins right now. If you go for the kill, there's another ten million in it if you deliver her research notes. It will be on a thumb-drive or may have been downloaded to one of the university's computers." Hauzer paused for a moment to let the assassin digest what he'd said. If you get into trouble, we have successfully blackmailed a Dr. Kenneth Thompson. He's a biology professor on campus and the only person we've been able to manipulated in that damn place."

"I won't need his help." In a hotel room in Fort Collins, a tall, powerful-looking man hung up the phone. He pulled a large duffle bag out of the closet and walked out the door. The man moved as gracefully as a big cat as he made his way through the hotel lobby and out into the street to hail a cab. When a cab finally responded to his hail, he tamped out his cigarette on the duffle bag and threw the butt on the ground.

"Airport," he said to the driver.

"Yes, sir. Which one?"

"Fort Collins Municipal."

The cab driver glanced into his rear view mirror and thought better of trying to strike up a conversation. The man in his back seat didn't look like the talkative type. Mcorp knew him only as Mr. Lunt, and they didn't need to know any more. All they knew was that he always got his mark, and he never left a mess.

As the cab raced to the airport, Lunt thought about the job. *I won't bother trying to make an offer or kidnap her,* he thought, *it would be too risky.* He'd done work at the UST before, and the kill had been unexpectedly difficult. He remembered being surprised at the level of security the university had, which had complicated his plans. That had been ten years ago. In the end, he'd got his mark and had enjoyed the challenge of doing it. *This time I will be ready for them*, he thought.

Dr. Vonstrausberg died well, he remembered. He respected men who didn't beg for their lives and who were defiant up to the very end. He looked forward to besting the university's security team again. He pulled a picture of Dr. Ford out of his pocket and examined it.. *Pretty lady,* he thought. *Should be an easy kill... too bad.* The taxi came to a stop in front of a sign that said, "Loveland Airport."

"Which hanger, sir?"

"Drop me off over there." Lunt pointed to a hanger with a QSST-AI jet parked in front of it.

The cab driver flashed his ID to the guard at the gate, and parked the cab under the nose of the private jet. "That'll be thirty-one bucks."

Lunt pushed a Ben Franklin through the panel and got out of the taxi without saying a word. By the time the taxi driver figured out the change, Lunt was walking up the aft stairs to the jet. They taxi driver shrugged and drove away and Lunt settled into his seat in the empty jet for the short flight to Texas.

Chapter Twenty-Seven

"Prototype"

Dr. Conner returned from helping Ann get settled into her new lab and had barely closed the door to his office when someone started pounding on it. "Come in."

It was Justin Woodward. "It looks like we are going to have company."

"Who?" asked Dr. Conner, standing up from behind his desk.

"We intercepted several communications from both the FBI and CIA. They will have people on campus in the next few hours. Our people at the Hilton just reported that the FBI commandeered the

Presidential Suite and a dozen other rooms, and are moving in a thousand pounds of gear."

Dr. Conner picked up the phone and dialed President Kane's office. "Carson, this is Brock. It appears that we have a bit of a problem. I'm coming up to your office with Justin."

"Sounds serious," said President Kane, "I'll see you in a minute."

On their way up the stairs Justin told Dr. Conner all he knew about the situation at the Hilton.

"I knew they'd eventually find her," said Dr. Conner, "but I was hoping it wouldn't be until tomorrow or the next day."

His sentence was interrupted by President Kane's voice. Rather than wait for them in his office, he had started down the hallway to meet them. "What's going on, gentlemen?" he asked, motioning them into his office.

"We've intercepted several transmissions from the FBI and the CIA that suggest they'll have agents on campus in the next few hours."

"How did they find her?" asked President Kane.

"Image or heat signature," said Justin.

"I was hoping it wouldn't come to this," said President Kane, frowning. "I was counting on being able to give Dr. Ford enough time to reconstruct her research and make an announcement before anyone figured out where she was. How much do the Feds know about our satellite capabilities?"

"They have the information we gave them, but I highly doubt they've figured out the breadth and depth of our technology. We've been very careful not to share our latest shielding and laser abilities beyond a few trusted people," said Justin.

"How do our birds stack up to theirs?"

"Well, sir, forgive me for sounding arrogant, but our satellites are equipped with the most advanced surveillance and weapons technology out there. Most of them have been upgraded with the F501 laser array we developed last year."

"I didn't realize that had been approved by the board."

"It was approved shortly after some space debris did a million dollars worth of damage to one of our research satellites. If you remember, the F501 allows us to track, target, and destroy space debris as small as a paint chip from twenty-three thousand miles in space to the surface of the earth. To date, we've destroyed over ten thousand objects in the flight path of our satellites. We've even gone out of our way to clean up space debris headed for satellites we don't own in an effort to build up some interstellar goodwill and create another revenue stream."

"What are these lasers capable of?"

Justin smiled like a boy with a fist full of firecrackers. "Well, we've done tests on everything from field mice to an old M2 Abrams tank we bought from a salvage yard."

"And?"

"In an area being overrun by vermin, we were able to eradicate fifty-two thousand field mice in one afternoon with no misses."

"From twenty-three thousand miles in space?"

"Yes," said Justin, still unable to suppress a grin, "and without endangering another satellite."

"And the tank?" asked President Kane, with boyish curiosity.

"Well, it was like cutting butter with a hot knife."

President Kane looked at Dr. Conner. "Did you know about this?"

"I thought everyone knew about it," said Conner, with a smile.

President Kane laughed, "Next time you play with one of your man toys, please don't hesitate to invite me. I may be old, but there is a whole lot of boy left in here," he said, tapping his chest. "So, can I assume that our satellites can protect themselves from about any threat that's thrown at us?

"With adequate warning, yes."

"Well, we have adequate warning now, so let's bring our defensive lasers on line," he said, emphasizing the word *defensive*.

"We already did that when you raised the security level on Dr. Ford. It's part of the Level One Protocol."

"Are our satellites already in orbit over the university?"

"Six satellites are in orbit above the university, sir."

"Easy on the sir, Justin," said President Kane with a smile.

Justin continued. "Positioning the satellites over the university is also part of the Level One Protocol."

"I hope there is enough room up there for all of them."

Justin smiled, "Plenty of room."

"It sounds like we have a technological edge over the Feds."

"We do," responded Justin, the schoolboy grin returning to his face.

President Kane stared out the window of his office, trying to figure out the right course of action to take. "If the FBI, the CIA or anyone else for that matter breaks the International Institute of Space Geostationary Satellite Treaty, you have my permission to cripple their satellites enough to send them out of geosynchronous orbit. We cannot afford to have our satellites in any danger at this time."

"Understood."

"How many of the six satellites are equipped with shield technology?"

"All of them are equipped with the experimental satellite shield technology, but only one has a shield that can extend down to the university," said Justin, with a curious look. "I should remind you that the shield technology is relatively new, and is not something we should count on. Remember it had a few glitches during Hurricane Derek, and it got in the way of that Russian GLONASS satellite's orbit."

"How could I forget! I learned some Russian words I didn't need to know. But, if we are going to have unwelcome visitors on campus, I want to know what all our options are. Let's turn on the shielding for each of the individual satellites."

"Already done."

"As part of the Level One Security Protocol?" guessed President Kane.

"That is correct," said Justin.

"If our FBI and CIA friends decide to operate on campus without a search warrant, assign a drone to each of them to keep them company, and make sure you don't let them get out of visual range. Don't use lethal force for any reason, but if things get out of hand, hit the perpetrators with enough ketamine to knock them out for a few hours."

Justin raised his eyebrows, a little surprised.

"I don't ever want to lose another professor to an assassin, so make sure we are prepared for all the scenarios we can think of. Make sure we have every inch of this campus covered with satellite and ground camera video so we can record what happens. We may need the footage to convince the media that we've not done anything wrong."

"Are you sure we need to take all these precautions?" asked Dr. Conner

"Better to be safe than sorry," responded President Kane. "I've got a sick feeling in my gut that tells me there are forces at play here that run as high as it gets in the United States Government."

President Kane's military instincts had kicked into overdrive. He felt like he was prepping troops for battle. His gut told him the Feds were about to overreact, and he didn't like the feeling.

He turned back towards the window. "Justin, we need more intel on what is going on out there. Triple the number of drones we have in the air and make sure each one has a full support and command contingent. I don't want any inexperienced drone operators flying drones until this fiasco is over."

"Understood," said Justin.

"The only people I want to see on campus are security details and SH701 drone controllers."

....

Unaware of the situation that was developing outside of the lab, Ann was hard at work reconstructing her hydrolyser. She stood facing a whiteboard with a marker in one hand and a dry eraser in the other. As fast as she filled up the board, the lab staff printed out her notes on giant eight-by-six-foot sheets of paper and taped them to the walls of the lab. Professors and graduate students were gathered around a table in the middle of the lab assembling the prototype Ann was outlining on the whiteboard. Every once in a while, Ann would leave the whiteboard and give clarifying instructions to those who were building the prototype. Excitement started to build as both students and faculty began to understand the genius behind Ann's research.

"Nine hours until morning, boys and girls, and we still have ten hours of setup and configuration to do," chirped Ann.

....

Jack's helicopter pick-up and corresponding jet ride went seamlessly and left the federal agents who'd been tailing him perplexed. Jack arrived on campus at 8:05PM, and spent the next forty minutes working his way through the Level One Security Clearance.

After clearing security, he was introduced to President Kane, who briefed him on what Ann was doing and that she planned on broadcasting a complete unrestricted disclosure of her work at 6:00 the next morning.

Jack nodded as he listened. "Giving her research away is a little anticlimactic, don't you think, especially since it's worth billions?" asked Jack trying to get a feel for the university's position on the subject.

"That was Ann's call," said President Kane, a little surprised by the comment. "In my opinion, there is nothing else she could do. The FBI already had one imposter try to kidnap her. Can you imagine what would happen if she tried to sell her technology to the highest bidder? I'm not entirely sure the United States Government would even let her sell it."

"You're probably right," responded Jack, rubbing his hand through his hair nervously. "There are a lot of inventions the government has put the kibosh on because there considered a threat to the public or to national security."

"There certainly have been a few."

"I'd really like to see my wife now. Is she in a secured area on campus?"

"She's as secure as she can be in this country."

"Forgive my skepticism," said Jack, "but I'm having a very difficult time believing that a university has enough security expertise and technical sophistication to protect anyone from a serious threat."

"That's probably true for every university in the world except for this one. Ever since we lost Dr. Vanstrausberg to that group of thugs who call themselves Mcorp," said Kane, shaking his head, "we've spent over eight-hundred-million dollars developing a security detail that has the experience and equipment they need to protect our people."

"And what are you going to do about the Feds who are parked outside your door?"

"Rest assured that we are not giving up Ann without her explicit permission. And if they come on campus they'd better do it by the book."

"Or what?" asked Jack.

"Or they won't make it past the front door."

"That's pretty tough talk for a university president. I'd like to see what you've got up your sleeve that gives you so much confidence."

"Everything we do here is transparent, so you will find out soon enough."

"I look forward to it. Back when I went to college, our campus security's biggest threat was late night beer parties and rival schools trying to paint our mascot purple."

President Kane laughed and shook his head in agreement. "Those were the days, weren't they?"

Jack followed President Kane down the hall to the elevator. As they walked, they talked about Ann's research, campus security, and the expensive transportation that had delivered Jack to the university an hour earlier.

Inside the elevator, Kane inserted his security card into a slot, then pressed his thumb against a biometrics reader while looking into an eye-level panel.

"Pretty fancy," said Jack, scrutinizing the bio-reader.

"It scans your fingerprint, retina, body temperature, and DNA all at the same time."

The elevator descended to a level that did not register on the elevator key pad, and the door opened into a brightly lit corridor. They walked briskly down the hallway, passing several empty labs.

"Where is Ann's lab from an above-ground perspective?"

"Underneath the left wing of the science building."

"Underground?"

"Yes. We have tunnels that connect all our buildings on campus. They keep us from getting sweaty during the warm, humid months."

The so-called tunnel they were walking down didn't look like a tunnel at all. There were laboratories on both sides of the well-lit hallway, and the only hint that they were underground was the fact that none of the laboratories had windows.

Jack was still thinking about the underground passageways. "Did you build these passages after the death of Dr. Vanstrausberg?"

"His death was certainly the catalyst that started the project, but we also needed several labs that could be completely blacked out."

Jack vaguely remembered the newspaper reports about Dr. Vanstrausberg's kidnapping and execution. The memory made the hair on the back of his neck stand up. The thought of Ann being in a similar situation made his jaw clench tightly. She was about to make an announcement that would put a good portion of the Middle East out of business, and it spiked his anxiety meter.

"I hope this isn't a mistake."

"We'll keep her safe or go down fighting," said President Kane, trying to build Jack's confidence. "We can't be any worse than the FBI or the CIA. If her security were left solely to them, she would already be in the custody of Black Gold, or dead. We've already saved her once, and we'll keep it up until this is over."

Jack didn't respond. *Maybe the FBI just dropped the ball on this one,* he thought as he followed President Kane down the hall. "Maybe the FBI's network doesn't have as many holes in it as you think it does," said Jack out loud.

"I hope you are right," said President Kane, "but I'm not willing to trust them at this point. If we trusted everyone that flashed a badge right now, your wife would be in serious trouble."

"Have you engaged the press?"

"Absolutely," said President Kane, "Whatever the Feds are scheming will be on public display."

They came to another set of elevators labeled, 'Secure Labs,' and President Kane once again went through the security routine. The elevator came to life with a low mechanical whir. When the door opened, they were greeted by two security guards and a couple of drones. The security guards stepped away from the elevator doors to make way for Jack and President Kane. The drones hovered at about shoulder height, flanking them like a couple of well-trained German Shepherds.

Down boy, thought Jack to himself.

One of the security guards stayed with them during the short elevator ride to the lab, and the other one stationed himself just outside the elevator door. The security guard that stayed with them motioned for President Kane and Jack to follow him down the hallway.

Jack was impressed by the drone technology, but wondered how effective they'd be in a firefight against a bunch of highly trained FBI agents.

"Who controls the drones?" he asked.

"Each drone has an independent support team that controls it. One team member drives the drone from a remote console, and the other team members act as supporting cast and as a communication link with central security."

"Interesting," responded Jack. "How many drones do you have?"

"Around two thousand or so," responded the security guard.

"Two thousand!" exclaimed Jack in surprise. "That's a lot of team support!"

"There are only fifty full-time teams," said the security guard, "but the rest of the campus staff and students are trained as backup drone controllers."

"I don't think I've ever heard of a university with its own army."

"I wouldn't call it an army," interrupted President Kane, "but the drones do give the campus staff a sense of security. It makes us feel like someone is looking out for us. Unfortunately the terrorist activity within our borders has made them a necessity."

They approached a series of rooms where there was a steady stream of people going in and out. "Here we are," announced President Kane. "It looks like you're wife has the lab humming like a beehive."

They stood in front of two double doors labeled 'Lab One.' Four security guards stood outside the doors, two on each side of the hall. Each of them had a drone by their side. They were carefully watching every person who entered or exited the lab. Every few minutes, people would come and go carrying various odd shaped pieces of equipment. Some of them looked familiar to Jack, like they'd been taken out of his wife's lab in Fort Collins.

President Kane nodded to the security guard and started to walk into the lab, but he was almost knocked over by a man carrying a large ring of compact lasers. "Coming through," he said, and disappeared down the hall.

The open door revealed a sophisticated lab full of people in white coats, bustling around a familiar-looking apparatus. Ann was right in the middle of it all pointing her finger at something on the table with one hand while writing on the whiteboard with another. *Damn, she's sexy*, Jack thought. He was barely able to restrain himself from running over and giving her a huge embrace, but he decided to watch her work for a minute instead.

A lump formed in his throat and he sighed with relief that Ann was safe. Watching her in her element overwhelmed Jack with a feeling of pride that almost edged out the anxiety he'd been feeling.

Two people were typing every word that Ann said into a couple of laptop computers, while another leveraged a CAD program to create a blueprint an object in the middle of the room. It was similar to one Jack had seen in his basement for the last couple of years, but a little larger in design.

Ann was so busy directing traffic; it took her a few minutes to see Jack standing in the doorway. When it finally registered, she ran over and threw her arms around his neck. Jack reciprocated with a long heartfelt hug, then planted a romantic kiss on her lips that lingered long enough to make the few people who noticed smile.

"Are you sure you want to do this?" he asked.

"What, trust these people, or give you another mushy kiss?"

"Both," said Jack.

Ann promptly pulled Jack in close and planted another heart-felt kiss on his mouth. "As far as trusting these people, we are pretty much out of options—besides I like them. We can't trust the Feds after that incident in Colorado almost got me killed?"

"I understand," said Jack, "but this whole thing makes me uncomfortable. I'm not sure these guys can protect you."

"You may be right, babe, but at this point who else can we turn to? Listen... I've got a couple more hours of work to do before I can get this thing running. In about half that time, there will be twenty more people in the world who know how to build one and then nobody will be able to suppress my research!"

Jack looked into his wife's bright eyes and believed her.

"Do you want to help?"

"Not sure I'll be of much help," said Jack, "but I will do what I can."

"Good," said Ann, handing him a crescent wrench, "follow me."

Jack followed Ann into the fray. He'd never seen so many excited people in one place at one time. Professors and students worked feverishly side by side, many of them too pumped up to take a break.

Dr. Conner and President Kane were just as anxious to finish the prototype, so they stayed in the lab to help.

At at 3AM Ann declared the hydro-electrolysis prototype to be complete. She carefully inspected the apparatus and made a few last minute adjustments. When she was done, she put her hands on her slim hips and smiled.

"What's stopping us from giving this thing a whirl?" asked President Kane.

"Not much," replied Ann. "The only things we are waiting on are the temperature control for the water tank and fifty gallons of distilled water."

"The water is ten minutes away," said Doctor Conner. "That's the only thing you stumped us on. Thank goodness for Wal-Mart."

"I'm pleasantly surprised you had so much laser equipment and people that know how to use it on hand," said Ann.

"We have a number of projects that use lasers technology," he responded. "I'm just happy we were able to put this thing together so fast."

President Kane looked at Ann. "Please pardon my lack of faith, Ann, but I haven't been so anxious to see something work in my life. Where is your confidence level?

"It's a little rough around the edges," she said pointing at the device on the table, but I'm 100% confident it will work."

Truth be told, Ann was every bit as worried as Dr. Conner. *How could it not work?* she thought, *it's exactly like the prototype I built at home*. The good thing was, a dozen professors and students in the room were getting a firm grasp on the logic behind her research, and were gaining confidence that her approach had merit.

Chapter Twenty-Eight

"Operation UST"

Agent Porter looked at his watch: it read Thursday, September 11, 12:01 AM. The Presidential Suite in the Corpus Christi Hilton felt jam-packed with personnel and equipment. The agents standing around him looked a little uncertain. They were the best undercover operatives the FBI had, and they didn't like the idea of going into UST with so little intelligence. Their mission—as they understood it— was find Dr. Ford, protect her, and bring her in for questioning. They'd been told that this mission was high profile, and that Dr. Ford's safety and the security of her research were paramount. The most uncomfortable thing about the operation was that Director, Rick Jefferson, was overseeing it in person, which validated everything they'd been told about the importance of the case.

The agents in the Presidential Suite were clustered in small groups discussing the details of the mission when Director Jefferson entered the room. He looked like he hadn't slept in two days, and his temperament showed it. "People!" he said, clearing his throat. "We have a situation here that is of the utmost urgency, and it is paramount that we execute this operation with absolute precision. We cannot afford to have any loose ends on this one."

He cleared his throat and took a sip of his coffee. "Dr. Ann Ford, a professor at Colorado State University, is a person of interest to us." He pointed to a poster-sized picture of her on the wall. "She's been doing research on a hyper-efficient petroleum substitute for a couple of years, and we believe she's had a major breakthrough. To be clear, if she's created a replacement for fossil fuels, her discovery will change the balance of power on this planet and rock the world economy overnight."

A murmur of surprise rippled through the group of agents. Jefferson was relieved that the agents understood the ramifications of what he was saying because he needed them to act with conviction.

"We got involved because we discovered that she's been under surveillance by Mcorp and Black Gold. Operatives from both organizations have been spotted in the Fort Collins area during the last few days, which is highly unusual considering they don't have any business in the area.

At approximately 8:40 on Tuesday morning, Dr. Ford burned her computer and her research notes in her fireplace. Shortly thereafter, operatives from Mcorp trashed her house looking for something. We chased them off fifteen minutes later, killing one of them in the process. We did a thorough search of her house and found absolutely nothing of interest. We left agents in the neighborhood in hopes that we might apprehend another Black Gold or Mcorp operative, but they did not make another appearance until Ann returned to her home that evening. The CIA is involved because of the consequences Dr. Ford's research could have on our foreign allies and enemies."

Jefferson paused for a minute and took a couple of sips of his coffee. "At approximately 8:00 PM on Tuesday, Dr. Ford arrived home from school, and discovered that her house had been broken into. She immediately called a friend and then ran to a neighbor's house street—who by way are not on the public registry by their neighborhood names. At 8:45 PM, she called the local authorities. We took over the investigation shortly thereafter. Dr. Ford and her neighbors showed up at the house about 9PM to survey the damages. Porter, here, did the meet-and-greet, then left them alone long enough for them to be accosted by our most recent imposter."

The agents in the room grew quiet and uncomfortable. The thought of the FBI being infiltrated again created instant feelings of disdain for the individual. A few of the agents glanced around the room, looking for an unfamiliar face. Jefferson shared their concern, but decided against saying what he was thinking. He continued his debrief.

"While trying to kidnap Dr. Ford, the rogue FBI agent shot Agent Porter, then got his face smashed into the kitchen sink by one of Dr. Ford's neighbors who we have yet to identify. After the first shot was fired, gunfire opened up in the front of Dr. Ford's house between the FBI, the CIA, and the accomplices of the would-be kidnapper. According to Agent Porter, Dr. Ford and her neighbors exited the kitchen area through a door leading to the basement to avoid the gunfire. Approximately five minutes later, Dr. Ford's home blew up and burned to the ground."

Jefferson paused for a minute, giving the agents in the room time enough to digest what he was saying and take another drink of coffee. "We now know that the rogue FBI agent was employed by the Arabic oil cartel, Black Gold. Thank goodness Porter here isn't quicker on the draw or we may not have been able to question him."

Porter tried not to blush, but failed and a couple of agents standing next to him gave him a bad time. Jefferson let the men beat up on Porter for a minute to ease the tension. Porter was well-liked and handled it fine.

"In Porter's defense, our rogue agent already had his gun drawn when he came through the front door, so he didn't have a chance to draw his weapon before he was shot in the shoulder. To his credit, he was able to take out three of the five Black Gold agents that had us pinned down out in the yard, even after being shot."

"Is that what Porter told you, or do we have this on film?" asked one of the agents.

Laughter rippled through the room and Porter's face reddened even more.

"That's where things get fuzzy," said Jefferson. "Porter is lucky he didn't follow Dr. Ford into the basement or he'd be dead right now."

"What caused the explosion?" asked one of the agents.

"We still don't know, but we do know that it originated from the basement. A careful investigation of the backyard has revealed six sets of tracks leading from Dr. Ford's backyard up into the foothills behind her home. The tracks dead end where we assume Dr. Ford was picked up by UST."

Jefferson paused again, letting his people get their minds around what he was saying. "If our assumptions are true, then it's obvious that Dr. Ford had some pretty sophisticated help. We can't figure out how the University of Southern Texas had enough information to know they'd need to evacuate Dr. Ford out of the Fort Collins area that night, unless they were being blackmailed into helping Black Gold with their kidnapping operation."

Jefferson shook his head as he thought through the evidence again. "In any case, the one thing we do know for sure is that Dr. Ford is on campus right this minute, and we have reason to believe that she has the discovery of the century on her person or in her head. It is absolutely imperative that her research not be stolen or destroyed by foreign powers, so she must be protected at all costs. The wholesale proliferation of her research would upset the very foundation of the world financial community for several years, so the United States cannot allow her research to be released without adequate laws in place to manage it. We are so concerned about containing and protecting Dr. Ford's research that we are jamming all radio, phone, internet, shortwave, and satellite transmissions to and from the university until this situation is resolved."

The agents in the room seemed to be getting more comfortable with the FBI's position. "As mentioned earlier, we picked up Dr. Ford's heat signature and matching profile on the University of Southern Texas's campus a couple of hours ago. There is no evidence that she is being held against her will, but we have to know for certain. If she's here of her own free will, there is nothing we can do but to offer our protection, and demand that she not release her research without the proper protocols in place. If she's being held here against her will, then we need to take her into protective custody."

Jefferson paused, "Are there any questions so far?"

Those in the room shook their heads.

"So our objectives are twofold. First, we need to establish whether Dr. Ford is being held against her will. If she is, we need to take her into protective custody. If she is not, we need to persuade her that she is in great danger and needs our immediate protection. If she so much as hints that she is being held here against her will, you have the green light to use lethal force to protect her. Remember, she cannot be harmed in any way, and must be protected at all costs. Under no circumstances are you to identify yourselves as FBI agents, unless it is to Dr. Ford or her husband, Jack."

Director Jefferson handed out a stack of Dr. Ford's pictures to the agents that surrounded him. "We believe that Mcorp and Black Gold will try and insert operatives on campus, so pay attention!"

He handed out several pictures of the Black Gold and Mcorp operatives who were known to be in the United States. "If you see any of these people on campus or in Corpus Christi, take them out and we'll clean up the mess later. Black Gold and Mcorp would rather kill Dr. Ford than allow her research to go public, so be aggressive."

Jefferson surveyed the group of agents, looking for any signs of confusion. They were all nodding their heads in the affirmative as they memorized the faces on the photos that were being passed around.

"Students generally start arriving on campus around 7:00 AM, so you have a few hours to get briefed and ready."

Jefferson motioned to Agent Porter to take over, and retired to the hotel room adjacent to the Presidential Suite.

Chapter Twenty-Nine

"Assassin"

In the lobby, a few floors below the Presidential Suite, Mcorp's most trusted and capable assassin was checking into the Corpus Christi Hilton. He passed the ID of the man he'd just killed across the counter to the desk clerk. It was the first test to see how well his disguise resembled that of the late Professor Stanley George Richardson III. He asked for the Presidential Suite, but was informed that it was already taken. His next two requests for deluxe rooms where also denied.

"I'll take the best thing you've got then," said Lunt coldly. His calloused tone made the seasoned desk clerk's head jerk up.

"Sorry for the smaller room, Dr. Richardson, but we have a pretty full house tonight."

"What is the occasion?" asked Lunt, raising an eyebrow.

"I'm not sure," said the clerk, "just a bunch of small conventions, I think."

Lunt knew the FBI was aware of Dr. Ford's whereabouts, and he suspected they were holed up somewhere in Corpus Christi. *Wouldn't it be ironic if we were under the same roof tonight,* he thought as he sorted through the credit cards in his wallet for the one with the correct name.

Lunt handed Dr. Richardson's credit card and driver's license to the clerk. The clerk made a few more entries in his computer, swiped Lunt's credit card, then compared the photo to the face of the man standing in front of him.

"Do you have a room facing the university?" asked Lunt.

"I believe we do, sir," said the clerk. After a few minutes of clicking, he nodded his head in affirmation. "Here you go, Dr. Richardson," said the clerk and handed Lunt his room key. The elevators are down the hall, to your right. Breakfast will be served from 6:30 to 9:30 AM."

Lunt stuffed the credit card and driver's license in his front pocket and hoisted his huge duffle bag over his shoulder as if it were as light as a feather. With the other hand, he picked up a long golf club travel bag that had "Ping" written in white lettering on the side.

Lunt's attempt at mimicking the look of the late Dr. Richardson had been successful enough to get him a room at the Hilton, and he was certain that Richardson wouldn't be missed for at least ten hours, which would give him the time he needed to take out Dr. Ford.

Lunt exited the elevator on the ninth floor and walked down the hallway in both directions to get his bearings. He carefully noted the location of every room, employee work area, vending machine, window, fire alarm, and exit on the floor. When he was satisfied he understood the layout, he unlocked the door to his room.

He dumped his luggage on one of the queen beds and immediately synchronized the clock on the night stand with his watch. After setting the alarm clock for 4:00 AM, he unzipped his duffle bag and took out a very impressive-looking night vision monocular and set it on the desk. After turning off all the lights in the room, he carefully parted the window blinds so he could observe the university.

The generous lighting on campus made the visibility through his night vision monocular nearly as good as if it were broad daylight. After twenty minutes of observation, he shut the blinds on the window and lay down on the bed. He was comfortable with the area and was confident he could get the job done. *Not much has changed since the last time I was here*

As a backup to the alarm clock, he called the front desk and asked them to wake him up at 4:00 AM. He lay staring at the ceiling for a few minutes before his eyes grew heavy with sleep. He didn't mind working for Mcorp. They paid well and stayed out of his business.

Chapter Thirty

"Definitive Proof"

Ann glanced at the clock on the wall. "3:45 AM," she muttered under her breath. *Where is the distilled water?* The past few hours had flown by like a dream. True to his word, Dr. Conner had been able to provide everything she had needed, and she hoped the makeshift hydro-electrolyzer would work despite the corners she'd cut to get it done quickly.

"Dr. Ford?" said a voice from the hallway. "Your water is here."

Ann directed the men carrying the distilled water to dump ten gallons of it in the chilling tank. The activity in the room had slowed to a crawl as Ann made a final inspection of their work.

The scientists in the room backed away from Ann's apparatus out of respect for the amount of hydrogen that would be distilled from ten gallons of water. While Ann waited for the water to chill to 31.85 degrees, she walked around the hydrolyser making sure they hadn't missed something. The room grew quiet with anticipation as the thermostat on the water tank dropped closer and closer to the desired temperature. The tension in the room was palpable. Everyone was thinking similar thoughts—*if this thing works, we will have witnessed one of the most amazing breakthroughs of all time.*

Finally, Ann stepped back from the hydrolyser.

"Where is President Kane and Dr. Conner?"

"Over here."

"I think we are ready to go," said Ann, unable to mask the excitement and anxiety in her voice.

Dr. Conner made his way through the crowd to where Dr. Ford was standing. "I've been waiting to see this thing work ever since I read your first white paper. What are we waiting for?"

He circled the apparatus, admiring its simple, yet elegant design. "Brilliant," he said, "absolutely brilliant. Who would have ever thought that a vibrating laser funnel that looks like a giant ice cream cone would do the trick?"

Ann looked around the room until her eyes met Jack's. She motioned him over to her side. "This is it," she breathed, holding his hand tightly.

"Looks like the one you built in the basement," was all Jack could say.

"Aren't you the observant one," said Ann, squeezing his hand.

Jack was beaming like a father at a talent show. "Show them your stuff, girl."

Ann stepped forward, smiling at the professors and students around the table. "Thank you for spending a late night with me to construct something you don't even know will work. Thanks for being patient as I extracted this thing out of my head, and thanks for all your suggestions on how to make it better. I'm kind of scared to pull this switch because if it doesn't work you might throw me out of here, and I was just getting to like you." Everyone in the room laughed.

"Well, I can't stall anymore, so here we go. "Counting five, four, three, two, one," and she pulled the lever.

Every person held their breath as they watched the crystal clear stream of water hit the laser funnel and disappear into the invisible gases of hydrogen and oxygen.

The room was silent for a few seconds, then broke into enthusiastic clapping and cheers. Ann smiled, and her shoulders sagged with relief and satisfaction. She leaned against Jack, who put his arms around her waist.

"I'm more proud of you right now than I have ever been proud of anyone in my entire life," he whispering into her ear. He turned Ann towards him and gave her a kiss. Ann responded in kind.

"I missed you," she whispered, looking up into his eyes.

"I missed you, too," he said.

Nobody noticed their romantic exchange because everyone in the room was crowded around Ann's hydrolyser like it was the Wright brothers' airplane. They were all talking at the same time and pointing out different aspects of the apparatus's construction. President Kane put his fingers to his lips and whistled loudly. Nobody seemed to hear. He tried again, but to no avail. In desperation, President Kane walked over to the light switch and turned off the lights. The lab had no windows, so the room went completely black except for the twinkling lights of the electronic equipment and the golden, cone-shaped image of the laser grid. Immediately the uproar died down.

"Now that I have your attention, ladies and gentleman, I'll turn the lights back on. I don't need to tell you this, but today is a day never to be forgotten. This is one of those once-in-a-lifetime moments that you'll proudly tell your grandchildren and great-grandchildren about. In my humble opinion, witnessing this event for the first time..."

Ann held up eight fingers, and President Kane nodded in acknowledgement. "Dr. Ford is telling me this is the eighth time this experiment has worked, but the first time in front of witnesses other than God?" he said, smiling.

A chuckle rippled through the room. "Am I correct Ann?" He glanced at Ann, who affirmed his statement. President Kane finished what he'd started to say a minute earlier. "Standing here watching this experiment succeed publicly for the first time will be no less impressive to our kids and grandkids than if we told them we were standing on the moon when Neil Armstrong stepped off Apollo 11 in 1969. The financial and economic implications of Dr. Ford's research will change our world beyond what we can now comprehend. This is the biggest scientific breakthrough this university has ever participated in, and I want to express my heartfelt appreciation to the Ford family for sharing it with us…"

Cheers and applause interrupted Kane's speech, and he waited for the noise to die down. "Now, I need all ya'll to pay close attention to what I'm about to say next, because I believe that Dr. Ford's life depends on it." He glanced down at his watch. "In about two hours, NBC News will be arriving on campus to interview Dr. Ford. At that time, she plans on giving away the specifications of her invention to the world."

The audible gasps of those present spoke of their admiration for Ann's generosity. Applause broke out again; evidence that the position she was taking with her research was widely supported.

President Kane waited patiently to be heard. He raised his hand, indicating that he wanted to speak, but the applause continued. Kane raised his hand again, and the applause died down.

"Before Dr. Ford can post her research on the internet, we'll need to package the content in such a way that it can be easily understood and reproduced. Our plan is to publish the research on the most popular scientific message boards, blogs, tweets, and websites, and give Dr. Ford the opportunity announce her findings with Dan Johnson on the morning news.

It is imperative that her research go viral for all of our sakes. President Kane looked at Ann. "What is your code name for this thing?"

Ann paused for a moment, then smiled. "My husband is the one that financed the emotional aspects of the research, so I will defer to him."

Jack was speechless. "Well, I don't know," he stammered. "Ah... a... how about..." Jack didn't say anything for twenty seconds and everybody in the room stood in silence looking at him. "Talk about pressure," he said, half to himself. A mild chuckle rippled through the room. "Well, you mentioned Apollo 11, and it is the 11th of September, so why not call it Apollo 11 or just Apollo?"

President Kane looked at Ann for approval. Ann shrugged and nodded her head. "Apollo, it is," said President Kane.

President Kane went on to explain what had happened to Dr. Ford during the last couple of days so the people in the room had better understanding of why speed was of the essence. He included the details of how Ann's home had been destroyed and how her life had been threatened. He cautioned everyone to remain in the science building until the NBC press release was officially aired. He provided details on the security measures that were in place to protect Dr. Ford and the university faculty. When he was done took a few minutes to answer questions.

"If there aren't any more questions, then let's get snapping. It would be wonderful if we could get this research packaged up and published on the internet with a fully functional schematic before NBC News graces us with their presence." The room came alive as people were instructed on exactly what needed to be done.

President Kane asked Ann and Jack to join him in the hall. "I want to update you on a couple of things. The FBI has over forty agents in the hotel across the street, and it appears that they are going to pay a visit to our campus."

"How did they find out where I am?" asked Ann.

"I would be guessing, but we think they picked up your heat signature this morning. If you are like me, you probably took one too many looks up our giant flag pole?"

"Guilty as charged," said Ann.

"Not to worry, they would have figured it out eventually anyway.

"Why are you telling us this?" asked Jack, a feeling of panic rising in his chest.

"Well... we pride ourselves on being transparent, and we wanted you to know exactly what has been going on. I also wanted to remind you that you are free to leave the campus anytime you want."

"How can you possibly stop forty FBI agents?" asked Jack.

"Forty agents is not a problem for us," said President Kane. "Two hundred might be a challenge, but forty we can handle."

"I would prefer to stay," said Ann, "and get this research out, then we'll re-evaluate the situation."

"Do you want us to do everything within our power to keep you out of their hands?"

"Yes," said Ann, with a determined look. "I trust you a lot more than I trust them. In fact, I would prefer not to speak with them directly until my research has saturated the internet, and someone outside this university has validated it."

"Do they have any legal grounds to take Ann into protective custody against her will?" asked Jack.

"Our legal team is telling us they don't have a leg to stand on. More than likely, they'll try and use your sudden disappearance from Colorado as an excuse to make sure you're not being held against your will. We're very confident that that they don't have probable cause, and we're one hundred percent sure there isn't a judge in Texas that would issue a search warrant against this university."

"I've made my decision," said Ann. "I believe if we release my research into the public domain the FBI won't have any reason to stay, especially when they see my smiling face on the news."

"I agree," said President Kane.

They walked back to the lab to help tie up any loose ends her new-found associates might have uncovered with the packaging of her research.

"When you are ready for a break or want to freshen up, Kellie has you all set up in Conference Room B. She had your stuff from the hotel brought over, so you should have what you need until we find more permanent accommodations for you."

"I could use a brush, comb, hair straightener, pair of warm-ups, tooth brush, etc. Don't forget you blew mine up.

"Not sure you'll let me live that one down anytime soon."

"Not for a while," said Ann giving him the stink eye.

"I'll have Kellie round up a few things so you are more comfortable, said President Kane with a smile." He left the lab and headed back to the command center.

Chapter Thirty-One

"Bending the Law"

Lunt's alarm clock went off at 4:00 AM sharp, followed by a call from the front desk a few seconds later. He sat up, swung his legs over the side of the bed, and sat there until his mind cleared and he'd gone over his plan for the day.

He picked up the night vision monocular on the bedside table and went to the window. He parted the blinds enough to get a good look at the university grounds. He scanned the campus until he had memorized the location of every building and walkway within his view. He compared what he was seeing with a map of the university that was laid out on the table beneath the window.

He was especially interested in the administration building since that was the last place Dr. Ford had been picked up by satellite. He knew the university had several underground hallways connecting most of their buildings, but was fairly certain that Dr. Ford would be hanging out in either the administration building or the adjoining science building.

He reasoned that if Dr. Ford had discovered an efficient way to extract hydrogen from water, the university would want empirical proof that her research worked before going public with an announcement. *Empirical proof means they'll want to reconstruct her project in one of their science labs,* he thought, *and that means she'll more than likely be in the science building.*

Lunt shut the drapes and threw the monocular on the bed. He took an extended shower, then pulled a chair over to the window, where he sat in his briefs and continued to scan the campus. When he was satisfied that he'd come up with a plan of attack that was low-risk, he began to dress for the day.

He pulled a business suit out of the closet and put it on. Mimicking the dead professor's mustache and beard was no problem given his years of expertise in deception and disguise. After he was satisfied with his appearance, he pulled a chair over to the bed where he'd tossed the bag of golf clubs the night before.

One by one he took the drivers out of the bag. Carefully he unscrewed the head of a Callaway driver to reveal that it concealed a rifle barrel. The rest of the components of the rifle were hidden in various aspects of his golf equipment. He quickly and easily assembled the weapon, having done it many times, then laid it on the bed and began to put together a pistol. Both guns were equipped with silencers, which would allow him to work on campus without drawing attention to himself.

Once he had his equipment in order, he sat back in the chair by the window and watched the university, waiting for the perfect opportunity to strike. At 4:30 AM, a news truck and crew showed up at the south entrance. He watched as a security guard came out of the guardhouse and walked around the truck, scanning its exterior and interior. The security guard held a mirror under the truck and walked around the vehicle, carefully inspecting its undercarriage, then extended his arm to the driver and his passenger and asked to see their IDs. When he was satisfied he motioned them to step out of the vehicle, then patted them both down.

When he was finished, he motioned for them to walk through the security scanners. They did so, then returned to the truck. With the security guard's permission, they pulled slowly through the gate in the direction of the science building.

Only two people? Budgets must be tight, Lunt thought to himself. He did not recognize the driver, but after zooming in on the man in the passenger's seat, he let out a low whistle. *Dan Johnson. Something big must be going down. I'll bet Dr. Ford is going to make an announcement of some sort,* he mused.

"If they set up outside, I won't even have to leave my room to kill her," he muttered hopefully. Lunt looked down at his watch. He knew the sun wouldn't be up until approximately 7:00 AM, which meant the interview would be handled inside if they were going to broadcast on the 6:00 AM news. *Too bad,* he thought, *it looks like I'm going to have to work for this one.*

The truck went slowly across campus and pulled up to the side of the science building. The driver backed the truck gently down a loading ramp until it touched the dock bumper pad.

A door opened on the right side of the dock and a couple of college students stepped through the opening to greet the news crew. They chatted for a minute, the students periodically pointing in the direction of the door. The driver and Dan Johnson opened the rear of the truck and began handing equipment to the students, who took it inside. Gauging from the time it took the two students to return to the loading dock for more equipment and based on how hard they were breathing,

Lunt estimated that the interview room was within two hundred yards of the loading dock and on the third story of the science building. Lunt left the window and went into the bathroom to check his disguise. *I make a pretty good professor,* he thought, as he adjusted his mustache and ran his fingers through his hair. *This is too easy.*

He held the visitor's ID he'd taken from the body of Professor Richardson and compared it to his reflection in the mirror. *Good enough for a bunch of campus security.* He adjusted his mustache a little more and tried out a smile in the mirror, then slid the ID back into his pocket.

He pulled the pistol from its shoulder holster and loaded nine shells into the clip, which he slid into place. "One shot, that's all," he said out loud and jacked a bullet into the chamber. "Thirty minutes from now, I should be well on my way to the George Bush International Airport for a well-deserved vacation." *This is going to be like taking candy from a baby.*

Lunt left his hotel, walking briskly like a professor who had a busy schedule and wanted to get a jump on the day by coming in early. He was a professional killer, perhaps the best of his kind. What he didn't know was that the university had just installed new scanning equipment at each gate, capable of taking a DNA scan on the spot and detecting a myriad of weapons. A long line of successes had made him cocky and careless.

....

Agent Porter had set his alarm for 5:00 AM so he could get up, get dressed, and have an hour or so to go over the campus building layout ahead of everyone else. Before his alarm could go off, his phone rang, jarring him out of his sleep.

"Sir," a voice said on the phone, "there's a person approaching the south gate and it's only 4:59 AM."

Porter looked at the alarm clock on the night stand and yawned, "Maybe he's a professor trying to get a quiet moment before his students arrive."

"You told me to call you when the first person arrived on campus, and I am."

"I was going to get up in a few minutes anyway," said Porter.

Porter got out of bed, showered, and put on the clothes that would make him appear like a student. He walked across the hall to the Presidential Suite, which had been retrofitted into a command center.

An agent immediately informed him that an NBC News truck had arrived on campus around 4:35 AM.

"I thought you were going to wake me up if anything suspicious happened?"

"Sorry, we didn't think a news team was a big deal."

"Where did they end up on campus?"

"They parked in the loading area of the science building and have been unloading equipment ever since."

Porter looked annoyed. "Has there been any other activity?"

"Nothing other than the professor I mentioned earlier."

Porter looked out the window, but couldn't see the NBC News truck. "I wonder what NBC is doing here today," he mumbled. "What happened to our early morning professor?"

"It took him forever to get through security, but you can see him walking towards the science building now."

....

President Kane had dozed off, but the ringing and buzzing of his cell phone brought him into a semi-conscious state.

"We have company, boss," said Justin. "Our south gate security guard says that someone pretending to be Dr. Stanley George Richardson III is on campus. The guard said that Richardson didn't pass the scan, and when the guard turned around to confront him, he smacked him on the head, so he played dead until the professor was out of sight. He said the imposter was packing a weapon under his left arm and was as strong as a mule."

"Doesn't sound like he's planning on teaching a class now does it?... Where is he?"

"He is taking a confident stroll towards the science building."

"Really?" said President Kane, showing no apprehension. "Have we been able to match his DNA?"

"No, there is no record of this guy in the public database."

"Then try the not-so-public database," suggested President Kane. "The minute he's out of the sight of the FBI agents on the roof of the Hilton, take him out. Let me know when he recovers from the anesthesia because I have a bad feeling that the real Dr. Richardson didn't give him his ID voluntarily."

"I agree," said Justin. "We're going to have to let him get inside the science building before we take him down or we'll alarm the FBI."

"Be very careful," said President Kane, "This guy is more than likely a trained killer and not just a cheap thug. He has a plan, and we need to make damn sure he doesn't execute it. I'm very uncomfortable having him in the same building as Dr. Ford, so use extreme caution, even lethal force if necessary. Let me know when you have him. I would like to talk to him myself."

"Don't worry," said Justin, "he'll be greeted by a full contingent of drones the minute he sets foot in the building."

....

Agents Porter and Thackery watched as the first professor to arrive on campus walked towards the science building. Rather than use the front door, the professor opted to enter the building through a door on the docking ramp where the NBC news truck was parked.

"What's he doing?" asked Porter.

Both Porter and Thackery zoomed in on the professor using their night vision binoculars. Lunt stopped near the loading bay and lounged against the wall like he needed a smoke. He casually pulled his Smith and Wesson out of its holster and held it against his leg as he walked towards the door.

"He is pulling something out of his jacket."

"Looks like he might need a smoke..."

"Dammit!" interrupted Thackery, "That's too big to be a lighter. I think it's a gun!"

"Let's move," said Porter to the men who were on the morning shift in the Presidential Suite. "Move,

move move! Keep Dr. Ford alive at all costs, and bring down that bastard who just went in the science building! Move, move, move, and screw the 'student' cover!"

The agents in the room hurried into the hallway, each taking a different exit out of the hotel. Within minutes, several agents had flashed their FBI IDs at the gate and moved towards their assigned positions on campus.

"It looks like the campus security guard took a knock on the head," said one of the agents into his radio.

"Is he going to be ok?" asked Porter.

"He appears to be shaken, but isn't leaving his post."

"Where are all the students?" asked an agent over the radio. "Is today a holiday?"

"Not that I'm aware of," said Agent Porter.

"It's still a little too early for students to be arriving," offered another agent.

"Stay focused!" snapped Porter, "Something is not right here!"

....

Lunt checked the chamber of his modified M&P Nine Smith and Wesson to make sure a cartridge was loaded, then held the gun out of view while walking casually toward the dock door. He was certain that he'd avoided the much-too-obvious campus security cameras and the FBI agents perched on top of the Hilton hotel. After taking a casual, but good look in all directions, he walked through the door next to the truck ramp.

The room behind the door was filled with packages of various sizes stacked in neat little piles, destined for different areas of campus. Lunt grabbed a package that fit securely under one arm and headed for the door that said "To Labs." The door opened into a well-lit hallway that continued right and left for a hundred yards in both directions. His eyes adjusted quickly to the light, and he walked nonchalantly in the direction of a staircase leading to the upper floors. He'd gone about thirty feet down the hall when he noticed two objects coming towards him, hovering about five feet off the floor.

"What the hell?" he muttered. He'd heard about the University of Southern Texas's security drones, but had never seen one other than in a Popular Science magazine. The drones continued towards him, but he kept walking like they were nothing out of the ordinary and he'd seen a million of them before.

"Welcome, Dr. Stanley George Richardson III," said a pleasant, but slightly sarcastic voice from one of the drones as it passed him. Lunt whirled. "Your DNA does not match that of Dr. Richardson," continued the voice from the drone.

Lunt was speechless, but his natural instincts took over and he leaped across the hallway, drawing his Smith and Wesson from its hiding place beneath the package he was carrying.

He twisted in mid-air to fire at the drones, but his fingers didn't respond fast enough and his shots went into the wall and then the ceiling. He hit the floor and tried to roll into a better firing position, but his body was unresponsive. There was a sharp pain originating from his neck and a cold feeling spreading down one arm.

He groped for the object in his neck causing the discomfort, and his fingers closed around a thin cylinder lodged right above his collar. He jerked it out and stared at it stupidly. He struggled to bring his eyes into focus... He squinted at the object in his hand with all his might... "A tranquilizer dart?" he muttered, somehow impressed. The look of surprise slowly vanished from his face and he slumped into unconsciousness, the dart clenched tightly in one hand.

....

The two FBI agents tailing the phony professor were two minutes behind him. They didn't wait a second after reaching the science building door before entering the building. As their eyes adjusted to the light in the hallway, they could see a body lying on the floor with two drones hovering over it. Both agents drew their weapons and walked towards the body.

"What should we do?" asked the junior agent.

"These things are supposed to be controlled by a small crew located in a command center somewhere," said the other agent. "Let's see if we can talk to the man in charge." The agents came within ten feet of the drones and stopped. A voice from the drone on the right drew their attention.

"What are you doing here and why do you have loaded weapons on university property?"

"We were following the man lying on the floor over there because he had a gun and we assumed he had the intent to do someone harm."

"Good answer," said the other agent sarcastically. "Listen, whoever you are, we are federal agents and we have been following this guy for several days."

"We know who you are, but we are curious as to why you feel you can operate on the property of a private university without a court order or a search warrant. As you can see, we have the situation under control."

One of the agents started to speak, but a drone voice cut him off.

"There has been so much disloyalty and infiltration within your agency that we have a hard time trusting your organizations. We are going to have to ask you to disarm and leave."

"Or what?" blurted the younger FBI agent.

"Or we will assume that your intentions are hostile, and we will be forced to take you down."

"We're here to protect Dr. Ford, not to harm her," said the senior agent.

"You've had plenty of chances to protect her and you've failed."

"We're not leaving this campus without our weapons," said the senior agent.

"Is that your final answer?" asked the drone controller.

"No," said the agent in charge, "this is my final answer." The senior agent fired his semi-automatic into the drone. Both men emptied their clips into the drones while they backed rapidly in the direction they had come. Their bullets bounced off a shield of some kind that was protecting the drones and fell harmlessly to the floor.

"Bad call," said a voice from one of the drones, and it fired darts into the necks of both agents.

The last thing the agents remembered hearing before losing consciousness was a voice saying "UST 3, FBI 0..."

....

The security center monitors displayed the action unfolding in the science building hallway like it was a sci-fi movie. Justin had been the director of campus security for several years, and the last few minutes of his tenure encapsulated more action than all the other years combined. His hands trembled as he tried to maintain his composure. "Good work, guys," he said to his drone control teams, then he looked at a couple of his veteran security guards. "Go down and lock them up. Don't forget that they are highly trained and dangerous, so be careful."

Justin glanced over at President Kane's stern face. "Well, it looks like we have just bagged one assassin and two FBI agents," he said. "What do you want to do with them?"

President Kane shrugged. "We don't have any options other than locking them up."

"Hey, at least we got to try out the drone shielding," said Justin dryly.

"That's just great," said Dr. Kane sarcastically, "I can't wait to have a conversation with the FBI. I'm sure they'll be happy to hear our shielding is working as designed." President Kane looked at the monitors on the wall and the three men lying in the hall. "Let's prep our FBI friends so they are ready to transport to the front gate the minute they wake up. I'd hate to give the FBI a legitimate excuse to storm our gates."

"I agree," said Justin.

"Let's be ready to engage our shield technology around all campus assets if things escalate any further."

"Seriously? Do you think it will come to that?"

"I hope not, but let's be ready, just in case."

Justin changed the subject. "The camera crew is set up and ready to roll when you are."

President Kane breathed deeply and turned away from the monitors. "I'll go get the Fords."

"Before you do that, you might want to take a look at what is coming through the gate," said Justin, pointing to images that were emerging from the south entrance.

Several FBI agents had entered through the south gate and appeared to be converging on the science building, weapons drawn.

"They must have been monitoring the two agents in the hallway."

"It appears that way."

"Lock down our building access points to approved personnel only."

Justin walked over to a computer console and typed in the command. In an instant, all building access across campus required a retina scan.

Justin and Kane watched as the agents moved around the science building, checking all the entrances.

"It looks like they are pretty intent on retrieving their comrades," said President Kane. He didn't hide the agitation he was feeling towards the FBI for being on campus without a search warrant. He stood with his hands on the command center rail for a moment, weighing his options. "I'll go out and have a little chat with them, but please be ready to take them all down if they show any aggressive behavior."

....

"Someone is coming out the front doors of the science building," reported an agent.

Agent Porter looked at the image on his monitor in the Presidential Suite. "That's President Kane."

"He is motioning me to come over and speak with him," said the agent closest to President Kane. "Should we exit the operation theater or engage him?"

"Shit!" breathed Porter, feeling like he was being forced into a corner. He paused, trying to figure out the best course of action.

"Agent Porter, I'm waiting for your orders," said the agent, a little uncomfortably.

President Kane stood on the bottom step of the science building and motioned again for the agent to come over and talk to him.

"Agents Jiles, Hastlehoff, Buechart, Thayne, and Jackson—approach President Kane and engage him in conversation and I will be there in two minutes. The rest of you, retreat back to the hotel. Somebody wake up Director Jefferson so he doesn't miss the entire show!"

Porter straightened his tie and rushed out the door of the hotel room, frustrated beyond belief. Not a single thing had gone as planned with this operation. Now his cover was blown, he had two missing agents, and they hadn't seen hide nor hair of Dr. Ford.

Porter walked quickly up the cobblestone sidewalk in the south entrance and nearly knocked over several of his agents who were retreating back to the hotel. He passed the security shack on the run, flashing his FBI badge to the campus security officer as a courtesy, but didn't slow his pace.

....

"Let him go," said Justin's voice coming through the speaker in the security building. "He must be Agent Porter—the one we just heard over the radio—who wants to speak with President Kane." Justin looked down at his drone teams. "Keep within dart range of each of those agents! This could get dicey. If these guys so much as cough in the wrong direction, drop them where they stand, but do not, under any circumstance, use lethal force," he reminded them.

Justin paced back and forth, his eyes shifting between monitors.

"Dan and Chris, bring your drones to bear on Agent Porter."

"Yes, sir."

The command center balcony where Justin was standing had room for about ten people. From his position, he had a clear view of all the wall monitors in the room, as well as direct eye contact with each drone team.

President Kane walked a few feet closer to the group of FBI agents that were converging on him. "You boys got a search warrant?" he asked boldly. His voice echoed through the command center as if he were a movie star in an IMAX Theater.

"We are here to inquire about Dr. Ann Ford."

"With drawn guns?" asked President Kane.

"Two of our agents entered this building and we haven't been able to make contact with them."

"They're all right," said President Kane, "We had to disarm them since we didn't know who they were or what they were doing on campus."

"What about Dr. Ford?" asked an agent.

"She is here as well, and is a few minutes away from doing an interview with NBC News."

"We need to speak with her immediately!"

"You are more than welcome to speak with her after she's finished her interview."

Porter reached the group of agents that had surrounded President Kane. He was out of breath from his quick walk up the hill, but had been monitoring the conversation via radio. The outside lighting in front of the administration building was bright, and he had to shield his eyes to see President Kane's face clearly. "With all due respect, sir, I don't think you understand our perspective in this matter."

President Kane shrugged and waited for Porter to continue. "Dr. Ford disappeared from her home on Tuesday night and nobody has seen her since. We know she's been working on some highly sensitive research, and we're concerned that she's been kidnapped or coerced.

President Kane shook his head. "Your information is spotty, at best. Our people were in contact with her before and after her home blew up. In fact, it appears that we saved your agency a great deal of embarrassment by foiling a kidnapping against Dr. Ford that may have been a threat to her life!"

"So it *was* you who orchestrated her flight down here?" responded Agent Porter, confirming his suspicion.

"She chose to come down here. All we did was offer her a ride."

"I would like to hear that from her own mouth," retorted Porter. "You guys aren't being blackmailed are you?" Porter watched Kane closely for any sign that the man was under duress.

President Kane shook his head. "After she's done with NBC News, you're more than welcome to speak with her—if she wants to talk to you. The interview will be over in a few minutes."

"We need to see her now," said Agent Porter.

"That ain't gonna happen, boys, until her interview with Dan Johnson is over," said President Kane, breaking into a Texan drawl.

He had been watching for the FBI agent's reaction to Dr. Ford's pending interview with Dan Johnson, but was puzzled by the lack of one. Porter didn't look surprised, alarmed, or bothered. Kane couldn't understand why the information hadn't caused more alarm. *I wonder if they plan on jamming our broadcast signal?*

"We don't care what Dr. Ford is doing, we need to see her now!"

"I'll bet you're having an impossible time getting a Texas judge to issue a search warrant for this university, aren't you?"

The agents looked at each other, but none of them other than Porter knew how close to the truth President Kane was. "If you gentlemen don't have a search warrant or a court order, you are going to have to leave!"

"We can't do that, sir, without seeing Dr. Ford." There was dead silence. President Kane was wracking his brain for a way to diffuse the situation. *This is how wars start,* he thought to himself.

Suddenly, an agent lunged towards President Kane, put him in a choke hold, and pressed his gun against his temple.

"What are you doing?" shouted Agent Porter, who was taken totally off guard.

"This diplomacy approach is bullshit," said the agent. "I'm tired of talking." He pushed the gun harder against Kane's temple. "Either bring out Dr. Ford, or I'll start blowing off body parts!"

"Come on Jackson... Stand down!" Porter drew his gun and pointed it at the agent. "I said, stand down!"

"I've got this handled, sir," he said to his superior. Jackson turned back to President Kane. "I'll give you two minutes to bring out Dr. Ford."

In the command center, Justin couldn't believe what he was hearing and seeing, and went into instant battlefield mode. He made eye contact with the drone controllers in the room. "Prepare to fire!" Then he yelled into the microphone that connected him with President Kane, "Drop and roll!"

President Kane didn't respond.

"Now!" shouted Justin.

At two-hundred-and-eight pounds, President Kane was not a little man, and even at sixty-seven he was a force to be reckoned with. He elbowed Jackson as hard as he could to the ribs, then dropped like a rock to the ground and rolled to his left.

"Fire on all agents!" shouted Justin. With absolute precision, six drone controllers brought their targets to their knees. All six agents collapsed in a heap around President Kane, each with a red feathered dart protruding just above the collar line. President Kane didn't stopped moving, and was halfway up the steps to the administration building before the darts took full effect.

In the command center, Justin was barking orders. "I want twelve drones at each gate, and another fifty drones monitoring the campus perimeter." Justin looked across the command platform where the drone manager sat paralyzed, staring at the monitors. His eyes shifted back to Justin when he heard him yelling in his direction.

Justin repeated himself, "I want twelve drones at each gate and another fifty posted on campus and around the perimeter! Get this room filled to capacity with drone support teams immediately—we need to be ready for anything!"

Justin turned to Dr. John Tate, who was the professor who had developed and now managed the university's space program.

"John, can you get a full contingent of satellite controllers in here? We need every satellite station fully manned." John nodded and pulled out his phone.

The command center had accommodations for one hundred drone teams and a team of satellite jockeys for every satellite that was in the air. Similar to drone teams, a team of satellite jockeys consisted of three people: one controlled the satellite's altitude, orbit speed, and positioning; another managed the onboard equipment, both weapons and scientific; and the third helped relay orders and manage the overall system. Drones always required a full-time contingent, but satellite teams were generally only staffed by one person, as needed, and usually by the science department.

Justin was as hyped up and as anxious as he'd ever been. He felt like he was in the control room at NORAD during the Cuban Missile Crisis. He reached into his pocket, fished out his cell phone and pressed it to his ear.

"All lines are busy, please try again later," said a prerecorded voice. He dialed another number to double check the first response. The dial tone failed and he got the same canned message as he had earlier. *Are they jamming our phones?*

He turned his phone to radio mode and started barking orders. "Bring the six FBI agents inside until we figure out what to do with them," he snapped into the phone. "Disarm them and put them in separate holding cells."

Justin glanced up at the balcony where the satellite jockeys sat. Dr. Tate was standing with his hands on the rail, looking at the screens in front of him. The screens in the command center had never been so full of action-packed content as they'd been in the last twenty minutes. "John!" he shouted, to get his attention over the buzz of activity in the command center. "How long has it been since you tested the lasers on the shield satellite?"

"Last week," yelled John, "when we blew up that piece of space junk that was on a collision course with satellite #57. It worked flawlessly."

"Remind me how many of our satellites are equipped with shield technology?"

"Only one has the shield type that extends to the university, but they all have the experimental shielding that protects the satellite itself."

"Did we fix the glitches we experienced during Hurricane Derek?"

"Yes, and we added a bunch of new capabilities as well. We upgrade it once a month."

"Good," said Justin, giving him a thumbs-up. *Because I've got a feeling we are going to be testing your upgrades before the next storm.*

President Kane entered the command center at the ground floor level and ran up the stairs to the balcony. Justin looked at him in admiration.

"Not too bad for an old guy. I think that FBI agent is going to have sore ribs and sorer ego in the morning."

"I hope so," Kane gasped, and leaned against the railing to catch his breath. He was breathing hard, partly because of his run from the front of the administration building and partly because of the adrenaline that was pumping through his body. He fumbled for his phone, then punched in a number.

"That won't work," said Justin, "they're jamming our signals."

"And the NBC broadcast?"

Justin shook his head grimly. "Unless something changes, it won't make it out."

Kane looked at Justin. "Does your phone have a radio?"

"Yes," he said, and handed it to President Kane. He buzzed his office until his office manager answered. "Call a special meeting of the general board ASAP. I think we are going to have to put up the shield."

"You're kidding!"

"Not kidding," said President Kane.

"Why are you calling me on the radio?"

"Because the FBI is jamming our cell phone signals. I'll explain later—just get the general board assembled as soon as you can."

I'll have them together within the hour," responded Margaret. She had been President Kane's office manager since he was hired by the university, and she had never heard him sound so tense.

The strain of the last twenty-four hours was starting to show on President Kane's face. He couldn't figure out how to stop things from spiraling further out of control. He hated being strong-armed by the feds, especially when they were braking their own laws and trampled the Constitution in the process. What the feds would do next was anyone's guess but they'd proven once and for all that they were not reliable.

He had no idea what to do with the eight FBI agents they'd knocked out, except to get them off campus as soon as possible. The university had never held anyone for more than an hour unless they'd broken some civil law—in which case they had always turned them over to the local authorities—and he couldn't remember the last time that had happened.

"This is out of control," he mumbled.

Justin turned when he heard President Kane speak. "What was that?"

"How did this thing get so far out of control?"

Justin shook his head. "I don't know, but if you keep punching FBI agents, you are going to start a war."

"What are you talking about? I've only punched one, and you've knocked out eight!" President Kane took on a more serious tone. "Get the FBI agents we've knocked out cuffed and ready to bus to the front gate." He glanced up to where the satellite jockeys and Dr. Tate were sitting, then looked back at Justin. "Are we ready to deploy the shield if we have to?"

"Not only are they ready, but John told me he's been upgrading it and testing it ever since Hurricane Derek."

"How long would it take to deploy?"

"Better ask John."

Justin motioned for John to pick up his radio. "John, how long would it take you to raise the campus shield?"

John shrugged, "Since I've already got the satellite in a stable orbit above the university, I just need you to tell me how wide you want the diameter and where to establish the fulcrum. Once I have that info, I could have it up in ten minutes."

Kane and Justin were impressed.

"Set it up with the dimensions you had for Hurricane Derek."

Justin looked a little surprised, "That means we'll cover a number of non-university properties with the shield."

"How many?" asked President Kane.

Wrinkles appeared in John's forehead as he considered the question. "During Hurricane Derek, I think we included about one hundred and two properties that didn't belong to us."

Kane didn't like the number. It was too high, and would be one more easy target for federal and press propaganda. "Do the best you can to involve the least number of privately held properties as possible, but we have to cover the university housing and faculty complexes."

"I agree," said Justin.

President Kane thought for a moment, then looked back up at John. "Let's configure the shield so that only people with G-Scores of seventy or higher can get in and out. All the other filter configurations should be set to match what we have at the university entrance gates."

"I like it," said John.

President Kane looked around the control room at all the people who were bustling about and realized that hardly any of them had ever seen any serious crises or combat before today.

"Fantastic," he muttered to himself, "nothing like going to war with a bunch of rookies." He prayed it wouldn't come to that, but things were not looking good. *If things get any worse we will have to raise the shield again—and not for bad weather.*

....

From the roof of the Hilton, Agent Thackery could barely see what was going on in front of the administration building because of the shrubbery and trees. He could hear what his agents were saying, and from the sound of things, he knew they were in trouble.

"Agent Porter! Agent Porter!" he yelled into his radio, "Can you hear me?" There was no response.

"Agents Jiles, Hastlehoff, Pugh, Buechart, Thayne, or Jackson, can you hear me?" Again, no response. *"Dammit... I knew this was a bad idea."*

Thackery shook his head as he left the roof and headed for the Presidential Suite. He wasn't looking forward to explaining what had just happened to Agent Porter and his five associates. He wished he was a thousand miles away enjoying a leisurely walk along Daytona Beach where he'd grown up. He pushed his way into the presidential suite just as his earpiece exploded with a barrage of questions from Jefferson. "What the hell happened out there?"

Thackery ripped out his earpiece and looked around the room for Jefferson. He headed in the direction of Jefferson's voice, and the second Jefferson caught sight of him, he started yelling.

"What happened?"

"From what I can tell, it sounded like Agent Jackson flipped out, sir, and tried to force President Kane to cooperate."

"You're kidding me!"

Jefferson was irritated, angry, and embarrassed. The last thing he needed was another news story about a federal agent who'd been overly aggressive. *That's what happens when you don't have enough funding for proper training.*

"What's the situation now?"

"Agents Jiles, Hasselhoff, Buechart, Jackson, Thayne, and Porter appear to be down, sir," said Thackery.

"Appear to be down?" asked Jefferson, his voice rising.

Thackery shook his head, trying to remain calm. "They're not responding to the radio, and I heard at least one of them say they'd been hit."

"Did you hear any gunfire?"

"No. From my vantage point on the roof, I couldn't see enough to determine how they were brought down. All I know for sure is that they're all on the ground."

"Who fired the first shot?"

"There was no shot, sir. Everyone had their weapons drawn and Agent Jackson had President Kane in a headlock, threatening to blow off body parts unless he brought out Dr. Ford. Then they dropped like flies."

"What happened to Kane?"

"I'm not sure. He fell out of my line of sight."

Jefferson could not believe what he was hearing, but in some ways he was glad there had been an altercation. "Well, we sure as hell don't need a warrant now, do we? We have probable cause."

"For who, sir, them or us?" he asked sarcastically. Jefferson looked away from Thackery, ignoring the comment, and mulled the situation over in his head. He quickly made up his mind and his focus snapped back to Thackery.

"Get our men out! I'm gambling that whoever is in charge across the street will at least let us retrieve our people without an incident—it's in both our best interests. After they are out, we'll decide what we should do next."

Thackery shook his head in disagreement. "Sir, I highly advise against going in again, until you talk to someone over there. They immobilized eight of our best agents with hardly any effort at all, and with technology we don't understand. We don't even know how they did it."

Jefferson looked incredulous. "What do you want me to do? Leave my men lying on the ground in there?"

Thackery shrugged. "It may be better to leave them there than provoke further action and add to the number. What if our retrieval unit doesn't get out? Why not go in with stretchers and a white flag?"

"That's pathetic. We can't afford to show that kind of weakness." Director Jefferson had convinced himself that the right course of action was to get his people out so he could start over with a clean slate. "How long have they been down?"

"Going on nine minutes, sir," said Agent Thackery.

Jefferson glared at Thackery as if measuring his competency. "Go get our agents, and I'll see you back here in five minutes."

"Yes, sir," said Agent Thackery with as much enthusiasm as he could muster. Agent Thackery and five others left the room on the run and fully armed, each carrying enough guns and ammo to start their own private war. *Six stretchers and a white flag is a better approach,* he thought as he ran across the street to the south entrance.

....

President Kane leaned against the command balcony railing, trying to clear his mind. Justin had just confirmed that the FBI was jamming communications to and from the university, and he couldn't comprehend why they were being so aggressive. *Is the United States Government that afraid of change?* he wondered silently. *If we can't get a signal out, Dr. Ford's research is in danger of being suppressed or destroyed.* A thread of fear began to creep into his mind. He was worried that the university wouldn't be able to hold off the feds long enough to get Ann's research into the public domain. *We cannot allow them to win this one!* His personal thoughts were interrupted by Justin, who was shouting something to him.

"President Kane, it appears we are about to have more company!"

"What?"

Justin pointed towards one of the flat screen monitors as six fully armed FBI agents charged through the south gate. "Are these guys stupid? What part of the Fourth Amendment don't they understand? You'd think we were having brunch with a bunch of terrorists.

Six agents reached the place where their comrades had gone down a few minutes earlier. They formed a tight circle with their guns pointed away from their center and slowly spread out. It was obvious that they were surprised not to find their fallen comrades.

"They're gone," shouted Agent Thackery into his headset. His voice echoed through the University of Southern Texas command center and into the Presidential Suite of the Hilton hotel.

"Withdraw," commanded Jefferson in a voice of authority.

"They haven't figured out that we can hear every word they are saying, have they?" asked President Kane, not expecting an answer.

"It doesn't look like it, sir."

With their weapons at full readiness, the agents started to retreat back towards the south gate. The command room was silent and every person watched the FBI team in retreat.

"Who is that?" asked President Kane.

"For the love of Pete!" said Justin in exasperation, "That's Joe Summersten." Joe was an emeritus professor of horticulture who enjoyed working in the university gardens.

"Obviously he didn't get the memo." said President Kane.

"What's he doing out this early anyway?"

President Kane shrugged, "He picked the wrong morning to mess around in his garden, that's for sure."

"Well, he's going to get himself killed," said Justin.

The FBI agents hadn't seen the retired professor because he was bent over some shrubbery directly in their line of retreat.

"Unbelievable," said President Kane, holding his breath.

The agents were thirty feet away from the gardener, then twenty, and then fifteen.

"Take them out, or we are going to lose old Joe," said President Kane. His command was a few seconds too late, because Joe did exactly what President Kane feared he would. Straightening up, he gave the FBI agents a hearty Texan welcome. "Good morning, gentlemen," he said enthusiastically.

The FBI agents swiveled as one. "Hold your fire," shouted Agent Thackery, but his order was too late. Somebody leaned on their trigger and a shot was fired. Joe fell, and a single red dot in the middle of his shirt pocket grew until the whole left side of his shirt was saturated with blood. Joe stared at them, confused.

"Why did you shoot...?" He looked down at his shirt, then slowly fell forward.

Agent Thackery leaned over the fallen gardener and felt for a pulse. He bowed his head, then looked up angrily at the agent who had pulled the trigger. "Does this look like a threat to you?" He looked at the rest of his men and yelled, "Retreat!" They hadn't taken a dozen steps before several drones materialized from behind buildings, trees, and shrubbery.

Thackery looked wildly from the drones to the gate and panicked. "Fire on the drones!" he commanded.

The words had hardly escaped his lips before a wild array of automatic weapon fire filled the air.

"Fire tranquilizers," commanded Justin coolly. Without hesitation, the drone controllers responded with impressive precision. All six agents dropped in their tracks, firing their weapons into the air until the nerves in their trigger fingers failed to respond and they passed into unconsciousness.

The silence in the command center was tangible. Every eye was frozen on the giant monitors showing six FBI agents crumpled on the sidewalk and Joe Summersten looking up into the morning sky.

The silence was broken by President Kane. "Damn them! Get a medical team out there and save Joe!" His hands were trembling with frustration and anger. Kane was a gentle, peaceful man who valued human life, and his mind wouldn't process what he'd just witnessed. He watched a medical team approach the garden area where Joe was lying, hoping for a miracle. His face stiffened with resolve. *We can't tolerate this incompetence for one more second,* He thought. His eyes met those of Dr. Tate and he shook his head sadly.

"Raise the shield!"

Dr. Tate nodded his head and keyed in the command. When he was through, he leaned over the railing. "President Kane... it's up."

Kane turned back to the monitors and watched the medical team working on Joe. It was obvious that things were not going well. After a few minutes, a man in a bloody white smock stood up and shook his head. The team covered Joe's body with a blanket and slowly carried him back to the building. The only thing that was audible in the command center was the hum of high-tech computer equipment as the team watched Joe's body disappear out of view.

President Kane shook his head and looked at the floor, his jaw muscles clenched in frustration, shock, and anger. He wanted to grab whoever was in charge of the FBI's investigation and shake them.

Raising his head, he looked at the team of people in the command center and could see they were experiencing a similar flood of emotions. He raised his hand to get everyone in the control room's attention. Anyone who didn't see him was nudged by someone who had. The team positioned themselves so they could see and hear President Kane clearly.

"Most of you are volunteers or are fulfilling your service quota to the university, and we appreciate all you do. I highly doubt any of you expected to see someone who you've grown accustomed to seeing in class or on the grounds—who greeted you with a warm hello—killed this morning. And I highly doubt any of you ever imagined that this university would openly defy the United States Government—at least I didn't until an hour ago."

President Kane could see that he'd struck a chord. "I just wanted to let you know that none of this was premeditated and that we are trying to make the best decisions with the information we have. Honestly... I don't know what to think! I'm surprised that the our government is being so aggressive with a university with such a long history of collegiate and academic excellence. Two Supreme Court justices, four presidents, and over two dozen representatives and senators are alumni of this institution!"

Heads were bobbing in the command center in support of what President Kane was saying. "My decisions this morning were made in the spirit of defending the rights of Dr. Ford and this university, of which you are a part. If you have the courage, I ask you to join with me and this university in open defense of our Constitutional rights. If you don't agree with the decisions that have been made, you're free to leave at any time and we will totally understand. I, for one, will not allow Joe's blood to spill into the soil of our gardens without redress!"

A respectful applause started somewhere in the room, rippled through it, and subsided. "Neither I nor this university has any intention of usurping the power of the United States Government, but we will hold them accountable! I'm done feeling politically impotent! I'm done feeling like my voice is too small to be heard, and I hope the shield we've raised in defense of our rights will send a clear and unmistakable message to our government, that we have had enough! They have forgotten the very purpose for which governments are instituted, and..."

Roaring applause from the faculty and students present interrupted his words. President Kane looked at Justin with surprise. "I thought I was the only one who was feeling this way."

"Apparently not," responded Justin.

President Kane raised his hand and the applause subsided. "I will be meeting with the general board within the hour to discuss the decisions that I've made this morning and to formalize a course of action going forward. Per our university's bylaws, once a decision has been approved by the general board, we'll publish it so the rest of the university can review it."

The students and faculty in the command center looked at one another in approval. "In the meantime, we have a lot to do. We cannot afford to make any mistakes that will agitate the feds and give them justification to take any further action against us."

He went on to assure the students and faculty in the command center that they were free to leave the university at any time if they didn't agree with or were not comfortable with the position the university had taken with the FBI. He let them know that the university would keep all communications with the federal and state authorities open so they would feel in-the-loop. A number of students and faculty had questions, which he took the time to answer the best he could.

President Kane looked at Justin. "We've got to leverage everything we learned from the last time we raised the shield against Hurricane Derek and improve it as we go. If we don't keep it up and operational, the government is going to overrun this campus and we'll lose the chance to make a statement or negotiate."

"I understand," said Justin. "We'll keep it up, no matter what."

"How close are we to being able to communicate with the outside world?"

"We have our best people working on it, and they've identified a couple of telecommunication satellites they think they can hack. It's totally illegal, but under the circumstances, I think everyone will understand."

"How long is it going to take?"

"They're telling me it will take eight to ten hours to do it right so our signal won't be interrupted."

President Kane shook his head. "If we don't get word out sooner than that, somebody is going to run into our shield and we'll risk losing any support we hoped to get from the general public."

There is one idea that surfaced from one of our students."

"I'm afraid to ask," responded President Kane, "but I'm desperate."

"The suggestion was to send thirty or forty students out into Corpus Christi on foot, on bicycles, mopeds, and motorcycles. Each one would be carrying an information packet about the shield's location and capabilities in both digital and hard copy formats."

A smile tugged at the corners of President Kane's mouth as he considered the suggestion. "What if they get arrested?"

Justin shrugged. "I think you'll find plenty of students and faculty who are over twenty-one and willing to take that risk. We could even send out a copy of Dr. Ford's research if we wanted to."

"No," said President Kane, "That would put too many lives at risk. I'm afraid that if a courier is apprehended with Dr. Ford's research in his backpack, someone might assume they know more than they do. I like the motorcycle idea though... Let's send out our motorcycle team with the coordinates of the shield, so nobody runs into it, and we'll wait to send everything else the minute we hack the communications satellites."

"I like it," said Justin, checking his watch. "The shield has been up too long already, so we'd better get moving." Justin radioed one of his security managers and told him exactly what needed to be done. "When you're ready to go, call me so I can review the information packet. President Kane and I will come down to talk to the team before they ride out."

"Is there an official code word for this operation?" asked the security manager, trying to insert a little humor into the situation.

"Not yet," responded Justin flatly. "Motorcycle team should do just fine." He hung up the phone and looked at President Kane. He could tell by the look on the president's face that he was deeply troubled at the loss of Joe.

"You know as well as I do ole Joe is laughing about being in the wrong place at the wrong time, don't you?"

A reminiscent smile appeared on President Kane's face. "Yea, you're probably right… And no doubt he's in the arms of his sweetheart as well. He's missed her in the worst way since her passing."

"I'm sure going to miss his cheerful attitude," said Justin.

President Kane nodded. "I'll miss his friendly greeting every morning." His smile faded into a look of determination. "Let me know when you're ready to send out the shield coordinates. I'd like to speak with our volunteer couriers before they go out. I'd also like to speak with the FBI agents before you toss them out the front gate, if they're coherent."

"Right," said Justin looking at President Kane's phone. I'll have a phone with a built-in radio brought to you so we can keep in touch

"Ok," said President Kane. "Hey... how hard would it be to get a high-definition copy of our surveillance footage put on a bunch of thumb-drives? Maybe if the Feds see the footage of how bad they screwed up, they might back off a little."

"Not hard at all."

"Good, then let's burn a personal copy for all of our FBI friends so they're not tempted to cover up what happened today."

President Kane knew he'd done everything in his power to diffuse the situation with the FBI, and his shoulders relaxed a little. He breathed in deeply, then exhaled slowly.

"Has anyone notified Joe's family of his passing?"

"No," said Justin, "I thought you'd want to do that yourself."

"I would," said President Kane. "He was a dear friend and I know the family personally." Kane dreaded the thought of having to tell Joe's family of his passing, but it was the least he could do, and it would be better coming from him than anyone else. His mind shifted back to Dr. Ford and her research. "Has NBC News started recording yet?"

"Not yet," said Justin, "I told them you had a couple of things to attend to, and they couldn't start without you..."

"Good," said President Kane. "I'll meet you down there in a few minutes."

....

Director Jefferson stood on top of the Hilton Hotel straining to see the location and source of the gunfire. "Agent Thackery, report!" Thackery did not respond. "Agent Thackery!" yelled Jefferson into his radio.

The agent standing next to Jefferson nudged him. "Hey, I think I can see something!

Jefferson raised his binoculars. "There behind the shrubs. Can you see them?"

Jefferson focused his binoculars and scanned the body of the agent lying beneath the shrubbery. He could see a couple of red feathered darts sticking out of the man's neck.

"Those arrogant sons-of-bitches. Are they trying to provoke us? Who in the hell do they think they are?

Jefferson stormed off the roof and started barking orders into his cell phone. "I don't want anyone coming in or out of the university until this is sorted out! No one!"

"Sir, it will take thirty minutes before we can have enough feet on the street to make that happen."

"You have fifteen!" snapped Jefferson.

Chapter Thirty-Two

"First Amendment"

President Kane knocked on the conference room door before entering and found Jack and Ann spooning on the couch, fast asleep. He cleared his throat, trying to wake them up. "Uh hm."

Jack jerked awake and took a second to recall where he was and what he was doing. He looked at the clock on the wall. It read 5:35 AM. "Hi, I guess you're ready for us?"

"We are."

Jack shook Ann's shoulder gently until she was awake. "It looks like they're ready for you," he said, smiling. Ann yawned and sat up on the couch. She stood up and stretched her athletic body. "Give me two minutes in front of the mirror and I'll be ready to go."

"Take whatever time you need."

Ann smiled and headed for the bathroom. "Be out in a jiffy."

"I'll come get you in ten minutes," said President Kane, leaving the room.

Ann went into the bathroom and fluffed her hair until it looked like she hadn't just slept on it. She straightened her outfit and smiled at herself in the mirror. *That's as good as its going get with no sleep and a borrowed hairbrush,* she thought. She stepped out of the bathroom and posed for Jack.

"Not bad for no sleep or shower."

Ann walked over to the couch where Jack was sitting and extended her arm. "Let's get this over with. I can't wait for everything to get back to normal again."

Jack rolled his eyes. "Your definition of normal is going to have to change. From now on Albert Einstein and Ann Ford are going to be used in the same sentence.

"It's not going to be that bad."

Jack looked at his wife, a little perplexed. "You're kidding, right? Do you think the world's going to let the girl who single-handedly toppled the oil empire just slip away into oblivion?"

Ann smiled wistfully, "I was kind of hoping so."

Jack smiled and scooped her into his arms. "You are such a noodle head!"

"If there was any way to release this information without all the attention and press, you know I'd do it," said Ann seriously.

"I know you would."

A knock sounded on the door and Jack opened it with Ann hanging on his arm. President Kane was standing there in a fresh shirt and sports coat. "Are you ready to do this?"

"I am," said Ann.

President Kane was still debating whether he should fill the Fords in on the events of the last hour, but decided to hold off until after the interview. They walked down the hall to the interview room that had been prepped for NBC News, and President Kane introduced Ann and Jack to Dan Johnson.

"So you have something earth-shaking to announce to the world?" asked Dan.

"Yes," said Ann.

"Would you like time to prep for your announcement, or are you ready to go?"

"I'm ready to go when you are."

"Ok," said Dan.

Dan introduced his cameraman to President Kane and to the Fords. "Phil has been with me for over ten years and never fails to make me look good."

Phil mumbled something inaudible and wiped sweat from his forehead with his shirt sleeve. Dan noticed the excessive sweat and looked at Phil with concern. "Are you ok?"

"Yeah... just an upset stomach," said Phil uncomfortably. "I'll be ok."

Dan looked at Ann and President Kane. "I don't know what the problem is, but we can't seem to get a broadcast signal, so this take is only going to be live on your internal network."

President Kane didn't want to take the time to explain what had been going on with the FBI, so he told Dan to go ahead with what he'd planned, and they'd figure out how to get the news snippet to the NBC Network when they were done.

Dan looked around the room to make sure they were ready to shoot. "I think we are ready to rock-and-roll. Remember, that we're 'live,' so any sounds you make will be picked up by the microphone."

Dan Johnson was the university's news reporter of choice, and had a reputation for being objective and fair. He turned to Ann, "I'll sit in the barstool on the right, and you sit on the barstool on the left."

Ann made herself comfortable while Dan gave a few last minute instructions to Phil, who looked really pale. "Are you sure you're all right?"

"I'm fine," said Phil through gritted teeth.

"Okay." Dan motioned to Phil to roll his camera.

Dan wiped his brow with the back of his hand and cleared his throat. "I'm Dan Johnson from NBC News, reporting live from the University of Southern Texas. I'm here with Dr. Ann Ford—an expert in molecular science—who has an announcement about a technological breakthrough she'd like to share with us."

Phil zoomed in on Dr. Ford.

....

In the command center, a drone controller waved at Justin to get his attention. "Hey boss, are you watching this interview with Dr. Ford?"

"No," said Justin," I've been busy getting tranquilized FBI agents ready to transport to the south gate. What's wrong?"

The controller tilted his head towards the monitor. "The NBC cameraman looks as nervous as a polecat, and he's sweating up a storm for this time of the year."

"Maybe he has the flu."

"He was scanned when he arrived on campus and he was fine."

"Maybe he ate something that didn't agree with him."

The controller shook his head. "He hasn't eaten anything since he got here."

"What was his heart rate when he arrived?"

"Seventy-four beats per minute."

Justin looked at the vital readout streaming in below the cameraman's image on the drone screen. "One hundred and twenty-two beats per minute! Has he been jogging in place?" asked Justin, his curiosity on the rise.

"Nope, he's just been standing there."

Justin looked around the room. "Hey, Drake, bring your drone into the interview room and focus it on the cameraman so we can see him from two different angles.

"Will do," said Drake, and flew his drone into the interview room as ordered.

Justin and his staff watched as Dan Johnson continued the interview with Dr. Ford. Justin could see President Kane, Dr. Conner, Dr. Sellers, and Jack standing off to the side of the interview area.

"The university tells me you have something to announce that is very exciting."

"I do," said Ann. "I've been working on a research project in the area of hydro-electrolysis, which is nothing new, except that nobody has ever come up with a super-economical way of doing it."

"Would you mind giving us a brief overview of this technology so those of us who don't know what you're talking about don't get left behind?"

Ann smiled. "Of course. Water is made up of three basic elements—two hydrogen molecules and one oxygen molecule—held together by a covalent bond. Up until Monday night nobody had been able to figure out how to split the water molecule apart efficiently so the hydrogen could easily be used as fuel…"

"So… how will your breakthrough affect the average person?" asked Dan for the benefit of his audience.

"By providing a very cheap replacement for gasoline, diesel, propane, natural gas and jet fuel."

"How cheap?" asked Dan skeptically. "Give us a meaningful example."

"Preliminary estimates suggest that we'll be able to produce hydrogen to run automobiles for less than thirty cents a gallon."

Dan wasn't easily surprised, but Ann caught him completely off guard. "Less than thirty cents a gallon?"

....

In the command center, Justin was still puzzling over the cameraman's behavior. He studied the man and his equipment carefully. "Zoom in on the camera. What's that quarter-inch tubing alongside the mike boom?"

"I don't know for sure, but it kind of looks like one of the tranquilizer tubes we have on our drones."

"I think you're right!" said Justin in alarm. "Park a drone in front of that camera now!" he yelled. "If that cameraman makes a wrong move, drop him!" A drone zoomed in front of Phil less than two seconds later.

Justin and two security guards sprinted down the hall to the interview room. By the time they got there, the room was already in commotion. Dr. Conner was on the floor, and President Kane was kneeling beside him, tightening a tie around his upper right arm in a tourniquet.

Jack was kneeling next to Conner and had just removed a black dart from Dr. Conner's forearm using a garbage bag so the fluid on the end of the needle didn't touch his skin.

Justin hustled Ann into the hallway to protect her, and left her with a couple of his men. "What happened?"

"A security drone flew in front of the news camera just in time to deflect a dart intended for Dr.

Ford," said President Kane as he tightened the tourniquet on Dr. Conner's arm.

Justin was giving orders into his radio before President Kane finished speaking. "Dr. Conner has been shot with some kind of poison dart, and we need medical assistance in the science building interview room ASAP. Bring your anti-venom and poison kits, and anyone who specializes in neurotoxins!"

"Where's the cameraman?" asked Justin, searching the room.

"I've got him over here," said Dr. Sellers, who had knocked the cameraman across the room with a well-timed punch to the jaw.

Justin bent over the man, who was starting to come to his senses. "The camera," he stammered, pointing, "has a bomb in it. It's programmed to go off if I'm more than four feet away...!"

Justin leaped over a fallen table and grabbed the camera, pinned it against a rolling desk chair, and raced towards the nearest window. Without slowing down, he flung both the chair and the camera through the window, which shattered into a thousand pieces. The chair and camera plummeted to the ground, bouncing a couple of times on the grass below.

Justin looked out the window, not knowing what to expect. Seconds later, the camera exploded, throwing bits of camera and chair all the way back up to the floor where Justin was standing. He ducked back into the room, just in time to avoid the flying debris. Smoke billowed up from where the camera and chair had landed, creating a mini-mushroom cloud. Justin's knees were knocking and his heart was pounding. He looked down in disbelief at a Volkswagen Bug-sized crater that had materialized where the camera and chair had landed.

....

"What the hell was that?" asked Director Jefferson from the Presidential Suite of the Hilton Hotel.

"I'm not sure, sir, but there is a ball of smoke rising from somewhere in the vicinity of the science building."

Jefferson finished a conversation he was having on the phone, then scanned the university from his window with his night vision binoculars. He palmed his radio and clicked the transmit button. "What can you see from up there?"

"Not much sir, but it looks like there was some kind of explosion outside the science building."

"You've got to be kidding!" said Jefferson. The man on the roof didn't answer. Jefferson shook his head, wondering how things could get any worse.

"There doesn't appear to be anyone moving around the explosion, so I don't think anyone was injured," said the man on the roof.

The fact that nobody was on campus finally registered in Jefferson's mind. He looked at his watch—it was 6:10 AM. His eyebrows bunched together as he tried to remember if there was a holiday he'd forgotten, but shook his head in frustration.

"Where are all the students?"

"Don't know, sir, but the campus should have some activity by now. Maybe word got out about the gardener being shot?"

Jefferson looked skeptical. "There are over thirty thousand students and staff on this campus, and there's no way they could've contacted everyone already."

Jefferson shrugged, then squinted, trying to pick up some details from the explosion site, but from his vantage point, all he could see was a smoke cloud slowly being dispersed by a light breeze.

He lowered his binoculars, exposing a smile.

"What?" asked the agent.

"That explosion just gave me the concrete 'probable cause' I've been looking for to get our men on campus without a search warrant."

"Not having a search warrant didn't stop you earlier."

Jefferson chuckled, "I think you're missing the point. The explosion supports my earlier decision to infiltrate the campus and is rock solid evidence that we have a right to be there. Something clearly is not right, and we are going to figure out what it is. Maybe they are being blackmailed and they are fighting back! Tell me the minute our boys from San Antonio and Houston get here, and we will get to the bottom of this."

The agent standing next to him nodded his head.

....

University hospital paramedics rushed Dr. Conner out of the room. Phil, the cameraman, was talking loudly and waving his arms in an animated fashion. "They told me they would kill me and my family if I didn't cooperate," he was saying.

"Who?" pressed President Kane.

"I don't know who they are, but they said they would kill my family!"

President Kane shook his head. "Get him out of here, and see if you can get a message out to the local authorities to check on his family. I'll join you once I have this mess cleaned up." A few minutes later he was back in the command center, standing next to Justin. "How are things going?"

"Ok for now."

"Were you able to check on Dr. Conner? How is he doing?"

"Not good," said Justin. "His body is not responding well to the antidote... Our scanners should've picked up the toxins on the camera when Phil entered the university, but they didn't."

President Kane put his hand on Justin's shoulder. "We are a university and shouldn't have to be taking those kinds of precautions. Adjust your scanner configurations and move on."

"We still should've caught it."

President Kane shook his head. "Even the best security systems in the world have flaws, so stop beating yourself up about it."

Justin was still mad at himself. *I'll never forgive myself if Dr. Conner dies.*

"Look," said President Kane. "It's a miracle you and your team even figured out that Phil was messed up in the first place. Conner will be ok. He's one tough cookie and is in the hands of some of the best doctors in the country."

Justin clenched his jaw and nodded his head, but he was still upset.

President Kane changed the subject. "Have your boys figured out how to penetrate the FBI's jamming technology yet?"

"No, but we have several ideas."

"Good." said President Kane. "It is critical we get Dr. Ford's research out as soon as possible so the Feds will ease up.

They stood in silence, unaware that they were processing the same thoughts: both were wondering how so much violence had happened on their peaceful campus in such a short amount of time.

Justin's radio started to buzz and he answered it. "We have thirty of our top athletes prepped and ready to ride," said the security manager.

Justin bobbed his head. "Excellent. Where are you?"

"We are in the football training facility."

"President Kane and I will be right down."

"Sounds like our couriers are ready to go?"

"Yes," said Justin.

They walked down to the training facility where they were greeted by thirty athletes who were pumped and ready to ride. Their enthusiasm and fearless attitudes made President Kane smile.

Even though they'd already been prepped by Jed, the athletic director, President Kane gave them his version of the events that had transpired during the morning hours and emphasized the importance of the task that was before them.

When he'd finished, he asked if any of them had a change of heart about the university's position with the United States Government or the dangerous assignment they'd accepted. He reminded them that they had the freedom to choose whether to participated in the assignment or not, but he could tell from the looks on their faces that they weren't going to change their minds.

"You know the FBI may shoot at you when you ride through the shield and interrogate you if you are caught?"

"I'd like to see them catch me on this," said a young man, revving his engine.

"Does everyone understand exactly what their destination is and what you're supposed to do when you get there?"

They all nodded.

"If you are apprehended, tell the truth as you understand it. Keep in mind that the University of Southern Texas is not at war with the United States. We're just sending them a defiant message. Are we clear?"

A linebacker from the varsity football team took off his helmet and looked around at the group. "Don't worry about us. We've seen what the FBI did this morning, and I think I can speak for everyone here—we support the decisions you've made and are honored to be able to deliver the shield information to the outside world."

President Kane could see that they all agreed with the linebacker. He turned to Jed. "Has everyone been equipped with bulletproof vests, chaps, and helmets?"

"Yes, sir. We are ready to go."

"All the bikes have been checked and their tanks topped off?"

"Yes."

"Have we given everyone sufficient cash to get them where they are going and back again?"

"And then some," said Jed.

President Kane looked pleased.

The linebacker raised his helmet. "President Kane? How did it feel elbowing that FBI agent in the ribs this morning? I heard you lifted him clean off the ground."

The serious look on President Kane's face softened into a Texan smile. "It felt pretty good actually." The boys had a good laugh. They loved the sincere, open, and down-to-earth nature of President Kane. He was like a father to them.

President Kane glared at Jed and Justin. "Did you have to tell them that?"

Before either one of them could answer, a rugby player spoke up. "Nice drop and roll, too, for an old far..." Before he could finish his sentence, someone elbowed him in the gut.

"Don't mind him, President Kane, we've got your back," said a first-string baseball player. Everyone in the group laughed, while the rugby player gasped for breath.

President Kane smiled... "All right people, when we open the doors I want you to blast out of here as fast as you are comfortable. Exit the campus at the location you've been assigned and we'll catch the FBI completely off guard. I'm counting on you to get this information out quickly so nobody runs into our shield. Today I won't mind if you break the speed limit."

The boys let out a whoop.

"Once you've delivered your package, you're welcome to return to the campus if you'd like to. And if for any reason you cannot make it back, it will show on your attendance record."

The boys looked at him to see if he was kidding. President Kane held a straight face for a few seconds, then grinned. "We might even be able to work this project into some extra credit if you need it. Just be safe, ya hear!"

Jed and Justin double-checked each athlete to make sure their information packets were secure and that they were wearing their protective gear. When they were satisfied that everything was in order, Jed raised the huge roll-up doors of the football practice facility and waved them through. As they left the practice facility in a cloud of exhaust, revved up engines, and wheelies, they raised their fists and shouted, "DUST! DUST! DUST!" and then they were gone.

President Kane's brow furrowed, and he looked at Justin. "Dust?"

Justin stared at Jed, who was grinning from ear to ear. "One of the athletes came up with it," he confessed. "DUST stands for **D**efiance of the **U**niversity of **S**outhern **T**exas."

President Kane's grin broadened. "I kind of like it. Where did you find so many volunteers?" he asked, changing the subject.

"Fifteen minutes after the word went out that we were looking for volunteers, I had two hundred students here with their bikes. I was able to select thirty who were over twenty-one and had significant motocross experience."

They watched as the last of the motorcycles raced from sight. "I'd hate to be an FBI agent in charge of rounding up that bunch," said President Kane with a tired chuckle.

"No kidding," said Justin, "but I wished we'd have sent a drone out with each of them."

President Kane shook his head, "A drone would've ruined their cover and drawn too much attention to them. Besides, we have a satellite jockey tracking each of them, right?"

"Yes," said Justin.

"Then there is nothing else we can do."

Chapter Thirty-Three

"Aggression and Defiance"

Director Jefferson had been able to recruit sixty more agents from the Houston and San Antonio areas, and he'd personally debriefed them on the events that had happened since Dr. Ford's disappearance.

"What's the big deal?" asked one of the agents. "We have probable cause, so let's bust some chops and go in and get her."

"We tried that," said Jefferson, "and we have fourteen FBI agents missing in action." Jefferson showed the new recruits the limited voice and video intel they'd gathered thus far around the missing agents.

"As you can see, our men were knocked out with remote-controlled drones armed with some kind of tranquilizer darts. Once the dart penetrates the skin, the person goes out like a light."

"It sounds like we need to use a bigger stick," said an agent.

"I couldn't agree more. I want this university strip-searched and every one of those damn drones in a scrap pile by the end of the day."

"Yes, sir!" said the agents in unison.

"This time we go in with full body armor," said Jefferson. "The university has twelve major entrances and I want three or four agents at each gate. Each group needs to be armed with at least one stinger so you have something to take out the drones if your MP 5/50s don't do the job. Keep your eyes and ears open because I don't want to lose one more man to these techie nerds."

Jefferson handed each team a map of the university so they understood where to position themselves and specific instructions on what he expected from them. "When you're in position, check in with me. All commands for this mission will come directly from me. Our primary objective is to bring out our men and Dr. Ann Ford alive. It's absolutely imperative... Remember there is a distinct possibility that either she is being held against her will or President Kane and his staff are being blackmailed. Why else would a bomb have been tossed out the window of the science building this morning...?"

Jefferson's sentence was drowned out by the roar of motorcycle engines.

"What the hell...?" Jefferson raced to the window, knocking over his chair in the process. It wasn't light enough to see anything but the headlights of a dozen motorcycles leaving the campus at audacious speeds. "Can you see what is going on from up there?" he shouted to the agents on the roof.

"It looks like a bunch of motorcycle riders just left campus at the same time."

"How many?"

"At least thirty, maybe more."

"I thought I could hear them shouting something. What was it?"

"I'm not exactly sure, sir, but it sounded like 'dust.'"

"What?"

"It sounded like they were saying 'dust' or 'eat our dust,' sir."

The agents in the room struggled to maintain their composure, but the second Jefferson whipped around, there was no hint of a smile on anybody's face. He was furious. His bomb theory had just been dowsed if what they had heard was true. He'd been outsmarted again by a bunch of weak-kneed geeks. "Get a satellite heat and dimension signature for anyone riding a motorcycle within five miles of campus, and let's track the little rat-bastards and pick them up."

"That is going to be tough, sir," said the agent in charge of satellite imaging.

"It's always tough, so don't waste another second talking about it—just get it done! If they're carrying Dr. Ford's research, we'll all be looking for a new job in the morning, or be posted to Utah." Jefferson's body language screamed how agitated he was and he made no attempt to mask it. "Where was I?..."

"You were just starting to say something about locking down the campus so nobody could get in or out," responded an agent, completely straight-faced. Jefferson glared at him, daring him to smile, but the agent wasn't foolish enough to even look him in the eye. Jefferson gave each of the FBI teams a critical once-over, as if he was trying to ascertain their competence, and was satisfied with what he saw.

"Let's make an example out of these intellectual sons-of-bitches," he growled. "Now, go get our men."

Jefferson looked at his watch. It was 6:35 AM—within twenty minutes this would all be over, and he could get out of this god-forsaken town. The sun hadn't come up yet, but the eastern horizon had turned a light blue, and it was humid enough to make a fish suffocate.

"I want this done fast and by the book," said Jefferson into his radio. "We need to be in and out in less than fifteen minutes. I want our men and Dr. Ford off campus before this city wakes up... Let's do this!"

At his command, a fully armed FBI contingent stormed the university at every major entrance. Jefferson watched as three agents rushed the south gate. They moved like a well-oiled machine, each man packing enough fire power to bring down an entire platoon. The agents he could see moved quickly, positioning themselves to be able to charge the south gate. Jefferson's confidence soared as he watched them work their way towards the university entrance.

They waited behind bushes and parked cars across the street from the entrance before they charged. When the leader of the team was satisfied that the entrance was clear, he motioned for his men to move forward.

They charged the gate, two men running in the front and two men covering the rear. They made it halfway across the street at full speed when the two agents leading the charge slammed into an invisible barrier and went down hard. The men bringing up the rear were so focused on what was behind them that they tripped over the men that had gone down and bounced off the invisible barrier like rubber balls off a brick wall.

From seven stories up in the hotel, Jefferson could see that the FBI team assigned to the south gate had run into trouble, but he couldn't tell what it was. He squinted through his binoculars so he could get a better look at what happened, but a hotel canopy was blocking his view.

"What's going on?" he shouted into his radio. There was no understandable response. All he could hear through his earpiece were sounds of surprise, shock, and groaning.

"Damn, that hurt…..we hit something, sir. Some kind of shield is blocking the south gate." Jefferson's radio came alive as every agent reported a similar story.

"Did anyone get in?" he bellowed. Nobody responded. "Team one?" questioned Jefferson.

"No, sir, we hit some kind of shield."

"Team two?"

"No, sir, we hit the same thing."

Jefferson questioned each of his teams, and every team reported hitting a virtually invisible shield.

Jefferson couldn't believe what he was hearing, and left his chair on the run, cussing up a storm. He pounded on the elevator button. "I'm headed down to the south gate to see this thing for myself." His patience ran out and he took the stairs to the lobby two at time. When he reached the street, the agents who had tried to enter the south gate were back on their feet.

"Where is it?" asked Jefferson.

"Here, sir," said one of the agents, pounding his rifle butt against the shield. "If you look along the edge of it, you can see it shimmer."

"What is it made of?"

"I've never seen anything like it, sir."

An agent who was rubbing his head looked at Jefferson. "It's got to be related to that shield technology they used when that hurricane pounded the Texas coast last year."

Jefferson shrugged. "I thought that didn't work."

"I heard it worked just fine until they had to lower the shield to let a Russian satellite through."

"You watch too much Sci-Fi... Let me see your rifle."

Jefferson grabbed the rifle and pounded on the shield with the butt of the gun. It was like pounding a cement wall that was wrapped in an inch of foam rubber, except it was crystal clear, and you could see right through it.

"Stand back," said Jefferson.

The men moved back from the shield to where Jefferson was standing. When they were safely behind him, he pointed the MP5/20 at the shield and let loose a ten-second volley. The bullets hit the shield, disintegrated, then slid to the ground in a pile of dust.

"What the...?" He fired twenty more rounds into the shield with the same results, then handed the weapon back to the agent. "I'll be damned," he muttered, and they all backed away from the barrier. Jefferson was speechless. He stood looking at the shield for a minute, then reached out and touched it with his fingers. "Shit! It's like an LCD screen with a lot of static electricity on the surface, but backed by solid rock."

All four agents came over to where he was standing and cautiously extended their hands toward the shield. Each of them experienced the same thing, except for Agent Cherrington, whose hand penetrated the shield.

"Sir, look at this!" he said, pushing his arm through the shield up to his elbow. They all stared at him as if he were a freak.

"Keep going," said Jefferson. Agent Cherrington tried walking through, but his ammunition belt, pistol, rifle, and Kevlar jacket wouldn't pass.

"That explains why you don't have a goose egg on your forehead," said Jefferson. "Strip down to your basic uniform and see if you can get through."

Cherrington stripped off all his gear and stood in front of the shield. "I hope this doesn't hurt," he said, looking back at his comrades with a weak smile. "For God and country," he said, saluting, and stepped towards the shield. His whole body made it through except for his left boot, which got hung up in the shield like it was clamped to a vice grip. He yanked on the boot, trying to free it from the shield, but it wouldn't come through.

Frustrated, he returned to the side of the shield where Jefferson and his two comrades stood staring. He stood looking down at this left boot trying to figure out what the difference was between the two.

"My knife," he exclaimed, "it doesn't like my combat knife." Cherrington rolled up his pant leg and unstrapped the combat knife from his leg. "Let's try it again," he said confidently, and this time he walked through without a problem.

"Well, aren't you the golden boy," said Jefferson sourly. "At least one of us can get inside the damn thing. Get your gear and let's see if anyone else was able to make it through the shield. We've got to figure out how to bring this thing down."

Cherrington returned to Jefferson's side of the shield, picked up his gear, and followed him into the hotel. As Cherrington was going through the revolving doors, he looked back over his shoulder at the shield and noticed a white bus approaching the south gate from the university's side. "Hey, there's a mini-bus coming towards the south entrance," he yelled to the guys already in the hotel.

Jefferson and his agents looked back at the gate. The mini-bus rolled to a stop several feet in front of the shield, a white handkerchief tied to its antenna. A man wearing a campus security uniform got out and motioned for Jefferson and his agents to come back out to the street. "What does he want?" asked Jefferson.

"I don't know, sir, but it appears that he is motioning for us to come back."

Jefferson and his agents moved cautiously out into the street and to within few feet of the shield. The man disappeared into the bus, but soon reappeared steadying a very groggy Agent Porter. Holding Porter by the arm, the security guard walked him up to the shield and then gave him a little push. Agent Porter stumbled through the shield and fell on his knees.

Agent Cherrington knelt beside him, steadying him with his hand. "Are you ok?"

"I'm, ah, I'm ok," he said, shaking his head from side to side. "I'm just feeling a little drowsy and nauseated. Wha... where am I?"

"You're at the south gate," said Cherrington, lifting him to his feet and helping him across the street.

One by one, the campus security guard helped the other thirteen agents out of the van, walked them over to the shield, and pushed them through. After pushing the last agent through, the guard came and stood a foot away from his side of the shield. He tossed the keys to the handcuffs at Jefferson's feet.

"Next time get a warrant," he said.

Director Jefferson stiffened, but he couldn't think of anything to say.

The security guard held up a thumb-drive. "Surveillance footage of your team shooting up our place and killing a very popular emeritus professor will be broadcasted on NBC News before noon. A copy of some of the footage is on this thumb-drive," he said, tossing it to Jefferson, who caught it deftly with his right hand.

Director Jefferson smiled to himself. *The man is obviously oblivious to the fact that we are jamming all transmissions to and from the university.*

The security guard pointed to the shield behind him. "This shield originates from a satellite that we have in geosynchronous orbit above Corpus Christi. It's a little unstable, and could destroy anything that hits it at a high velocity, so assume that anything that runs into it has the potential of being obliterated. You might want to get on the phone and let your armed forces air traffic controllers know where it is. It will be visible on your radar if you look closely. We tried to send out a warning, but you're jamming all our communications. Hopefully one of our motorcyclists made it to a location where they could broadcast the location and capabilities of the shield; otherwise, you'll be liable for any injuries sustained by the people who run into it."

The security guard's eyes twinkled with amusement as he turned and walked back through the south gate without saying another word.

Jefferson looked in bewilderment up into the sky where the security guard had pointed. *How could we not have known about this?* His eyes shifted back to the guard, who had disappeared into the security shack. The guard's nonchalant manner brought his blood pressure back to a boiling point. The idea that he, the Deputy Director of the FBI, had just been casually dismissed by a mere university security guard was more than he could stomach. "Get these men back to the hotel for a debriefing," he said through clenched teeth as he walked past his men on his way to the hotel.

Jefferson dialed the personal line of the President of the United States and waited for him to pick up the phone.

Chapter Thirty-Four

"Weak Faith"

Dan Johnson, President Kane, Ann, and Jack left the interview room so the maintenance crew could replace the window and clean up the glass. President Kane led the way back to the command center and took the opportunity to radio the head of the film department to see if he could round up a camera and crew to help Dan out.

After he finished, he took a few minutes and briefed Dan and the Fords on everything that had happened since the assassin and the FBI trespassed on campus. Dan looked like he'd been slapped. "That's absolutely unbelievable! You seriously have a shield that is repelling the FBI right now?"

President Kane smiled weakly. "It has so far."

"Must be an improvement from that technology you tried to use on Hurricane Derek."

"That's correct. We've been working feverishly to perfect it before there's another weather emergency."

"I'm still a little unclear on why the Feds are passionate enough about Dr. Ford's research to blockade this university. Are they doing the same thing at Princeton, Harvard, and Yale?"

President Kane forced a smile. "I hadn't thought of that. Maybe they've declared war on all higher institutions of learning. Seriously, though, we don't know what's got them so wound up, but we suspect they believe Ann's research will cause a wholesale meltdown of the oil empire and the world economy."

Jack shrugged. "Maybe you're right. I know they can't be too excited about losing billions of dollars in gas tax revenue."

"I think they're also worried that Ann's technology will be so disruptive that it might throw us into another great depression."

"I thought we were in one," retorted Jack sarcastically.

President Kane and Dan both nodded. President Kane's eyes were bright, but his face was serious. "I've decided, and I believe the board will support me, that we should stand behind Ann's decision to give her technology away, regardless of the consequences."

Dan grimaced. "From what you've already told me, the Feds aren't going to like that decision. Are you sure you want to push them that far? They've already killed one man trying to get their hands on her technology.

"I'm sure. And in a few minutes we'll know if the general board feels the same way. To be frank, their aggressive behavior and casual interpretation of the law makes me furious. It's got to stop, and why not here?"

Ann hadn't said a word because she felt somewhat responsible for the situation the university was in. She felt horrible that Joe Summersten had lost his life and Dr. Conner's life was in peril because of her research. "Maybe I should've kept all my research in my head. Is any technology worth a man's life?

President Kane shook his head. "That's nonsense. For every life that's been lost trying to preserve your research, ten thousand will be saved or benefitted because of it, and I know that both Dr. Conner and Joe would agree with me. Getting your research out to the public is more important now because it will help bring them justice and honor." He turned to Dan and the broadcast crew. "Now, we could really use some help getting Ann's research into enough hands that it becomes viral."

Dan smiled broadly. "If there is one thing in the world I excel at, it's knowing how to make a story viral. If you can get me a link to the outside world, we'll broadcast and send the Feds scrambling back to their cave with their tails between their legs. By the time we are done, every citizen in this country will be screaming for justice."

President Kane nodded and clapped a hand on Dan's shoulder. "That's exactly what needs to happen."

"There's only one thing I'm a little concerned about," said Dan.

"What's that?"

"I'm a little worried that I'm going to get bumped outside the shield and won't be able to get back in because I have a low G-Score."

President Kane grinned. "Do you really think we would've asked you to come over if your G-Score wasn't high enough? People with G-Scores of seventy-five or higher aren't perfect, they're just great people."

Dan looked at Justin. "Is he telling the whole truth?"

"He shore is…" said Justin, exaggerating his Texas drawl.

"When did you get my DNA?"

"A few years back, when you did that piece on Dr. Hamilton's Parkinson's cure."

"Ah yes, I remember… So you're one hundred percent confident I can get back in if I leave? Because if I can't get back in, I'm staying in."

President Kane assured him that he could get back in, but warned him that the FBI might be less accommodating.

"When can I get my hooks into the surveillance video you were telling me about?"

"We'll give you an ID and Password for the material and you can access it anytime you want."

"Perfect," said Dan, "but I still can't believe you have a shield sophisticated enough to keep out the FBI." *I'm going to have to go out and touch it before I can talk about it,* he thought.

Justin's radio buzzed, and he took the call. The expression on his face turned from concern to sadness. His shoulders sagged forward and he turned away from the group.

"What's the matter, Justin," asked President Kane, walking over to him.

"We lost Dr. Conner," he said, trying to choke back the tears. "They couldn't save him. The dart that hit him had enough pancuronium-potassium chloride in it to kill an elephant."

President Kane's knees failed him and he grabbed the balcony railing. Dr. Conner had been one of his closest friends. His emotions were already raw from the senseless death of Joe Summersten, and the news of his good friend's death stirred feelings inside him that he hadn't felt since his military combat service. Anger simmered deep within him for those who'd so casually taken his friends from him.

Seeing that something was wrong, the Fords approached the two men for an explanation. "Did you say something about Dr. Conner?" asked Jack. President Kane could not answer, but nodded his head.

"Yes," said Justin, "we lost him a few minutes ago due to complications from the poisons that were used in the dart."

Jack looked at Ann with wide eyes. He had not fully appreciated how close to death she'd been during the interview until that moment. He grabbed her and held her tight. *One more inch to the left and I would have lost her,* he thought. His lips quivered at the thought of someone perpetrating such a senseless, vicious, and cowardly act.

They stood in silence in the command center, each wrestling with their emotions. For the second time that day, President Kane was forced to deal with the loss of a close friend while trying to show strength for those who trusted him as their leader.

Ann stepped between Justin and President Kane, putting a hand on each of their shoulders. "I'm so sorry for your loss; Dr. Conner was a generous and thoughtful man. If it wasn't for him, I would not be alive right now on two accounts."

Neither man could muster a response, but both nodded in agreement.

"I would like to finish my interview with Dan so their deaths are not in vain. We need to release this technology before another life is endangered."

Taking Ann's lead, Dan offered his condolences. "I'm terribly sorry for your loss, gentlemen."

President Kane acknowledged the sentiment. "Let's do this," he said in a hollow tone. "Let's finish this interview."

President Kane felt like he had been kicked in the gut by a mule. The last time he had felt so empty inside was when his wife had passed away several years ago.

Unable to speak, he motioned for everyone to follow him back to the room where the interview with Dan Johnson would be finalized. He stayed far enough ahead of the group that they couldn't see him struggle with his emotions.

President Kane's radio started buzzing, and he answered it. He listened for a minute, nodding his head. "So you are set up and ready to go?" He listened for a few more seconds. "That's perfect. We'll be there shortly."

Dan caught up with President Kane. "Are they ready for us to finish the interview?"

Kane nodded, and they walked in silence. President Kane slowed as they approached the room that had been outfitted with the equipment Dan needed. Dan inspected the room and the equipment. "All right... let's get this interview done." Dan smiled at the volunteer students and professors in the room. "Follow my lead, and this will go off without a hitch."

....

Director Jefferson looked down at his watch. The display said it was 6:50 AM, but he felt like he'd been up for three weeks. The phone call with the president had been a disaster. President Buchman told him, in no uncertain terms, that he was to cease and desist from any further action against the University of Southern Texas until he was explicitly ordered otherwise. He'd ordered Jefferson to maintain a five-hundred-foot defensive perimeter round the university's shield to ensure that the public did not run or fly into it, and insisted that no one else be allowed in or out of the shield. The president had told him he'd been out-smarted, out-maneuvered, and made to look like a complete fool by the University of Southern Texas, and expressed his profound disappointment that the FBI didn't have better intel on the university's technologies. Jefferson didn't take correction well and was livid.

....

Ann and Jack talked quietly with Dr. Sellers in the hallway while they waited for Dan to brief his volunteers. President Kane and Justin were a few feet away, talking about the problems the shield was creating with the morning traffic. "Is the mayor aware of these problem areas?"

"He has crews headed to the areas of concern to put up barricades and detour signs."

"That's good," said President Kane.

"He would like to talk to you in person about the shield."

"I'm sure he would," said President Kane. "See if you can put him off until this afternoon. How have you been communicating with him?"

"We've been sending a runner back and forth."

"How are you getting past the FBI?"

"There are a couple of underground emergency exits that dead-end in buildings we own off campus. The FBI has not discovered this yet, so until they do, we have at least a couple avenues to the outside world."

"Let's make sure we only use them if absolutely necessary."

"Understood," said Justin.

Justin's radio buzzed again. He bobbed his head as he listened to the person on the other end of the phone. "Keep your eye on it," said Justin, looking grim. He was hesitant to give President Kane any more bad news, but he had no choice. "Somebody is moving a US Armed Forces satellite into orbit above Texas."

"That's not surprising," said President Kane. "Have they broken any satellite proximity laws?"

"Not so far."

"How well is their satellite armed?"

"It is equipped with several different types of missiles, a non-nuclear EMP cannon, and a rail gun."

"Can any of these weapons bring down our satellite?"

"It would be a long shot."

"What does that mean?"

"It means that we have tested the shield against all of these weapons, and so far none of them have been able to penetrate our technology.

President Kane frowned. "Our shield is the only thing empowering us to take a stand against the federal government. If that satellite gets within firing range of ours and points any of those weapons at us, blow it out of the sky."

"Technically, they already are within range. They could take a shot at us from anywhere with any one of those weapons. They could even take a shot at us from the ground, for that matter. Remember when the Chinese and the US shot down a couple of satellites with decaying orbits?"

"I forgot about that. They were low earth orbits though... correct?"

"They were, but the altitude of the orbit won't make too much difference other than in reaction time. We don't believe they can hurt us, but they can definitely fire on us from about anywhere."

"Are we good enough to intercept a missile that's launched from the ground?"

"We can hit and destroy space junk that's as small as a marble and that travels anywhere from five to thirty thousand miles an hour, so we should be able to hit a missile that's fired at us from ground or space the moment we detect it—especially considering how old and slow the technology is."

President Kane looked impressed. "In that case, let's intercept and destroy anything that's shot directly at our satellite or the shield. I want to send a strong message to anyone who thinks they can push us around, and I don't want to take any chances."

Justin seemed relieved. "That, I can live with. It also positions us as the party being attacked, not perpetrating the attack."

A student from the broadcasting department came out into the hallway and smiled at Dr. Ford enthusiastically. "We're ready for you."

Ann smiled back, relieved that the students were so excited to participate.

President Kane sighed, "Shall we try this again?"

"We have no choice?" said Ann. She straightened her jacket and turned to Jack. "How do I look?"

"As sharp and gorgeous as always."

Ann walked over to where Dan was sitting. Her emotions were all over the place, and she hoped with all her heart that the announcement she was about to make would stop the violence.

Dan motioned for her to sit in the chair next to him. "Are you ready to try this again?"

"Yes, I am."

"Since the FBI is jamming our communications, this will only be live on the campus network, so if you don't like something, we can edit it before sending it out to the rest of the world."

"This whole signal-jamming thing is a little alarming, isn't it?" asked Ann.

"That's an understatement. I feel like I did when I was trying to broadcast out of Jerusalem a while ago."

"Hopefully once we get this broadcast out, everything will settle down."

Dan looked a little worried. "My biggest concern is that we won't be able to get the message out. It sounds like the Feds are pulling out all the stops to keep us from broadcasting."

Ann smiled tentatively. "After all I've seen here, I have a lot of faith in UST's technology department. If anyone can hack the FBI's jamming technology, it's them."

"Can't be too soon for me," responded Dan. "Now what do you say we get this show on the road?"

"Let's do it!" said Ann confidently.

Dan motioned for his inexperienced film crew to start the countdown, "Five, four, three, two, one...

It's Thursday, September 11th, I'm Dan Johnson, and this is NBC News. I'm coming to you this morning from the University of Southern Texas, where we will be broadcasting off and on throughout the day, so stay tuned. Over the past two decades, I've had the unique privilege of introducing new technological breakthroughs on behalf of UST and its brilliant students and professors. Today is one of those occasions."

Dan smiled with his trademark smile. "I would like to introduce Dr. Ann Ford, who is solely responsible for some research that is about to change the world as we know it. She's been researching potential energy alternatives for fossil fuels for the last few years and had a recent development that may break OPEC's heart," he said, turning to Ann. "Dr. Ford, why don't you tell us about your research?"

Ann thought she knew what she wanted to say, but the trauma of the past hour had shaken her. She paused for a minute to gather her thoughts. "Let me put it this way; the solution I've developed is so efficient, it could replace fossil fuels as our primary energy source within eighteen months."

Dan wasn't prepared for such a dramatic declaration, and it showed on his face. "I appreciate your confidence, Dr. Ford, but is that possible? Every hydrolyser on the market that I'm aware of requires almost as much energy to run as it produces. Are you sure your calculations are correct? I mean, you're talking about putting OPEC out of business."

Ann smiled knowingly. It wasn't too often that the famous Dan Johnson looked rattled.

"We're getting way ahead of our audience. Let me explain what I've done."

"Fair enough," said Dan.

"First of all, let me start by saying that I was as surprised as you were when I had my breakthrough. Don't get me wrong, I knew exactly what I was trying to accomplish, but I was shocked at the level of efficiency that was achieved."

Ann paused and looked at the camera. "Everyone is familiar with water, but sometimes we don't stop to think about what it's made of. Water is made up of three elements—two hydrogen molecules and one oxygen molecule. I've simply figured out how to remove the hydrogen from water so it can be used as a fuel source. Hydrogen is an extremely clean fuel to burn, and it has the potential to replace gasoline, diesel, jet fuel, propane, heating oil, and coal."

"So... you think you have come up with an efficient way to extract hydrogen from water?" said Dan, trying to digest what Ann was saying.

"I haven't just thought it." said Ann confidently. "The university has helped me build a working prototype."

Dan blinked several times before responding, then looked over at President Kane for confirmation. President Kane smiled and nodded.

"When I say it is an efficient solution, I mean it's hyper-efficient. Using approximately one gallon of water, we will be able to run a hydrolyser that can distill twelve hundred and fifty-one gallons of hydrogen!"

Ann let what she'd said sink in, then served up a few more facts for people to chew on. "Let me say it another way, Dan—my solution is so efficient and easy to reproduce that automobiles, airplanes, trains, eighteen-wheelers, boats, and electrical power plants around the world could be running on hydrogen for less than thirty cents a gallon. In fact, the technology is so simple that you could literally have a hydrolyser at your home capable of filtering the water from your garden hose. You could store the hydrogen in a tank and use it to power your car, heat your home, barbeque a hotdog, run a motorcycle…"

"I get it, I get it… but I don't know if I believe it! If you really have done what you say you have, it's going to disrupt the global economy!"

"Yes… It will be wonderfully disruptive!" said Ann enthusiastically. "All the turmoil and bloodshed over Middle Eastern petroleum will come to a screeching halt. Crude oil prices will no longer be manipulated to influence the world economy, and our carbon footprint will lessen dramatically. Imagine the millions of new businesses that will spring up overnight to capitalize on this new technology!"

Dan started firing off questions. "Who are you going to sell the technology to?"

"It is not for sale," said Ann. "I'm going to give it away. In fact, with the help of the University of Southern Texas, I'll release blueprints for the working model shortly after this broadcast."

"Aren't you concerned that your research will wipe out the economies of some oil producing countries?"

"Maybe they can tweak my technology to take the salt out of seawater and become farmers," laughed Ann. "Seriously, though, they've ruled the world for nearly a century without having to do much innovation, so this will give them an opportunity to try something new."

"Are you concerned about everyone who is employed in the oil industry?"

"No," said Ann. "Just like the people who built wagons, shoed horses, built type writers, carried coal, made candles, and rode for the Pony Express, they'll move on to other things."

Dan watched Ann talk and couldn't help laughing. He could see that her passion was contagious and had an effect on everyone in the room, including himself. "I have one last question for this segment. Are you at all worried about the billions of dollars that state and federal governments will lose in tax revenues?"

Ann laughed out loud. "I won't bother to honor that one with a response."

"Well then, thank you so much for joining us, Dr. Ford," concluded Dan. "For those of you who are interested in understanding more about Dr. Ford's research, please go to the University of Southern Texas's website located at www.newscience@ust.edu This is Dan Johnson reporting from the University of Southern Texas for NBC News."

Dan jumped off his chair. "Cut!" he said to the student running the camera, and walked over to President Kane. "Tell me this isn't a hoax. Does Dr.

Ford's hydrolyser really have the efficiencies she is claiming?"

President Kane forced a grin. "I kind of like seeing you this intense. Now you know how the people you interview feel."

Dan wasn't in a joking mood. "No, really. How much did I stretch the truth just then?"

President Kane slapped Dan on the back. "This is no hoax. We've already lost a couple of good friends because of this technology and we need you to understand it. Trust me, we didn't believe it either, but Dr. Ford rebuilt her hydrolyser in our lab late last night, and it does everything she claimed it would."

"She rebuilt it in a night? Why didn't I pick up on that in our earlier conversation?"

"I don't know," said President Kane, "but she rebuilt it with the help of a handful of our students and professors in less than ten hours."

"I would really like to do a follow-up segment by filming Dr. Ford's hydrolyser in action."

President Kane grinned tiredly. "What's wrong, Dan? Is your faith a little weak?"

"You might say that," said Dan.

Kane still had his hand on Dan's shoulder. "We'd love to have you film Dr. Ford's hydrolyser in action, especially if it gets the Feds off our back."

President Kane looked over at Ann. "Doubting Thomas here wants to see your device in action."

"That's totally understandable. I didn't believe it myself until I ran the experiment a few times, so let's take him down to the lab and show him."

Dan stared at her as if he were seeing her for the first time. He thought he'd understood what Ann had accomplished before the interview, but had somehow missed the part about how efficient it was. *If she's right about this, she's about to turn the world as we know it upside-down.*

Ann and President Kane stared at Dan, waiting for a response. "If this is real," said the newsman, shaking his finger at Ann, "the next couple of years are going to be amazing to watch." Dan held his hands about a foot apart. "Were you serious when you said this technology could be bundled in a small enough unit that I could buy it online or from your local hardware store?"

"Yes," said Ann, "and that's another reason why the technology is so disruptive."

"That's amazing." Dan frowned in concentration. "I was trying to calculate how many people your invention is going to put out of work, and I can't begin to put a number to it."

Ann shrugged. "Like I said earlier, people will adapt. Henry Ford put wagon and harness makers and horse breeders in a bind, and they recovered."

"This is a billion times more disruptive than that," responded Dan. "Everybody in the oil and gas business will be affected. Even gas stations will lose a portion of their revenue."

"But on the positive side, at least the price of fertilizer, synthetic fibers, plastics, wax, solvents, dish soap, tar, roofing, tires, rubber, and a million other things will go down," said Ann.

"Why is that?" asked Dan.

"Most of a barrel of crude oil is used for diesel, gas, jet fuel, heating oil, and other related products. Once hydrogen replaces these fuels, oil will only be useful for plastics, fertilizers, tar, asphalt, lubrication, and other bi-products."

"I guess I wouldn't mind paying a little less for things."

"We shouldn't feel too bad," said Ann. "It will take at least eighteen months for the world to adapt to this new energy source. Things won't change overnight."

"In the oil industry, eighteen months *is* overnight," said Dan.

President Kane asked the camera crew to pack up whatever gear they needed to film another segment in Ann's lab. Once he was sure his instructions were understood, he motioned for Dan and the Fords to follow him. When they arrived at the lab, it was still buzzing with activity.

As Ann entered the lab, she was greeted by a round of applause. Most present had watched the internal news broadcast, and they were all excited about the ramifications of the new technology. President Kane grinned and waited for everyone to calm down. "We are honored to have Dan Johnson from NBC News here to help us broadcast this event. His faith is a little weak, and he's looking for empirical evidence that Dr. Ford's research is not a hoax."

A sympathetic chuckle rippled through the room. "Dan is feeling the same way we were last night when Dr. Ford told us what she wanted to do, so I hope you have this gadget in working order or you'll be making a liar out me."

A white-haired scientist named Dr. McNally stepped forward. "Not only do we have it in working order, but we've already tweaked it a little and increased its efficiency by twelve percent!"

Ann looked pleasantly surprised. "Awesome. I can't believe you guys mastered the technology so quickly!" She hurried over to the prototype to see how they'd improved it, and one of the scientists filled her in on the details.

The team was delighted and relieved at her favorable response, as they'd been a little nervous about tinkering with her prototype. Dan rolled his eyes at all the techno talk while he positioned his crew so that the prototype was directly behind where he would be doing the follow-up interview. After he had everything in place, he took a minute to inspect Ann's hydrolyser. When he was satisfied that it didn't look like a complete sham, he looked at Ann a little more impressed. "So this is it?"

"Doesn't look like much of an empire killer does it?"

"No, but if it does half of what you say it does, it's going to do more than kill an empire."

Dan turned to his camera crew and gave them some last minute instructions. "Do exactly what you did in the last interview and everything will be fine. Remember we are semi-live, so anyone watching UST campus cable this morning will see all our screw-ups! Are you ready?"

He motioned to the cameraman that he was ready to start. "Counting five, four, three, two, one... Like many of you who watched the last segment on Dr. Ford's energy solution, I was a little skeptical about her claims, so I've asked her to give us a live demonstration and show us how her hydrolyser works."

Dan looked away from the camera to Ann. "From what I gather, you and a handful of students and professors from the University of Southern Texas assembled the prototype behind us in a little less than ten hours." Dan pointed to the table were the hydrolyser prototype was sitting behind him.

Ann smiled. "That is correct. These fine people, who I didn't know until last night, were gracious enough to supply me with the equipment, muscle, and brain power I needed to get a prototype built in record time."

"Tell us a little about this device of yours, Dr. Ford."

"Well, to be frank, there is not much to tell. This thing is just a bunch of lasers in the shape of a cone that vibrate at an incredibly high frequency. When water that's slightly colder than freezing is poured through the laser's filter, it separates into hydrogen and oxygen molecules. Oxygen molecules have eight protons, eight neutrons, and eight electrons, so they are significantly larger than hydrogen, which means they are easy to filter out. It's as simple as separating base balls from marbles. Then the "marbles" can be used for fuel."

"You have got to be kidding me!" said Dan in surprise. "Why hasn't anyone thought of this before?"

"Electro-hydrolysis is nothing new. It's the hyper-efficiency that's new. I've been working on this process for several years, as have many others." said Ann with a smile. "The trick was finding the right type of lasers, spacing them the right distance apart, finding the right vibration frequency, and using water that is just the right temperature, or it's not efficient."

"Why the sub-freezing water?"

"When water is near freezing, it is approximately nine percent less dense than when it's at room temperature and the hydrogen and oxygen atoms are the farthest apart from each other, which makes their covalent bond much easier to break."

"Can we see it work?" asked Dan, who was doing his best not to look skeptical.

"Of course," said Ann, and she jumped down from her stool.

Dan followed Ann around as she checked the apparatus. "Would you mind telling us what you are doing?" asked Dan.

"Sure," said Ann. "I'm checking the water temperature to see if it's reached the magical temperature of 31.85 degrees... Hey, why is this water colder than 31.85 degrees?" She looked at the scientists in the room for an answer.

"Sorry, Dr. Ford," said a man in a white smock, stepping forward. "We've been playing with the water temperature in an attempt to increase efficiency," he said, looking a little embarrassed.

"And…?"

"Well, we think we may have increased the efficiency of the system by four percent just by changing the water temperature to 31.25."

"Excellent!" exclaimed Ann. She walked around her device checking everything and looking for the other improvements the team made to the system, talking to Dan as she went.

"Are the hydrogen and oxygen tanks empty?" asked Ann.

"They are," said Dr. McNally.

"Then let's give this baby another whirl," said Ann.

Ann pointed to the water tank above her head, "I'm going to release ten gallons of 31.85… I mean 31.25 degree water from this tank, and it will pour through the laser funnel below it…"

"Whoa, there," said Dan pointing at the hydrogen tank. "How do I know there isn't already hydrogen in the tank?"

"This is how you know," said Ann, and she opened up a bleeder valve, lit a match, and held to the end of the copper tubing. The match sputtered, then died out. "In a few seconds we will do this again, and you'll see the difference."

"Another way you know," said President Kane, "is that you're at the University of Southern Texas, and we have a reputation to protect."

Dan bobbed his head and smiled mischievously. "One can never be too careful."

Ann continued. "When the water hits the laser funnel, it will separate into oxygen and hydrogen.

The hydrogen will rise to the top of the tank on the outside of the funnel and be siphoned off and compressed. The larger oxygen molecules will percolate to the top of the tank on the inside of the funnel..."

Ann paused to see if Dan was keeping up. He looked at the apparatus, then back at Ann, and shrugged his shoulders. "Okay."

"When I pull this lever and the water hits the laser grid, it will appear that the water just disappears because hydrogen and oxygen by themselves are invisible. It'll look like the best magic trick you've ever seen, except that it's real."

Ann looked around the room. "Folks, let's make Dan a believer," she said, and pulled the lever. A perfectly cylindrical stream of water poured into the middle of the laser funnel, and just as Ann had described, it disappeared into hydrogen and oxygen gas.

The second the water disappeared, applause and cheers broke out in the room. Dan stood with his hands on his hips, staring at the apparatus and shaking his head in amazement. "This is monumental!" he said, sitting down on the stool in front of the hydrolyser. "Do you know what this means?" he asked, turning to Ann.

Ann laughed. "I think we've been over that."

Dan turned back to the camera. "Folks, I doubt many of you realize it, but what you've just witnessed is bigger than Neil Armstrong stepping foot on the moon or Henry Ford rolling the first Model-T off the assembly line. I'm truly honored to have the opportunity to be here. Any of you who are in the oil or petroleum industries should start polishing up your resumes and familiarizing yourselves with hydrogen, because you are about to have the ride of your lives. Hold on!"

Every eye in the room was directed at Dr. Ann Ford. She beamed with happiness and satisfaction as she accepted hugs, handshakes, and congratulations. She felt like a massive burden had been removed from her shoulders now that several of the top scientists in the country thoroughly understood and could reproduce her research.

Dan waited for the room to quiet, and then turned back to Ann. "I understand that it's a tradition at this university to give code names to every project?"

"Apparently so," said Ann.

"How will history books refer to this one?"

Ann looked at Jack apologetically. "Early this morning, my husband suggested the project be named Apollo. However, in honor of our own Nobel Prize winner who lost his life because of this technology, and an emeritus professor who got caught in the line of fire, I'd like to change the name to 'The Summersten-Conner Project.'"

The room was silent for a minute. President Kane broke the silence with a slow, but respectful clap, clap, clap, clap. Tears ran freely down his face at the thought of his good friends and of the generosity and thoughtfulness of Dr. Ford. Gradually everyone in the room joined in the respectful applause. Even Dan Johnson stood and joined in the ovation.

Seeing that the applause was not going to die down anytime soon, Dan wrapped up the interview over the applause. "I doubt that I'll ever have the privilege of announcing a more profound piece of news than what I have today. It is certainly a day to remember. I'm Dan Johnson, and this is NBC News."

Dan walked over to President Kane and leaned in close to him. "It will take me twenty minutes or less to edit both segments of this story, then I'll be ready to upload it in the medium you need. How far away are you engineers from restoring communications?"

"I'm not sure," said President Kane, "but I'll let you know the minute we figure something out."

Chapter Thirty-Five

"Free Market and Capitalism Suppressed"

President Buchman was nearing the end of his second term as President of the United States, and he felt sorry for the person who would be elected after him. The government was in big trouble. They'd gone too long without balancing the budget and had ignored the infallible laws of supply-demand and capitalism. They had participated in too many bail outs, had created too many jobs by taxing the people they were created for, and had pork-barreled too many useless projects, programs, and research.

A wave of organized crime had its tentacles in every facet of the federal government—special interest groups, lobbyists, unions, FBI & CIA headquarters, senators, and congressional offices were all infected—and there was not enough manpower or resources to eradicate it.

Tax revenues were at a thirteen-year low, federal debt was at an all-time high, and several cities and states had gone bankrupt.

On top of it all, disaster and emergency funds had hemorrhaged to the point of drying up, due to the increased number of natural disasters that had hit the country. Governors from several states were even questioning the value of federal government. They viewed the federal government as a liability rather than a partner who could help them maintain the rule-of-law, stabilize the economy, and promote economic prosperity.

The president stared dismally out the window of the Oval Office, trying to make sense of the intelligence he was receiving from the FBI about the University of Southern Texas. What he heard was so alarming, he had called an emergency meeting of his Joint Chiefs, the Vice President, the Director of National Intelligence, the Secretary of Defense, and a handful of advisors. One by one, they filed into his office, avoiding eye contact and conversation. The Joint Chiefs stood out in their meticulously tailored uniforms, but sat uncomfortably, waiting for him to get started. He didn't make any attempt to hide his frustration as he put Jefferson on speakerphone. "Jefferson, would you tell these men what you told me a few minutes ago?"

"Yes, sir."

The President's body tensed as he listened to Jefferson explain what had happened during the last few days on the Ford case. Jefferson summarized how someone had trashed and blown up the Ford's home and concluded by describing how a UST security guard had tossed fourteen FBI agents out through the shield.

When he was finished, the president asked him a few clarifying questions about the sequence of events that had happened at the Ford residence on Tuesday and Wednesday, and a question or two about the assassin who'd been seen on campus.

Director Jefferson was about to bring up the NBC News broadcast that they had just jammed, but was interrupted by the president, who was still thinking about the FBI agents in Corpus Christi.

"Are all your men off campus?"

"Yes, sir."

"Have you had any further contact with the university?"

"No," responded Jefferson. "The last dialogue we had with them was with the security guard I just told you about."

President Buchman shook his head and looked at the group of men and women in his office. "How did this get so far out of hand? This is the University of Southern Texas we are talking about, not some wacked out religious cult!"

The Oval Office was full of frustrated people who were looking for someone to blame, and President Buchman wasn't an exception. "What time is it there?"

"7:15 AM, sir."

"Is the press aware of the shield?"

"No... No one other than Dan Johnson."

"That's like saying nobody important is on the opposing basketball team other than Michael Jordan!"

Out of self-preservation, Jefferson did not respond to the comment. "There are a few people out and about who have been directed away from the shield, but things are pretty quiet for the most part."

"Keep the public away from that thing like we discussed earlier until we figure out what to do. If anybody asks about it, tell them it's part of an experimental emergency response system for extreme weather. Tell them that it triggered accidentally and the university is trying to shut it down. We should also leak that the shield is interfering with some of the university's communication systems."

"Is that the official story?" asked Jefferson.

"It is until we get a hold of someone at the university who can tell us what their intentions are," said the President. "Besides," he paused and a little optimism crept into his voice, "didn't they raise the shield a year or so ago when Hurricane Derek was threatening Corpus Christi?

Director Jefferson had a vague recollection of the university trying out some shield technology. "I think I remember something like that."

President Buchman shook his head, but didn't say what he was thinking. *It's pathetic that we don't know anything about a technology that just kicked our butt!* "We'll contact you within the hour and let you know what we decide to do going forward. Until then, don't let anyone run into the shield, and don't say anything to the press without my explicit consent."

"Yes, sir."

President Buchman hung up the speaker phone and moved around to the front of his desk. "It's obvious we're not going to resolve this issue in twenty minutes, so why don't we move to the Situation Room where we can be more comfortable. You might want to clear your schedules for the next couple of days."

Once they were all comfortably seated in the Situation Room, President Buchman's frustration exploded in a tirade of angry words. "Is it just me or am I the only one surprised at the effectiveness of the university's shield?"

He didn't give anyone time to respond. "I'm not only shocked about the effectiveness of the damn thing, I'm embarrassed that we don't know more about the technology. Hell, can you imagine what would happen if this technology got into the wrong hands? Maybe it's in the wrong hands now.

Several people in the room shifted uncomfortably in their chairs.

"Are you telling me this technology is a surprise to all of you? What did I hire you people for anyway?" Everyone in the room sat quietly, not wanting to expose their ignorance.

"I hate to admit this, Mr. President, but I'm as surprised as you are," responded the Vice President.

One of the Joint Chiefs cleared his throat. "We knew UST was playing around with some experimental shield technology because they tried to use it to ward off Hurricane Derek. At the time, we concluded that Corpus Christi got more protection from the Mustang, Padre, and San Jose Islands than it did from the university's shield. Apparently it went down several times during the storm and ended up providing little, if any, protection for the university."

"Sounds to me like we are so full of arrogant intellectual bullshit, we can't see the forest for the trees!" shouted President Buchman.

"We definitely had no idea they intended to repel anything other than water," said General Sacket, the Army Chief of Staff.

"And you didn't stop to think that something that could repel water might be able to be configured to repel bullets and have military applications?" The President was fuming. "What about their drone technology? Did we minimize that as well? If what Jefferson told us is true, the university disabled fourteen of our best FBI agents and nonchalantly tossed them into the street using another technology we know nothing about!"

The room was silent. The facts were on the table, and they revealed a startling level of incompetence. "Every one of you should be embarrassed. Hell, if the American people knew how incompetent we've been on this one, we'd have another million-man march on Washington."

President Buchman could see that he wasn't going to get any more information about the university's shield and drone technology out of the people in the room. "Is there anyone on our payroll who knows about this technology? If there is, I want them in this room now! If there isn't... God help us."

A number of people palmed their cell phones and made calls, trying to find someone familiar with the university's shield and drone technology. President Buchman looked over at the Chief of Naval Operations, Admiral Sorensen. "Wasn't President Kane a roommate of yours at college?"

"I was hoping you wouldn't remember that," said the admiral dryly.

"Give President Kane a call and ask him what the hell is going on."

"Now, sir?"

"Now would be a great time," he said, turning to the Director of National Intelligence. "Can we poke a hole through the communications channels we are jamming and get through to President Kane's office?"

"Yes, sir," replied the Director. "Give me ten minutes." The Director turned away from the table and started barking orders into his cell phone.

The president pushed the speaker phone on the conference room table closer to where the admiral was sitting. "Since nobody in the United States Armed Forces seems to know anything about this shield technology, we might as well go to the source."

"What do you want me to say to him? It sounds like we killed one of his emeritus professors and an FBI agent put a gun to his head," said Admiral Sorensen in frustration. "If I'd been through what he has in the last couple of hours and I had access to drone and shield technology, I would've used it too."

Before the admiral could continue, the giant flat screen in the room flickered to life, interrupting the conversation.

One of the president's staff entered the room and whispered something in his ear.

He nodded his head. "Run it." President Buchman stood up. "It appears that UST tried to broadcast a two part-segment about Dr. Ford's research. Even though we prevented it from airing on the public networks, we need to take a look at it so we understand what they're trying to communicate to the world."

He'd barely finished speaking before an NBC news brief started playing on the monitor. The familiar face of Dan Johnson flashed on the screen. "It's Thursday September 11th, I'm Dan Johnson, and this is NBC News. I'm coming to you this morning from the University of Southern Texas. There will be several amazing stories coming out of the university this morning, so stay with us. Over the past two decades, I've had the unique privilege of introducing new technological breakthroughs on behalf of the University of Southern Texas and its students and faculty. Today is one of those occasions. I would like to introduce you to Dr. Ford, who is solely responsible for some research that is about to change the world as we know it..." The news story continued to play until it was finished and the monitor went blank.

President Buchman turned to the room of people. "Most of you don't know about Dr. Ford and her research, but we've been keeping an eye on her ever since she published a white paper on it a few years ago. During the last few days, we discovered that Mcorp, Black Gold, and the University of Southern Texas were showing increased interest in her, so we upgraded her status to that of a person of significant interest."

"So, we've been keeping an eye on her for some time?" stated one of the Joint Chiefs, making a quotation sign with his fingers.

The president sighed. "We've stretched the Patriot Act to its limit in order to keep an eye on a handful of scientists who are working on projects that have the potential to cause severe economic and diplomatic disruption."

A member of the president's staff entered the room, and whispered in the president's ear.

"Please repeat what you said to the group."

"We just confirmed that the University of Southern Texas has published the design, schematics, and a blueprint for what they claim is a working model of Dr. Ford's hydrolyser on their website."

"We've temporarily blocked their website from being available to the public, right?"

The staff member nodded her head. "We have our best people on it." She smiled and left the room.

"As if the shield wasn't a big enough problem," said an economic advisor.

"What do you mean?" asked one of the Joint Chiefs.

"If Dr. Ford has created a viable fossil fuel substitute for twenty to thirty cents a gallon and the refining process can be handled at a local level...

well…" He paused, feeling totally exasperated. He searched for the right words to accurately describe the economic disruption and transformation Dr. Ford's research would have on the world economy. He shook his head after a minute, and then looked up. "I could sit here for a week and not be able to explain the size of this economic tsunami."

"Just give us the highlights, Wally," said the president impatiently.

Wally swallowed and pursed his lips, trying to figure out where to start. He decided to explain how the technology would hit the president's pocketbook.

"I'll start with the basics. Approximately eighty-five percent of all crude oil is used for transportation, agriculture, and heating. Most of the taxes and lease revenues we collect from these sources will evaporate within a couple of years or less."

"Why couldn't we levy a tax on hydrogen use?"

"If the technology is simple enough and can be distributed at a household or local level like Dr. Ford claims, it will be impossible to manage. It would be harder than managing the tax on marijuana or enforcing the prohibition in the 1920s. If the average person is able buy a device online that can distill hydrogen from water out of their garden hose, how could we possibly tax it?"

One of the president's advisors shook her head in disagreement. "We can figure out some way to tax it. We'll do something like we did for propane and refrigerants, and introduce a few laws making it illegal to handle."

"That's a poor comparison because propane and refrigerants can't be grown or distilled in your backyard like marijuana, alcohol, or bio-diesel," said Wally, not wanting to have an open debate on the issues. "Regardless, the demand for oil will decrease by approximately eighty-five percent, along with products and services from related industries like drilling, refining, oil-distributing, trucking, etc."

"Eighty-five percent? Really?"

"Yes, and that's a well-known, if not conservative number."

Wally waited a second to see if anyone else had an objection. "The decrease in gas, propane, natural gas, diesel, and jet fuel consumption means we could lose well over two hundred billion dollars a year in state and federal tax and lease dollars."

A number of people in the room looked at each other in surprise. They all knew the federal government couldn't pay its bills with its current tax revenues, and a two hundred billion dollar drop would be disastrous.

Wally could see that he'd struck a nerve. "If hydrogen replaces oil, there will be hundreds of billions of dollars lost in the private sector as well."

The room was silent as people tried to grasp the immensity of what he was saying. President Buchman motioned for him to finish.

"In addition, the over-supply of crude oil will drive the prices, profits, and taxes of anything made from oil or its derivatives down to rock bottom for many years to come. Prices would plummet on things like fertilizers, adhesives, plastics, feedstock, artificial hearts, pacemakers, tooth brushes, aspirin, contact lenses, bandages, surgical equipment,…"

President Buchman interrupted his exuberant advisor. "I think we get the picture, Wally. It sounds like we'd be in for some serious economic disruption if we allowed Ford's research to free-fall into the world market."

"That would be an understatement," said Wally. The economic advisors in the room nodded in agreement.

"How will this affect the natural gas and propane industries?" asked the Vice President.

"It will definitely affect them, but it's hard to say how much."

"It will be significant," said an advisor who was punching numbers into his handheld device.

Another advisor cleared his throat, indicating he was about to say something. "This isn't all bad. The country will adjust, and there will be hundreds of new businesses springing up all over the place."

His words were met with skepticism. He stammered, but kept talking, not wanting to lose his momentum. "Another positive outcome from Dr. Ford's research will be the elimination of wars over oil. We might even save what we lose in gas taxes by not having to fund so many damn war theaters in the Middle East."

"Tell us how you really feel, Henry."

"I lost a boy and several friends in the oil wars," responded Henry bitterly. "That's how I really feel!" He glared at the man who had made the comment.

"Sorry, Henry, I wasn't thinking."

The Vice President, sensing the need for a change of subject, verbalized his opinion, but ended up opening another can of worms. "Since I wasn't aware of how close we've been monitoring Dr. Ford and her research, it appears from my perspective that we have gone beyond stretching the Patriot Act."

"Are you kidding me?" exclaimed the Director of National Intelligence. "Ford's breakthrough will literally wipe out several Middle Eastern countries."

"Give me a break," said the Vice President. "Since when did any of those countries give a shit about the American economy? You're starting to sound like a damn communist!"

"When I say wipe out, I mean there are over a dozen countries whose sole income comes from oil revenues."

"Do you really think we can control this technology? If we succeed in suppressing Ford, someone else will have a similar breakthrough tomorrow, and they might be a citizen of Saudi Arabia or China. What are we going to do then? This change in our primary energy resource was going to happen sooner or later, and we should embrace it."

"Gentlemen, gentlemen," said President Buchman. "The question in my mind isn't *if* we should be involved in controlling this technology, but *how* we should be involved. According to our Deputy Director of the FBI, we are already involved up to our eyeballs. What I want to do is make damn sure we manage the situation the best we can moving forward. It's not just our allies in the Middle East that I'm worried about. I honestly believe that the combination of a sudden replacement for oil and the shield in Texas that's defying the United States military is the most serious threat to our stability I've ever seen."

He looked around the room to assess who agreed with him, and he could see that he had some work to do if he was going to get everyone's support. It was imperative that they all agree on a single course of action or the situation with the University of Southern Texas would explode into a media nightmare.

He summarized the intelligence they had available to them using his most logical, calm, and persuasive voice. "Let me restate what we know about this situation so we're all on the same page. One, we know that the University of Southern Texas has backed Dr. Ford's research, so we'd better count on it being real. Two, the university has thrown up a shield that we know very little about and it stopped the FBI dead in its tracks. Three, the university is in a highly agitated state considering they've had an assassination attempt on Dr. Ford, an explosion on campus, an FBI agent attack their university president, a professor killed by the FBI, and a visiting professor is missing in action. Four, the university disabled fourteen FBI agents and tossed them out the front gate using drone technology we have underestimated for years. Am I missing anything?"

The Vice President looked up. "Don't forget they have a lot of what you just described on surveillance tape, and have already tried to broadcast Dr. Ford's breakthrough. Undoubtedly they've discovered that we are jamming their signal too."

"They will definitely throw the Constitution at us over that," said President Buchman.

Several people shifted in their chairs uncomfortably.

"Don't forget that there are over thirty thousand students and faculty who have heard what's going on from UST's news network. Every one of these people has friends and family around the world, and a cell phone, so there is no way for us to stop them from talking."

General Sacket looked annoyed. "I have a daughter on campus, and I've tried to call, email, and text her, but I can't get through."

"I thought you understood that we were temporarily jamming their communication capability," responded President Buchman.

General Sacket stared at the Director of National Intelligence with a menacing look. "Cell phone and landline communications?"

"What did you expect us to do?" asked the director sarcastically. "With everything that's at stake, it's the first thing we did when we discovered we couldn't penetrate the shield and secure Ford's technology!"

Trent, one of the president's advisors, burst out laughing. "It won't take the university more than a couple of hours to hack whatever it is you are doing to block their communications."

"We've got our best people on it!" snapped the director defensively.

"Don't be naïve. UST has the best computer programmers in the world, and half the software you're using to block their communications was probably written by them. Besides, I heard the university has already broken your impenetrable communication barrier."

President Buchman collapsed in his chair and put his head in his hands. The conversation was headed in the opposite direction he'd intended. "What's Trent talking about?"

The director's day was getting worse by the second. "Thirty motorcycle riders left campus this morning with a message about the shield. We apprehended four of them, and they were all carrying the same information packet. All the packets contained were details about the shield's coordinates and capabilities."

"Are you sure?" asked President Buchman skeptically.

General Sacket shook his head. "That makes no sense to me either. If I were President Kane, I would've included information out about the death of Dr. Summersten, Dr. Ford's research, and the FBI's blockade."

The director shrugged. "Either it was a bad call on their part or they just felt they needed to get information out about the shield's location before someone ran into it. It's also possible they didn't have the documentation on Dr. Ford's research ready when they sent the motorcycle riders out."

The president rubbed his forehead with his hand. "It doesn't sound like the university is locked down tight enough to keep a herd of elephants from walking out!"

"The motorcycle riders left campus before we got the reinforcements we needed to make our perimeter defenses airtight."

"Maybe we'd better come clean and admit we screwed up," said the Vice President.

A few heads around the table nodded in agreement. The President of the United States shook his head skeptically. "Let's get President Kane on the phone and see if we can talk him into lowering his shield before we make a decision. If we can get him to lower his shields and work with us on a controlled release of Dr. Ford's technology, I'd be happy to admit we screwed up."

Director Mason's phone rang and he answered it. He listened for a minute then hung up without saying anything. "We've got President Kane's office on the line," he said, looking at Admiral Sorensen, "and the call's being transferred to this room."

Admiral Sorensen was not happy about the President using his personal relationship with President Kane to discuss the current situation, which, in his opinion, the FBI had totally screwed up. Despite his personal feelings, he leaned over the speaker phone on the conference room table. "Hello?"

A pleasant voice on the other end responded. "Hello, President Kane's office, this is Margaret. How may I help you?"

"Would you tell President Kane that Admiral Sorensen of the United States Navy, the Joint Chiefs, the Secretary of Defense, the Director of National Intelligence, the Vice President, the President of the

United States, and several of his economic and defense department advisors are on the phone?"

"It would be my pleasure, Admiral Sorensen and Mr. President," responded Margaret, trying to sound calm. "It may take me a few minutes to locate him. He's had a very busy morning, as you probably know."

"We'll wait," said Admiral Sorensen flatly. "Oh... and we'd also like to speak with Dr. Ford if she's available," he added without asking permission.

"I'll see what I can do," said Margaret.

They waited without saying any thing for several minutes. Everyone in the Situation Room was deep in their own thoughts, trying to figure out a way to resolve the situation before it escalated any further. None of them felt secure enough to go head-to-head with the University of Southern Texas on their own. It was political suicide.

"Admiral," drawled a tired, yet sarcastic Texan voice. "I've been expecting a call from you or your boss."

"We're both here," Admiral Sorensen replied, scowling.

"How is the family?" asked President Kane.

"They're doing fine," responded Admiral Sorensen, ignoring the glare he was getting from the President. "How about your family?"

"We're doing great," responded President Kane. "I think..."

"That's good to hear," said the Admiral, knowing the President had completely run out of patience. "The reason I called was so we could get your perspective on what's been going on the last couple of days."

President Kane hesitated while he gathered his thoughts. "It's quite simple, really. We made an offer of employment to Dr. Ford—who is on the phone with me—on Tuesday morning and everything has gone to hell in a handbag since."

"It is good to have you on the phone, Dr. Ford," said President Buchman, motioning for Director Mason to get a voice match.

"It's good to be alive, Mr. President," said Ann, her voice dripping with sarcasm.

President Kane nodded in agreement, then continued. "Unfortunately, Dr. Sellers's presence at CSU and an anxiety-stress reading someone took off Dr. Ford's personal phone threw Mcorp, Black Gold, and your people into an adolescent, paranoid frenzy."

Director Mason ignored the insult, but fired back, "What makes you think Black Gold or Mcorp were involved?"

"We were able to ID the guy who impersonated an FBI agent on Tuesday night—you know, the guy who shot Agent Porter and put a gun to Dr. Ford's head? He's been working for Black Gold for several years, and unless he's had a change of employment and started working for you, Black Gold was involved."

The director's neck and face turned red, but he suppressed his desire to lash out in defense of his organization. "You're certain he was working for Black Gold?"

"Yes, and you will be too, once you run an image match on him. The five guys you killed in the front yard also worked for Black Gold, if you haven't figured it out already."

"How did you ID them so fast?"

"The old-fashioned way. We had a forensic sketch artist work with the people who were with Dr. Ford when it happened," said President Kane trying not to disclose the fact that they'd gotten positive IDs on both the agent in the house and the five operatives in the yard from their satellite infrared and image-matching software.

"Who was the guy in the house?" asked the director, testing to see if President Kane really had gotten a positive ID.

"A thug who goes by the name of Harper. His real name is Lance Hodgkin."

President Buchman had reviewed the Ford file before the meeting, and knew there were five people with Dr. Ford the last time she was seen and he knew that none of the corpses had been positively identified by the FBI yet. "So who were the people you were with the other night?"

"You lost me," said the Vice President.

President Buchman explained that Dr. Ford had entered her home accompanied by five people on the night of the explosion, and the FBI had yet to identify who they were.

"Were all five of them friends of yours?" asked President Buchman, directing the question at Ann.

"I'll let you figure out who they are on your own. I just feel extremely fortunate that the university had a couple of people in the area or I would be dead right now and my research would've been lost forever."

"I don't understand," said President Buchman.

"I destroyed all of my research notes and counted on being able to rebuild it from memory."

A couple of people in the room shook their heads doubtfully and President Buchman glared at the phone. Director Mason gave the President a nod, indicating that the woman on the phone was indeed Dr. Ford.

"I suppose it was your high-tech helicopter that tied up traffic on the interstate, jammed our communications, and transported Dr. Ford to Corpus Christi?" asked Buchman, directing the question to President Kane. He continued to vent, not and didn't give Kane a chance to respond. "What gives the University of Southern Texas the right to interfere with CIA and FBI business?"

"When they are so incompetent they can't protect a professor in Fort Collins, Colorado!" retorted President Kane sharply.

Director Mason came off his chair in an angry lunge. He moved around the table to get closer to the phone mike, but President Buchman waved him back to his seat. "It's unreasonable for you to expect us to protect every professor in the world who might have a good idea.

"I agree," said President Kane. "But when you think they've discovered the biggest breakthrough of the century, I fully expect you to protect them."

President Buchman was fuming, but needed President Kane to keep talking until they figured out what he was going to do with the shield. "When did you figure out that she'd had a breakthrough?"

"After she arrived on campus and told us."

"So you believed her without any evidence?"

"No," said Ann interrupting. "They were so skeptical they insisted that I build a working model before they'd back me up."

"Which she did, by the way, in less than eleven hours, with no schematics, blueprints, or supporting documentation," said President Kane, trying to make a point of how simple the technology was to reproduce.

"It was really that easy?" asked one of the president's advisors.

"I could have done it faster," responded Ann, "but we needed to document the reconstruction so my research could be widely distributed and easily reproduced. Thanks to UST, a dozen top scientists are now up-to-speed on the technology. Oh, and speaking of scientists, is General Sacket in the room?"

The general grimaced, guessing what Dr. Ford was about to say. "Yes?"

"You should be pleased to know that there was a very impressive young lady who was of immense help during the reconstruction of my prototype. She hung in there without sleep for the full eleven hours and now she knows as much about my research as I do."

General Sacker's jaw tensed. "Her ongoing safety is my only concern," he snapped, showing the emotion of a concerned father.

"She's perfectly safe with us, just like she has been for the last four years. The only thing you need to worry about is making sure the FBI doesn't shoot her," said President Kane tersely, "especially now that she knows how to reproduce Dr. Ford's technology." President Kane needed an ally in the room and was counting on General Sacket and Admiral Sorenson.

"Is she free to leave the campus if she wants to?" asked the General.

"Of course. As usual our students and faculty are free to come and go as they please."

"Even with the shield up?"

"Even with the shield up," responded President Kane.

Intent on keeping President Kane talking he pressed him with another question. "What are your intentions with the shield, and why did you feel the need to raise it in the first place?"

"After losing two good friends to your organization's incompetence and having a gun pressed to my head, I decided we had to protect ourselves. It was fortunate we raised the shield when we did because it prohibited fifty fully armed FBI agents from storming the campus without probable cause or a search warrant."

President Buchman was feeling defensive and countered back. "The Patriot Act relaxed the warrant law, and the FBI acted well-within its expanded guidelines."

"How do you twist 'Intercepting and Obstructing Terrorism' to justify your involvement with Dr. Ford and UST?"

"A foreign and domestic cartel threatened an American university and an American citizen's life. What more do we need?"

President Kane could see how easily the events of the last few days could be twisted when taken out of context. "You're quite the spin doctor, Mr. President. Don't forget we have it all captured in a nice neat digital format for your review if you forget how things really happened. You know as well as I do that the FBI and CIA were ramped up in Fort Collins without probable cause, which I will be more than happy to prove in a court of law. When did the United States Government start invading prestigious universities with the intent to suppress innovative technology? Last time I checked, we were still governed by a republic that upholds the Constitution, not a bunch of trigger-happy communists. Has our government become so morally bankrupt that it can't distinguish between right and wrong? Where are our Abraham Lincolns and George Washingtons, Mr. President?"

"Look, the agent in charge made the call to deploy men on your campus with the information he had at the time," responded Director Mason defensively.

"You mean the Deputy Director of the FBI," retorted President Kane quickly.

"Ah... right. The information that Director Jefferson had this morning convinced him that Dr.

Ford's life was in danger, so he sent agents onto campus to protect her. According to our agents, a man with a gun equipped with a silencer entered the science building on campus at 4:45 this morning, so we…"

President Kane rarely swore, but couldn't help himself and let loose with his Texan drawl. "Don't insult me with that crock of bullshit! You planned on mounting a full-scale assault on campus hours before the man with the gun showed up! You were set up at the Hilton before he even arrived in Corpus Christi! The really sad thing is; he booked a room in the Hilton one floor below you, and you didn't even know it!"

President Buchman and the Joint Chiefs shifted their gaze from the phone to Director Mason, waiting for him to deny the accusations. He didn't.

President Kane continued his rant. "At least be honest. You've been chasing Dr. Ford since Tuesday, trying to secure her technology so you can control it. I realize you're scared about the economic disruption her research is going cause, but she wants to give it away, so there is nothing you can do about it. Your fear of the unknown and naivety about being able to control supply and demand has clouded your judgment. You're acting like a communist government, that can't make its debt payments and can't enforce the rule-of-law. Look at yourselves! Are you so desperate, you're willing to sacrifice your morals and manipulate the Constitution to justify your baseless fears? You already have the deaths of two wonderful men on your hands!"

President Kane's words stung, and no one at the table could think of anything to say. President Kane took advantage of the silence to try and convince the Commander-in-Chief to reconsider the direction he was headed.

"You've violated our Constitutional rights, twisted federal law, demonstrated gross incompetence, and murdered an innocent man. Why don't you quit and go home before this escalates any further? Do you really want your names to be in the history books alongside Kim Chong-Il, Stalin, Lenin, Mao Zedong Fidel Castro and Mengistu Mariam fifty years from now!"

President Buchman didn't say anything for a minute and then leaned over the speakerphone. "That's not a fair comparison, but on behalf of the United States Government, I sincerely apologize for your loss. We will extend our most sincere condolences to the friends and families of the professors who passed away and make sure they are taken care of."

He paused and cleared his throat, carefully choosing his next words. He wanted to explain why the United States Government had acted the way they had in relation to Dr. Ford's technology, and disassociate himself from communist terminology.

"As you probably know, the American public is in a precarious state of mind right now. Our polls are telling us that their faith in our government is at an all-time low, and the approval rating of nearly every government official has plummeted. There are several cities and states that are extremely hesitant to have federal assistance in matters where they would normally be involved, which is a troubling sign. Internationally, the dollar is not nearly as strong as it once was, and countries who have traditionally held large reserves of US dollars are dumping them at an alarming rate."

President Kane grunted. "Is there any question in your mind why that might be the case, Mr. President? Hell, I'm almost embarrassed to say I'm an American these days."

President Buchman ignored the comment. "What I'm trying to say is, this is not the best time for UST to openly oppose the United States Government. If the general public sees your open opposition, we're afraid it will throw the nation into a state of uncertainty it hasn't seen since the days of Abraham Lincoln. You will inadvertently validate the public's distrust of our federal government."

President Kane delayed commenting while he considered what had been said. After thinking it over he responded. "I don't think a simple shield will be perceived as opposition to federal authority unless you continue to fire on it."

President Buchman looked surprised and turned away from the speakerphone. "Have we fired on the shield?"

"We have, sir. Several shots were fired on the shield in an attempt to investigate what it was made of."

The president rolled his eyes and stared at the ceiling, "For the love of Mary." He shook his head and turned back to the speakerphone. "It's also a bad time to introduce a technology that will interrupt the flow of trillions of tax dollars, corporate revenues, and personal incomes. No offense, Dr. Ford, but we need to control the release of your technology so it doesn't cause a complete economic meltdown. This clearly is not a good time for defiant behavior or disruptive technologies!"

Ann did not respond. Her worst fears seemed to be materializing, and at the highest levels of the United States Government.

President Kane was beside himself. He couldn't understand how people as educated and intelligent as President Buchman and his staff could have such a limited understanding and lack of faith in the free market and capitalism. *I've never seen such blatant stupidity and ignorance among the highly educated in my life,* he thought. *All he has to do to heal this country is uphold the Constitution, enforce reasonable law, not spend more than he collects in taxes, stop giving handouts and let the market take its natural course.* "Didn't he go to law school" he mumbled. "They still teach economics and logic at Harvard don't they?"

"He must have forgotten or he is someone's puppet," whispered Ann.

President Kane looked at Ann and muted the call, "Either he's lost faith in the free market or there's a puppet master with a hell of a lot of power pulling his strings."

Ann shrugged and shook her head.

Kane searched for something that would convince the president to reconsider. He looked hopeless for a moment then he brightened. "Mr. President, I would humbly propose that you withdraw from the perimeter of the shield and leave the city of Corpus Christi altogether. Let Dr. Ford release her technology to the world, and I pledge that the University of Southern Texas will dedicate a substantial amount of its intellect, influence, and resources to the development of this new technology on American soil, so that we, as a nation, can benefit from it more than any other country in the world. I'd also be willing to discuss how we can spin this little fiasco in a way that it won't alarm the American public or our international allies."

President Kane paused for a moment but there was no response.

"All you have to do is enforce the law, trust the free market and allow us to help American's take advantage of this amazing technology. You could single handedly save this country from the worst financial disaster in history. Why not take advantage of this situation, Mr. President?"

President Kane bowed his head and waited for an answer. There was silence on the call for a few seconds, so he continued.

"I'm not the only one that feels this way, Mr. President. Some of the brightest minds in this country share the same opinion. As harsh as it sounds, the government's corrupt fiscal policy and inability to enforce the law is the reason this country is on the verge of collapse—and it's going to take some pretty intrusive surgery to fix it. Don't let the robbers of Wall Street control you anymore. They've stolen and mismanaged the wealth of this nation long enough! Why not take her under the knife while you have the support of one of the most influential universities in the world?"

President Buchman's blood pressure was rising and his face was red. He looked at the people sitting in the Situation Room. Over three quarters of them were shaking their heads disparagingly. They were all scared. As much as they wanted to believe what President Kane was saying, it seemed much safer to stay with the status quo—the evil that they knew—than to risk allowing an unpredictable and highly disruptive technology to cannonball into an extremely volatile marketplace.

President Buchman bowed his head and exhaled slowly, but he couldn't maintain his composure. "We can't do that! We can't risk allowing the unpredictable and invisible influence of the market take its course with this technology right now. A free market can't miraculously take care of everything! It doesn't work. It has never worked!"

Kane shook his head in disappointment. It was apparent that he could not present an argument that would change the president's mind.

"It appears that we are at an impasse then," he said in a discouraged tone, trying with all his might to suppress the frustration and anger that simmered within him.

"Apparently so!" confirmed President Buchman, equally frustrated.

"Unless the UST general board overrides my decision or Dr. Ford changes her mind, the shield will remain up until we figure out a way to get her research into the hands of the general public. Hell, I'm half-tempted to leave it up until you regain convincing control of our government, purge it of organized crime and balance the budget!"

"You're insane!" said President Buchman bitterly.

"Maybe," said President Kane, "but not anymore than a guy who spends six trillion dollars more than his budget, then criticizes the other party's math! And definitely not as insane as a guy who is foolish enough to try and jam a well-respected university and news agency's freedom of speech! Listen to yourself Mr. President! Are you going to be remembered as the greatest president we've ever had or the biggest puppet?"

President Kane's words cut the Commander-in-Chief to the core, but he had no response for the accurate representation of his last four years—not to mention the last forty eight hours.

"Until now we've felt as helpless to influence our country's economic problems as most Americans, but our shield has given us the power to hold you accountable. You've pushed this university too far, Mr. President. Your bullying and reckless distain for our lives and constitutional rights stops here. We will publicize your unlawful actions against Dr. Ford and the University of Southern Texas until we've fanned the spark of freedom in enough American hearts to get your attention. This university will be the staff upon which the nation will lean, and we will bear the Constitution away from the verge of destruction if you will not. You've run roughshod over us one too many times Mr. President, and we, the people of the University of Southern Texas, have just fired a shot across your bow! I hope and pray you are not naïve enough to think you can suppress our voice."

All the hair on the back of President Buchman's neck was standing on end. Such passion coming from a single man wouldn't normally have bothered him. But in this situation—coming from this university president—it was beyond alarming. In a time when demonstrations against the government were becoming all too common, President Kane's passion could easily become come the catalyst for sustained civil unrest.

"You can't be serious! We need a short-term solution before we can even remotely consider releasing Dr. Ford's technology!'

"That's what people in your position have been saying for fifty years!" snapped President Kane tartly. "What you don't understand, is that it's not yours to release!"

"Like hell its not!"

"Time is up, Mr. President. If I were you, I'd take this opportunity to make real change. Together we can make it happen. This country is in dire need of great leadership. Why not do what you know in your heart needs to be done? Why not cut the puppet strings and be the George Washington of the twenty-first century?"

The tension was thick. President Buchman looked desperately around the room hoping that someone had an argument that would resolve the situation, but everybody was shaking their heads. "Is there any way we can convince you to lower your shield and consider a controlled rollout of Dr. Ford's technology?"

"Not if I have anything to say about it," said President Kane, without hesitation.

"Is that how you feel, Dr. Ford?"

"With all due respect, Mr. President, rolling out my research as President Kane has suggested would give the United States a decided head start and an incredible economic boost. I don't think you understand how much of an advantage the US would have if it was backed by the intellectual capital of the University of Southern Texas. It might be the only thing that can save this country from economic disaster. Please don't try and take away my freedom of speech by suppressing my work."

The Situation Room was silent as everyone waited for the Commander-in-Chief of the United States to respond.

He stood at the end of the table with his head bowed. Deep lines creased his forehead as he tried to determine if there was any way to bridge the chasm between them. After almost a minute, he shook his head.

"It is unfortunate that you both feel this way. I was hoping that you'd do what is in the best interest of your country. My only hope is that your general board reaches a more reasonable conclusion. If they don't, I'll be forced to take whatever action is necessary to get you to lower your shield and regulate your research."

He thanked President Kane and Dr. Ford for their time in a semi-cordial manner and ended the call.

President Buchman looked around the room at the men and women who represented the most powerful country on earth. "Ladies and gentlemen, we have a problem."

Everyone in the room agreed that they had a problem, but nobody had a solution. To some extent, they all sympathized with President Kane and Dr. Ford's position, but they feared that the combination of disruptive technology and the open defiance the shield represented was too big of a threat to the stability of the Unites States.

What bothered them the most was the passion that President Kane had demonstrated in support of his position. Such passion from a man so highly respected could easily become contagious, which, in and of itself, was extremely dangerous. Up until now, the demonstrations across the country hadn't had cohesive leadership or a focal point for their passion. President Kane and the University of Southern Texas would fill that void unless they were stopped.

Secretary Jacobs, broke the silence. "If we could knock out the satellite generating their shield in the next hour or so, we would hold all the cards and be able to manage this situation at our discretion. Their satellite is geosynchronous, so it'll be up at twenty-two to twenty-three thousand miles where nobody will notice if it blows up."

Several of the president's advisors nodded their heads in agreement. "If we can prevent the majority of the public from seeing the shield firsthand, it won't take long for us to propagandize this thing into an Area Fifty-One rat hole."

"Is anyone else uncomfortable with this conversation? The university has video footage that's pretty damning for the FBI. How can we possibly manage that—and should we even try to? The minute we step over the line and attempt to suppress the freedom of speech we risk starting a war," said General Sacket.

President Buchman shrugged. "Maybe we just explain the situation about the assassin going after Dr. Ford, admit we screwed up, and fire the FBI agent who overreacted."

Several people in the room were skeptical. "There are too many well-respected students and professors that witnessed and understand the success of Dr. Ford's technology. How can we possibly manage the opinions of so many people?"

"That's a tough one," said the Vice President. "About all we can do is suppress Dr. Ford's technology legally, like we have with nuclear power, automatic weapons, and a hundred other disruptive technologies until we figure out what to do with it."

President Buchman could feel the consensus building. "Better yet, we would assure everyone involved with Dr. Ford's research that we also believe it's in the best interest of the United States to roll it out, but in a moderated and controlled time frame."

Half the people in the room agreed—Secretary Jacobs foremost among them. "Maybe it's as simple as creating a contract with Dr. Ford and the University of Southern Texas that states how we intend to regulate this technology. We've done this with other technologies that have come out of the university, so it won't be a new concept for them. In the meantime, we'll figure out how the United States can be the first country to wean itself from foreign oil."

"What about the shield technology?" asked one of the military chiefs. "Clearly it cannot be allowed to get into the wrong hands?" In the right hands, it would go a long way towards promoting peace in the world and keeping our soldiers out of harm's way."

"The good news is they've kept it a secret and haven't shared it with anybody, so it'll be somewhat easier to contain."

"The bad news is they won't give it up without a fight," said President Buchman.

"We can always offer to pay for it," said an advisor.

General Allen, the Commandant of the Marine Corp, had gone thirty minutes without saying anything. "For over two hundred years, the government has limited or outlawed technologies in the best interest of the public's health and security. This shield technology is no different, and the university will have to get over it. It's just like the lasers they use to protect their satellites from space junk. Federal regulations define exactly how their lasers can and cannot be used. We could do the same thing with the shield technology. We let them keep the shield for hurricane, tsunami, and tornado protection and nothing else, and we leverage it to maintain our technological dominance in the world."

"I think you are onto something there," said the President. He could see that there was sufficient momentum in the room to get a unanimous vote to bring down the university's shield satellite, so he pushed in that direction. "I like your idea of bringing down the shield satellite," he said, turning towards Secretary Jacobs, "but can it be done quickly, and without the university mounting some kind of defense?"

The generals and admirals at the table looked at each other and shrugged. "When they built the shield satellite, they had no reason to build in any defense mechanisms."

"That makes sense," said President Buchman, "but what if they do have a defensive element built in to the system? For example, could the lasers they use to destroy space junk be used as a weapon?"

"Not if they followed the specifications that were approved by the Department of Defense. They've never breached a contract with us yet and there is no reason they would have on this project. Besides, it would've cost them hundreds of millions of dollars to bring their lasers up to weapons grade. I think we can safely assume that their lasers are only capable of short-range bursts on very small objects."

Admiral Sorensen raised his hand, indicating he had something to add. "Our satellites, outer-atmosphere fighters, and ground-to-air missile sites have the most advanced weapons and technology available, and it would've been impossible for the university to prepare a defense against them. We should be able to take their shield satellite down with little to no problems. As much as I like President Kane, taking the shield off the table is the only way we'll be able to negotiate objectively; otherwise, they hold all the cards."

President Buchman decided to strike while the iron was hot. "Is there anyone opposed to mounting a major offensive against the university's shield satellite?"

Every on except General Sacket shook their heads affirmatively, and President Buchman was satisfied.

"How close is our nearest armed satellite to the target?"

A faint smile tugged at the corners of the Director of National Intelligence's mouth. "We can be within comfortable weapons range in fifteen minutes, sir."

President Buchman raised his eyebrows. "In fifteen minutes?"

"I had my boys move our bird into position the minute the shield went up. Technically we are within weapons range now, but we'll be more confident once we match the speed of their geosynchronous orbit. We don't need the distraction of other satellites flying between us and our target."

"It looks like we are all in agreement then," said the President looking around the room at the men and women sitting at the table. "Unless I'm mistaken, anything we do at twenty-three thousand miles won't be visible to the general public or the naked eye— correct?"

The Joint Chiefs confirmed the President's assumption. "Let's knock their bird out of the sky and then give President Kane a call to see if his position has softened. Fire whatever we have at the thing, and don't hold back!"

Chapter Thirty-Six

"Skirmish"

President Kane was near exhaustion and couldn't wait for the general board meeting so he could share the burden of the decisions he'd made during the last few hours.

His thoughts were interrupted by the buzzing of his radio. He unclipped it and put it to his ear. "Hello?"

It was Justin, and he sounded alarmed. "You're not going to believe this... We're still tracking that US Armed Forces satellite and it is closing in on our position. It's been in weapons range for a while, but it's being maneuvered so it matches our orbit."

President Kane's shoulders sagged. "If they breach the International Institute of Space Satellite Law's proximity parameters, blow them out of the sky."

"They crossed that line several minutes ago."

"Damn them," said Kane. "They're not going to give me time to meet with the general board." He raised his eyes to stare at the ceiling. "I've done everything I can to avoid this."

"What was that?"

"Nothing," said Kane. "Can they damage or destroy our satellite?"

"We don't think so, but we haven't done extensive testing using DARPA's HEM, THEL, or EMP technologies."

"What?"

"The Department of Defense has a project that's evolved into an organization, called DARPA. If I remember right, it stands for Defense Advanced Research Projects Agency. They've been messing around with Magneto Hydrodynamic Explosive Munitions, Tactical High-Energy Lasers, Electromagnetic Pulses and other technologies for a while. I'm a little concerned they might throw some of unknown technology at us."

"I didn't think anyone had weapons grade lasers except us."

"I'm not sure they're equipped with any of the weapons I just mentioned, but I know they've been working on them for years. All I'm saying is that we aren't entirely sure what kind of armaments their satellites have, but since it's the United States

Government we're talking about, we should be prepared for anything."

President Kane had already started to walk towards the command center. "Have we tested the shield and satellite against an EMP burst?"

"Only a non-nuclear one."

"Aren't they the same?"

"Kind of," said Justin, "but we don't know how much explosive power they'll throw at us. If they fire on us, should we disable the satellite or destroy it?"

"We can't risk having them damage our satellite, or we'll lose all our negotiation power. They've already broken several satellite treaty laws so we are well-within our right to defend ourselves. For all we know, they may have lost control of their satellite and it's on a collision course with ours."

"Right..." said Justin sarcastically.

President Kane had a feeling of impending doom in the pit of his stomach, so he picked up his pace and jogged in the direction of the command center. The exhaustion he'd been feeling earlier was replaced by another surge of adrenaline.

He was surprised that President Buchman had decided to take such an aggressive position. *He must be confident he can bring down our satellite,* he thought to himself. *He must think he can and do it without creating a public outcry. Maybe he does have technologies that we don't know about.*

He entered the command center just in time to hear Justin give the instruction to fire. The giant screens in the room lit up as a US military satellite exploded into a thousand pieces.

President Kane's eyes widened in shock, as did everyone else's in the command center. "What happened?"

"They fired on us!" said Justin, "and it appears that the shield took the hit without any problem."

"What did they use?"

"They hit us with an EMP and then battered the shield satellite with several thousand rounds from a rail gun."

President Kane stared at the giant screens in the command center and watched as pieces of the Armed Force satellite hit the shield and were obliterated. Several larger pieces of debris hit the shield and slid rapidly into the atmosphere.

President Kane looked surprised. "That's weird. Did we shoot down their satellite or did it hit the shield?"

"When we returned fire it must have altered the orbit of the satellite because a lot of the debris is hitting the shield."

"Why doesn't the large debris disintegrate when it hits the shield?"

Justin shrugged his shoulders, "That is a question for Dr. Tate."

President Kane grimaced. "Our shield seems to be attracting the debris. I guess I have a couple of questions for Dr. Tate."

Up on the second tier of the command center, they could see Dr. Tate staring at the images on the monitors. "Dr. Tate, is it my imagination or is some of the debris being attracted to the shield?"

He shook his head. "I don't know for certain, but I'll get back to you when we have a theory."

President Kane looked worried. "Could any of it make it through the atmosphere?"

"Not unless it was a huge piece of debris."

President Kane watched as several larger pieces of debris slid into the atmosphere, turning red, then catching fire as they gathered speed. "I'd like to see all the footage of the attack so I can reference it when President Buchman calls. Would you mind rolling the video back so I can see it on one of the monitors?"

Justin directed a technician to roll the recording back to a few minutes before the attack had begun. The monitor went black, then lit up and played back the attack in crystal-clear detail.

President Kane shook his head in amazement. "What are they thinking?"

"I'm not sure. We've done nothing to provoke such an aggressive response. They must really be scared."

"I've been trying to put myself in President Buchman's shoes all morning. If I were him, I'd be sorely tempted to try and disable the shield without the public's knowledge so I could get my hands on both Dr. Ford's and the shield technology. At the very least, I'd want to shut down the shield so the university couldn't use it to bargain with."

"Explain." said Justin.

"Well, if I could get the shield down before the public actually sees it; I could discredit the shield technology, which would give me time to draw up legislation that would make the use of such technology illegal. Then I'd apologize for a month of Sundays about Dr. Summersten's death, and come up with a hundred reasons why I had probable cause to come on campus looking for Dr. Ford. Then I'd draw up some kind of complicated contract stating how and when I would release Dr. Ford's technology. As long as it was complicated enough, the scientists that worked on the project wouldn't feel like I was suppressing it."

"Interesting."

President Kane started to say something else when a huge explosion rocked the command center.

"What was that?" shouted Justin.

"A large piece of satellite debris slid down the shield into a couple of parked cars about a quarter mile from the south entrance," responded a satellite jockey.

"It should have taken longer than that," said Dr. Tate.

"Did anyone get hurt?"

"No," said the satellite jockey, "but it is bound to attract some attention."

What next... thought President Kane to himself. He looked over at one of the members of the security team. "Get the license plates of those two cars and call the owners right away. Tell them we're working on our shield technology and there was an accident. Assure them that we'll replace their vehicles with new ones. How long will it take us to clean up that debris?"

"Not long," responded the security guard. "We can have it cleaned up in a few minutes."

"Perfect," said President Kane. "We might even be able to learn a little about our shield technology if we have a chance to examine the debris."

Justin made eye contact with his man before he left the command center. "The FBI may try and stop you, so throw some cable on that debris and pull it under the shield as quickly as you can."

"It may have enough contaminants on it that we won't be able to get it back through the shield," replied the man.

"They may have burned off coming through the atmosphere, so let's give it a try." The man nodded and left the command center at a run.

President Kane didn't know what to think. "Are we prepared for anything else they might throw at us? Didn't you say the Army, Air Force, and Navy have anti-satellite munitions in the air and on the ground?"

"They do," said Justin, "but we should be able to detect them when they are airborne."

"Good," said President Kane. "Destroy anything you think is directed at us, as soon as it is launched."

All eyes in the Situation Room were glued to the monitor as the command was given to fire on the university's satellite. The Joint Chiefs were confident that several EMP bursts would be all that was required to knock out the shield satellite, but they decided to throw several thousand rounds from a DARPA's MAHEM at it for good measure. DARPA's MAHEM hadn't been tested against a live satellite before, but the data they'd gathered from other tests suggested it would be lethal.

The EMP bursts and the salvos from the DARPA's MAHEM hit the shield protecting the satellite repeatedly, one after another, for over a minute.

A few seconds after the volley ended, the military's hundred-and-fifty-million-dollar, class-one satellite exploded in a ball of fire.

Most of the debris incinerated, then disappeared, but several larger pieces burned like comets in the early morning sky. One large chunk of satellite debris made it through the atmosphere and slammed into a couple of cars, parked at the base of the shield. Smoke swirled around the smoldering cars, exposing the nearly transparent silhouette of the shield.

Many of the men and women in the Situation Room were seasoned veterans of war, yet none of them had ever seen anything close to what they had just witnessed. Not a single eye left the two hundred inch monitor until the last piece of debris disintegrated into the atmosphere.

President Buchman's heart almost stopped. He'd allowed the confidence of his Joint Chiefs to minimize his personal trepidations about the attack to the point where he'd convinced himself that failure was impossible. It took him a minute to regain his composure.

"How did they do that?" he rasped, barely able to speak. "What destroyed our satellite?"

General Lawson, the Air Force Chief of Staff, motioned for the recording to be played back.

Everyone watched as the Class One Military Satellite turned to face its target.

"Slow it down," said General Lawson.

Nothing obvious seemed to happen, yet the Class One Satellite blew into a thousand pieces.

"Play it again," said General Lawson. The recording started to play again. "Stop! Look, here," he said, pointing his laser pen at a beam of light coming from the university's satellite.

Everyone leaned forward in their chairs, trying to see what he was talking about.

"I see it," said the Vice President.

"What is it?" several people asked at once.

"It's a laser weapon of some sort," said General Lawson.

"I thought you said their lasers were equivalent to squirt guns," said President Buchman, rising from his chair. "Does anyone else have any brilliant ideas?" He felt nauseated.

General Allen of the Marine Corps cleared his throat. "Since we've committed to this course of action, perhaps we should try bringing their satellite down using technology that has been used for this purpose before. I recommend we hit them with a barrage of surface-to-air SM-IVs and a few SM-Vs if they're available."

"That's a good idea," said General Lawson. "I'll scramble a couple of X-38c OTVs equipped with our latest laser technology and we'll see how their shield handles it."

"How long will it take?" asked the President, looking at his Joint Chiefs.

"Twenty minutes or less," responded General Lawson. Admiral Sorensen nodded his head in support.

The president gave his approval, and the room fell silent, except for those who were giving orders on their smart phones.

Secretary Jacobs fidgeted with a sheet of paper in front of him, then crumpled it into a ball. "Mr. President, ah... we have some weapons that not everyone in this room has the security clearance to know about."

President Buchman shook his head. "Let's wait and see if our SM-IVs, Vs and X-38cs do the trick first."

Secretary Jacobs grimaced. "If you think we have time."

For a second, the President had forgotten that he was out of time. "How long will it take your boys to be ready to deploy?"

"Thirty minutes or so, sir."

President Buchman tilted his head indecisively. The weapons the Secretary was referring to were the modified ICBM Patriot Missiles and a series of nano-satellite robots that could attach themselves to a satellite in orbit and destroy it by physically cutting into its circuitry or by detonating an onboard explosive. The President was reluctant to use the new technology for fear of starting another arms race, but he felt like he had no choice. "Have both weapons ready to deploy in half an hour."

President Buchman turned and addressed everyone else in the room. "Some of you don't have high enough security clearance to know about our OTV lasers and nano-technologies. I shouldn't have to remind you that these technologies are classified as 'top secret.'

....

The students and faculty working in the university's command center didn't know if they should feel ecstatic or stunned. On the one hand, they had successfully defended the university's private property and constitutional rights, yet on the other hand, they'd just shot down one of their own country's military satellites.

There was no time to analyze the mix of emotions, however, because the radar monitors started to beep, and several red dots came into view, moving in the direction of the university's satellite.

"It appears that we have incoming surface-to-air missiles! Looks like they're SM IVs and SM-Vs."

"Put them on the screen," said President Kane. "Can we pinpoint and destroy them?"

"That won't be a problem."

"Let them get within a thousand miles, then knock them down."

Dr. Tate looked over the balcony. "Why wait?"

"The closer we let them get, the less chance their debris will damage neighboring satellites. We'll need all the allies we can get when this is over."

"Two more blips have appeared on the screen," said a young man from the command center floor.

"They're flying a lot slower than the missiles, so they must be OTVs."

Justin glanced at President Kane. "We believe the Air Force has several Orbit Test Vehicles that are equipped with weapons-grade laser technology. We know so little about them that I'm hesitant to let them within ten thousand miles of our bird. We have no idea how the shield will react to their lasers, and I don't want to find out today. In tests we ran last year, a variety of lasers just bounced off the shield, but we don't know how these OTVs are equipped."

Kane didn't have any suggestions. "As soon as you think they're a threat to our satellite, shoot them down, but try and destroy any debris they create so it doesn't damage other satellites."

Justin walked over to President Kane so he could have a private conversation. "The Feds have both surface-to-air and air-to-air launch platforms. Do you want to take out the delivery platforms that fired on us?"

President Kane instantly understood where Justin was headed. He wanted to destroy the launch capability that was being used against them, but was worried about killing innocent people doing it.

"Let's be very creative on how we disable any missile launch sites where we know there are armed force and civilian personnel. If we're careful, we can pinpoint and disable the platforms without doing any harm to the people who work there."

Justin agreed. "Then what would you like to do with the USS Zumwalt? All the SM-Missiles that were launched at us originated from her."

"Can you disable her radar system without doing damage to anything else?"

"If it's exposed on the exterior of the warship, it shouldn't be a problem."

"Let's do it. If that doesn't send a strong message to Buchman, nothing will."

Justin looked doubtful. "We might have been better off letting the FBI storm the campus. This feels too much like a war for my liking, and it's nowhere in my job description."

"If we'd allowed the FBI on campus, more than one person would've been injured or killed, and who knows what they'd have done with Dr. Ford and her technology. I highly doubt they would have encouraged her to make her discovery public. I'm even a little concerned about what they intend to do with our shield technology. I don't think they'll let us keep it after today," said President Kane tiredly.

They stood on the balcony and talked about various strategies that they could use for a myriad of scenarios.

A shout from the floor interrupted their conversation. "We have ten bogies closing in on ten thousand miles, and two others a few minutes behind."

"Let's take them out before they get any closer."

"Targeting ten bogies headed for our shield satellite," said the man on the floor, to be sure he'd understood Justin's order. "Eight appear to be SM-III and IV missiles and the other two are the newer OTVs."

Justin nodded. "Take them out." The man set the shield satellite's laser to target each of the bogies and fired a single three-second burst.

The images of the SM-Missiles sharpened on the giant monitors before they each exploded.

"This is not how I wanted to test our laser technology," said a grim-faced President Kane. They waited and watched as the two OTVs approached the invisible ten-thousand-mile barrier.

"The OTV's are closing in on the ten-thousand-mile mark," said the man on the floor. The monitors showed the two unmanned vehicles as they cruised in tandem towards their target. As they approached the ten-thousand-mile mark, they split and headed in different directions, as if they intended to attack the shield satellite from two different angles. The shield satellite's tracking system picked up the evasive maneuver without any difficulty and fired at the closest OTV. A three-second laser burst hit the OTV's propellant tanks and it erupted into a massive ball of fire, then disintegrated into a thousand pieces. The second OTV didn't explode from the first laser burst, but destabilized and ran headlong into the shield. The second it made contact with the shield, it burst into flames, sending several large pieces of shrapnel spinning off into space.

Justin looked up at Dr. Tate. "Excellent work! Can we destroy all of the debris the missiles and the OTVs left behind?"

"You bet," said Dr. Tate, who then proceeded to give the order. In an impressive series of laser bursts, the laser targeting system fired on any debris bigger than a pencil eraser. The sky around the satellite lit up like a planetarium show for several minutes, until every piece of OTV and missile debris was vaporized.

It was impossible for anyone to tear their eyes away from the giant monitor until the last fragment was destroyed and the laser stopped firing. The command center had never been so charged with emotion. The students and staff looked at each other, silently trying to process what they had just seen.

President Kane broke the tension by waving at Dr. Tate to get his attention. "How long can we maintain the shield if we have to fire our laser cannons at this rate?" Tate's head disappeared over the side of the balcony, and he typed furiously on his keyboard. Two minutes later he emerged. "If we have to keep the shield up and we fire 24/7 at our current rate, we'll have enough power for two or three months. We can go a little longer if we pick up some hydrogen in the scoop, refuel, or lower the shields."

Both President Kane and Justin shrugged.

"I hope this conflict resolves itself in a couple of weeks," said President Kane.

"I was hoping in couple of days," countered Woodward.

....

The Joint Chiefs and the President sat helplessly as they watched several billion dollars-worth of technology destroyed. Admiral Sorensen's phone started to buzz, and he answered it. It was the commanding officer of the USS Zumwalt, who described how a laser had destroyed their Spy-6 radar equipment with pinpoint accuracy without doing harm to any other systems or personnel.

"Can you tell where the shots originated from?"

"From the air, sir. We think they came from either a UAV or a manned aircraft."

"Did you pick up anything on radar?"

"Not a thing, sir."

"How long will it take to repair?"

"We'll have to dock to repair her, sir."

"Bring her in and get her repaired. When you get more information on the attack, send me a detailed damage report, and classify it for my eyes only."

"You don't seem too alarmed, sir."

"I'm alarmed, but I think I know who did it and why. I'll bring you up to speed in the next couple of hours."

Everyone in the Situation Room was looking at Admiral Sorensen when he hung up the phone. "I think the university is trying to send us a message. Unless I'm mistaken, they are responsible for taking out the SPY-6 radar system on the USS Zumwalt."

"I hope you're kidding," said President Buchman, "because that's an act of war."

Admiral Sorensen snorted. "Indeed. Unfortunately, we fired the first dozen shots, didn't we…"

President Buchman had never been so agitated in his life. "What are we going to do about this damn shield? Don't we have anything that can bring it down?"

"We haven't tried anything nuclear," suggested the General Lawson.

President Buchman rolled his eyes. "Our EMP blast didn't bring it down, so what makes you think a nuclear warhead will?"

"There's a big difference between the EMP blast we tried earlier and the blast that would originate from a series of nuclear warheads."

"Have we forgotten what happened last time we tried that in the outer atmosphere? Hell, I'm still worried the general public is going to unravel those records and sue us," said Buchman, his voice trailing off.

Another staff sergeant entered the room. He saluted and waited to be asked to speak.

"What is it, sergeant?"

"The shield is expanding."

"What do you mean?

"It's expanded a foot since they deployed it, sir."

"You've got to be kidding me," said President Buchman incredulously.

"If it continues to expand at this rate, it will expand about twenty feet an hour, which is about four inches a minute."

The sergeant's news was met with silence and stares.

"There is one more thing, sir. The shield appears to be repelling people with low G-Scores, as well as anything else that consists of dangerous or harmful elements and compounds."

"I thought President Kane was kidding about that," responded the President dubiously.

"No, sir, we don't know how they did it, but they built their goofy personality and character measurements into the shield's filter," responded the sergeant with disdain.

"That," said President Buchman, referring to the sergeant's sarcastic tone, "is precisely the intellectually arrogant bullshit I was referring to earlier. Up until today, the University of Southern Texas has never done anything even remotely offensive, illegal, or edgy. Apparently their personality and character measurements have been successful, or they wouldn't be kicking our butts and wiping the floor with us!"

The sergeant reddened. "I don't like the idea of a machine determining whether I'm a decent person or not."

President Buchman hesitated and almost didn't respond to the sergeant, but after reading the looks on a few people's faces, he concluded that a strong response might be necessary. "Why not? If a machine can tell you when your blood sugar is high, or when you have a bacterial infection, or if you have cancer, then why would you be offended by a technology that can determine if you are a jackass or not?" The sergeant looked like he wished he would have kept his mouth shut. "Besides, it's only programmed to filter out the most base and fundamental character flaws like one would expect to find in liars, murderers, rapists, child abusers, thieves, white-collar criminals, drug addicts, overly aggressive people, and the likes, right?" The sergeant nodded.

"Not a lot of people will be getting through the shield then," mumbled someone at the table.

President Buchman shrugged. "Do we know why it repelled our FBI agents, sergeant?"

"Well sir," said the sergeant, "the shield G-Score filter is set high enough to repel anyone who is overly aggressive, as you pointed out, and most FBI agents fit that description by design.

"What did you mean earlier when you said the shield is repelling anything that is dangerous or harmful?" asked one of the advisors.

"The shield is repelling any man-made or naturally occurring chemicals and compounds that are potentially dangerous, sir."

"What the does that mean?" asked one of the Joint Chiefs. "How is it doing that?"

"It appears that the shield has been programmed to block a list of potentially harmful compounds and objects like handguns, combat knives, plutonium, cyanide, and uranium. Some viruses and bacteria are getting through, but others are not. We're not entirely sure what the filter list is yet."

The sergeant paused and looked around the table to see if anyone else had questions.

"It also means that anything that is on the shield's filter list is literally being pushed out of the way at a rate of twenty feet an hour. This phenomenon is impossible to appreciate unless you see it, so I've brought some footage to show you.

President Buchman raised his hand towards the monitor. "Let's see it."

The sergeant punched a few buttons on the control panel and the monitor came to life. The image on the screen showed an almost invisible force pushing an M-4 rifle along the ground until it came to a cement wall. When the M-4 hit the wall it was smashed into a wafer-thin piece of metal, then vaporized into a pile of dust.

"That's not possible!" exclaimed one of the Joint Chiefs, "Did I just see what I thought I saw?"

The sergeant paused the recording so he could explain. "I'm not sure what you thought you saw, sir, but the shield repels dangerous or undesirable objects unless they are pushed up against something that is allowed through the shield. When this happens, the object that is being repelled is reduced to its base elements or pushed through the object that is allowed through the shield."

"That's a problem," said Admiral Sorensen.

"I'll say," agreed General Sacket. "So... what would have happened if a human being with a low G-Score had been trapped against that cement wall?"

"The same thing, sir, the person would have been reduced to the sixty-or-so chemical elements that make up the human body. In other words, they would end up as a pile of carbon and vapor."

"There are a couple more things you should see," said the sergeant as he fiddled with the buttons on the remote control. The screen flickered again and came into focus on an FBI agent with his back against the shield, slowly being pushed along the ground. Everyone stared at the screen with fascination.

The sergeant paused the recording. "Mr. President, I have one more thing to show you." President Buchman motioned for the sergeant to run

Defiance

the clip. "Sir, one of our FBI agents can walk through the shield."

"What?"

"Finding people who can get through the shield won't be too hard," said the sergeant. We estimate that between twenty to twenty-five percent of the United States population could get through the shield at its current configuration, so long as they aren't carrying something the shield rejects."

President Buchman looked hopeful. "Who is he?" he asked, pointing at the agent on the screen who'd just walked through the shield.

"The agent's name is Cherrington and he's been through a couple of times, just to check out how it feels. The problem is that anyone who can get through the shield isn't aggressive enough or willing to do any harm to anyone within the shield."

"How is that possible? He's an agent that carries out the orders he's given, isn't he?"

"People like Agent Cherrington don't have a mean bone in their body. They also require a lot of explanation, and have to really believe in a cause before they'll act aggressively. And even if we could get a bunch of them inside the shield, we would not be able to arm them. Without some kind of weapon, they would be at the mercy of the drones that knocked out our people earlier."

"If someone were to get through the shield who believed in what we are trying to accomplish, they could make their own weapon once they were inside if need be. What does Agent Cherrington do for us?" asked the President.

"He's part of our satellite team," responded the sergeant.

"Has anyone else been tested?"

"Yes, sir, we are in the process of testing more agents as we speak." The sergeant replayed the clip of Cherrington walking through the shield.

"What did he say it felt like?"

"He said it felt like nothing he had ever experienced before. The closest thing he could compare it to was walking through a waterfall without getting wet."

The president couldn't help feeling impressed.

"Let's get all our agents tested so we know what our options are."

"Yes, sir."

"Anything, else, sergeant?"

"No, sir."

"Let us know the instant there is more intel on this thing."

"Yes, sir," said the sergeant, saluting before he left the room.

"It will be interesting to see if President Kane throws the Constitution at us again, since he's now encroaching on private property," said one of the chiefs.

"He will," responded General Sacket, "since we caused the malfunction."

President Buchman looked around the room. "If we are going to get that shield down we'd better do it in the next few minutes."

"

Chapter Thirty-Seven

"Justification"

President Kane and Justin made their way down the busy hallway to the conference room. "This is not a good time to be yanking my chain," said President Kane.

Justin shook his head, "I wish I were, but unfortunately I'm not. The shield is expanding at a rate of about twenty feet an hour."

"Twenty feet an hour?" President Kane did some rough calculations in his head and frowned. "What's causing the problem?"

"Engineering is telling me there's a malfunction in the shield radius controller, so the problem appears to be mechanical, and not software-related. We think the EMP blast may have jarred something loose."

President Kane looked extremely agitated. "How do we fix it?"

"The faulty controller will have to be replaced manually or by remote control," responded Justin.

"Are those our only options?"

"We could send up a replacement satellite," said Justin, "but I'm not sure how long it would take to deploy."

"Find out," said Kane. "How long would it take to get a remote-controlled repair droid in the air?"

"About three to five days."

"Let's get the facts so we know exactly what our options are. It wouldn't hurt to start prepping a replacement satellite and a remote-controlled droid right now, don't you think?"

"Yes. It would be foolish not to."

President Kane stopped just before he entered the boardroom. "Did we notify the coast guard, port authority, and oil companies that have rigs in the Gulf that might be affected by the shield?"

"One or two of the motorcyclists had that assignment," responded Justin, "if they got through.

"I hope the Feds have thought about the consequences of jamming our communications, because I'm going to lay any accidents people have with the shield at the government's feet when this is over. I'm afraid this malfunction is going to give President Buchman the excuse he needs to be more aggressive. He is going to be tempted to bring this war down to the street level." President Kane put his hand on the doorknob. "Is there any danger that the malfunction will affect our ability to keep the shield up?"

"No," said Justin. "In the worst-case scenario, the shield will expand to its maximum diameter of three hundred and twenty miles, but that won't affect our ability to keep it functional. Mechanically, it can't expand any farther than that. It will consume a little more power, so it may not stay up for the full two months that Dr. Tate estimated, but it will stay up long enough for us to work through our issues with the Feds."

"What would happen if we decrease the shield's orbit altitude to compensate for the expansion?"

"It will take us out of the sweet spot of geosynchronous orbit, and we would burn more fuel staying in place over Corpus Christi."

"If we can't stop the expansion, it's going to encompass all of San Antonio, Houston, and a chunk of the Gulf of Mexico!"

"That's what our calculations show," confirmed Justin.

"If we can't hack the FBIs signal-jamming software soon, we'll be forced to send out more messengers to warn people about our expanding shield and what we intend to do about it."

"I agree, but let's wait an hour or so and see where we are."

"Ok," said President Kane as he stepped into the boardroom. It resembled the Senate floor in Washington, D.C. Each of the twenty-four general board members had two desks assigned to them. The paired desks fanned out from the podium where the board president, vice president, and secretary sat, like spokes on a giant wheel. The desks were positioned in four columns, six rows deep. Behind the desks, there were several more rows of deluxe leather chairs set up in auditorium-style—enough to seat another forty eight people. These seats were often filled by subcommittee members who were scheduled to address the general board. A balcony was suspended from the ceiling and rimmed the outside walls of the room with enough seating for two hundred people.

Most board members attended meetings with their chief-of-staff, who took scrupulous notes and relayed messages to other board or subcommittee members as necessary. Today the session was closed to anyone that was not a member of the board or a chief-of-staff.

President Kane climbed the steps of the slightly elevated platform and stood behind his desk. The responsibility of his office weighed on his shoulders like a ton of bricks. He was anxious to have feedback from the board, and hoped they would support the decisions he'd made. The noise in the room gradually diminished, then ceased as members became aware of his presence.

Kane straightened his shoulders and looked out over the men and women in who had been able to attend the last minute meeting. Some members had been waylaid by the FBI, but over half of them had made it. He'd come to admire and respect each of them for their dedication, values, objectivity, and expertise. Over the years, they'd become some of his closest friends. His eyes rested on the empty desk of Dr. Conner and he had a difficult time controlling his emotions.

He walked around his desk and stood in front of the hand-carved wooden podium, which he gripped with both hands. He took a couple of deep breaths and then addressed his associates. "Several disturbing things have happened while most of you were sleeping that culminated in me deploying the campus shield. I'd like to review these events in the order that they transpired and give you an opportunity to ask questions about them. Some of the things we will be discussing were captured by our surveillance cameras, and we will make the footage available to you so you can develop an unbiased opinion on what's happened."

President Kane stood silently at the podium, waiting for the room to quiet down before he continued. "Before we get started, I need to let you know that our good friend and colleague, Dr. Conner, passed away this morning as a result of poison from a dart intended for Dr. Ann Ford." Several gasps were heard from board members who had not been privy to this information.

President Kane's voice quivered and he lowered his head, trying to keep his emotions in check. All eyes were trained on him and not one of them was dry. Dr. Conner was widely respected and loved, and his absence would leave a void. "I will cover his death in more detail a later on, so bear with me."

President Kane fought to keep his composure. His voice was calm, but firm as he started to speak again.

"Due to the seriousness of what's happened, I will spend as much time as I can to bring you fully up to speed, but keep in mind that hounds are baying at our door so we need to be as brief as possible."

He paused to take a drink from a bottle of water that that was sitting near the podium. "I've asked Drs. Ann and Jack Ford, Dan Johnson of NBC News, Dr. Ben Sellers, and Justin Woodward to join our meeting today so that you can get a well-rounded view of what has happened and so you can ask them questions directly. Justin will join us in a few minutes, after he's coordinated a few adjustments to the shield."

He paused and took another drink from the bottle of water. He had been so busy the last few hours that he'd forgotten to eat or drink. He then proceeded to recap the events that had taken place during the last couple of days. The boardroom broke out into a jumble of conversations. President Kane raised his hand in an effort to bring the room to order.

"Ladies and gentleman, I will be happy to get into more detail about Dr. Ford's research at a later time. For now, all you need to know is that we've validated her research and have developed a working model with energy efficiencies high enough to know that hydrogen will replace fossil fuels as our primary energy source within the next two years, if not sooner."

The room buzzed with conversation, and President Kane had to raise his voice to get everybody's attention. "Right now we need to focus on several urgent matters that have arisen because of this research that require our immediate attention."

The room quieted and he continued. "Since our validation of Dr. Ford's research, a series of unfortunate events have endangered Dr. Ford's life, and culminated in the deaths of Dr. Conner, Professor Summersten, and possibly Dr. Stanley George Richardson III from MIT, and his wife, Teresa."

Very few of the members had heard the about Professor Summersten and Dr. Richardson so the news was troubling. President Kane went on to explain the events that had taken place during the last seventy-two hours. His voice grew firm as he described the last few minutes of Joe Summersten and Dr. Conner's life.

"Now you understand why we felt like we were under attack this morning, and why I made the decision to deploy the shield. I wish you'd all been here to help with the decisions that were made, but we did the best we could with the information we had at the time."

A hand went up. "What are the chances that they'll come up with something that can penetrate the shield or bring it down altogether?"

"I honestly don't know, but Dr. Tate and his teams are confident that the government won't be able to bring the shield down. They've already tried using a rail gun, several EMP blasts, two OTVs, and a hand full of SM-class missiles, which, so far, have failed."

"What haven't they tried?" asked a board member.

President Kane turned to Justin. "About the only thing they haven't tried is a nuclear device, but I don't think they're that desperate," Justin answered.

"Have we returned fire?"

"As of this moment, we've been forced to shoot down one armed force satellite, two orbiting test vehicles, and eight missiles. We also fired on the destroyer, USS Zumwalt, and disabled its missile-launching capability. No significant damage was done to the destroyer, and none of her crew were harmed."

Several board members looked alarmed. "So we fired on a United States warship?" someone asked.

"After it had launched eight missiles at us, we decided it was the only thing left to do. Justin, would you mind showing a few clips that include footage of what happened?"

"Give me a second to find it," said Justin, as he sorted through the video clips he had on his laptop. He found the clip he was looking for and played it for the board. There wasn't a single board member that didn't sit wide-eyed and speechless as the surveillance video played out.

Several seconds after the clip ended, a hand went up. "President Kane, is there any precedent supporting our actions against the United States government?"

Kane shook his head. "None that I know of; however, there is no precedent for what the United States Government has perpetrated against this university either. Our legal team is coming up to speed on what has happened, and so far they believe we've acted well-within our legal rights."

A distinguished-looking gentleman raised his hand and waited to be acknowledged.

"Yes, Dr. Anhder?"

"Would you tell us a little more about your conversation with the President of the United States and his Joint Chiefs?"

"I would be happy to. Less than an hour ago I got a phone call from President Buchman, who was meeting with the Joint Chiefs, Vice President, Director of National Intelligence, Secretary of Defense, and several other cabinet and advisory members. The President asked that Dr. Ford join me on the call and she did. The President feels that the university's use of a shield to protect its constitutional rights might aggravate existing anti-federal-government sentiments to an unhealthy level. He also believes that Dr. Ford's research cannot be dumped on the market at this time without causing a global economic meltdown."

"What does he think these anti-government groups will do?" asked another professor in the room.

"I'm not exactly sure," said Kane, "but they are scared enough to jam our communication to the outside world. I got the distinct impression that he believes there are several cities and states that have been making overtures about withdrawing from the Union because the federal government is not providing the protection and benefits it once did. He and his advisors believe that our defiance might be the catalyst that pushes them over the edge."

"Are his fears founded?"

"Ironically, Texas and South Carolina are among those that are the most vocal about their dissatisfaction with the way the federal government is being run, but I don't think they would actually secede. However, the last time there was this much dissatisfaction was in 1861, and we all know what happened then."

The room went quiet for a minute as the governing board digested what they were hearing. Jack leaned over to Ann and whispered, "You sure stirred up a hornet's nest this time!"

"Hush," said Ann, squeezing his arm. "I'm trying to concentrate on what President Kane is saying..."

"I have one more confession to make," said President Kane. "My conversation with President Buchman came right after we'd lost Dr. Summersten and Dr. Conner, so I was feeling very passionate and may have overstepped my authority." The room grew quiet with anticipation. "I told the President that he'd backed us into a corner and that we were going to leverage the power the shield gave us to fire a warning shot across his bow."

President Kane had struck a chord and the board members jumped to their feet, applauding his words. Ann was on her feet before she knew it and was clapping loudly in support of what President Kane had said. Jack stood beside her doing the same.

After a minute, President Kane attempted to continue. He looked a lot calmer than when he'd first entered the room. "I cannot tell you how relieved I am that you support the course we've taken, but there is one more piece of information that I need to share with you that significantly complicates our current situation. In the last clip Justin showed you, several explosions and an EMP burst hit our shield near the proximity of the satellite itself. We think that the reverberation of these explosions may have damaged a piece of hardware on the satellite. The motor that powers the control arm has been damaged in such a way that it's allowing the shield to slowly expand. As of a few minutes ago, we have been unable to stop the expansion, and as a consequence the shield's diameter is expanding at a rate of approximately twenty feet an hour or about four inches a minute."

A dozen arms flew in the air, and with Justin's help they were able to provide answers for all the questions.

"The good news is that we have several solutions for fixing the problem and we have time to do it," said Justin.

"The bad news," interjected President Kane, "is that the federal government will use the shield's expansion as an excuse to become more aggressive towards us, since it will temporarily take away the property rights of anyone who doesn't have a high enough G-Score."

President Kane scanned the room. A few more people had questions and he was able to answer them to everyone's satisfaction.

"If there are no further questions, I would like to call for a formal vote from the general board members who are in attendance. All those in favor of leaving the shield up for the immediate future, please raise your hand."

Every hand in the room went up. "Mr. Secretary," said President Kane turning to a man sitting behind him, "let the record show that on this date, all the board members in attendance voted unanimously to leave the shield up."

President Kane turned back to face the board. "As circumstances change and more information surfaces, we may decide to lower the shield; however, until such time, it will remain in place as it is currently configured.

Kane looked around the room at all those who were present. "Are there any further questions about the shield?"

No hands were raised so President Kane continued speaking. "The last thing we need to vote on is whether or not to support Dr. Ford in releasing her technology to the world, free of government restraints or intervention. Normally we would not vote on this, but under the circumstances, I want to see how many of you support her, because our support will have a significant impact on the university."

Again, and without hesitation, every hand in the general board room rose in favor of backing Ann's research, and President Kane asked for the results of the vote to be recorded in the minutes.

"Now that you are all up-to-date on the current situation, I would like to make one thing very clear. Our shield technology must continue to improve at a rapid pace and under absolute secrecy because it's the only thing guaranteeing our constitutional rights and freedom."

"Haven't we patented the technology?"

President Kane shook his head. "Thanks to the foresight of a number of people in this room, we never did. Several of you were afraid that the patent office would create too great of a security risk for us, and you were absolutely right... thank you. In the spirit of maintaining our shield I would propose that we triple our staff in this area to improve and support it? Nobody opposed the idea.

He waited for a minute to see if there were any other questions about the events of the last seventy-two hours, the shield, or Dr. Ford's research. "If there are no further questions, there are a few things we need to take care of ASAP." He listed numerous things that needed to be addressed, from shield policy to consumables that would be imported and exported through the shield, and recruited volunteers from the general board to create committees to address these needs.

"Since hydrogen will become our primary source of energy during the next couple of months, we desperately need someone to head up a subcommittee and provide us with leadership in this area. I would like to propose that Dr. Ford fill this position if she is amenable." President Kane looked at Ann, who he'd caught a little off guard. She looked at Jack, who gave her a supportive nod. Ann nodded her head and mouthed the word, *ok.*

"It appears that Dr. Ford is ok with this suggestion, so is there someone who will second the motion?" The general board was quiet for a few seconds as they considered President Kane's proposal, then two board members who'd spent the last several hours working with Dr. Ford jumped to their feet at the same time.

"I will second the motion," they said in unison. Both grinned and sat back down.

"Well then," said President Kane with a sigh, "according to our bylaws, her appointment will go to a vote."

Ann raised her hand, but President Kane didn't notice because she was sitting so far to the right of the platform. Justin, who was sitting within President Kane's line of site, cleared his throat a couple of times until President Kane acknowledged her. "It appears that Dr. Ford has a comment."

"There is one problem with your nomination," she said, a smile tugging at the corners of her mouth. "I was not aware that someone could serve on one of your subcommittees unless they were a faculty member."

The board members looked at each other and smiled. Several of them chuckled for the first time that morning, which broke the tension in the room.

President Kane grinned and looked at Ann, "You bring up a very good point. Since you've had so much uninterrupted time to think about our offer over the last seventy-two hours, what do you say... are you in?"

"I wouldn't miss it for the world." Her new colleagues showed their approval with applause and hearty words of welcome. Ann had never felt this level of camaraderie before, and although the attention made her feel uncomfortable, she felt a sudden sense of belonging.

When the meeting was over, President Kane came over to shake Ann's hand. "We are honored to have you on board. We've made temporary living arrangements for you until we can figure out something more permanent. I'll send someone to get you when your accommodations are ready."

"Thank you for everything," said Ann. Although her heart still ached over the loss of her personal belongings in Fort Collins, she felt she could really make a new home here.

President Kane had turned to walk down the hall when Jack stopped him. "Hey, I appreciate you taking care of Ann while I was in Kuwait. You and your team may have saved her life, and I'll be forever in your debt."

"I suspect you would have done the same thing," said Kane, "if our roles had been reversed."

"Seriously, Ann is the most important person in my life and I'm profoundly grateful for all you've done for her!"

"No... thank you," responded President Kane. "We're honored to have you and your wife on our team." He slapped Jack on the shoulder and walked down the hall to the command center.

Ann and Jack found the group of board members who were assigned to write the first draft of the Shield Policy. "Before we can write any policy," one board member was saying, "We need to understand exactly how the shield works." She turned to Ann, "Dr. Ford, do you have enough knowledge about the shield to give us an overview of how it works and what its limitations and capabilities are?"

"I would be more than happy to tell you what I know," said Ann suppressing a yawn, "but I'm not nearly as knowledgeable as Justin or Dr. Tate."

She proceeded to tell them everything she could think of that was relevant about the shield. She described how the shield could be configured to allow things to pass from the inside to the outside, but still be able to restrict things coming from the outside to the inside. Twenty minutes went by in a flash, and both Jack and Ann had to fight to stay awake.

President Kane appeared in the doorway of the conference room and motioned Ann and Jack to join him. "We've found a little home just off of campus where you two can stay until you find a permanent residence. It is well-within the shield, and will be easy for our security team to keep an eye on."

"As long as it has a bed and a warm shower, it will be fine," said Ann. "Point us in the right direction and we'll walk."

"Normally that wouldn't be a problem," said Kane, "but today I would prefer that we give you a ride. What we don't need is the FBI and the CIA knowing your exact location. If you walk, they will pick you up on satellite and get a lock on you."

"I thought we were safe behind the shield," said Jack, sounding a little nervous.

"For the most part you are," said President Kane, "but until we get a count of everyone who is currently inside the shield, we won't know with confidence who we are dealing with. It is possible that the CIA, the FBI, Black Gold, or Mcorp had someone on campus before the shield went up."

"I still don't understand," said Jack.

"When we put up the shield, there was no way for us to know exactly who was already on campus. We are ninety percent done with a scan that will give us an exact count and description of everyone under the protection of the shield, but until it's complete, I would prefer to be cautious and keep a very close eye on you. We will respect your privacy as much as possible, but we need to keep several drones and a couple of security officers in your immediate vicinity until we've had a chance to analyze the scan results."

"Do they have to be in the house?" asked Jack.

"No," said Kane, "but they will be right outside your window."

President Kane looked around for the security officers he'd mentioned and spotted them coming down the hall. He waved them over to where he and the Fords were standing. "Sarah, Joe, and Lance, these are the Fords. I believe you've been briefed on why they are here and on the importance of keeping a very close eye on them until the scan results have been analyzed."

"Yes, we have. Even after the scan is complete, we'll be standing guard outside of your home and following you around campus until we are satisfied it is completely safe for you to be on your own," said Sarah.

"I'll let these guys take you to your temporary residence and I won't bother you unless something important comes up. If you need me, call me on this,"

Kane said, handing Ann a radio. If I need to get a hold of you, I'll contact you on this radio until we have our cell phone service back up and running."

"I still can't believe the Feds are jamming our communications," said Jack.

"I can't either," said President Kane. "I feel like I'm somewhere other than the United States."

They parted ways—the Ford's escorted to their new residence by three security guards and a hand full of drones and President Kane to his office, where he could have a few minutes alone.

Chapter Thirty-Eight

"Tactical Adjustments"

Marlon Hauzer had gotten his hands on some FBI intel that described the shield UST was using to repel the Feds, so he called another meeting of the Mcorp principals. Although the shield technology didn't have as much profit potential as Dr. Ford's research, he knew several of the principals would find it extremely interesting and highly valuable.

The Mcorp conference bridge was silent as the principals listened to him describe the shield and its unique filtering capabilities. Their reactions were as varied as their interests.

"Didn't the university try to use this shield technology during the last hurricane?

"They did," said Hauzer, "and we've been trying to get our hands on the technology ever since. Unfortunately, they've kept it under such tight lock-and-key, we can't get close to it. They were so paranoid about it, they didn't even patent it."

"What happened to Lunt? Could he help us get our hands on this technology?"

"We lost contact with him a couple of hours ago and haven't heard from him since."

"Is he inside the shield?"

Hauzer shrugged. "We think he made it inside; otherwise he would've contacted us to collected a paycheck."

"Can't he contact us from inside the shield?"

"No, the Feds are jamming all communication in and out of the university. If he was outside the shield right now, we would have heard from him."

"What?" chorused a dozen voices on the conference bridge.

Hauzer filled everyone in on what was known about the FBI's activities in Corpus Christi. "Apparently they don't want Ford's technology getting out any more than we do."

"Maybe the Feds found out that Ann was trying to broker a deal with the university and are trying to intervene."

"This is crazy. UST won't tolerate anyone messing with their constitutional rights, especially if it's the federal government. Before this is over, somebody is going to hang, and it might be Buchman.

I wouldn't mess with Kane over his First Amendment rights."

"I wouldn't either," echoed someone on the call. "The man is a retired four-star general."

Random questions surfaced as the Mcorp principals tried to gain a better understanding about what was going on in Texas.

"Has anyone been able to get through the shield?"

Hauzer nodded his head. "A few minutes ago, we learned that the FBI and CIA have found a handful of people, not associated with UST, who can penetrate the shield."

"Let's get someone of our own in there if Lunt's gone off the radar."

Hauzer grimaced. "That's the rub. The university has somehow incorporated their G-Score technology into the shield so there's absolutely no way we can get anyone inside who has the intent to harm, kill, or steal. We might be able to get someone in who could broker a great deal for us, though…"

"We can certainly top anything the university can offer Ford," said a woman on the call. "So, what's the plan?"

"We're still hopeful that Lunt got onto campus before the shield went up, and we're trying to find a person with a G-Score over eighty who can get through the shield and deliver an offer to Dr. Ford."

"Are we still offering a billion?"

"Yes. We think that should clinch the deal."

"What are the FBI and the CIA saying about the shield? I'll bet Buchman wet himself when he heard about it." A chuckle rippled through the room and the conference bridge.

Hauzer scowled. "Our intel is a little sketchy, but we know he's pissed as hell and committed to taking down the shield by any means necessary. Apparently he's worried that the American public will perceive UST's actions as anti-government and that it will trigger more civil unrest."

"Is he more worried about the shield or Dr. Ford's technology?"

"From what we've heard, he's worried about both technologies for different reasons. Like I said, our information is a little sketchy right now."

"Every whack job in the country is going to be attracted to that damn shield," observed a principal

"That's too bad, because Corpus Christi is a great place to live." Several people in the room agreed, then there was silence for a few seconds.

"We need to get our hands on this shield technology!"

"We tried to buy it for an ungodly amount of money, but were turned down cold. We've tried to buy off a couple of the scientists that are working on it, but they won't give us the time of day. UST's raised the level of security coverage on the people we approached, so we know they know that someone with a lot of resources is interested in it."

"There's no way the government is going to let them keep it once this is over, so we'd better figure out how to get our hands on it before they shut it down."

A heavy-set man on one of the monitors cleared his throat to speak. "Imagine what we could do with technology like that."

A lady whose company contracted with the Department of Defense spoke up. "I agree. We could build all kinds of products and services from the shield technology if we could get our hands on it."

Hauzer shook his head. "There is no way we can get close to it, so forget it. We'll have a better chance of stealing it once the government knocks out the shield and suppresses the technology. It will be much easier to get it from the Fed's than from UST."

Hauzer wrapped up the meeting. "We've agreed to send someone onto campus to make Dr. Ford an offer. We've also expressed the desire to increase our efforts to try and get our hands on the shield technology, so we'll look into that again. There's still a good chance that Lunt made it onto campus before the shield went up and will succeed in persuading Dr. Ford to work with us, or put an end to her career. Did I miss anything?"

A CEO for a group of oil refineries spoke up. "I don't feel like we are doing enough here! There are literally trillions of dollars at stake—maybe even the future of my country!"

Hauzer shrugged helplessly. "Do you have an alternate proposal? The trillion dollar technology you are speaking of is locked up behind a shield created by some of the world's best scientists and the FBI is camped around it, trying to bring it down. We sent our most capable man to either kidnap Dr. Ford or kill her. He's never failed on an initiative in twenty years and there is a good chance he is already on campus. I'm also confident we can find someone who can deliver a financial offer that Dr. Ford will find difficult to pass up."

The CEO looked perplexed. "Couldn't we at least have several agents ready and waiting to infiltrate UST if the Feds bring the shield down?"

"They are already in place," said Hauzer, "so I don't think there is much more we can do at this juncture. Don't forget we also have the NBC camera guy under our thumb and we might be able to do something there." He looked around at the participants in the meeting, and the key players gave him their approval with a hardly noticeable toss of their heads.

He closed his laptop, which signaled the end of the meeting. "You will hear from me as soon as something new develops."

....

Lunt's body twitched several times before his eyes snapped open, but he continued to breathe as if he were still unconscious. He fought the effects of the tranquilizer until he was able to remember every detail of what had happened, right up until he'd passed out.

He didn't allow himself the luxury of becoming angry or annoyed—instead he began to carefully assess his situation without revealing that he was awake. He'd been stripped of all his clothes and was dressed in some kind of jump suit. His hands were shackled behind his back, but his feet were free. *Big mistake*, he thought to himself. He flexed his right calf muscle and could feel the implant still buried beneath the skin—a serrated wire that could be used both as a file and a lock pick. He closed his eyes and began to memorize the location, voice, and mannerisms of each of his guards. In his mind, he ticked off the minutes and calculated when the guards changed duty. *Mostly volunteer students*, he mused with satisfaction. *Who was the doctor that Mcorp had blackmailed in the past? Ah yes, Dr. Thompson in the biology department. I think I'm going to have a visitor.*

Chapter Thirty-Nine

"Governor of Texas"

President Kane shut the door to his office and asked Margaret not to bother him unless the President of the United States or God called. He hadn't had his eyes closed for ten minutes when there was a panicked knock on the door. "Sir, the Governor of Texas just walked through the shield and wants to talk to you. He's pretty upset that only half of his staff and none of his bodyguards could get through."

"He's going to be even more upset when I tell him *why* they didn't make it through, isn't he? Where is he now?"

"He's in the administration building lobby."

"Perfect," said Kane, "Tell him I've been up for twenty-four hours and just got accused of being a traitor to the United States of America by its Commander-in-Chief, and that I need a nap."

Margaret smiled uncomfortably. "I think I'll let you tell him that. When would you like to see him?"

President Kane could see that Margaret was as stressed as he was. It wasn't every day that someone had to answer a phone call from the President. He breathed deeply, then smiled. "Sorry, Margaret, I'm just venting. Tell him I'll be down to see him in ten minutes. That'll give me time to clean up and put on a new shirt. Does he have a gun?"

"That's not possible, sir, unless he picked one up on the inside from one of our security detail."

"I was just kidding," said President Kane with a smile, "and easy on the 'sir' stuff!"

Margaret rolled her eyes and left the office in a hurry.

President Kane looked in the bathroom mirror. A tired, but resolute man looked back at him. He had no idea how the governor would react to what he was about to tell him. *Thank goodness I've known Faust since he was in the Senate,* he thought.

He had no time for a shower, which was what he wanted and needed, but he put on a fresh shirt, topped it off with his favorite sports coat, and headed to the lobby to greet the governor. When President Kane entered the lobby, Governor Faust rushed over to greet him and shook his hand vigorously. "How you doing, Carson? It sounds like you've had a busy day!"

President Kane shrugged his shoulders and tried to smile. "That's the understatement of the century."

Ever since they'd been introduced at a fundraiser twenty years ago, they'd enjoyed engaging in sarcastic banter. During the last few years, Governor Faust had called on President Kane and the university's political science department to consult him on a number of civic matters. This arrangement had been a raging success for both the university and the governor.

Given how the governor felt about President Kane and the university, he was alarmed with what was going on between them and the federal government. He knew the university had always been critical of the government's fiscal policies, but he couldn't imagine how things had escalated to the point they had.

"My boys have been giving me a lot of spotty information about what's been going on over here. I've heard about a shield that's repelling people and a explosion that made a crater outside of the science building. Hell, they're even telling me you might be conducting a private war in my air space, so I thought I'd better mosey on over and get it straight from the horse's mouth since the only communication I've had is through a courier." Governor Faust had always been blunt, which is one reason why he was such a popular governor.

"You're lucky you even got through the shield. Usually it can sense a politician a mile away," joked Kane.

"And you're fortunate the shield went up with you in it. Hell, you've probably got someone on the payroll jacking up your G-Score so you don't get thrown off campus," bantered the governor.

President Kane laughed, then put his arm on the governor's shoulder and steered him a few yards away from the rest of the group. "Jim, you only know the half of it. I just got off the phone with the President of the United States. He's branded me as a traitor and is threatening to go to war unless we lower the shield."

The Governor laughed loudly. "Then you're in great company. If I'm not mistaken, George Washington, Ben Franklin, John Adams, and Thomas Jefferson were all labeled as traitors, but they are spoken of quite favorably in our history books today, unless you're reading the stupid revisionist crap put out by those damn liberals. To be honest, I'm not a big fan of President Buchman either since he ran up the national debt after promising not to. So what is the deal with the shield? Half my delegation couldn't make it through the damn thing."

"If you understood why they didn't make it through you might reconsider having them as staff."

"What do you mean?"

"One of the functions of the shield is to deny access to anyone whose poor character traits outweigh their good ones.

"You're telling me that half my staff has problems?"

President Kane tilted his head and smiled. "Let's be optimistic and assume that they've all come down with something that's contagious, or they're carrying weapons that are on the shield's naughty list. If you'd like, I can tell you what kept each of them out."

"I'd like that... But, hell, I swear like a banshee and get angry sometimes, and I got through. And look at old George over there," he said, pointing to a man over his shoulder, "he's been a lawyer for thirty years and he made it through."

"You may get angry once in a while, Governor, but you are not inherently an angry or a violent person; there is a big difference." President Kane looked at George. "As for George there, I have no idea why the shield let him through; it must have a glitch."

The governor laughed. "Your shield and its people-filter is way over my head, but considering the university's reputation and all, I'll take your word that it works for you. Send me an email detailing why some of my boys didn't make it through that cock-eyed thing so I can see who I need to send over to your hospital and who I need to fire."

The governor looked around at the people who were with him so he could remember who'd made it through the shield and who had not. "Figures," he muttered to himself.

President Kane looked at him, "What was that?"

"Oh," said the governor, "I was just thinking about the folks who didn't make it through your shield. So, have you decided whether you're going to lower the shield or not?"

President Kane took a deep breath, "Come with me, and I will show why we've decided to keep it up."

He escorted Governor Faust to the command center and spent the next thirty minutes explaining how the university had gotten itself into its current predicament with the federal government. His presentation was a shortened version of the one he'd given the general board. The governor and his staff asked dozens of questions and took pages of notes. President Kane decided to come clean about Dr. Ford's breakthrough, and spent an hour explaining how it would affect federal tax revenue, oil profits, and the state of Texas. At the end of Kane's explanation, the Governor looked satisfied.

"I think I get the picture now. Can we get a copy containing the footage you've shown us and a snippet of Dan Johnson's interview with Dr. Ford

Justin looked at President Kane, who nodded. Governor Faust turned back to President Kane and grinned. "Nice move on that FBI agent! You're lucky he didn't shoot you!" The governor put his hand on President Kane's shoulder, "Would you mind if we had a word in private?"

"Sure." President Kane instructed Justin to answer any questions the governor's staff might have and to give them access to all the video they required, then he jerked his head in the direction of his office. "Let's chat in my office."

When they were out of earshot, President Kane turned to the governor. "What would you like to discuss?"

"I'll cut right the chase, Carson. Over the last several years there have been a growing number of very influential people in Texas who are sick and tired of getting no bang for their buck from the federal government. They're fed up with the incompetence and corruption, and frankly, just pissed off about the misuse of their tax dollars. I've got a petition on my desk right now signed by five million of the good ol' boys, you know, the ones with all the money, and they're telling me that they don't want to pay any more federal taxes until the government has convincing control of its budget problems! They've even made a list of all the bullshit government agencies and projects that are flushing our money down the toilet and you wouldn't believe what's on the list! Hell, I didn't believe it at first, so I had my people validate the list. Guess what they found out?"

"What?"

"That they'd missed a couple hundred other ridiculous research projects the government has been funding!"

President Kane was a little surprised at how passionate the Governor was. "Five million influential people? That's a lot of people..."

"I know. Imagine what the number will be if the good ol' boys decide to educate the rest of the population on what's going on. What am I going to do if they stop paying taxes? Build a prison big enough to hold them all? I might have to put barbed wire around the entire state of Texas!"

Kane raised his eyebrows and whistled. How serious are they?"

The governor shifted uneasily. "They're dead damn serious! Most of them feel like their voices are not being heard and they want the state of Texas to make a statement."

"Are they serious enough to actually stop paying taxes?"

"No, they're not that mad, but they are getting damn close. They estimate that the government could easily cut trillions of dollars from its yearly expenditures and still be fat."

President Kane look surprised. "Their estimates are in line with what our political science department is coming up with."

The governor nodded his head thoughtfully. "I know that five million petitioners don't represent all thirty million people living in the state of Texas, but it's a pretty damn good sample of what everyone else is thinking, including me."

"So what does this have to do with the university, Jim?"

The governor wavered a little and Kane could see he was hesitant to come right out and say what he was thinking, which wasn't like him.

"Well... Now that you've confessed what's going on up at your twenty-three-thousand-mile Alamo, I want to know if it's going to be a repeat of 1836, or if you'll be able to hold off the Feds for longer than thirteen days."

President Kane didn't even flinch. "I just told the President that I am going to leave the shield up until he cleans up his mess. The only other way it's coming down is if they outsmart us technologically."

"How long do you figure you can hold them off?"

"We figure we can hold them off for at least two months, and maybe three. Since we engineered half of what they are firing at us, we're confident we can keep improving the shield technology and stay ahead of them indefinitely."

"I think you can too," said the governor. He paused and turned towards the window where he could see the giant American flag catching the full rays of the morning sun. "Do you support and uphold all the documents that are at the base of that flag, Carson?"

"You know I do," responded President Kane, a little annoyed at the question. "What kind of question is that?"

"What about the general board and the rest of the university?"

"The Constitution is core to our university policy and belief system."

"Then let your shield expand until it covers the entire state of Texas."

The governor's suggestion caught President Kane entirely off guard, and he was too tired to try and hide his surprise. "But what about all the people who would be displaced?"

"If our calculations are correct, your shield is expanding slowly enough that we'll have time to talk about that in the next couple of days. You're willing to help compensate anyone who is displaced, right?"

"Of course."

"Then we can work something out. Do you have a satellite with a backup shield?"

"Not in the air."

"Then I would strongly recommend you get it in the air before the air space around the university is swarming with F-22 II Raptors, 'cause I've got a feeling this little incident of yours is going to get real messy," said the governor thoughtfully. "You know, if you had a couple of shields going at the same time—one within the other—you could make the G-Score settings on the outer shield less stringent and displace a whole lot less people."

President Kane thought for a moment, then smiled hopefully. "That's not a bad idea."

"Don't look so surprised—even a politician can have a good idea once in a while. And don't forget that *this* politician got through your shield." The governor looked out the window again. "I'm not exactly certain how all this is going to shake out, but there's one thing I'm damn certain of and that is the United States Government has reached a point where it's completely impotent and incompetent. Don't get me wrong, I believe that we need a federal government, but we need one that has some clout, some integrity and leadership talent, that's run by people with a backbone."

President Kane looked a little confused. "I'm not exactly sure what you are suggesting, Jim."

"I'm saying that I support you putting a few more of your shield satellites in space, and I support your defiance of the federal government, but I'm going to sit back for the first thirteen days of your siege and see if you really can hold your own against the Feds. I'll refuse to help President Buchman if he asks, but I won't fully back you until you've proven you can keep Santa Ana out of the fort."

President Kane looked hopeful. "Thanks, I think. While you're waiting, do us a favor and evacuate anyone who is in the way of the expanding shield. I'm worried that it might injure someone or that more debris from our private war might slide down the shield and kill someone. For now, the story is that we have a malfunctioning storm shield that we're trying to get under control and we will compensate anyone that sustains damage because of it."

"That I can do," said the governor. "There is one more thing that might put a kink in my support."

"What's that?"

"The oil industry supports hundreds of thousands of jobs in Texas and is a major source of our state tax revenue. The primary reason the state of Texas is not bankrupt like everyone else is because of the huge oil revenues we've been collecting. Over twenty-three percent of the oil produced in the US comes from Texas, so Dr. Ford's little breakthrough is literally going to kill us. And since she is hell-bent on giving it away, I will need you to give the state of Texas special consideration when you release this technology."

President Kane grinned. "You are a consummate politician! I guess you want to buy futures from me as well. What exactly are you suggesting?"

"I'm thinking this breakthrough of Dr. Ford's would've happened sooner or later, no matter what— it's just the next step in our energy evolution. I believe I can sell this fact to the people of Texas if you promise to dedicate a significant amount of intellectual capital towards helping your home state excel at hydrogen production beyond anyone else in the world. I'd need your personal guarantee that you will assist us in making Texas the "Saudi Arabia" of hydrogen production. If this state were to advance more rapidly in hydrogen expertise than anyone else, we may not lose a bit of our hard-earned revenue. If you can deliver on that, I think I can sell it."

President Kane eyed the governor for a minute. "I'd have to run it by Dr. Ford and the board, but I'm pretty sure they'd go for it as long as the base technology is given to anyone in the world who wants it."

"We don't want to control the technology," said the governor. "We want to be the best in the world at using it."

President Kane smiled. "I'll tell you what. You figure out how to get a packet of information containing all of Dr. Ford's research out of the Alamo, here, and past the FBI, and I'll do my best to sell the board on your proposal."

"I know you don't need our money to further your research, but I bet you could use the strong Texas backs that'll be out of work when this technology takes off to build a production plant or two and some infrastructure."

"Oh, we'll be able to put the people of Texas to work, and could probably start doing it in the next few weeks. I'll let you know what the board says."

"Do you need me to pitch it to them?" asked the governor with a grin.

"I think I can handle it," said President Kane. "I don't want the idea sounding sleazy."

Governor Faust chuckled and extended his hand to his old friend. "I never thought we'd be in a position like this," he said a little more seriously. "I don't think either one of us has been this close to a hangman's noose, except when we were dating the Holman twins. You just keep that damn shield up no matter what, ya hear? I'd better get the hell out of here before President Buchman finds out we had a visit and tries to ambush me."

President Kane walked into the hall with the governor and they continued talking while they headed in the direction of the command center. "What would happen if they try and bring the shield down using a nuke?"

Kane shook his head. "Well, the only place they could detonate it without killing millions of Texans or frying all the electronics in Texas is out near the shield satellite itself, and my people are telling me that the shield would handle it without any problem. They say the blast would wash around the shield like clouds over Mount Everest."

"So, if they try a stunt like that we won't have any side effects caused by the electromagnetic pulse down here on the ground?"

"That's correct. And if any radioactive debris doesn't disintegrate on its own, we'll vaporize it with our lasers."

The governor slapped President Kane on the shoulder. "How does it feel to have the biggest gun in town?"

"We'd already be dead without it, and I'm finally satisfied that the money we spent upgrading our lasers was worth it. I've taken a lot of crap over the last couple of years for pushing that agenda—until today, anyway. Hey, you're welcome to stay for a while. Why don't we get some breakfast? I'm starving."

The governor smiled. "I'd like that, but I'd better get out of here before Santa Ana gets suspicious and parks a thousand troops on my doorstep."

Governor Faust had all the information he had come for and was feeling much more comfortable about the situation. Before he left the cover of the administration building, he shook hands with his friend and slapped him on the back. "Thanks for standing up for what you believe in. It means a great deal to the people of Texas."

The governor pointed to the area outside the east entrance. "When I leave the area of the shield, I'll have a sour, ornery look on my face, like you really have chapped my hide. President Buchman cannot think I'm supportive of the shield right now or I'll have bunch of FBI agents camped outside my office and I won't be able to assist you. My little act will also help me get by the FBI with these," he said, showing his friend the cylindrical tube filled with Dr. Ford's research and Dan Johnson's news broadcast.

President Kane grinned. "You keep it up and you might convince me there's an honest politician with backbone."

Chapter Forty

"Desperation"

The President of the United States, the Joint Chiefs, and the Secretary of Defense had been debating for thirty minutes about the next course of action that should be taken with the University of Southern Texas. In the end, they decided it was in the best interest of the country to bring the shield down, even if they had to use nuclear weapons.

"Sir, we will need to evacuate part of Corpus Christi if we're going to do this without risking civilian casualties."

"Let's get on the phone to the governor and enlist his help."

"You should know that he just left the shield a few minutes ago," said a sergeant that had just entered the room.

President Buchman looked surprised. "Did we stop and interrogate him?"

"He had a fully armed escort and we didn't want to risk making a scene."

"How long was he in there?"

"A little over an hour."

"Why did you wait until now to tell me about this?"

"Well, sir, we … we just found out ourselves."

"Is there anything else I should know?" asked the President.

"Not really, sir, but you might be interested to know that over half the governor's staff couldn't get through the shield, and he wasn't too happy about it. He was even less happy when he exited the shield," said the sergeant.

"How do you know?"

"Well, he looked pretty ticked off when he left the university, and he was cussing a blue streak. He didn't say a word to any of our people—he just got into his limo and drove away."

"I don't want one more person going in or out of that shield, do you understand?" said the President, his voice rising in irritation.

"Yes, sir," said Director Mason.

"This is the second time I've given you this order. Make it stick this time!"

President Buchman turned to the rest of the group. "I want this damn shield down within the hour, regardless of what it takes, even if it means detonating a nuke."

The Joint Chiefs looked uncomfortable, but none disagreed out loud. If it wasn't for the fact that the shield was expanding, violating property rights, and endangering the lives of American citizens, they would've questioned using nukes against the university, even if it was at a high altitude.

"What are you waiting for?" asked President Buchman, standing up. "Let's get that shield down before Corpus Christi wakes up. I want to know exactly what you plan to do, and when you plan to do it, within thirty minutes."

"Yes, sir," they replied as they stood with the President and watched him leave the room. After the he left, several people sighed and relaxed in their chairs. Others remained standing to stretch their legs and backs. The Joint Chiefs talked in hushed tones about anything else they had in their arsenal that might have the desired effect on the university's satellite.

General Sacket reminded everyone that only seventeen nukes had been detonated in space, and none since 1967, because of the damage that they'd caused to earthbound electronic systems and neighboring satellites. He pointed out that the use of a nuclear weapon in space would violate the Outer Space Treaty signed by the United States.

"General, although what you are saying is true, the highest altitude at which a nuclear device has been detonated is three hundred and thirty-six miles.

The satellite we're talking about destroying is around twenty-three thousand miles away from the earth."

"Exactly," said the general, "so we have no idea how such an explosion will affect the earth. One thing we do know for sure is that there are around forty-five hundred satellites that are currently in orbit around the earth in working or semi-working condition, and about a two thousand of those are in everyday operation. If we detonate a nuke at twenty-two or twenty-three thousand miles in the air, how many of these satellites will be damaged or destroyed? Are we prepared to deal with the political repercussions of such an action?"

Admiral Sorensen shared the general's concerns. "At last count, over one-third of those satellites were Russia's, and around fifteen hundred are American. China and Japan both have around two hundred satellites each, and France and India have seventy or eighty..."

"I think we get the picture," said Secretary Jacobs. "Is it possible to manipulate a nuclear detonation so it won't affect other satellites?"

"Look," said General Lawson, "if we are going to do this, let's do it right. I think we can do what the secretary is suggesting. We can detonate a couple of nukes so that the primary EMP blast is directed into outer space and won't affect any other satellites."

"What if the university shoots them down before they get into position?"

"Then they will endanger every satellite up there, including their own. None of their other satellites have shielding, that we know of, and they have billions of dollars of hardware up there."

"Are we sure that none of their other satellites have shields?"

"That's what our intel is telling us."

"It also told us that they didn't have weapons-grade lasers, either."

"Gentlemen, it doesn't matter if the rest of their satellites have shielding technology. All we need to do is disrupt the shield long enough to get our men inside it and put an end to this game. All I need is a few seconds of disruption to get my men inside."

The Joint Chiefs nodded their heads thoughtfully.

"How much time will it take for you gentlemen to rig up a couple of nukes and plot a solution?" asked Secretary Jacobs.

"We'll have something for you in less than twenty-five minutes."

"What about our surface-to-air lasers?"

"I don't think the president wants to let that technology out of the bag yet."

"Come on, every geek in the world knows that UST has been shooting down space junk. Hell, I'll bet I've read at least two dozen articles in science journals reporting that the US has had ground-to-air lasers since the beginning of the twenty-first century."

Secretary Jacobs and the Vice President were swayed by the logic and asked Admiral Sorensen to prep and position a warship equipped with the technology should the president decide to use it.

....

President Kane returned to the general boardroom to run Governor Faust's proposal by the members still in attendance. As he suspected, everyone supported the idea and he recorded an official vote. He checked on each of the teams who'd received assignments from the last meeting and was pleased to find that they had all made significant progress. Once he was satisfied that everyone was on track, he walked back to the command center to find that it was still buzzing with activity.

He spotted Justin staring at a flat screen monitor with Dr. Tate, and walked over to see what they were looking at. Justin saw President Kane coming out of the corner of his eye and turned to greet him. "There are a couple of old nuke silos at the Francis E. Warren Air Force Base with modified Minute Man IV ICBMs that just came alive with activity."

"Is that uncommon?"

"Yeah, they haven't been this active for years, and it can't be a coincidence that both silos have modified Minute Man IV missiles capable of hitting a satellite in a twenty-two-or-three thousand mile orbit."

"What kind of payload do they carry?"

"Anything from one to ten thousand kiloton bombs."

"I thought the START Treaty made more than one warhead illegal?"

"It would if they ever get the treaty finalized and signed."

"Is there any way to tell when they've committed to firing a missile?"

"Yes, when fifty feet of the rocket is out of the ground," said Justin with a smile. "They can have one of those things in the air in a matter of minutes, and there is no warning other than the opening of the silo doors."

"Can we disable them on the ground?"

"We can't risk it. The warheads are too prominent and too close to the guidance system."

"You disabled the radar guidance system on the USS Jason Dunham, which seemed like a precision shot. What's the difference?"

"These two ICBM silos are so compact there isn't anything to target until the missile tube is open, and even then it's unlikely we'll have the right angle to be able to see anything, much less target it. The risk of detonating a warhead is too high. If they launch either one of these babies, we are going to have to wait and destroy or disable them in space."

"Won't that set off an EMP burst that will damage our own satellites?"

"Our objective would be to disable them or jam the guidance system signal so they can't be detonated. Either way we'll do our best to create the least amount of damage to the other satellites in orbit. The good thing is that they are so old, slow, and out-of-date, plotting a defensive strategy against them is not too difficult."

"Good," said President Kane, leaning over to get a better look at the silos. "We are going to need all the allies we can get before this thing is over."

....

After making a few phone calls, President Buchman walked back to the Situation Room. "I was told that you have a solution?"

"Mr. President, our team of scientists believes the only thing that can bring down the satellite is a nuclear explosion. We are going to detonate two clusters of nuclear bombs in a pattern that we think will force the shield satellite out of geosynchronous orbit, or at least disrupt it long enough for our ground forces to secure the university," responded Secretary Jacobs.

"How are you going to shield all the other satellites in orbit from the EMP blast?"

"There are about one hundred satellites in geosynchronous orbit over the western hemisphere and we believe we can direct the EMP blast in such a way that it will not affect them."

"And there won't be any negative effects from the EMP blast on the ground? The last thing we need is a bunch of angry Texans brandishing their rifles."

"There is no danger of that at all, Mr. President."

"How long until we can launch?"

"We are ready to launch on your command."

President Buchman looked around the room. "Is there anyone who has any doubts or concerns about this course of action?"

Admiral Sorensen shook his head. "Would it hurt to give President Kane another call and give him one more chance to lower his shields?"

President Buchman bowed his head. "I think we are past that point, and I don't think he's going to budge. This has become a war of principles, and neither he nor the general board is going to back down."

General Sacket spoke up. "Are we prepared to shoot down any satellite or missile debris that might make it through the atmosphere?"

"We are, General," said Secretary Jacobs, "which brings up another point. The president turned his attention to the secretary. "We believe we need to leverage our ground-to-air lasers—not only to shoot down any radioactive debris that doesn't burn up in the atmosphere, but to try and disrupt UST's satellite."

President Buchman thought for a moment then nodded. "I can't think of a better situation to let that cat out of the bag. Do it."

"Is the FBI ready to send in men on the ground?" asked General Sacket.

"They are ready, sir, and are prepped to identify and secure the shield technology, Dr. Ford, and her research."

"What is our story to the press going to be?"

"Well, sir, that's a bit tricky. We are going to control the media around this thing with an iron fist, but our story is going to be that we're trying to help the University of Southern Texas bring down their faulty shield before it kills somebody. We've seen what will happen if someone with a G-Score less than eighty is trapped in a building or a car when the shield expands through it, and we are going to leverage that footage to its fullest. We are also going to use the footage we captured when the missile debris hit the ground to illustrate that the shield is blocking the orbits of several satellites and could create another collision that might result in falling debris. After all, the Russian GLONASS Satellite will hit the shield unless they change its orbit."

President Buchman liked what he was hearing. "That is a great starting point. If we build from there and agree that all announcements to the public and the press don't go out without this body's approval, we should be fine. Unless anyone has a vehement objection, let's proceed."

Secretary Jacobs looked at General Lawson and Admiral Sorensen. "We have a go."

....

President Kane had taken the stairs to the second level of the command center where Dr. Tate and his satellite jockey teams were located. He wanted to know more about the various outcomes that could result from a nuclear blast detonating near the shield satellite.

"They're launching from both silos!"

Dr. Tate stayed with his satellite team, but President Kane took the steps down to the command center floor two at a time. "Are we certain they're aimed at us?"

"We'll know in sixty seconds, after the first-stage rocket has fired." Justin gave a series of commands to the team who were manning the lasers on the shield satellite. "Lock on to the navigation systems on both of those rockets and stay locked on until we are ready to fire!" He turned to another group of engineers who were huddled around the controls for another university satellite. The second Justin was able to verify that the missiles were on a trajectory with the shield satellite, he gave the command to jam the communications of the launch site. "Begin jamming now."

Neither of the missiles was affected, and both rocketed towards the shield satellite at fifteen thousand miles an hour and climbing. "That's what I was afraid of. They're equipped with a built-in guidance system that requires no ground communication. How long until impact?"

"One hour, forty-two minutes, and thirty-one seconds," said a technician.

"How comfortable are you with that estimate?"

"Very comfortable, unless they've improved their technology significantly."

President Kane's tension eased when he heard how long the nukes would take to reach their target, and he remembered the Russian GLONASS Satellite they'd had issues with during Hurricane Derek. "Did we figure out how to maneuver that Russian satellite away from our shield?"

"We did, but they burned up most of their thruster fuel doing it, so we agreed to refuel them once this is over."

President Kane shrugged. "That's a lot cheaper than replacing the whole satellite."

"That's for sure," responded Justin. Too tense to accommodate any more small talk, he politely excused himself and joined Dr. Tate on the balcony. "I know we won't be firing on these missiles for a while, but have we successfully located and locked onto their guidance systems?"

"We have," said Dr. Tate. "And we are ready to fire at any time."

"How far away are the guidance modules from the warheads?"

"They are located about twenty feet below the cone."

Justin frowned. "What are the chances we will trigger a detonation?"

"I don't know," said Dr. Tate, sounding a little worried. "But what choice do we have?"

"Good point," responded Justin.

"We plan on disabling the missiles when they are five miles away from the shield satellite, so if we detonate one, there will be less horizontal impact on our satellite."

"I hope you're right," said Justin with a strained grin. Justin took a seat near Dr. Tate's desk where the team of scientists and engineers were debating the best way to defend the shield satellite. An hour went by, and a man on the floor started counting down the minutes until impact. "Missiles are at twenty thousand feet and closing—approximately twelve minutes until impact!"

There was nothing that Justin could do, so he sat back and let Dr. Tate do his job. President Kane joined him in the loft. "If they bring the shield down," said President Kane, "you'll come visit me in prison, won't you?"

Justin rocked back and forth in his chair. "No, because we'll more than likely be there together," he said nervously.

President Kane looked at Justin thoughtfully. "As soon as these nukes are destroyed, let's powwow with Dr. Ford and Dan. I don't want to wait another minute before we get her technology out to the world. I know our programmers will more than likely have hacked their way to the outside world within the hour, but I want to tell Governor Faust to release the hounds right away."

Justin had no idea what President Kane was talking about. "How is Governor Faust going to help us?"

"Oh... I forgot to tell you that he walked out of here with a complete copy of Ann's research, our surveillance footage, and the two news clips that Dan put together," said President Kane with a mischievous grin.

"You're kidding me."

"Not kidding. Faust was yelling and cussing so loudly about the university and our damn shield, the FBI didn't bother to search him."

....

The people in the Situation Room stared at the giant plasma monitor, hardly daring to breathe as they watched the two relic nuclear missiles climb closer and closer to their target.

"Less than five minutes until detonation."

"Fire lasers," commanded President Buchman.

Admiral Sorensen was on his phone, giving commands. "Several bursts from the lasers have been fired, sir." Everyone in the room waited for the Admiral to get word back on the effects of the lasers on the shield. After a minute, the anticipatory look on his face turned sour, and he hung up the phone. "The laser bursts just ricocheted off the shield into space. They want to try a more direct angle from one of our military satellites, equipped with the same technology."

"Dammit," said President Buchman, "We need a break here." He looked at Admiral Sorenson for a minute. "Do it."

The minutes ticked by slowly—every minute felt like an hour. "Three minutes to detonation."

The Joint Chiefs and the Director of National Intelligence all had their cell phones to their ears while they watched. "Jefferson, are you ready to go?" asked the director.

"I've got seventy agents ready to storm the campus the minute the shield goes down."

"It will be down in less than three minutes and counting."

....

"They're firing ground-to-air lasers at us!" yelled a technician.

"What?" said Justin and President Kane in unison.

The technician pointed to a screen on his right. "Watch." He'd slowed the images down so that the laser bursts could be seen by the naked eye. They watched as two laser bursts hit the shield and ricocheted into space.

Justin's heart was pounding and President Kane was gripping his chair so hard his knuckles were white. "Looks like they are throwing everything they have at us." Justin didn't respond. "How is the shield holding?"

"We had a little power fluctuation at the moment of impact, but everything seems to working fine now."

"We are ready to fire on the missiles' guidance systems," announced Dr. Tate.

Justin looked at Dr. Kane, who nodded his approval.

"Target and fire on the missiles' guidance systems," commanded Dr. Tate. His team responded by firing several laser bursts, as commanded. The desired result was to obliterate the automatic guidance systems on both missiles and have them blast into outer space where the university could detonate them at their leisure.

The lasers struck both missiles exactly as intended. On contact, the sky around the first missile erupted into a massive ball of flame, and a circular shock wave shot out from the detonation point, carrying smoke and debris around the shield and off into space. The second missile careened past the shield satellite, into the blackness of space, turning end-over-end until it was out of sight.

"Damage report!" shouted Justin. "Is the shield holding?"

"The shield hasn't moved an inch!" shouted a technician from the floor.

"Check its rate of expansion."

"Still holding...wait...! Expansion has increase to thirty feet an hour and climbing."

"Watch it closely," commanded President Kane, coming off his chair. "If it increases past one hundred feet an hour, shut it down."

Justin's face was pale, and President Kane was staring at the technician and gripping the rail. "Thirty-eight feet per hour and climbing."

President Kane was doing calculations in his head, trying to figure out the maximum expansion speed that that wouldn't endanger the people of Corpus Christi.

"It's stopped, sir! It seems to be holding at forty-two feet an hour," said the technician monitoring the shield.

"Watch it closely." President Kane turned to Justin. "Put a team on shield-expansion monitoring duty full-time until this is over." He turned back to the technician. "Is the radius or the diameter expanding at forty-two feet an hour?"

"The diameter, sir." Everyone listening to the conversation sighed with relief.

"What will they try next?"

"I don't know, but if this gets any more tense, I'm going to have a heart attack," said President Kane, collapsing in a chair. "Hopefully they'll get it through their thick heads that there is nothing else to try."

Justin looked skeptical. "As much as I hope you're right, I'm not holding my breath." He changed the subject and looked at Dr. Tate. "You just made history with your shield, doctor."

Tate winced. "Not like I'd hoped. But maybe history will be kind and remember this day favorably." Tate turned to his staff. "Let's check the shield integrity every minute for the next four hours until we feel confident we are out of the woods. And keep an eye on that army of FBI agents out there so we know what they are up to."

....

President Buchman and his staff in the Situation Room were stunned. They'd been out-smarted, out-gunned, and out-maneuvered by a university to whom they'd given millions of research dollars. The president pounded a fist on the table and looked angrily at the men and women in the room. "Terminate the command to fire satellite lasers."

President Buchman waited for the command to be given, then continued to pound on the table. "Nothing has changed! I want the perimeter of that damn shield surrounded immediately. Nobody enters or leaves it without my explicit authorization—not even the governor! Our story's the same—the shield is expanding and is a danger to anyone or anything that comes in contact with it, and we're doing our damnedest to assist the university in disabling it. I don't want any unauthorized personnel within five miles of it, so we'd better start evacuating Corpus Christi. To make sure that our story sounds authentic, we'll be pushing food, medicine, and anything else the university needs through the shield to ensure UST's survival, but nobody can leave the shield because they may have been contaminated with radiation of some kind. Are you all getting the gist of what I'm saying?"

The president looked through narrowed eyes at his Joint Chiefs. "You've just had your asses handed to you on a platter. I don't think I've ever seen the United States Armed Forces so humiliated! Get the shield perimeter secured and figure out how to get inside it! Dig under it! Put a sub under it... I don't care how you do it or how much you spend doing it, but get inside it and end this thing!"

He turned to the White House Press Secretary. "Craft an official release stating our position, then bring it to my office for review. I'd like to get something to the press before they start speculating about what's going on. I want it on my desk in twenty minutes."

The press secretary left the room on the run, and the Joint Chiefs filed out for a bio break, looking like a bunch of dogs with their tails between their legs.

....

Justin Woodward leaned back in his chair. "So... what now?"

President Kane had slumped forward in his chair with his eyes closed and rubbed his temples. "We'd better get the students and faculty together in the football stadium so we can explain what's going on."

"What time do you want to do that?"

"How about 10:00 a.m.?"

"Ok... I'll make it happen."

Kane opened his eyes. "How long can we survive with the emergency food and toiletries we have on campus?"

"When we started goofing around with this satellite technology, we decided we'd better have at least a month's supply of food for everyone on campus in case one of the active volcanoes in Mexico blew its top and we had to leave the shield up for a while. If I remember right, they went a little overboard and we ended up with a two month's supply, plus anything the university agricultural department can grow or we can catch out of the Gulf of Mexico. We'll run out of toilet paper, milk, cheese, and eggs, before anything," said Justin with a smile. "Hey, at least we have an endless supply of hydrogen and fish."

"Hopefully it won't come to that," said President Kane sourly. "But if we can't resolve this thing within a few days, I'm going to have to develop a love for fish."

Justin chuckled tiredly. "You've got President Buchman so wound up, the only resolution he's going to give you is at the end of a rope."

"On a more positive note, how quickly can we have the rest of your motorcyclists saddled up?"

"I can have them ready to ride in fifteen minutes."

"I'll meet you in fifteen minutes down at the practice field."

"Works for me."

Chapter Forty-One

"Whispers of Secession"

Deputy Director Jefferson smiled to himself. His boss told him they'd failed to bring down the shield and that a contingent from all the armed forces would be on site within a couple of hours under the command of one of the generals. *Perfect,* he thought, *I'm more than happy to fade to the background of this nightmare.* He hoped everyone would forget how it all started.

Rapid knocking on the door snapped Jefferson out of his daydream. "What is it?"

The agent was breathing hard. "Six more motorcycle riders just left the university. We've already caught four and are in hot pursuit of the other two."

"How did they get off campus? We've got the place blockaded."

"They jumped the barrier, sir. The four that we caught didn't have anything on them except for the shirts on their backs."

"No information packets or thumb-drives?"

"Nothing, sir!"

"Bring them to the hotel. I'd like to interrogate them myself."

"They're on their way here as we speak."

Jefferson glared at the agent as if it was his fault the riders had gotten through. "What direction are the other two riders headed?"

"One was headed north on Highway 281, and the other was headed north on Highway 77."

"Put whatever resources you need on those two until you pick them up." *What's north of here that is so damn important?* he wondered.

. . . .

President Kane stood in front of the faculty and student body of the University of Southern Texas. Jason Woodward, Dr. Tate, Dan Johnson, Jack, and Ann sat behind him. His face filled the giant VTX monitors at both ends of the stadium as he re-hashed everything that had happened during the last few days and disclosed how the university had become involved. When he got to the part where the faculty and staff had successfully built a working prototype of Ann's research, the crowd came to their feet in a wave, congratulating the participants with loud applause.

President Kane motioned for Ann to stand. "This is Dr. Ann Ford, our newest faculty member." The response was deafening.

When the noise had diminished enough for President Kane to continue, he described how Ann's research had cost the lives of Dr. Summersten and Dr. Conner. He explained why their deaths and the protection of Ann's research had been his justification for raising the modified weather shield. The stadium grew deathly quiet as thirty thousand people tried to reconcile the deaths of two men many of them knew and respected.

President Kane described how Ann had renamed her research in honor of Dr. Conner and Summersten, and committed that he would not rest until those who were responsible for their deaths were brought to justice. "As a result of these events, the United States Government has decided that both Dr. Ford's technology and our new shield technology are too disruptive and dangerous to be allowed onto the open market."

The crowd's displeasure was evident from the angry rumble that echoed through the stadium.

"In a meeting a few hours ago with President Buchman, his Joint Chiefs, and several other key officials, I stated that that we would not be lowering the shield, and that it would remain up until Dr. Ford's technology was widely distributed to hundreds of scientists around the world, and until I have proof that they've been able to reproduce it. I told him we would uphold the Constitution of the United States and publicize his unlawful actions against Dr. Ford and this university until we'd fanned the spark of freedom in enough American hearts to get his attention. I told him that he'd run roughshod over us one too many times, and we, the people of the University of Southern Texas, had fired a shot across his bow!"

The stadium reverberated with thunderous applause and it took a full five minutes before it quieted to a point where President Kane could continue.

"President Buchman defines my position and the position of this university as 'treasonous,' but I beg to differ. What we do now will stand equal to what Thomas Jefferson did when he penned the words, *"We hold these truths to be self-evident, that all men are created equal, that they are endowed by their Creator with certain unalienable Rights, that among these are Life, Liberty and the pursuit of Happiness. That to secure these rights, Governments are instituted among men, deriving their just powers from the consent of the governed, That whenever any Form of Government becomes destructive of these ends, it is the Right of the People to alter or to abolish it!"*

We do not intend to abolish our form of government, but to force our government to alter itself so that we and the generations that come after us will be proud to be Americans..." His voice echoed in the stadium. "Are you with me?"

The cheer that went up from the crowd was louder than any that had ever been heard for a touchdown or home run in school history. It was the sound of people expressing their pent-up desire for a responsible government. It was the sound of thousands of people who felt empowered to enforce change on their government for the first time in their lives. It was the sound of every hard-working American whose voice had never been heard. It was the sound of people who yearned to be proud Americans again.

When the crowd settled down, President Kane explained that everyone on campus was free to come and go as they pleased, but that the university could not control what action the United States Government would take against anyone who left the area protected by the shield.

He let them know that the university had enough food for several months and that it would be served out of the cafeteria free of charge until the current situation was resolved. He pledged that where possible, school would continue as usual, but that there would be plenty of new opportunities for students and faculty to volunteer for projects related to hydrogen production, water purification, agriculture, and fishing, which coaxed a chuckle from the crowd. He concluded by affirming that the university's policies, decisions, and procedures would be transparent and available for anyone interested enough to read them.

Thousands of students streamed onto the football field to shake President Kane's hand and pledge their support. As the crowd dwindled down to a few stragglers, a handsome man in his late forties approached Ann. In his hand he held a large envelope, which he presented to her.

"I represent an organization that would like to make an offer for exclusive rights to your research."

Ann, President Kane, Jack, and Justin all looked surprised and suspicious. Justin closed the gap between him and Ann in a couple of quick steps.

"There is no need for alarm. I sneaked through the shield this morning in hope of being able to present this to you in person. I can't stay long, but the company I represent is offering you one billion dollars for the exclusive rights to your research."

Ann smiled and handed the unopened envelope back to the man. "Please tell your employer that I'm not interested in their offer. My research is not for sale. As soon as possible, I will be releasing it to the world for free."

"Do you realize that your research is so disruptive it may cause the downfall of some of the oldest businesses and most successful countries in the world?"

"I do," said Ann with a smile, "and I'm hopeful that they'll consider farming—it's a lot less stressful."

"It's hard to switch from oil to agriculture when there is such a shortage of fresh water in the Middle East."

Ann put her hand on the man's arm. "You, my friend, need to dig into my research. It can be tweaked to enable the purification of seawater for virtually nothing, just as easily as it can be used to filter hydrogen from water."

The man looked amazed. "You are full of surprises, Dr. Ford. Thank you for letting me barge in on you unannounced."

With that, he turned on his heel and walked off the football field in the direction of the shield, clutching the envelope to his chest.

"I wonder who he represented?" said Jack.

"Could be any one of a hundred organizations or countries," responded President Kane.

They chatted as they walked back to the command center. "Were you serious about being able to purify salt water?" asked President Kane.

"There are a lot of things you don't know about my research," Ann said, squeezing Jack's arm.

President Kane chuckled and kept walking. Dozens of students and faculty interrupted their walk to the science building to pledge their support.

"I feel like I'm at a wedding reception and there is a guest line forty-thousand-people long."

President Kane grinned. "That is not too far from the truth. By the time you are done, your smiler might be broken."

....

Governor Faust sat in his office listening to the news, hoping that a news agency would break the story on the university so he wouldn't have to. He wanted to talk to a few of his key people about what was going on before he came out in open support for President Kane

He nodded when his staff informed him that the US Armed Forces had failed again to bring down the shield. *Texas three, Santa Ana zero,* he thought to himself. *If they can just keep the shield up long enough for the American public to actually see it and to become aware of what's going on, it will be game over for the United States Government. Hell, they might even be forced to make the changes necessary to keep this country intact!*

His thoughts were interrupted by one of his security staff. "You might want to see this, sir."

"See what?"

"A young man rode his motorcycle up the steps of the capital building and is insisting on seeing you. We tried to take him into custody, but we are at a standoff with six FBI agents who are telling us he is their responsibility."

"Where is he?"

"He's in the lobby sir, but…"

"Show me!"

Governor Faust followed the security officer into the lobby at a run, and found six FBI agents with guns pointed at a stocky young man with wind-blown hair. His security staff had their weapons pointed at the FBI agents, but their lack of confidence was showing.

"Lower your weapons! All of you!"

"We can't do that sir," said one of the FBI agents. "This man is a fugitive and is in federal custody."

"Since when?"

"Since he left the campus of UST about an hour ago," responded the agent.

"I don't think so," retorted Governor Faust, "he is coming with me."

The FBI agent in charge pointed his gun at the student's chest. "If he doesn't come with us, he will die right here. He has information that will drastically affect the security of this country."

"If he dies right here, so will you and all your FBI friends," said Governor Faust.

"You wouldn't dare… that would guarantee you a life-long sentence in prison," threatened the agent.

"My men have armor-piercing rounds, so your vests will not protect you. Drop your weapons now!"

The FBI agents stood their ground.

"Take a look up at the balcony, and at the red dots on each of your foreheads before you pull that trigger. You are in the state of Texas, boys, and we will cut you to shreds without so much as getting blood spatter on this boy."

The agent looked at one of his comrades to validate what the governor had said. There was a red dot on each of their foreheads, and he assumed that he had one on his as well. His jaw tightened, but he made the right decision and lowered and holstered his weapon.

Governor Faust grabbed the boy by the arm and pulled him out of earshot of the FBI.

"Why are you here, boy?"

The kid smiled, "President Kane says to release the hounds."

The governor's face hardened with resolve as he turned to address the FBI agents.

"Tell your boss that the FBI is no longer welcome in the State of Texas." He started to turn away but stopped abruptly. "Oh, and give him this," he said, walking up to the agent who had pulled his gun on the boy and hit him in the jaw as hard has he could.

A couple of agents started to reach for their guns, but Faust jerked his head towards the balcony to remind them his security staff already had the drop on them. "I wouldn't do that if I were you. My boys are a little better armed than you, and you'd be dead before you cleared leather. Leave your weapons on the ground and take care of your associate before he bleeds all over my place."

"You won't get away with this."

"Shut up," said the governor, "and get your law-breaking trash out of my house before I shoot it full of holes."

The FBI agents retreated, dragging their wounded man behind them.

"Make sure they leave the premises, then call up the Texas State Guard. I want this building sealed off immediately, with ten thousand times the firepower we had at the Alamo. I need my State Guard, National Guard, and National Air Guard Generals in here on the double, before they get conflicting commands from President Buchman. You tell them that their governor has never had more urgent business for them to attend to than I do right now!"

"Yes, sir," said one of his security team, and left the building on the run.

"One of you take care of this boy and make sure he is fed. I want to see him in my office in twenty minutes. I'll be in there preparing a statement for the press, and I want to know everything that's going on inside UST."

....

The President of the United States sat in his oval office, alone. It was just a little after noon on what had started out to be a beautiful Thursday. He had no idea how history would refer to this day in the future, but he'd done what he was told was best for the country. The words of President Kane echoed in his mind, and he wondered which one of them was right. It was too late to turn back now. The die had been cast, and the wheels of government were in motion.

A knock sounded at the door. "Come in," he said.

His chief-of-staff walked quickly to his desk and handed him a piece of paper. "This was just emailed to us from the office of the Governor of Texas."

President Buchman took the paper and read it out loud. "If I were you, I would take a moment and watch NBC News. The network is about to interrupt their normal programming." It was signed, Governor Jim Faust.

"Turn it on," said the president, motioning to the flat screen on the wall. NBC was in the middle of broadcasting the local news, and the president and his chief-of-staff watched until the interruption of the normal programming happened as predicted.

A man in a tweed jacket walked in front of the camera and handed the anchor a piece of paper. The news anchor stopped what he was saying, read what was on the paper, then looked up at the camera. "We are interrupting our regular programming to bring you some breaking news from Austin, Texas. This is coming to us live from the office of the Governor."

Governor Faust's face appeared on the screen, and he immediately began to speak. "Early this morning and without probable cause, the FBI stormed the campus of the University of Southern Texas and killed one of their emeritus professors, Dr. Joseph Summersten. Shortly thereafter, one of their agents put a gun to President Kane's head and tried to force him to surrender up Dr. Ann Ford, who has recently discovered some phenomenal and ground-breaking technology."

"In addition, and as a direct consequence of the FBI's incompetence, Nobel Prize recipient, Dr. Brock Conner, also lost his life this morning, and a visiting professor from MIT and his wife are still missing."

"The FBI has surrounded the UST campus and is jamming their communications in hopes of suppressing the technology developed by Dr. Ford. Luckily, a young man who starts on UST's football team was able to get through the FBI's barricade and give me permission to release Dr. Ford's research that I received earlier today. He took a huge risk riding his motorcycle up here to deliver this information, and almost lost his life doing it, but he's going to be ok."

"I've forwarded a copy of Dr. Ford's research to many of the top universities in the world via email and posted the information is on the website of the State of Texas if you would like to download it.

"Because the federal government was so aggressive this morning and has demonstrated such a blatant disregard for our lives and our freedom, the University of Southern Texas put up their weather shield with a few modifications. These modifications not only allow the shield to keep out bad weather, they give it the ability to keep out certain kinds of people, such as murderers, rapists, con-men, thieves, anyone who is violent, overly aggressive, a consummate liar, etc."

"Now... what we don't need is a passel of curious Texans or other yahoos coming down to Corpus Christi to see if they can get through the shield. Until this conflict is over, I need you to go about your regular business, and I promise to keep you posted on what's happening down at the University of Southern Texas."

Governor Faust took a drink from a bottle of water sitting on his desk, and then continued. "The shield covers the university's property and extends into the Gulf of Mexico on the east. If there is anyone who can't access their property due to the shield, the university has promised to work out some kind of compensation with you until this crisis is over."

"The University of Southern Texas has decided to take this opportunity to send a strong message to the United States Government. President Kane and the general board of UST have agreed to leave the shield up until Dr. Ford's technology saturates the scientific community and the federal government has publically apologized and repaired the damages they have perpetrated against them."

The governor paused, searching for the perfect words. "In the spirit of maintaining the constitutional rights of every citizen in the great State of Texas, we will follow the lead of the University of Southern Texas and start eliminating our dependencies on the federal government immediately. Until they withdraw from the City of Corpus Christi, make adequate reparations for the damages they've perpetrated this morning, and alter their form of government so this type of thing cannot happen again, they are not welcome in the state of Texas."

He paused to let his words sink in. "If I were an employee of the federal government and lived in Texas, I'd start looking for other employment. As your governor and fellow Texan, I pledge to support you, and will be setting up a referral program to help you find and secure another job. If you are in the oil industry in the state of Texas, please call my office immediately because I have some breaking news that's going to pitch you off the bronc you're riding."

"I just met with the Texas State Guard, National Guard, and National Air Guard a few minutes ago, and have put them on high alert. They will not be assisting the FBI, the CIA, Home Land Security, or the armed forces with their assault on the University of Southern Texas. In fact, they'll be making it pretty damn difficult for them to do their jobs."

"We are *not* seceding from the Union, but, like the University of Southern Texas, are firing a shot across your bow, Mr. President. We will hold you personally accountable for every life that's been lost this morning, and for every life that is lost hereafter because of your foolish actions. When you do what we've asked, we'll be more than happy to see you in the great state of Texas. Until then, you, the FBI, the CIA, Homeland Security, and the Armed Forces are not welcome here."

....

The NBC News anchorman came back on the screen, and it was fidgeting with the papers on his desk. It was obvious that the governor's message had rattled him.

"Thank you Governor Faust I ah... It sounds like mmm... It sounds like you've been inside the shield and spoken with President Kane?"

"I have."

"Aren't you longtime friends?"

"We are..."

The commander in chief of the United States turned off the broadcast and walked into the hall. "Damn him and his arrogant Texan pride!" he said under his breath, "who does he think he is?"

President Buchannan walked back to the situation room with the bad news, muttering to himself. "I didn't sign up for this..."

End of Book One

This concludes book one, *Defiance*, from the *Fall of the Empire* series. The story will continue in book two, *Patriots Blood*.

Praise for "Defiance"

"Readers be warned! *Defiance* will commandeer your free time and any other moment you might risk sneaking in a page or two. *Defiance* is truly captivating straight out of the gate. Get ready for a great ride. Bring on the next installment!"

Jeff Ankder, CIA, CPA

"*Defiance* had me hooked from the beginning. With its fast-paced, thriller style, I couldn't put it down. Ryker's introduction of groundbreaking technologies and their possible ramifications, both ethical and economical, grabbed my attention and kept me guessing at what might happen next. I want to see them work in real life! An excellent, thought-provoking read."

Annie Morgan, Actor, Singer

"*Defiance* was thrilling from page one till the end, a definite two thumbs up!"

Amberlee Cope, Rock'n Hairstylist

"*Defiance* will grab you in the first chapter and won't let go until the last page is read.
It is intriguing, smart, and a powerful reminder of the values that make our nation great!"

Kayloni Hansen, Teacher

"I so much enjoyed reading *Defiance*. It started right in with action, and as I finished one chapter I had to keep going on to see what would happen. I enjoyed the idea that "good" could prevail and would fight for the cause of that which is right.

Francine Sorensen, Grandmother

"What a fun ride! The suspense keeps you reading to the end. If you like Tom Clancy, you'll be sure to enjoy this read. Bring on the sequel!"

Jaynalee Peterson, Mom, Teacher

"*Defiance* not only stimulated the techno geek in me, but simultaneously quenched my thirst for intrigue, suspense, and patriotism. It resonated soundly with this true-blooded American who roots for the little guy and loves to see arrogance and corruption brought to its knees."

Steve Griffiths, Engineer, Avid Reader

"I loved the twists that developed from chapter to chapter. I truly enjoyed reading *Defiance*."

Wayne Sorensen, Coach and Grandfather

"This book is an action-packed ride that delivers nonstop intrigue peppered with warnings regarding the degradation of the principles upon which the United States was founded. I loved every page of it and am anxiously looking forward to the next book in the series."

Jason Cowley, Film Editor

"*Defiance* is an exciting debut novel packed full of suspense and drama. Tom Ryker has put a fresh new spin on the technological thriller with a strong, gutsy female main character that readers will love. Definitely worth a read!"

Talei Lawson, Mom and Master Chef

"*Defiance* is a thriller that will capture your imagination! It's an adventure with a gravity field that will suck you into its pages. It's intelligently written, with enough octane to put Tom Ryker at the top of your 'must read' list!"

Randy Jones, Literary Agent and Grandfather

"Prepare yourself to be captivated by the beautiful and brilliant scientist, Dr. Ann Ford, whose invention could literally change the world. It's imperative that she share her knowledge before something happens to her. Who can she trust...the FBI...the police...her husband? This book is so compelling it leaves you wondering if it's real or fiction. The author's writing is reminiscent of John Grisham and Dan Brown... a powerful suspenseful page-turner. I couldn't put it down."

Kathy Jacobs, CPA

"On the surface, this is an exciting page-turner. But it's more than that. Much more."

Elise Brown, Liberal Arts Graduate

"An entertaining blend of intrigue, action, and cutting-edge science. *Defiance* is a compelling technological thriller that grips the reader from beginning to end—and puts them in keen anticipation of the sequel."

Jon Elliot

"*Defiance* is a fantastic thriller that hooks you from the start and doesn't let you go."

Ben

Tom Ryker's love of storytelling and deep concern for the current state of the union prompted him to take a break from corporate America and write his first novel, *Defiance*, book one in the *Fall of an Empire* series. He is currently writing book two, *Patriots Blood*.

Tom lives in the foothills of the Rocky Mountains with his wife and two youngest children. For more information about Tom, see tomryker.com.

When any form of government becomes destructive of these ends, it is the Right of the People to alter or to abolish it, and to institute new Government, laying its foundation on such principles and organizing its powers in such form, as to them shall seem most likely to effect their Safety and Happiness. Prudence, indeed, will dictate that Governments long established should not be changed for light and transient causes; and accordingly all experience hath shewn, that mankind are more disposed to suffer, while evils are sufferable, than to right themselves by abolishing the forms to which they are accustomed. But when a long train of abuses and usurpations, pursuing invariably the same Object evinces a design to reduce them under absolute Despotism, it is their right, it is their duty, to throw off such Government, and to provide new Guards for their future security. . . .

Declaration of Independence – 1776